SILVER EVE

GUARDIANS OF TARNEC

Lark Rising
Silver Eve

GUARDIANS OF TARNEC BOOK II

SILVER EVE

SANDRA WAUGH

RANDOM HOUSE 🏠 NEW YORK

Text copyright © 2015 by Sandra Waugh
Jacket art copyright © 2015 by Marcela Bolivar
Map copyright © 2014 by Rhys Davies

Visit us on the Web! randomhouseteens.com

Educators and librarians, for a variety of teaching tools,
visit us at RHTeachersLibrarians.com

Library of Congress Cataloging-in-Publication Data
Waugh, Sandra.
Silver Eve / Sandra Waugh.
p. cm.—(Guardians of Tarnec ; Book 2)
Summary: Seventeen-year-old Evie Carew travels to Rood Marsh, where she is hunted by Breeders of Chaos because she is a Guardian of Tarnec, one of four who can save the world from destruction.
ISBN 978-0-449-81752-0 (trade)—ISBN 978-0-449-81753-7 (lib. bdg.)
ISBN 978-0-449-81754-4 (ebook)
[1. Fantasy.] I. Title.
PZ7.W351Si 2015 [Fic]—dc23 2014011624

Printed in the United States of America

10 9 8 7 6 5 4 3 2 1

First Edition

for Christopher and Jeremy,
with all my love

Moonlight on water brings Nature's daughter,
Swift-bred terror and sorrow of slaughter.
Silver and sickle, the healing hand,
Find the shell's song; bring rain upon land.

1

SUMMER'S WANE

"YOU HAVE NO fear of death."

The woman lay wide-eyed on the ground gasping this at me—gargling, really, for her throat was torn open, her voice shredded. She'd not last two breaths beyond those words; 'twas sad she had to waste them on me. But there was no one familiar left with whom to share meaningful last speeches of love or regret, nor anything that might ease her mind. Just the stranger who held her hand.

I smiled and soothed as I'd done through the final moments of all the dying, kneeling next to her on the hardened earth while she struggled, our fingers linked. I said softly, as if we'd continue this conversation, as if we took afternoon tea and commented on the dearth of rain, "There is nothing to fear."

The woman looked to challenge, but then her eyes drifted from mine and stilled. I kept my hand on hers for a moment longer, slumped back with a sigh. And then all that moved was the smoke.

Smoke. It filtered through the 'dull green of the trees, carrying the stink of burning things. We were a distance from the ruined village, but the gray wisps slipped through, swirled and surrounded, blinding the eye and polluting the soul. My soul.

"Mistress! Mistress Healer!"

I'd been called that since I first entered Bern, since I dropped my satchel in what remained of their growing fields and kneeled to assist those sprawled among the charred stalks. That I no longer cared about the title made no difference. One is born with one's gifts.

"Mistress! Here, *please!*" The brown-bearded man was crouched by some little tumble of clothing. He'd been zigzagging about the field ahead of me, avoiding bits of lingering flame, yelling and pointing at anyone who still breathed. How he'd spied survivors through the choking fog, had found the few among so many, I didn't know.

I shut the staring eyes of the woman, crossed her arms over her heart, then scrambled up and ran to the man, shoving up my sleeves once more. I forgot my satchel, hastened back for it. The satchel had been light in weight when I abandoned my own village of Merith; it was even lighter now. I'd taken only herbs— minion, yew, and heliotrope—hardly intending they'd serve anyone but me. Now I was nearly out. Three of five villages I'd passed through had been ravaged, the wounded begging to be tended back to life or eased into death. It was a trail of destruction, of pure savagery, witless and cruel. I'd never seen such except in my little town, never imagined that the vicious Troths would attack any defenseless community other than mine. But this time the creatures had run beyond Merith, burning and slaughtering for no fathomable reason. As a Healer I'd seen my share of violence from accident or misfortune; I had no aversion to it. But this was different. This was violence for pleasure.

"Here! Here." The brown-bearded man clawed at my skirt, pulling me down next to him at the side of a small boy—limp but seemingly unharmed.

"Is he the last?" I asked. I kept my voice light and calm to stave off Brown-beard's mounting anguish. He'd been far too eager in his assistance searching through these fields. Now there were the first trembles in his hands and face. Despair, catching up.

The man nodded awkwardly at my question, eyes darting about. He'd given me his name somewhere in the frenzy of tending: *Rafinn.* I had not used it. "So many dead." He fidgeted. "So many."

I touched the back of my hand to the boy's temple. "He might live, this one, if we are quick."

"As if that is good news."

True. Only seven villagers remained, by my count. This was hardly a triumph.

The man's voice dropped to a pathetic quiver. "Why did they come?"

"I don't know," I answered honestly, peeking under the boy's eyelids. The whites were still pure.

"But you are from Merith," Brown-beard muttered. "I heard you say it. I know the story of your village. The beasts came out of the Myr Mountains, attacking you fifty years back, then fifteen years back—"

"Thirteen," I corrected.

"And then midsummer. *Three* attacks." He said it roughly, as if he were jealous of our plight. "Merith survived the Troths *three* times."

"They only killed those of childbearing age before." I opened the boy's mouth to check his tongue, that his throat was clear. "And this time . . ." My voice hitched. "This time . . ."

This time we'd had warning. That was how we'd survived. My cousin Lark had come back from our field not three months past carrying a severed hand. Lark had the Sight—a rare gift that included the ability to sense people's histories—and she'd told us how the hand belonged to the kind old tailor, Ruber Minwl, how he'd been killed by the Troths and how the beasts had once again turned their vicious gaze to our town. We'd had ten days of warning to ponder, to worry. Ten days to hope.

Lark was the one who sought help for our defenseless village—bound to the task for which she should never have been chosen. She was Merith's most timid member, had never ventured beyond its rose-hedged borders. Yet somehow she pushed herself north into the hills, found and persuaded the Riders (the twelve of legendary might) to come and protect us. Eleven of them charged into Merith with horse and sword just as the Troths attacked, saving us from the worst. Lark returned afterward with the twelfth Rider in tow, both gravely wounded. And then it was our turn to save—Grandmama and me healing the two of them to the best of our abilities. Shy, beloved Lark, my almost-sister, my dearest friend, had rescued our home.

It seemed a good story. But neither did I attempt it for Brown-beard, nor was he interested in hearing it. "*This* time? This time is different!" He shuddered. "They've gone beyond your Merith; they've gone beyond child bearers! Look around. They killed everyone they could!"

"You must think what to do now." I changed the subject firmly, wiping my palms on my cloak. "Rebuild. Regrow. You'll need shelter from this sun at least. You'll need to find clean water." I dug into the dusty satchel for the vials of herbs, spilling them on the ground in front of me. I selected one and pulled its stopper. Minion. The most healing of any plant we knew.

"No purpose to rebuilding." The man was whimpering. "No purpose. We are lost. Drought, death, savagery—there is nothing more to suffer. There is nothing to save!"

"Here." I took Brown-beard's hand and sprinkled some of the dried bits into his ash-smeared palm. There was no water; we'd use his spit. 'Twould give him something purposeful to do. "Chew those, counting to ten. *Slowly.* Do not swallow any." He obliged, eyeing the little bottles. I pushed the minion under the satchel, out of sight.

I lifted the boy's shirt from the front—pale little belly, pale chest, unmarred. Very gently, I rolled him to one side, my fingers instantly sticky with blood. I tore away the shirt. There, by his left shoulder blade, was a jagged rip of skin. A Troth's claw had snagged him—a single claw thankfully, or he'd not have a shoulder blade . . . or a back. I'd seen close-up the brutal results of a Troth's hard swipe. The boy had not been the target of those slug-skinned creatures; he'd just been in the way.

"Spit into your palm," I told Brown-beard, lifting the boy's arm and draping it over his head. I wiped away the blood and dirt and pointed at the soft underarm. "Spread it here. Make a thin coating, cover all."

Brown-beard was sweating now, a cold sweat in the aftermath of shock, a bad sign. "Focus," I urged. "Focus." His hands shook as he smeared the mess onto the boy's skin, and then I had to pull those hands away as the man seemed to forget he'd finished.

I tucked the boy's arm down, then cradled his cheek against his palm and brushed the hair from his brow. It was feather-soft, and for just a moment I lingered, combing back the fine curls, thinking this must be what it was like to tuck a child in to sleep, to watch him sweetly dream.

Yearning pierced through, sharp as any needle; I swallowed it down . . . away. 'Twas quick—only a breath, a moment to steel myself. Then smoke wafted over and I looked at Brown-beard. "Clean your hands," I told him, pointing at the blackened grass.

He did not hear me. His hands lay limp on his knees, the corners of his mouth twitching with words that didn't come. I ripped tufts of the grass and did it for him, scrubbing the herb from his palms; he didn't flinch.

"Do not falter now," I warned. And I clutched his shoulder, willing my own energy to seep in and erase the stupor. "You are whole. You can help."

He turned his head and looked at me strangely, this man with the too-close name, Rafinn. The smoke fingered between us, the last hisses of flame like an ugly, mocking whisper: *Ruin and death, ruin and death, all gone, all gone, all gone.* I let my gaze slip, scanned the charred field we crouched in. The other survivors had long stumbled off, and I did not like that I was suddenly alone with the one whose name was too painful to use, who had the stare of one who needed to confess. "Listen to me," I gritted, turning back abruptly. I gave his shoulder another shake and squeezed harder. "*Listen.* You are all right. 'Twill be all right."

"All right . . . ," Brown-beard echoed. "All right . . ." My grip was stirring something at last, my energy igniting his. Guilt burst open, a whisper running to a shriek: "I am whole because I *didn't* help!" he blurted out. "I am whole because I was afraid! I ran. I let my village burn . . . and I ran! Do you hear me? I *ran.*"

The man broke down in wrenching sobs. I held still, half sorry for him, half revolted. I should have liked to pull my hand from his shoulder, let him bear his shame alone. I should have liked to run far from this seeping darkness and nurse my own grief. But that was not what Healers did. He ran. I could not.

I waited until his breath calmed, then released my grip and brushed his misery from my palms. "What was before makes no difference," I said. "You are helping now. Look."

The boy lay soft and still in his lullaby pose, but the wound was bubbling along its jagged edge. "There is poison in the claws of the Troth," I said low. "The minion is pushing it out." I took the warm little hand and pressed it within my own to speed the process. As we watched, purple-black blood dripped from the wound and was replaced by a bright, clean red. It quickly scabbed over.

"Do they all react like that?" The man gulped.

"Different poisons respond to different herbs." I glanced up at the ash-dead fields and added, "Some poisons do not respond at all." Hukon, of course, was the vilest poison; nothing could completely cure it.

I wondered if anything could cure fear.

He looked sideways at me, then touched where I'd gripped his shoulder. "You—you hold much ability for one so young." There was a hint of awe in his voice now, like the dead woman's. "I thought Healers were of great age."

"I am seventeen nigh two months." That seemed substantial enough. What I'd witnessed in those months had aged me greatly, and I was done with it all anyway.

Once more I took the boy's arm and raised it, wiped the smear of minion off with a clean patch on my cloak. My cloak was turquoise—or had been before I left Merith. The minion went black against the brilliant blue. "This child is small. The medicine cannot be kept there too long or he would not wake again," I explained. "Things that heal will themselves become poison if used unwisely. And they are not for *you*."

I said the last bit severely because the man had cast his eye on the vials of heliotrope and yew that lay in the dirt. There was a new eagerness in those furtive glances. He might have recognized one of them, known either of those plants wrongly used could put out his fear forever. 'Twas like that, healing and death. They were always near one another.

I slipped the vials back in my satchel along with the minion and slung the thing over my shoulder to keep them safe. *Safe*—I'd never thought like that before. In Merith, my home, my past, we'd never barred a door; we'd never argued in anger; we'd never even feared Dark Wood at our doorstep. Now in this blackened, empty field, I felt the first prickings of danger. Not from the bloody ravaging of Troths, but from what remained in their wake.

Another feeling to push away, sweep under the mat of rigid focus. I was sick of being stoic. Still, I turned to Brown-beard with no expression to betray me. "Let the child's eyes open on their own," I instructed. "Find something to feed him, to feed all of you. A broth is best. You'll have to make a fire. You'll have to find water, a pot. Put whatever food you can scavenge to steep. Do you understand?"

He nodded, shivering. I pushed myself from the ground.

"You are leaving?"

I nodded back. I was late enough for my own destiny.

"But you cannot leave! Not yet!" He shouted it, jumping up. "You must help us finish what we started. We—we do not know what to do. You can help."

No. I closed my eyes. *Let me be done. Let me finally be done.*

But Brown-beard turned me to him, all nervous and eager

again, and easily forgetting the boy that lay at his feet. "You *must* help," he insisted. "This way." And he set off at a skittish pace.

"Wait!" I called. "Take the child!" Brown-beard returned and impatiently scooped the boy in his arms as I bade him take care. 'Twould have been better to let the boy heal where he lay, but he'd have been forgotten. I wasn't even certain the man would do anything more than dump the poor little thing on some cold cobblestone. I had to follow.

I shook off the burr of disappointment, crunched over smoldering stalks and blackened leaves to the closest body for something to cover the boy. The old man there no longer needed his coat, so I slid it gently from his shoulders. I took as well the apron from the corpse of a woman.

"This way," Brown-beard said as I neared. He led me back toward the ruin of Bern, where we laid the boy in the market square by the well, pillowing the apron under his head and draping the jacket. "This way," Brown-beard repeated, edgy and hushed, and continued. I followed, blurring the footprints he left in the ash.

It was near the last cottage, a long garden shed at the very end of the village, one of the few structures not destroyed. Five remaining villagers mingled there, hobbled and restless, away from its shut door.

"What is it?" I asked. "Is another hurt?" I was at the door lifting the latch before Brown-beard yelped, "No!" He grabbed my wrist, yanking me back. "Not one of us! A—" He could barely name it: "A Troth."

In perfect response, a howl curdled from the shed. The crowd gasped and stumbled closer together. Even I reeled a little at the suddenness of the revelation, the threat. *Troth.*

"Wounded," someone whispered.

"The first beast to arrive. Tamel managed to stick it with a hammer before he was killed," said another. "It ran in there. Then the rest attacked. . . ."

That was two days past, from what I'd learned. I straightened. "Has no one opened the door?" I asked. "Has no one looked? Where was the creature wounded?"

They shook their heads at my questions, and I shook my head back at them, upset. "You cannot leave the Troth like this."

"We thought it would die—"

"Except it hasn't!" someone broke in. "And what if it's mended—"

"'Twill burst through the door and kill us all!"

"'Twill have its *revenge*!"

Their words scrambled over one another in fearful spurts. Six adults—four men, two women—and the little boy asleep in the market square. Seven left. A sad straggle of survivors. The Troth keened, rattling the shed, and panic shivered through those standing, fevered their stares.

"You could cast a spell to keep it inside, to keep the door bolted hard, couldn't you?" the youngest man there begged.

"She's a Healer, fool!" A second man knocked his shoulder angrily.

"A Healer, nonetheless! They weave spells!"

"A Healer is no wizard!" I exclaimed.

"But she has knowledge of *herb*," Brown-beard announced to a chorus of gasps. He turned to me, echoing my own warning with jittery enthusiasm: "You carry things that poison, no? That thing must be parched or starving. If we mashed your herbs, smeared it on some meat—"

A woman shrieked, "Meat! When we starve?"

"There are dead things all around us," Brown-beard hissed back. "Take your pick."

The angry man would have none of it. "Too easy after what they've done! As painful a death as we can make for that thing!" He turned. "*You*, Mistress Healer, have you something in your bag for that?"

Someone giggled wildly in agreement, saying "If poison contorts even a little, we can pull the tools from the shed and finish it!"

"Finish *slowly*!"

"*Our* revenge . . ."

It. Thing. The opportunity to pay back suffering with suffering. "The herbs are not for that," I bit out over the ugly chatter. "You cannot ask me to take a life." Defense, yes, but not cruelty.

"It's a *beast*," one woman muttered.

"No more than any of us," I muttered back, repulsed. I'd had enough of violence. I pushed past the closest man by the door and grabbed the latch. "I will finish this my way."

No one stopped me this time; instead, they ran back a distance and fell into a huddle. They cried to me, a mix of fearful voices: "Do not let it out!" " 'Twill kill us!" "Tear you in pieces!" "You'll be raven pickings!"

"I do not fear any Troth," I called back. I opened the door and shut it hard behind me with grim relief. Better to face a wild brutality than a reasoned one.

The interior was dusk-dark. The windows were patches of gray from the smoke. A tumble of rakes, hoes, and shovels clotted the planked floor like jackstraws; wheelbarrows and carts were tossed upside down—the Troth had crashed into everything in a fury of pain. I could smell the leaked blood, hear his sharp panting, but I could not see him.

I kept my hand on the latch and whispered to test: "Where do you hide?"

A low growl emitted from the back shadows. Then nothing. I waited, learning by that eerie silence what I needed to know—'twas a warning only; the Troth could not attack. I let go of breath and latch, began climbing over the mess with as little noise as possible. Halfway, the stench of blood and beast stopped me cold. I swallowed, hitched a little to the left, and peered into the dimness, watching shadow resolve into form.

"There you are," I murmured.

The Troth was horribly wounded, his left arm half ripped from the shoulder, the blood smearing him more black than red. Two days he'd lasted like that, an impressive feat. But it left him more dangerous—he'd die soon enough, but not before becoming even more ferocious in a final gasp of agony. The

Troth would explode out of the garden shed just as the villagers feared and take them down. And he *would* take them down. Even one-armed, the Troth could take us all.

I studied him, wondering how a physique no greater in size could hold more strength than any human. The goblin-hunched frame; the mottled, spongy skin; the strings of hair and dagger teeth; the slits for a nose. And those eyes—they were meant for the dark. They caught the gray light in sudden gleams and flashes. It made me vulnerable that the Troth could see better and kill with a single blow. But I held my ground, held my gaze, wanting to see this foreign creature up close and wanting to *know*—as if somehow in the dim light and mess of blood I might recognize this Troth as the one who killed the young man I loved. And if I might recognize, then . . .

The end of the story I did not tell Brown-beard: that the Riders had saved Merith from the worst. Almost.

It was not two months since I saw the Troths leaping from Dark Wood, through the gardens and growing fields, through barn and cottage, thudding over the pretty paths that led straight to our village square. But then the Riders stormed in and . . .

And compared to Bern we'd been spared.

There was one slaughter, though, that stood out as breathtakingly cruel. A young man lay with his chest ripped open in the middle of Merith's market square. Raif—*my* Raif. A Troth had slain my love, whole claw.

Perhaps this Troth.

We eyed each other. The Troth was cornered; I was exposed. An unfavorable standoff, truly. For him.

In that moment, in that space of wonder and possibility, I was invincible—a strength not from knowledge of cures or fearlessness, but from rage. I had a culprit to take it out on, finally, a way to release the screams I never screamed. My blood was heating, surging through veins, flushing cheeks, quickening heart—expanding until I dominated the shed and could crush this puny creature without a flicker of movement, and in silence.

The Troth sensed it. He remained wary; those luminous disks fixed on me. I returned his stare with arrows of ice-cold fury and a fierce smile.

"I would leave you like this," I hissed. A minute ago I'd shunned such viciousness in the frightened villagers beyond the door. Now I wished and whispered a similar curse—a glorious, livid, and far too brief curse: "I want you to suffer. I *want* you to hurt."

His gaze stayed fixed. The Troth didn't understand me . . . or maybe he did. For though I might pretend I'd entered the shed with dark intent and hurl hate-filled words, Healers could not act out of malice. I could not harm, nor prolong agony. I could not even leave this creature to those villagers outside.

I could not avenge Raif's death.

Still, rage illuminated, awed me, even—pure and fleeting like a shooting star. And then it was done. Smile gone, I settled to the task of ending his suffering quickly. My eyes roamed the room for something to use. There—a scythe. Sickle-shaped, with a sharp tip, honed blade, and sturdy wood handle. It hung on the back wall. Behind the Troth.

Healer's task . . . I eased forward; the Troth shifted. I stepped over a rake, and he growled—a little game of dare, with me unafraid and he so very wary—ever closer until we were face to face, my cloak almost brushing his feet. I wondered that he neither attacked nor ran—wondered if he was truly too exhausted from pain and loss of blood. But the Troth stayed hunkered against the wall, snorts of breath flexing those ugly little slits, leaving me to stretch over him for the tool. The rank breath and the stench of his grisly wound mixed in overwhelming foulness. I swallowed against it, then slowly reached my hand above his string-haired scalp. Those orbs slid up, tracked my move—

"Mistress Healer!" Cries came pounding through the shed, shocking both of us. "Mistress Healer! What happens?"

With a hideous shriek, the Troth sprang and I lunged for the scythe. Then his claws were gripping my throat and it was I who was pinned to the wall, dangling, my fingers scrabbling for the sickle blade. And still the villagers shouted for me, their terror whipping frenzy. "Hush!" I tried to yell. There was barely a voice, barely air.

He used the wounded arm, yet the Troth kept rigid hold, his snarl curling a lipless mouth over those dagger teeth. I gasped and choked and strained for the scythe, stunned at how quick it could all be over. How easy. And then I stopped struggling, remembering that moment two months back when a Troth sprang for me as I kneeled by Raif's lifeless body.

My useless wish now was the same as then: *Kill me. Kill* me.

But this Troth waited. Maybe he fed on fear and was surprised that I held none. Maybe he smelled the Healer, the herbs, and wondered what I could offer to cure. Or did he feel the same hate I did, and enjoyed that for me the pain of living was far worse than a quick death? Speculations only. The Troth was a wild thing, a killer, and I was prey. Eye to limpid eye, we stared, judged.

And there it was: the recognition that I should be killed. The creature's grip tightened; I felt the claws digging in, forcing me sideways. The back of my neck grated against the planking. My fingertips touched the scythe. *Now. Do it now.* I was begging for him to win. His good arm went up to slash—

Instinct swept in. I ripped the scythe from the hook and had it to his throat before he could finish me. The tip of the blade pierced the small, soft fold in his neck, the point where blood would flow out fastest and without sting.

How quick it could all be over. How easy. How unfair. The orbs stared at me—no shock, just an easing of torment . . . and, finally, release. Then the luminous glow faded and the claws unclenched. The Troth thumped to the floor in a hiss of dark blood, and my feet touched down.

There was a moment of pure silence—even the villagers had stopped. Slowly, I wiped the scythe on my cloak and hung it back on the wall. I pressed my fingers against the splinters of wood where my nails had scraped and I exhaled . . . but not with relief. Healer nature always prevailed. No malice. No harm. Not even to myself.

The shouting began again.

Well, perhaps a tiny spark of malice: I clambered back over the wreckage, flung open the door, catching the villagers by surprise. They started and stumbled back, cringing with shrieks of terror, and I let them, before shouting over all of it, "It is done."

Slowly they righted themselves, releasing fear in gasps, then choking with helpless laughter.

"You killed it!" The angry man wheezed. I nodded and brushed some cobwebs from my cloak, smearing all the Troth blood, which I'd yet to wipe from my fingers. One of the women turned to retch.

But the other woman wiped her eyes and looked at me in wonder. "How? How did you manage? You waded through our destruction, you helped, you killed . . . but your pretty face is so brave and still. You have no tears? No tears for sadness, or worry, or fear, or relief?"

No. I had no tears. Another thing: Healers did not cry.

"I did what you asked," I told them instead. "I'll leave you now." I moved away from the garden shed. *West*, I remembered, and turned in that direction, then looked back at them all. "You will not forget the boy back in the square," I said to the man named Rafinn. "You will not forget to make a broth, to *feed* him." He nodded. They all did.

I would not be sorry to leave this village, that name. Each of them grinning now like fools over the death of one Troth. A tiny, ugly victory in a sea of despair, those grins highlighting bleak stares. Maybe mine was as bleak. I suppressed a shudder, said as fairly as I could, "Farewell, then. Good luck to you."

Charred grass, charred village. Not sorry to leave this place—

But they did not like to lose me so quickly. They trailed me a little ways, chattering: "Won't you stay?" "Where do you go?"

No, I will not stay. I go to my end.

"Wait, *please,* Mistress Healer!"

That was Rafinn. I stiffened, then turned.

"Your name," he said, eager and nervous. "At least give us that. We must thank you by name."

"Eve," I told him after a moment. It was not my full name, or my nickname. But it made me sound older, more like the aged Healer he'd expected.

"Then thank you, Mistress Eve." The remaining villagers murmured the same in turn, "Thank you, Mistress Eve."

I nodded to each, then walked on alone.

"Mistress Eve," I heard Rafinn say admiringly to the others. "The one who is unafraid of death."

No. No tears, no fear of death. Grimacing as I left them in the distance.

Then, a little farther on, I smiled. *Fear* of death? Nay. I would be glad of it.

2

I WOULD BE glad of it.

That ran as a little song. Kept me company all the way to
the mossy edge of a drought-diminished river. I stopped there
to wash away the filth of the past days, shedding my clothes
piece by piece—cloak and frock and undershift and sandals. I
scoured the blood and ash from each using river stones in slow,
methodic circles. Scoured myself with the stones until I, like
the cloth, was scrubbed clean, and my hair was silver-blond
again.

I left everything to dry on the bank and plunged into the
river, diving straight to the bottom. Swimming was my favorite idyll, once—the clear water, the sun-sparkled droplets on
skin, the peace—it was my shedding of a day, my healing. But
now the quiet of it made my ears ring with memory: the clash

of sword, the shriek of beast, and the roar of fire in Merith's square. Things I could not shed or heal.

I would be glad of it. I sang it underwater, watching the bubbles rise and pop, like splatters of blood beneath the red sunset.

Later, I spread myself out to dry like my clothes and waited for the light to die. And even later I gathered watercress and fennel and a wild carrot for a meal, adding in a bit of dried meat that one village had spared me as thanks. Methodical and neat and emotionless. I scraped some oil from a berrit leaf onto a stick and lit it as a candle.

Functions of survival that I no longer had use for yet performed without thought.

A bitter truth: I might chant that I would be glad for death, but to offer myself to it was a near-impossible effort—even in the grip of a Troth. I was no good at it, at this decision to be done; I could not let go.

'Twas weakness, not cowardice. Call it duty, or the fault of my gift. Healers knew too much. An affinity with the workings of Nature: we could spot the greens and herbs to eat or mend with. We could find water easily, light a fire, fashion a storm-proof shelter, gauge direction. . . . Our hands bestowed calming energy to others or sped the healing process. We protected ourselves instinctively, with little effort. The effort was in trying to take life prematurely.

Next to my little salad I placed two of the vials of herbs from my satchel and stared at them as I ate. Only two vials.

The minion was too precious to misuse; I left that in the bag. But the heliotrope and yew were lovely poisons. I took them out often, unstoppered them to smell the dark-deep earthiness of one and the cherry scent of the other. I imagined fading into sleep.

Fade away: 'twas what I planned, why I left Merith, why I'd abandoned Grandmama and Lark one early dawn without goodbyes and walked away from my life. I could not stay, mend into some half existence. 'Twas like finishing a tapestry with the color missing, and I could not bear to weave such a dulled, lonely picture. I wanted Raif. I wanted not to have let him die.

My hand reached for the yew, disembodied. I touched a fingertip to the smooth glass, rolling the vial a little to watch the dark bits tumble inside. Some plants' poisons fade when cut and dried. Never yew. *Chew thoroughly, expect gastric distress, death comes quickly* . . . I'd done this so many times: stared at or smelled the vials, recounting the effects, intending to stuff their contents in my mouth. Each time I was sure I could confound my instincts, I only found myself packing up and traveling on in a daze. Another meal, another night, another devastated village.

My fingers found the stopper. I squeezed it between my thumb and forefinger. *This time, Evie. If this time you could just* . . .

The fennel went bitter. I spit it out, wiped my mouth, and was stuffing the vials back in the satchel before I even realized.

But then I caught my breath. It was too forceful, that shove.

My fingertips brushed things I'd tucked under the satchel's bottom seam. Mementos of home I'd taken with me, things to keep close yet out of reach, things far more potent, more painful than any poison.

A lark feather and a braided leather ring.

The feather was for Lark. I picked it from the garden path not long after she'd gone for the Riders. It was no sign, but lark feathers were rare, so an auspicious find nonetheless. And the ring? The ring had been worn by Raif's grandfather, the tailor who was mutilated by the Troths. During the attack on Merith, Raif grabbed back the ring the Troths had kept as a prize. And I, in turn, took it from Raif's lifeless hand.

Hand to hand to hand—a circle of leather, a circle of victory and of death. My own hand was cold, frozen by that accidental touch. Memories were building now like rain clouds: first a sprinkle, then a shower. I squeezed my eyes shut and tried to force them back, but they were bursting over me, as fresh as yesterday's happening, brutally sweet and heart-scraping. Raif—my loyal comrade in Merith, my partner in all the exploits I could not share with my shy cousin. Every field and garden, every tree had been explored and picked and climbed together. He was the best part of my every day.

A downpour of memories now, drenching, drowning. So I gave in, hugged my knees close to my chest, and braced.

"Look up, Evie! Look where I am!" Raif calling from somewhere in the canopy of Jarett Doun's apple trees. Six years old and so proud of his squirrel-like agility. "Hold out your apron!"

Fruit raining down before I had a chance to lift the hem of my blue apron. . . .

"'Tis Evie, you dolts!" Raif at ten years, snorting with laughter at our group game of blind man, when I'd put on little Wilby's eyeglasses as a disguise. We were too familiar with one another to ever win at it; Raif was pulling off his blindfold with one hand and tugging my long braid with the other. "You cannot hide from me . . . !"

One hand usually pulling my braid, the other shoving his own shock of black hair from his brow. At twelve years we goaded one another—happy, carefree, busy bodies, just longer-limbed and wild-spirited. Raif constantly pointing over my head so I'd turn, and then stealing my hair ribbon to wave in victory. I'd leap for it; he'd feign surrender to my strength. We'd scuffle for the prize. . . .

And three years later came ridiculously fateful words: "Cath! Stop giggling!"

Voices—filtering from the orchard where I'd gone to welcome Raif home. He'd been away in Crene for eighteen months apprenticing with the treekeepers, and I'd waited impatiently for his return—both wanting to prove myself his superior with my own Healer knowledge and to have our teases again. But there was the flirting, silly Cath arriving first, eager to claim the so very handsome and newly grown-up Raif. And he was happily obliging: "If you want a kiss, then let me do it properly. . . ."

I caught their kiss, gawking like a fool. And what was familiar was suddenly lost in queasy strangeness—of heart, stomach, and limb—a sickness I could not cure. Seeing Raif in the orchard, at Gatherings, or by any accident became both brilliant and awkward. He stood out, suddenly, not as my friend but like some beacon too bright to look upon, yet impossible to avoid. And then it was even more strange and awkward when at sixteen he stopped at our booth one market day to smell Grandmama's lavender soaps and lemon balm possets—

Raif said my hair smelled of those things. He said it shone as silver as the full moon. And then all the feelings were no longer strange, but delicious and thrilling, and as necessary as breathing.

Tall, dark-haired, and pale-skinned, even in midsummer. Quiet, patient, more serious, with a wit too subtle to be much recognized in our guileless village. I knew Raif's face better than my own, for I could not help but watch him—learning to observe in secret from the corner of my eye. I observed as Cath lost his fancy. I observed as he contrived reasons to visit our booth or arrive to draw water from the common well at the same times I did. I observed him observing me, sometimes, and was secretly glad. I lay in bed at night picturing his smile, wanting that kiss he'd given Cath. I'd construct the moment when he might profess, and shape our future into pretty pictures—husband, wife, and babies gathered around a hearth. And I kept it—*all* of it—secret.

My stupidity, such secrets. My loss. I was blunt and forthright about most things, but I never spoke of love. 'Twas a choice I made when very young. I liked being a Healer; I wanted to be best at it, maybe even to earn the status of White Healer, so I'd decided never to betray my feelings—that I might always appear impartial, look fairly to all. If Raif asked for my hand, that was a fine thing, but I'd not choose him first. I thought I was being brave and selfless. I thought it didn't matter.

Grandmama would say, "Loving freely will not weaken one's gifts," as if she suspected my desire. But I stayed rigidly quiet. And Raif was patient.

It was not until that last day, when the threat of Troths weighed heavy in anticipation. It was after market; I'd repacked the basket, said my daily—and more earnest—farewells, and was just past Dame Keren's cottage when Raif met me and pulled my elbow so that I swung around the side of her chimney and into his arms.

He kissed me. It was not my first kiss, but I thought it the best. And he kissed my cheeks and my hair and held my face between his hands to look me straight in the eye, to memorize me. Then he left quickly without demanding my response.

Soon after, the village bell was clanging in warning, the Troths were howling, Raif was lying heart open in the village square, and my moon-colored hair was red with his blood. And then I hung, half surprised, half eager as a Troth sprang for my throat, undone when that Troth was stabbed dead by a Rider charging past.

Words of affection, of pledge, were never shared. 'Twas Lark who told Raif I loved him, as she told me the same. *Love cannot die,* Raif bade her tell me in return. And even that Lark intervened for our sakes was a lost effort, for it was too late for anything but words. All of it was too late, too secret, wasted and unfinished.

Love cannot die. But it did die. And I was left with these fierce memories and a ring.

My arms were clasped so hard around my legs that my limbs were white. I slowly let go, slowly tied my satchel closed over the unused herbs. But I smiled a little, for I was not yet defeated. I had an alternate plan for death: Rood Marsh. I'd heard it talked of at market—'twas a place so wide and so empty, a person would lose her way in the reeds with little there to sustain her. It gave purpose—like a little glow beyond all the numbness— for if I could not struggle free of Healer instinct on my own, this marsh would do it for me.

West, I was told. I was getting closer. And my clothes were dry.

Moonlight made for easy travel. I walked through the night and the next one, slept some, and continued west. I was far enough from Merith that I could no longer guess at which village I passed or recognize the ribbons of their market tents. I aimed away from the sunrise, keeping a little to the south. If I strayed north I might reach the city of Tyre. That was a vile place, I'd heard; I had no wish to lose myself there.

Once, I happened upon a troupe of mummers who were

camped on the banks of a shrinking pond. Their bells jingled faintly merry in the breeze, a reminiscence of festivals, of acrobats and pantomimes. "What news?" they asked me of the towns to the east. My answer was the same as theirs was from the west: too meager a harvest to celebrate, farmers too poor to pay for treats.

We shook hands all around in place of food to share, as none of us had any to spare. I started off, but a little farther on one of the children waved at me, pointing to the water. She wanted me to fetch some little waterfowl she'd spied drifting in the middle, struggling to stay upright. The pond was not deep, but none of them could swim. I kicked off my sandals, bunched up my skirts, and waded in. Black and white, the thing was like a large duck, but not one I'd ever seen. I slid my hand under his firm belly and towed him slowly back to shore. He waddled up the bank a ways and crouched silent, so we kneeled by him. "Is it dead?" the girl asked, frowning.

I shook my head. "Nay, look." I brushed the edge of one wing so it stretched out long in reflex. But then I too frowned. Something else I'd never seen: the bird's feathers were singed as if by a hot blade—a dark straight line sheared the tips, a harsh scent of metal still potent.

We banked the little fowl with handfuls of grass and moss for cover and left him there. "There's no medicine for this," I told her. "A burned wing will refeather. But he is far from his home, and that is something we must let the bird find on his own." She skipped off, pleased enough to have saved him. I walked on, wondering.

A waterbird that drowned; wings clipped by strange fire. This was way beyond the violent reach of Troths.

Something dark was coming to our little world.

A day and night and day again, a plain landscape with food scarcer to forage. The last green tints dissolved into brown, and I was left with a few lone skyhawks. Then the skyhawks dropped away, and out of the dullness appeared something else altogether:

Rood Marsh.

I had to stop first and simply stare at the dense stand of reeds that confronted me, jutting up from the mud, twice a man's height. They spread far to the north and west, breaking the landscape. I scouted along its border. Trails were cut into the marsh; most were abandoned after a few paces. One opening, though, pushed farther, cutting a narrow trough that disappeared into a wet dimness. It seemed a better start than simply plunging in. The marsh seemed to think so too. There was a shuffling of canes in the faint breeze, their humid breath on my cheeks. An applause of sorts, a welcome.

I opened my satchel, took out the water flask and the last bits of dried meat and carrots I'd saved, and placed them on the edge of the grass as a gift for whatever creature might pass by. Nothing left for me except the keepsakes, the minion, and the poisons. I closed my eyes, lifted my face for a last drenching of sun, and smiled.

Then I shifted my pack and walked in.

The path followed the only solid ground. Other trails were

cut here and there, and at first I paused to peer into each dark winding, to finger the pale brown wands. But then the trails fell away, leaving only one narrow gap between towering walls. I trekked on. It turned silent, save for the whispers. There were no shadows, just gray light. Minutes passed, perhaps hours. Eagerness dwindled against monotony. I imagined Raif with me; I imagined Lark. I imagined journeys I'd not have to make alone.

Somewhere I remembered I was thirsty. By habit I broke off a stem to suck out the moisture—a worthless puddle-taste of rotting leaves. Without thinking, I turned and began walking back the way I came, then stopped, snorting. How foolish— I'd been too safe by staying on the path; Healer instinct would march me straight out of the marsh. I could feel it even then: the tug for water, for the little necessities I'd left behind on the grass. I'd have to fight myself to stay.

And so I did it fast, the only thing I could think to make myself hopelessly lost, before I could reason my way into returning: I shut my eyes and spun in circles until I was wildly dizzy . . . and then crashed into the reeds. Hands out, pushing at the forest of stems, I slogged ten steps, twenty, as many as I could before my eyes sprang open.

I was shin-deep in mud. There was another trail in front of me, so I took it and ran a little ways, then broke through the walls again. *No paths!* I had to go deeper.

Reeds caught and tore, feathering down their fluffy crowns like snow. I stumbled upon a third path, crossed it, and farther on crossed another. *"Stop!"* I hissed fiercely. *"Stop finding me!"* Who had been through here? There was nary a reason to come this far—no one would willingly choose this way to travel. And yet ahead was a rudely made footbridge laid over a deep puddle. I swore at it, turned, and went knee-deep into green-slick muck. I stumbled up, slashing at the canes. I crossed more paths and more until I raged at this invisible crowd of explorers, feet stamping, splattering mud into mud.

"Claim me!" I shouted to the marsh. "Go on. *Claim* me!"

I waited. There was the faint brush of applause.

I turned and ran again. Broken stems, shards of reeds flaking and sticking. *Deeper, Evie. Deeper.* And then I tripped flat onto the stinking ground. Panting and spitting, I raised my head, wiped the slime to look at what had sent me sprawling.

There was the footbridge again, and the path. The *only* path. All the others I'd made myself, circling and recircling. Healer instinct—I kept coming back.

A bitter, ugly little noise curled from my throat. I was not lost but found; I could not shake any trail, any opportunity to return. I pushed myself up, not bothering anymore to smear the mess away, and sat down on the bridge. I pulled the satchel around front, untied it, and took out the yew, determined. There was no more applause from the crowd of reeds, but whispers of disappointment. I growled at them, and they sighed back, hollow and forlorn. I yelled out, "You don't understand: I *want* this! Raif is gone!" My voice was as forlorn as the reeds: "You like this solitude. But it is not for me, this being alone."

But then I was no longer alone.

It made no secret of its approach. It was simply coming, an uneven tread of foot on mud and straw, limping, gaining.

Intruding. Annoyed, I slammed the yew back in my bag and stood up to confront.

Not more than a minute and then the louder whisper of reeds rustled in passing—

An old man stepped into view.

3

NOT JUST AN old man. A terribly old man. Stooped and scrawny and ugly. He wore a robe wrapped nearly twice around and tied with a bit of leather. Whether he wore leggings underneath, I could not tell. And, as if that were not enough, he was made more absurd by the sky-blue dunce cap stuck on his greasy head.

The old man had stopped short, a little surprised by me—black with filth, arms akimbo, blocking the path. But then he limped forward, pulled off his cap, and held it out all meek and cringing.

"A penny a fortune, mud poppet."

I stared for a moment in disbelief. Then I burst out laughing.

"One penny," he wheedled. "You will know your future."

"Here, in the midst of nothing you want to barter! What are you? A seer?"

He smiled, a mouth of darkly yellowed teeth. "Some call me so. I am named Harker."

"Well, then, Master Harker—"

"*Not* Master," he said sharply.

"Harker, then. If you are a true seer you would know I have no future."

He peered at me. "And if you were a seer you might know differently."

"You are not here for fortunes. I can divine *that* much." Humor was gone. "Why do you follow me?"

"Follow! 'Tis a path," he said with that hideous grin, evading. "Why are you the only one to walk it?"

"There is no reason for you to come this way."

"And you have reason where I have none?"

"More reason than you."

The old man inched closer. " 'Tis not reason that brings you here. You push reason away."

"You cannot say that. You do not know me." We were speaking coyly, both of us, like a little game. I did not like it. And I was sorely disappointed—I'd been so close to an ending.

"Ah, but I do know you," he said solemnly. "You are the Healer."

I sniffed. "There are many Healers about. That was but a guess."

"No. You are *the* Healer. The one of ones."

"And you are the riddle maker." I turned and pointed

at the bridge. "Go on. I will wait until you are past. Go on your way."

He did not move. "You dictate? You make a choice for me?"

"I only let you go first."

"Nay, you pointed with your finger. You choose my direction. If I step past you it is because you directed."

"You make your own fate, Harker. You are the seer."

That made him suddenly sad. "True." He nodded slowly, no grin now. "If I follow your pointing finger it is because I choose to follow. But . . . what if you pushed me forward? Then is it my choice? Or is this where one's fate takes a turn by another's choosing?"

That he was more than a little mad was clear. I sat back down on the footbridge, leaving him room. "You do what you wish. But I hope you will go."

Harker shuffled very close. I watched his feet in their broken leather sandals—all trussed with cords of hide and plant. "Your cousin will make a choice for you," he announced.

"Cousin!" I looked up. "You know my cousin? How?"

He only eyed me slyly and held out his cap.

"That is no fortune." I pushed his hat from me, looked away again. Better to wait for him to tire of this play.

"I hope," he said very slowly, "that she chooses well."

I laid my chin in my hands and studiously ignored him. But it shook me that he used those words. *She did choose well, Seer, but for naught.*

"Nay." Harker answered my thought as if he'd heard me.

He leaned close. I could smell on him the filth and disease gathered from a long time of wandering, but I also smelled a wiry, tenacious strength. The opposites battled one another—he would live out countless years but be riddled with pain. A sad existence.

He hissed in my ear: "Nay, Evie Carew, the one Healer. I do not speak of your dead man. I speak of what's yet to come."

I jerked my head up, mouth open. "How do you know my thought? My name?"

"For one who wanted no fortune you have now asked for three!" He grinned. "Three questions and not one penny? *There.*" He stuck his cap almost under my nose. "Spare my fee."

"I have no penny," I said.

"Thief!" Harker shouted. I jumped a little, but he jumped farther. "You'll beg me. You'll all beg me!" He started off up the bridge where I'd pointed. It wasn't really a walk, but more like a puppet's dance with that limp—his feet on tiptoe, barely touching down, making the stands of rushes whisper as he passed.

I sat hunched for a while longer, upset that he'd interrupted my efforts but more disturbed that he knew me, that he knew Lark. And he'd said Lark would choose for me—something yet to come.

"She chose Raif," I whispered after him. "Lark already chose Raif for me. What more can she do than that?"

Oh, that I was like my cousin! Lark would have waited long for the seer to disappear and be soothed once more by the quiet and solitude. But I was left with my intentions in ruins, curiosity running like tendrils of ghisane, reaching to clutch at the speculations of this old man. Thorny, dark, incessant. What he meant I had to learn.

It was not long, then, before I picked myself up and started after him.

There is a secret in the middle of Rood Marsh.

It was an island in the sea of mud and towering reed: a broad scape, unaffected by drought, of bright green grass and clover, with a stream of clear water bubbling from a spurt in a choke of rock, and three trees: apple, beech, and willow. A border of brambleberries and cattails and woodbine defined one edge; borage and thyme grew wild at another. A tiny hut was built from timber and thatched with the reeds. And two goats and their kid roamed freely, grazing under a sky that was clear of the marsh gray.

The old man, Harker, sat by the stream on a large flat stone and watched the water.

I walked straight to him, surprised. "Is this your home?"

"I have no home," he said without moving.

"Others must come, then. The wilderness is well tended. There is all one needs to thrive here."

"Few bother the marsh. A herder from Bullbarr left the goats, and returns to cull the flock. Mostly it sits unknown. But those who find it can find peace." He turned his head to look at me. "You will not find peace."

I frowned. He'd been speaking lucidly. Now he was back to coy innuendos, and I was too easy a target.

"Why do you know my name? Why do you say I will not find peace?"

"Because you run from one reason and not the other."

"Harker!" I stamped my foot.

"You must pay me for your fortune, Healer."

"Please, I have no—"

"I give away no news for free." It was a loud, a bitter declaration. The old man choked a little upon saying it, and added, harsher, "I *cannot* be tempted. Never again."

I turned away, frustrated, but then spun back. "Seer that you are, you must know I have no coins. So you must content yourself with something else."

He waited. I said, "You have blisters on your hands. I can heal them."

Maybe he'd known I'd reach this stage of barter, but not this particular offer—there was an eager spark in his eyes. He dismissed it quickly, though, with a sharp little bark: "Do you think so?"

"Hold them out," I insisted.

He did. I kneeled down at his feet and took up his hands. They were worn and spotted and gnarled, made horrible by red-rimmed blisters, and he shivered under the inspection. I had expected to smear some of the heliotrope, or mix a poultice from the goat's milk and borage. I could shape an arch of the blackberry bushes and have the seer crawl beneath three times—such were medicines for skin boils. But what Harker suffered was nothing I could repair. This was pain that goaded and punished.

I said to him, "These wounds are magic-made. You gave or held something that you should not." Then I ducked a little so I could catch his eye and speak straight. "You were burned because of a mistake you made."

His returning stare was bleak. "How long have you suffered these?" I asked.

"I am old. These are not."

I looked again at the blisters, wondering what ill he'd done to carry such a reminder. "Well, I'm sorry. I cannot heal such wounds."

He jerked his hands away with a sly little smile. "Are you sorry for me or for yourself?" And then he was chuckling at my frown. "You still want to know what I can tell you."

"Yes." I tugged my satchel closer and dug in, pulling out the vial of heliotrope buds and offering it. "Here. You may have these. Roll one around in your mouth 'til it is fully dissolved before you swallow. One at a time *only*. 'Twill bring you a full night's sleep at least. Make them last."

Harker took the vial. One of his blisters brushed my skin; it burned cold. He put the little jar into the folds of his robe—some pocket hidden within—and said, "You give the heliotrope; you give me your own escape. Why not the jar of minion? You are shrewd, Healer."

I pressed the satchel against my cloak. "The minion is too precious to trade." I said it firmly, disconcerted that he knew I carried minion and that I wanted the heliotrope for my own end. He was the shrewd one.

"True," he was answering. "But that is not why. Still, a

penny's worth of sleep for a penny's worth of fortune." Harker pushed himself up from the stone; I saw how it hurt to use his hands. A constant suffering. "Stand away from me, Evie Carew. Step into the stream."

I knew what he meant. Running water held no intent, no spells good or bad. It was a fair place to wait, fair of him to ask. I stepped back into the cool shallows and felt the pebbled bed loosen around my toes and disperse. I held my breath, held in my eagerness for his words.

Harker too stepped back. He lifted his face to catch the dying sun full on it, his scrawny little frame stiffening. And he waited. But he was not drawing his words from the sky, rather waiting for them to form within him and bubble up.

And then he spoke, stilted, reading from a page that did not exist:

> *Moonlight on water brings Nature's daughter,*
> *Swift-bred terror and sorrow of slaughter.*
> *Silver and sickle, the healing hand,*
> *Find the shell's song; bring rain upon land.*

I waited, then burst out: "That is no fortune. That is a verse of poem."

"Nonetheless it belongs to you."

"But it means nothing to me!" I came out of the water, shaking the wet from my sandals. "Can you not say that I will die here? That the marsh will swallow me—something that makes sense?"

"Those would be the things that do not make sense, for that will not happen."

"Why not? Because you speak some fanciful words? Because I gave you my heliotrope? If this is not your home, then I will make it mine. I will stay here, grow old here. Tend the goats." I'd made that up. I was disappointed he'd given me no clear fortune, annoyed that my own choices were so simply negated.

But he laughed at me. "You will not, the one Healer, any more than you will take your own life with an herb. You toy with your little idea of death, thinking you are sad to be left alone. You blame your gift of healing for your hesitation, but that is not why you hold on to life. You do not see—"

"Don't say that! You know nothing of me!"

"I will say it. It is you who know nothing, silly girl. This is not your time. You are needed."

"Needed?" How dare he talk of changed fate, so smugly dangled like bait! "How am I needed?"

Harker walked back toward me and inspected me for a minute. "You are not shy like your cousin," he said. "You are hardly timid. Yet you share some of her stubbornness, and maybe more. Not unlike the others."

"What others?"

"Your cousin told you nothing of her journey!" The seer announced this with delight, but immediately contorted in agony. He swerved, swore, and spun around, crying to the space around us, "I do not have to tell! I do not have to tell!" And in the next breath he cringed, hissing to himself: "Your fault, so your duty to bear . . ." The protests grew to indistinct whines and faded. Then the seer shook himself, recovered, then looked at me coyly again. "She told you nothing, Healer, which makes you most ignorant. Unfortunate for one so curious."

I *was* curious, gruelingly so. But I changed tactics, refusing to ask anything more, since the more I questioned the more he evaded. After a moment he repeated, taunting: "Nature's daughter, one of the *four*."

I bit my tongue, waited.

He moved a little then, fixing me with his gaze. "Single daughters of twin mothers, born on the same day in the same hour. Alike and yet opposite."

Harker was speaking of Lark, of me, of our nearly sister connection. He said it like a chant:

"Her hair runs brown like the falling leaf, and yours is the rippling moonlight on a lake. Her eyes are the hazel of a new acorn and yours are the blue of the sea. Her skin is touched by sun, yours is the pale of the full moon." He shuffled a little more, circling slowly so that he was almost behind me. "She stays quiet like a fawn; you move easily in company. She wears her feelings; you suffocate yours. So different. And yet . . ." Harker lifted his scarred hand to point at my back. "What is alike between you? What do you share with your dearest Lark?"

I knew, small as it was. "We share a birthmark."

The seer nodded. "Yes. A mark. Just there above the blade edge of your left shoulder." He reached a finger to touch it; I shivered, jerked away, and turned on him—

He pulled back, cowering and shouting, "I am sorry! I am sorry! I am sorry!"

"You did nothing . . ." I protested, but stopped. Harker was not apologizing to me; he was looking up to the empty, intense blue.

There was silence while he searched, waiting for some answer, and then suddenly he fell to the ground with a scream of anguish and began writhing in pain. He held his hands out in front of him; there was a shimmer of heat rising from his blisters. They were burning. I grabbed his wrists, dragged his racked body to the stream, and plunged his hands into the cold water. "Hold them there, it will help." Running water could wash small magic away. But I doubted it could this.

He lay there, hands in fists underwater, convulsing and sobbing into his shoulder, "I am sorry!" What he was sorry for I didn't know, but I was sorry for him. He was too old yet too far from death to be enduring such agony.

At length old Harker worked his way to his knees and drew his hands from the water. They were raw but no longer on fire. Sober, quiet, and suddenly very sane, the seer murmured, "All want me to share what I know; all want me to help them face their fates—as if fates could not be changed in an instant! And yet . . . And yet no one cares for my fate. No one wishes to help me."

He raised his head, looked straight at me. "Except you, Eveline Carew. I did not foresee your kindness to me." Then, sitting back a little and squaring his shoulders, the seer said, "You have earned this, young Healer. I tell you this freely, so listen well:

"You see that a darkness is coming. I will not call it by name, but know that this darkness begins as a violence of Nature and becomes the violence of Man. It will consume us all if it cannot be stopped. But you, Evie Carew, are one who can help stop this darkness. You asked three questions before, so three things I will share. Not your questions, nor things that are in and of themselves your fate, but knowing these three things will help guide you:

"You must find the shell amulet. And if you love your cousin you will not ask for any help.

"Secondly, you believe you are hiding because you feel grief at a death, but that is not what you truly hide from. You must open your eyes.

"And lastly, they will strike you where you are weak."

Harker cringed then, as if he knew what weakness was, as if he expected his hands to burst with new pain. But nothing happened, and so he straightened and made a funny little bow and began walking away.

I followed. "Am I supposed to thank you for this? For leaving me with more questions?"

"Yes."

"But that is no gift—"

"I did not say I would give you a gift, I said you earned these."

"But then can I not barter for more earnings? Will you not say more?"

"No."

And Harker brushed off his filthy robe and, avoiding the single path, turned to the wall of reeds.

"Harker!"

He ignored me. Yet I couldn't let him leave; burden me with more questions. "Harker!"

I ran to catch up but he turned on me fiercely, hissing, "They will strike you where you are weak! Where are you weak, young girl?" He grinned meanly, stuck his face too close. "Where. Are. You. *WEAK?*"

I held my ground. The seer was mad, maybe, but not harmful.

He answered for me. "Curious—too eager for knowledge, Healer! And longing for what was. Curiosity sways emotion, as does longing, Healer; they are *needs.* Be careful what you need!"

The seer whirled then, spiraling back, railing to the marsh, "I have given her more than I dared! I will suffer. I will suffer." He parted the brittle stems.

"Milkweed, Harker," I called out abruptly. "Break milkweed stems, smear them on your hands. The milk might ease a bit of your pain."

Harker paused and looked back. "That," he said, eyeing me sadly, "I already know." He turned around again and pushed in.

His drab robe was quickly swallowed by the forest of brown. Then all that was left was the faint applauding of the reeds.

4

THERE WAS NO sign of any threatening darkness on this little island. I sat in the middle of the green lawn looking at silly, fat clouds huffing across a lucid blue sky, listened to the *brr* and shrill of redwings as they conversed clinging to the velvet tips of cattails. It was sweetly pastoral: a bee drunkenly weaving through the clover, the kid bleating after his mother, the stream bubbling quick and clear and cold; none showed concern. Harker's ominous foreboding had echoed mine—that something dark was coming to our little world—but it was not present here. Perhaps I'd lost myself at last.

Except that Harker had said those words: *You will find no peace here.* Prophetic or mocking, they were more than a little thorn. And his cryptic verse, his challenge and warnings made everything unsettled and wanting. It burned me that he said I *earned* those things. He knew questions would bubble up in me, eat away at any peace. I should defy his words to prove him wrong; stay here in this spot until whoever owned this hut and these goats returned in a week, a fortnight, a lifetime.

I lasted two days.

Two days: milking the nanny goat, collecting berries and salad greens, gathering dead branches and fishing cinder stones for fires out of the stream. The hut had a cup and a plate and a broom for sweeping; I wove a basket from the willow to add as way of thanks. I cleaned my marsh-filthy clothes. I played with the kid, or rather, he ran from me as I chased him. And I slept under the stars, for it was so pretty, and too warm for the hut. Lark would have loved this solace.

But while my hands were useful, my mind was fixed on the old seer. What had Harker meant by not letting Lark help me? What had he meant by *find the shell*? Why did he say to open my eyes? No chore, no sleep helped me escape his words or the want to understand his prophecies. . . . I finally had to surrender in agreement with the seer, the sweetness of this place paling as I fretted: There was no peace here.

Another battle raged inside as well: I already knew how to find answers to the seer's offerings. I had the yew and minion still; they could be combined in a spell to create a powerful mind opener called the Insight. Except it was a dangerous crafting, and something for a magician, not a simple Healer.

They were different, magic-makers and Healers. Healers were born with their gift, while a magician was someone who learned the craft. A Healer's work was limited to the ways of Nature; the magician's not. A magician was a conjurer, but, then, he did not have the Healer's hands, the natural instinct for rescue, for assuaging pain. Either way, efforts done in ignorance made for danger.

But, if a Healer chose to study the ways of magic beyond her innate understanding of herb and mineral, then she blended simple instinct with learned technique—a most powerful combination, far more powerful than any magician. And the title of White Healer was bestowed.

I knew the makings of the Insight spell. Certainly not from Grandmama, who had no use for curiosity-soothing enchantments. Grandmama was not curious; "necessary knowledge" was all she wanted. I was not so calm—though I knew Lark thought me so. For Grandmama it was enough to be a Healer, but I wanted to be a White Healer. I wanted to learn magic.

'Twas not difficult to search out such knowledge. Market days brought any variety of mysticism mixed into gossip. Someone could be pointed to if you asked, or eagerness might draw someone to find you. Dame Gringer was a White Healer from the village of Crene who traded geese at market. She'd enjoyed my interest and had lent me metal-bound books of spells and potions, which I'd pored over in between barters. At the end of the day I'd return the books and ask a handful of questions. "You have potential," the dame would always encourage.

Herbs and minerals used for simple healing had much greater powers when combined with the proper spells. I learned that yew could be used to raise the dead, or, combined with minion and with proper crafting, yew could make the Insight spell. I learned as well that using such a spell could be life changing. Not even a year back Dame Gringer made the Insight spell because she'd wanted to learn why her son had abruptly left their village. Ever after she was mute and came no more to market. No one knew if this was brought on because of what she saw or the spell itself. Eowan Holt said she'd uttered a last word about *breeders;* he laughed that she was struck dumb for a gaggle of geese. But whatever the reason, it cut short my studies. Had Dame Gringer not gone silent, I might have learned how to use the yew to raise the dead.

I might have saved Raif.

Two days I lasted, arguing every reason why I should neither attempt something beyond my gift nor use up my remaining poison—my *escape,* as Harker said. But the answers to his portents were too great a temptation.

Besides, every ingredient for the spell was at hand, and that seemed no coincidence.

On the third day of my sojourn I undertook to cast the Insight spell. The preparations began at dawn—the importance of which Dame Gringer had impressed upon me above any actual casting. "Show that your intention is sincere," she'd scribbled in the margins of her books, "The rest will follow." And so I woke at first light and carefully laid out all the mal stones that I'd gathered the day before in a wide circle on the lawn to create the neutral space, sweeping out any bits of pebble and twig and seed from the grass within. I milked the nanny goat and drank the first cupful with a handful of blackberries. Then I tethered the goats far from the circle with strands from the protective willow tree, so they could neither interrupt nor fall prey to the spell's workings. I set a cinder stone, a hard stone, the yew, and minion just inside the circle and added the second cup of goat's milk within as well. I took the last things from my satchel and laid them down: the lark feather and the leather ring. I felt some guilt to use them for this, but mementos made spells most powerful.

I washed in the stream, then laid my cloak and frock and sandals to the side, wearing only the white undershift as a show of humility. I brushed my hands over my body to shed old energy. Then—with an earnest wish that I'd done well—I took a deep, shaky breath, picked up the branch I'd broken from the beech tree, and stepped inside the circle.

With the beech I scraped a cross, quartering the circle. In one quarter I carved the word *Shell;* in the second, *Lark;* the third, *See,* defining the questions that I wanted answered. I did not ask to learn my weakness; the seer had already told me that. I kneeled in the remaining quarter.

Minion first, I reminded myself. *Minion shields Earth from yew.* I opened the tiny vial of dried minion and divided it equally, mounding a tiny heap of minion over each of the three words. Then I picked up the vial of yew and poured all of it into my palm. I sorted equally the needles, bark, and wizened little drupes that still burned rich red in color. I saved three needles, three chips of bark, and three drupes, which I dropped into the goat's milk. The rest of the yew was portioned atop the minion heaps.

"*Representations of intent,*" I murmured; items to focus each answer. I pulled a strand of my hair and placed it on top of the

Shell pile. 'Twas the weakest offering, since I had no idea what this shell was, but if I was meant to find it, then the answer would be within me. I placed the feather for *Lark* and put Raif's woven leather ring on *See*.

Glass for clarity. I took the hard stone and smashed the empty vial of yew, then equally sprinkled the shards. One shard I used to pierce my little finger, adding a drop of blood to each pile. *"Life's blood,"* I murmured. Then I pressed my hands into the earth by each word, saying aloud three times, "Show me the reasons; show me the whys."

I went over the steps in my head one more time for good measure, then picked up the cinder stone and struck it on the hard stone next to the first offering. I watched it spark and flare into a little flame before going on, until three little herb piles burned white-hot and then fizzled. As soon as the flames died, I swept the piles into the center so the smoking ash mingled. Then I tipped the goat's milk over my scalding hands—all but the last bit, which I drank, taking care not to swallow any yew.

Finished. The cup placed outside the circle. Fingers laced in lap. I breathed—in, out, in. . . . The exhale was so very loud. Another breath, and another, and then I could not stand the silence. Had I done well? Would I have to wait? How long? A plea was already forming—

Then only half uttered. The poisoned milk seared my belly, raced fire through my veins. I wrapped my arms around my stomach, gagging against the burn, and maybe I tipped to one side, to stop the world from spinning, but none of that was important. . . .

I was flying, the earth racing far beneath. There was the marsh, then solid ground, a canopy of trees, and a lake hemmed by rock and fed by countless waterfalls all thundering down the face of a cliff. 'Twas a bird's flight, this. I recognized the flash of wing—*my wing*—from the corner of my eye, the black feather above white. The bird I'd rescued was the form I'd taken in this spell; burned wing and all, I was flying. In a heart-stopping breath, I skimmed the cliff of waterfalls, turned to sweep far out into the center of the lake, and then shot straight toward one furious torrent.

No easing of speed, no gasp for air. I burst through the fall and landed in a hollow behind the sheet of water, into blurred sight and deadened sound. There was a ledge of some sort, a faint shimmer of light. Red, slime-slicked rocks before it . . .

It lay there, the answer to my first question: a whelk's shell—pinkish gray on the outside, pearlescent within. I'd seen pictures of them in Dame Gringer's books. This one was no different, small and ordinary, discarded on the damp shelf. And yet a feeling stabbed through me with sudden force—that this insignificant object wanted rescue from the cold and dripping walls, that I should scoop it up and carry it home. But even as I moved closer, a protest began—a faint rumbling of sound, which grew into shadow form, bellowing huge and black and utterly horrifying. A stench burst out from it in revolting waves, swallowing all the senses, and I rolled to avoid it and fell straight into cold blackness before another spiral of flight began. . . .

I spun upward out of water. Slick stone became hard-hewn

rock—a warm gray splattered with onyx and mica—rock that was cut, stacked, designed. My gaze traveled up, up, following battlements and turrets and banners all spilling precipitously above an enormous canyon. A castle, carved from the very stone it was so precariously built upon. It stood majestic, strong, and wholly stunning. The sky was a luminous backdrop, the sun slanted finely etched shadows in curves and corners. I soared straight up the east bulwark, and then made a dizzying fall between its tallest turrets. The dive sent my stomach into my throat. I shut my eyes, then blinked wide, for I was crossing a small bit of green—an interior courtyard bursting with white blossoms. I spied the blue of a stone-rimmed pond, and then went racing up and out, over the west turrets to a broad scape of grass.

Two horses stood stark against the lush green—dappled gray and brilliant white—with two riders who'd paused midride to share an embrace. I remembered those horses, remembered their startling visit to Merith. And I knew their riders: my cousin, Lark, and the Rider Gharain.

I swept right over their heads and flew on, no voice, no hand, nor anything to call to my cousin. I'd only a glimpse to barely think silly things: How was she riding a horse? What were those leggings she wore? Where was her moss-green frock? And then to understand: this castle, this canyon—this was Tarnec. It meant Lark had left Merith, as I had. She'd found a new home. She was with her love.

My second question answered. And I thought, briefly, gladly: *She is happy.*

I soared toward the clouds, leaving behind the beautiful castle. But then it seemed I hit some invisible wall, for I stopped hard in one searing jolt, thrown off flight. A jerk, a pause, and then a freefall; I went crashing down toward the couple, screaming and putting my hand out to break the fall. Only my voice was a caw, my hand a wing.

Wing or not, Lark sensed something. Her head shot up; she lurched forward on her horse to reach up. And whatever she saw—the beaded black eye of a seabird, or my own sea-blue gaze—she knew me. Eye to eye we clung, connected.

A sadness, sharp as any blade, stabbed through, a longing for the *before*—before Lark discovered the severed hand, before her journey and our terrible birthday, before the wound on her shoulder that would never quite heal and the young man who would take her heart . . . before the Troth would kill the man who'd offered me his. Lark felt what I felt, for there was longing in her eyes as well. She missed me as I missed her. And however happy, however beautiful this castle, however strong her love for Gharain, something else had been ripped away:

Innocence.

And then it was gone and there was something else in her stare—fear. "Evie," she gasped, "what have you done . . . ?" Her eyes lifted to something beyond, behind my wing. She screamed in warning, *"Evie!"*

I looked up to see some hideous bird, grizzled and sharp and human-eyed. I spun sideways, flight recovered, and was winging fast away over the castle's wide terrace toward the dizzying cliff. Lark came galloping after, crying my name. I was high up; I could do nothing but watch as she raced across the grass, hair flying. She would go straight over the edge. Gharain was shouting her name, too far behind to catch her. And there were others it seemed, streaming suddenly from everywhere to chase her runaway speed with warning cries: "My lady!"

Yet her shining horse did not take her over the cliff, but ground to a halt. Lark slid off him, falling straight to her knees then stumbling up again, staring up, reaching arms high to where I circled.

"No! Evie, don't! Stop!" Lark begged until she was hoarse. Gharain was shouting too, galloping forward, sword drawn. Alarm rang all the way to the castle—people were spilling into the back courtyard, running to assist. . . .

"'Tis but a shrieking fowl, my lady," one old woman was calling. "No harm, no harm!"

But someone else was pointing beyond. "Not a fowl, a harbinger! They come!"

"Evie, look out!" Lark screamed. And I wheeled on my little wings as that hideous bird-thing swooped straight for me. I passed just under its breast, scorched by the heat. The creature swerved to attack again, but an arrow loosed from somewhere below shot the thing straight through the heart and it exploded above me in a crash of light and sound.

Gharain had raced in on that gray steed, his chestnut hair blown back. He clattered across the courtyard to the edge of the cliff, was off his horse, throwing his sword and running to scoop Lark in his arms in one sweeping move. And she half clung, half pulled from him, sobbing, "She's cast a spell,

Gharain. Evie cast a spell! Look—the bird! Now they've spied her. They're coming—she's in danger!"

"It's all right, love. He is near. He will reach her."

"How? He cannot know where she is! *We* don't know where she is!" Nothing would calm her, though an army of concerned faces surrounded. They murmured, soothed, and fussed while Lark reached up, imploring, "Stop now, Evie! Stop what you do!" Then she turned, frantic, looking to the others as if someone else would be able to speak to me.

But now their eyes were not on her, but on the sky beyond where I circled. Fussing turned to urgent warnings; the horses were sent galloping to their stables; Gharain was shouting, "Inside, everyone! Dartegn, find Ilone!" Lark spun back to look as well, her face turned dreadful. She screamed: "Run, Evie, run! The Breeders come!"

Two men lifted their swords, shielding Gharain as he grabbed Lark by the waist and tried to hurry her away. But Lark held, begging, "He *must* hurry! We must make him hurry! Laurent must find her!" She wrenched away, furious at her helplessness. "I have to see! I have to *see*. . . ."

Gharain pulled her back into his arms and together they ran for the safety of the castle. I could not see if they reached it nor could it matter, for at the name *Laurent* I was winging up and away and swirling back to witness the answer to the last question, back to an image that I could not bear. . . .

Smoke whipped around me. I was no longer high above the earth, but grounded flat against cobblestone, eyes stinging and choking for breath. I recognized Merith's market square and the confusion of the day of the Troths' attack. I recognized the blood that stained those cobblestones.

Raif was there, eyes closed, lifeless. Shock slammed into my gut again, then the dizzying spiral of agony, the horror that I was too late to help Raif, that there was nothing I could do to save him.

And . . . that I had not told him that I loved him.

Brutal knowledge, bitter pain. They overwhelmed, consumed, left me stunned and empty. The rampaging Troths had been forgotten. I'd not thought to look if I was safe. I'd not thought at all. And even when I did look up in that sudden moment and saw the Troth leaping for my throat with teeth and claws bared, I felt only mild surprise, and then the fierce wish: *Kill me now.*

But my wish went ungranted. The Troth was stabbed through in midleap and gone, and in his place was the one who'd saved my life. A Rider. The strong, dark-haired, blue-eyed one. The one I learned was named Laurent. Our eyes caught briefly in that moment. Only briefly.

See was the last question. I thought I'd been thrown back to Merith to relive Raif's death, to witness once more his prone body and my terrible regret. But the spell was showing me something else: what I'd truly seen in that frenzied rush of battle and despair and never before recognized.

It was Laurent's gaze I met, clear-eyed, raw, and nakedly honest.

And then that moment too was ripped away and I was flinging back—from cobble, to sky, to stone, to water, to earth.

With a great shudder and gasp my eyes flew open and I gagged for breath, hard-slammed into the ground as if I'd been thrown down from the heights I'd flown.

Night. The Insight spell had held me from morning until past sunset. Stars twinkled above; the grass was soft beneath. Something was different, though—maybe it was the marsh. Maybe it was I. I blinked and gingerly turned my head at the sound of a bleat. There were the goats still tethered as I'd left them. And there, the little stream was still bubbling its way along its banks. I lifted my arm to inspect: arm, hand. No more wing. I was whole. I was alive. I'd survived my spell making.

But not unscathed.

5

LAURENT.

A hollow whisper in my ears. I ignored it, stood up, wobbly and dazed, and began unmaking the circle as ritually as I'd fashioned it. I struck the cinder stone and lit the beech limb, then stuck it into the ground to burn as a torch. I returned the stone, the singed lark feather, and ring to my satchel, gathered the remaining ash from the three offerings, and sprinkled it into the stream. I scoured the cup with sand from the stream bottom and brought it back to the hut. Stone by stone I undid the circle and scattered them into the stream as well, the way one might sow a field.

Laurent.

The second whisper caught me by surprise in midstride; I had to stop to shake it away before continuing on, to clear the fog. I untethered the goats, went to my store of provisions, and ate handfuls of blackberries and dandelions, breathing deep while my body slowly calmed and righted. The kid was there, nudging for some of the greens, and then the whole goat family surrounded me with hungry interest, and so I shared my store. Then I scrubbed my teeth and hands in the stream, spread my turquoise cloak on the grass, and lay down for sleep.

Laurent.

"Stop!" I hissed loudly to the night sky. But the name only whispered again, so I shut my ears and closed my eyes to will the name away. Still it stayed.

"What is this?" I muttered, sitting up. It made no sense. I should not have survived the spell only to have this name take all the space in my head. There was a shell behind a waterfall, there was Lark in her castle, there were rumblings of something monstrous, and Lark's terrible fear. . . .

And I was thinking on a name.

I'd shared a single glance with that Rider—even if I now recognized how powerful that glance, 'twas still only the briefest of moments. He'd caught the Troth with his sword, caught my eye as he flung it away, then galloped on while I sat with Raif until Quin and Kerrick Swan came to carry him from the square.

Eleven of the twelve Riders came that day to Merith, *eleven,* not one. They all did their part in saving our village. None stood out more heroic than the next. Food was prepared when the dead beasts were carted away, when the smoke cleared and the stone was swept. The Riders stayed for that, grateful for a hot meal as we were grateful for our rescue, but I was not there.

I stayed with Raif—washed his body, sewed the gaping wound shut, and dressed him while they supped in grim celebration. The eleven were gone soon after, their hoofprints soon erased. Later I asked Quin the name of the Rider with the dark curls and bluest eyes. I asked, because it seemed polite to do so, to put a name to the one who'd erroneously spared my life.

A name—it meant nothing. So why should a Rider be the answer to Harker's challenge to open my eyes?

I got up from my makeshift bed and paced the perimeter of the little island under the starlight. I trailed my fingertips along the rushes so that their rustlings drowned the whisper of his name. Still, I tasted the word on my tongue, whispered it myself once, then twice. Laurent. *Laurent*—

I stopped my mouth with my hands. I loved Raif! I would have been *glad* to wed him—his warm smile, his calm strength, bountiful harvests from the orchards and market days, the cottage at the west edge of the village, and pudgy, red-cheeked babies and an herb garden—to fill our world with laughter and sweet fragrance. I yearned for those lost plans; it was ridiculous to focus on a name, as if it took precedence.

"There, and be done with it!" I clapped my hands three times and threw them wide to dispel the thoughts. But there was still a whisper in the air. So I chafed my bare arms and legs with my palms to still the trembling and erase the Rider's name forever. But when I stood up, the whisper lingered.

"A fool's suffering," I bit out, walking away from the reeds. But the whisper suddenly wafted from the far edge of the marsh, and I could not help but turn to look. Nothing was there. But then another whisper hinted from the near border, and then again behind me. I turned, turned again—

Whispers were floating from all around the marsh. I almost laughed at my obsession, except the sound was curdling, resolving into something else entirely—

She . . .

Whispers doubling, then growing tenfold. *She . . . She . . .* I stopped and stared into the wall of reeds. Darkness, all of it; there was nothing to see. The whispers rebounded now, bouncing from one end of the little island to the next. And there was too the faintest rattle of stems—a rattle when there was no wind.

And then, not just a rattle, but a cracking, a breaking of stems. The night lost its hushed privacy. Three days I'd spent in silence, but now things were in the marsh. Things that sensed.

Things that searched.

She . . . She . . . She . . .

I backed away from the boundary, stunned by the suddenness of company, the little thrill of threat that ran with those whispers. Not Troths, Troths had no words. Not Kelpies, for they were singular menaces. But these whispers were likewise hostile. *She . . . She . . .* A drumbeat. Ominous and closing in.

And then I remembered Lark's terrified cry: *Run, Evie! Run! The Breeders come!*

I whirled, unprepared, standing empty-handed in my undershift. My mind worked fast—there were none of the plants I'd need to fashion a barrier, but there was a broom in the hut. I ran across the grass, pulled on my frock and cloak, crammed into my sandals, and threw my satchel over my shoulder. The rustlings were louder—how much time? How many were coming? I raced to the shelter of the hut and felt my way in the darkness, sending a brief thanks skyward to the owner who'd left a simple tool, something that might fend off an attack.

Attack—a shuddering, unexpected word. It made me think, suddenly, of Raif's grandfather suffering the first attack of the Troths. Lark said the old man accepted his death with noble dignity, as any villager of Merith might. I didn't think I could stand still like that, didn't think I could surrender. I'd planned my death over and over these months, wished for it, but the Healer in me immediately armed against it.

I found the broom, stamped on it to splinter the handle for a spear. It was the best I could do. No one from Merith ever learned how to fashion a weapon properly. To us, violence was appalling.

I stepped back outside and held, listening. A silence had taken hold of the marsh—an abnormal silence. I looked up. The stars seemed fainter in the rich blue expanse, which meant the moon was rising. I looked at the goats. They huddled at the side of the hut, panting and restless, so I walked away from them toward the center of the lawn and planted the spear at my feet like some makeshift soldier, ready to defend.

Our little island waited, poised. The silence deepened—a held breath. Then—

The goats bleated in panic, shattering quiet. I spun to catch the first intruder; but it was just a shadow skittering across the grass, gone before I could blink. I whisked the other way as another little blur darted out of the reeds and was gone, and then another and another. Shadows, 'twas all, harmless little swipes as quick and silent as bats. But then a thousand hisses of *She!* exploded from the reeds, and dark things poured out of the marsh aiming straight for me.

I swore and took off running. They pursued—shreds of darkness, racing fast. No faces, no true arms or legs, just wisps—brushing across my face and arms like a sweep of stinging nettles. I yelled and lashed out with my broom handle. I hit some of them, I think, for there was an ugly ripping sound and a stink of sulfur. I stumbled forward, hacking at the air, trying to beat back the shadows, but I was already surrounded—they hovered and swallowed. Their sheer numbers turned the night black like some turbulent and hostile cloud that lifted me off my feet and hurtled me, dangling, through the miles of marsh at breakneck speed, leaving a wake of broken reeds.

I kicked and slashed, but anything struck was only replaced by countless more, an endless swarm of shadows buzzing *She! She! She!* until the word blurred into a single drone. I was gasping from the struggle, the speed, the suddenness—

And then, just as sudden, we broke through the end of Rood Marsh, where the moon ascended above a wide, shallow pond that bled from the rushes. It lit the surface in a sweep of silver. It lit my hair silver too, a beacon in the midst of the black. The abundance of light seemed to shock the swarm, for they abruptly scattered in a fury of hisses, dropping me belly-first into the water.

I sank, resurfaced, and then stroked fast away from the marsh. They were shaky strokes—I moved by some mechanical reflex, hardly thinking. But it was a mistake, my release; the things were not done with me. In a shriek the swarm regathered and clouded above my head more frenzied than before. I ducked under. My cloak and satchel dragged leaden around my neck, but the water was only chin-deep. I half swam, half stumbled toward the shore, popping up for another gulp of air, and the things attacked from the left, propelling me back out to the center. When I came up for air a third time, they were there on the left again, pushing me north.

They were herding me.

I took a deeper breath and dove under, tacking back toward the marsh. I scrambled onto soggy ground and made for the reeds, but there the moon betrayed me. Even wet, my hair shone—I might as well have shouted, "Here!" for the swarm was on me, surrounding, suffocating, buzzing. . . .

"Get away!" I screamed, swiping at the wisps. "Get back!" I gulped a lungful of air and dove back into the pond, shooting to its deeper center. But it didn't matter; I wasn't escaping, only buying time. I could hold my breath long, but I couldn't think of what to do next. I opened my eyes underwater, trying to see where I'd lost the broomstick—

Help came least expected.

I have swum in the river at Merith and in Fresh Pond at Dann. There are crays and periwinkles and tiny green baits that nip and swim through the strands of my hair as if it were lakeweed. But I'd never before witnessed the glimmers of

light that sprinkled through this pond. *Moonwater.* I'd heard
of it—a phenomenon that happens only in full moon, only
in silted ponds, and so rare as to be more legend than truth.
Where moonlight washes a path over such water it frays into
fizzy spirals—*true* light, not merely reflection, trapped in tiny
droplets and set adrift. They shimmered and danced above me
so beautifully that for a brief moment I forgot the black swarm
and watched the little glowing swirls. I reached my hands up,
and they gathered at my fingertips and clung. . . .

Light. I burst up directly under the swarm, flicking my
fingers at the wisps. They bolted away before regrouping and
I shouted at the discovery—that these remnants of light disturbed them—and ducked under to do it again. And again. I
was exhilarated; the wisps infuriated. They splintered, returned,
splintered again. Each time I came up splashing, the swarm
scattered, enraged, their buzzing reaching some fevered pitch.

They'd have to give up; they'd have to wear out. I flung
the moonwater with a vengeance, saw the shadow break and
scatter, then ducked under once more to gather the fizz. The
hostile wisps had worked themselves into a fury, their buzzing
pounding like hooves upon stone—

I gasped, inhaling water and light, and came up choking.
Somewhere out in the darkness real hooves were pounding
closer. Hooves, carrying the weight of horses—*not* ponies, I
knew, for I'd never seen a horse until the eleven Riders came
galloping into Merith that day, and I would never forget such
a sound.

Galloping. The wisps sensed the approach. They lifted

as a piece, leaving me, and shot across the pond. Moon-light expanded over the water again; I could see the swarm rebuilding—shaping itself like some gargantuan creature with arms spreading wide to swallow whatever those hooves brought.

Hooves—and grunts. Grunts, shouts, and the faint clank of sword slashing at the suffocating folds. The stench of sulfur gagged; the swarm surrounded and smothered, too thick for me to witness the fight. There was a horse's harsh whinny, then his rider was swearing and shouting at the dark—and I realized there were not eleven as before, but a single steed and a single rider. One man alone had stormed into the fray.

He was not winning.

The man wasted his energy, for what sword could conquer things insubstantial as smoke, multiplying faster than they disappeared? The folds only thickened, choking. I could hear the horse in distress even as his rider refused to give in.

"Wait!" I shouted from the water. "Let me help!" I swam and slogged toward the shore. "I can help!"

"Stay back!" came an answering command. But I paid no mind to such a silly order. The man could not fight this alone; he could not fight this at all.

"Move!" I screamed. "I know how to stop them!" I was tearing at the knot on my sodden cloak, grabbing its deep hood to use as a pail and scooping the moonwater. I dragged the cloak to the shore, to the shadows, close to where I thought the hooves stamped. *"Move,"* I screamed again, and heaved the cloak at the blackness.

The exploding swarm knocked me back into the deep. I sputtered, fought my way up. The creature they'd formed had shattered like glass, dissipating in a thousand directions. My hand hit my broom-spear, which bobbed in the pond; I grabbed it, hurled it on shore, then yanked my satchel from around my neck and threw the sopping thing to the silhouetted man. "Get off your horse!" I pushed my streaming hair from my eyes and pointed at the satchel, spluttering indistinct directions: "Grab the cinder stone from it! They'll regather. I can hold them, but you have to start a fire—the spear will catch. They hate direct light!"

He didn't answer. There was no time to. The regrouped wisps came shooting at us like an arrow. I dove under, kicking hands and feet, splashing moonwater at the swarm. It was a blur of motion. I was shouting, the horse neighing, the wisps buzzing, and then—

And then there was a burst of light and a final hiss of wisps. I lay in the shallows, dragging deep breaths, staring up at the sky, where the moon spilled silver over the edge of marsh, the pond, and across the horse and rider who stood on shore by a burning pile of moss and cloth. Sweat frothed at the horse's jaw; his neck glistened in the firelight. The man in silhouette pulled the reins over the head of the horse and released the bit and bridle. He leaned heavily for an extra moment against the horse. Then the horse made his way to the water. The man made his way to me.

The battle had taken its toll. He aimed straight but his gait was unsteady. His breath shuddered.

And I? My breath shuddered as well. For as the man neared, the moonlight erased the shadows one by one, opening his features. I saw hair curling darkly and eyes of clear blue.

I struggled upright, stood ankle-deep and dripping wet. The man stopped at the lip of the pond, made an effort to grin. "You . . . are . . . a difficult . . . girl . . . to find. . . ."

And then the Rider Laurent pitched forward and fell face-down in the shallows at my feet.

6

HAIR DARK AS a raven's, falling in waves from crown to jaw. Face tanned and smooth-polished. A sweep of brow and thick lash covering those blue eyes. He was as tall as he'd looked that fateful day astride his horse.

I watched Laurent sleep off his exhaustion.

The wisps were gone. Vanished, as if they'd simply been some dream. I'd dragged the Rider out of the water and laid him on the mossy bank. I'd ripped reeds from the marsh, gathered pinecones, and built up the fire. I'd unlaced his shirt, removed it, and hung it on a stick to dry near the flames. And I'd gone to the horse—huge and black and heaving steam from his nostrils—and wiped down his flanks with my sodden cloak, checking for wounds. Superficial, those scratches the steed bore; I'd healed enough ponies to know this horse was not hurt, just worn out. They'd ridden hard.

Difficult to find, he'd said. Lark said it as well in the Insight spell: *Laurent must find her.* The Rider had come on purpose.

I'd gone back to him then and used the cloth that was tied to his belt to wash the blood and dirt from his cuts. I'd never been embarrassed or squeamish about a man's body. 'Twas healing work, simple and straightforward, and I'd swear I focused only on the beads of red crisscrossing the Rider's arms and chest. But even so, I stopped often and walked away to reclaim my breath, as if it was I who was overtaxed. I was keenly aware too that I both lingered and rushed, that I acted far less efficiently than I should. So I'd forced my hands, my breath, to behave, to pay attention to detail, to do all the things Healers would do for anyone, checking for a break of bone, for any wounds to clean or repair.

But finally I'd given up, frustrated at my sloppiness, sat back a little way from Laurent and simply watched him. 'Twas curiosity affecting me, I decided, and if I drank my fill of the Rider this once, then I'd not need to think of him again. It would take time, though. This Rider was a mass of curiosities—a history of pain imposed on gentleness, of strength built from necessary endurance. It was all there to be read from his body.

Hands that should have been a sculptor's, face and form that would have been a sculptor's muses. Square jaw, faint stubble, and hollow cheek—'twould be expected his mouth be grim, set in that hardened look, but it wasn't. Whatever a Rider was, Laurent was not born to it. There was the bruise at his left cheekbone from the fall—that would be gone by day's end. The deeper cut above his collarbone would last but a day longer if I found some mithren for a salve, likewise the raw scrape where his breath raised his chest. Nothing needed serious attention or my tending, honestly. But there too were fine scars from wounds that had been inflicted long before. Wounds that had been tended—by some other Healer perhaps—from some other time. Twenty-five year'd, I deemed this Rider. I wondered what other Healers he'd known in his life.

And then I wondered why I wondered that.

There was one scar in particular, a thin line that ran from just above his left eyebrow to his temple. It was old and very faint; most would not notice. But my eye was sharp for such marks that did not belong. The wound had been severe. Laurent would have lost too much blood before any herb or hand could have sealed it—a spell had to have been involved. A White Healer treated that wound. A thorough, perfect job. I reached my hand out and drew a finger across the scar, sensing warmth and the life force of this Rider—

I pulled back, got up, and stormed across the bank. Why had I done that—touched him not as a Healer? This was a betrayal to Raif, to my own calling. I should have left then and there. Still, I paced back again, swore at Laurent for having come, and then (with stern focus) forced myself to finish what I'd started. I rinsed his cloth, spread it to dry, then worked the saddle from his steed and dragged it to rest by his head. There was a cloak rolled with a small pack, which I unstrapped from the saddle. I opened the pack. There was food—a tough bread of sorts, a cup and knife, and some sort of cake that smelled distinctly of oats, which I tossed to his horse. I placed the bread atop the pack ready for him and filled the cup with water. I spread the cloak. I would drag Laurent onto it and be done; walk away. He did not need further attending; his life force was strong.

It burned a little that what questions I had for the Rider would go unanswered—but it was a far lesser hardship than to actually speak with him. I already bore the memory of his gaze and seared the feel of his skin against my fingers; I didn't want the cadence of his voice to ring forever in my ears.

The reed fire spit and fell to smoking. I'd not rekindle it. Dawn was nearing anyway. I crouched down and caught under the Rider's shoulders to drag him onto the cloak. A simple move, one I'd done often: with the right leverage even bodies twice my weight could be slid evenly—

And then suddenly it wasn't simple. *"What—?"* *"Ow!"* His yell, my gasp, a thud. One moment I was dragging the man, the next moment he had me pinned underneath him—a swift, hard move—his hand on my throat. I'd surprised him and he was quick to defend.

But I was quick too, reflexes taking over. My hand was there, digging under his ribs, pinching the place that would incapacitate him long enough for me to wriggle free. He swore and flinched, but it seemed Riders were well trained to withstand, for he grabbed one of my hands and then the other, yanking them out of the way, pressing me down with his full weight.

And all of this took but an instant. He growled, "Who . . . ?" then his eyes widened; he pulled abruptly away. I scrambled back and faced him, breathing hard, wary as his expression went from battle-ready to surprise, then almost—almost—to humor as he took in the spread cloak, and his own bared torso.

But then the humor fell away and he turned his gaze back on me. "Lady," he murmured with a respectful nod. He brushed his hair back from his eyes.

Lady was ridiculous. "My name is Evie Carew." But then I wished my name back. Wished I'd called myself Eve again to sound older.

The Rider nodded, then turned quick to look for his sword, disturbed that I'd placed it just out of his reach. He leaned, caught it up and stood in one fluid movement, testing its weight—or maybe his own tired strength—by sweeping the blade through the air. And then he looked about; I wondered if he expected the swarm to return.

"You said that I was difficult to find," I blurted, watching him. "Why were you looking for me?"

The Rider's brow creased, as if the question made no sense, or else the sword—or something—felt wrong. So I added, "My cousin, Lark, might have asked it of you. Please let her know that I am fine." *There.* I considered us done. I brushed my wet skirts to look busy, hoping he would find something to do— tend to his horse, inspect everything that I'd unpacked for him.

He sheathed the sword. "Nay, my lady, I do not return. I am here to protect you."

"Why?" It came out something like a gasp. I was forgetting my vow of no questions—not to ask, not to learn anything that might make it difficult to leave this Rider. I shook my head to clear it and found a firmer, harder voice: "I journey alone, and there is no reason to protect. I need no help."

"We all need help," he said pleasantly.

"*You* might."

There was a flash of a grin at my bluntness, but then the Rider asked quite seriously, "You did not fear that attack before?"

"I have no fear of death."

"There are worse things than death." He raised a brow, implying how curt my response was and his own impulse to remark in kind. But then came something else: recognition and sympathy and regret, as if he suddenly remembered Raif's body in the market square and that maybe I'd already faced worse things. The brow dropped; the grin faded. Silence expanded the space between us and yet the moment was suddenly too intimate.

I said quickly, "Your wounds are not deep. You will heal. Your horse as well." I tipped my chin in the direction of the steed. "What's his name?" *No questions, Evie!*

"Arro."

"Arro," I repeated, then rose to my feet, picked up my cloak and satchel, and turned, realizing suddenly I had no direction. The marsh had lost any appeal, my poisons were gone, and I'd never retrace my steps home. 'Twas a hasty choice: there was some shadowing to the west beyond the pond, a forest maybe. So I started off, then stopped and turned back—too aware that he watched. "Thank you," I said as evenly as I could, and rounded once more, heading away from sun.

"My lady," he called after me. I bit my lip and kept walking. "What of you? Will you heal as quickly?"

That stopped me. What did he know of my wound, my loss and anguish? I paused and whipped around. 'Twas on the tip of my tongue to say something harsh to end such nosy concern. The Rider was standing, a figure brilliantly lit by moonlight.

"Your injuries," he said, gesturing. "Look at them."

I looked down at my arms, where my sodden cloak hung away from them. They were covered in long, fine scratches, rivulets of dried blood. I reached my hands to my face, my neck, and drew away smears of red. I'd not even noticed.

"The reeds." My indignation deflated. I simply felt exposed.

"Or the wisps," he suggested with a nod to the pond. "You might wash."

As if he needed to tell a Healer what to do for this. Nonetheless I walked to the pond, dropped my satchel and cloak, and pulled off my frock and dropped it as well, realizing later there was no point in removing anything since all of it was wet anyway. I was not acting myself.

Wisps. He'd named them as I had. "Those wisps," I began, splashing off the blood. "What are they?"

"Vestiges of the Waste. They come from underground and are rarely seen above, but if they are stirred to swarm . . . Shadows, seemingly nothing, but needle-sharp when threatened or spurred to aggression. When massed they can overwhelm, whisk you off your feet. Easy enough to be rid of, but you have to be quick." He said a little ruefully, "I was not quick."

"Quick?" *No questions, Evie!* I bit my tongue before I could ask what the Waste was.

"Fire, any sort of light—as you said. I knew better than to fight the swarm. Though I do not know why water worked."

" 'Twas moonwater."

Laurent looked hard at me, but then nodded as if he'd heard of such a serendipitous occurrence before. He said more solemnly, "Thank you for coming to my aid."

"Then we are even." I sloshed out of the pond, dragging my clothes behind. "Should these wisps return, I'll know how to stop them."

"They will not stop."

"But you have just said. Easy enough to get rid of." I was impatient, pretending to be calm when I was not calm. I wanted to go. I'd had enough challenges this night.

"Wisps are the least of our worries." The Rider was matter-of-fact. "*They* can raise the earth and build firestorms, gather the most vicious creatures, or pull the worst from humans—"

"They?" I'd misunderstood. "Who are *they*?"

"Breeders. They will find you. They will not stop."

The tiniest breeze ruffled over us. I said, "You found me, Rider Laurent. Are you one of these Breeders who will not stop?"

"No." He made the slightest hesitation, as if confused that I suggested it.

"Then how *did* you find me?"

The Rider looked up over my head toward the pond and said softly, "Moonlight on water brings Nature's daughter."

The breeze chilled my skin. *Moonlight on water . . .* 'Twas what the seer had said. I turned around. There the sinking moon carved a path of silver straight across the water. From where I stood at water's edge it trailed right to my feet.

I looked back at him, then shivered. He asked suddenly, "Do you not know who you are, my lady? What it is we fight? Can it be that no one has told you?"

I said, "I am a Healer." A tainted one by now, but I kept that to myself. "I do not fight."

It was not enough. "Your cousin returned to Merith not long after the battle with the Troths. She didn't speak to you?"

"Lark was wounded, and when she was better—"

"You left."

I looked away. "There wasn't time to talk . . . of much."

"Then, my lady, where are you going?" the Rider asked softly. "Do you know?" A second shiver rippled over my skin, but not from the breeze. His voice was rich.

I hadn't answered, so he asked another: "Do you think your cousin, Lark, is still in Merith?"

I said, "I think she is with one of your Riders. Gharain."

"She is."

"Except . . . I saw walls, a castle." I couldn't help telling it, for the image of Lark at home there was so strange. I glanced at him. "'Twas not what I imagined for her." *Or for the Riders.*

But Laurent was frowning. "What do you mean 'saw'?"

"I made a spell. I saw Lark in a castle. And she saw me."

In the barest hint of dawn, Laurent's face went dark. He took a slow breath; his hand found the hilt of his sword. "So that is what the queen meant in her message, why they come so quickly."

"Who? These Breeders? What queen?"

"Your spell—'twas not luck they found you, you opened passage for them. We need to leave here." He looked around, realizing I'd undone all his packing, and shook his head, muttering, "We stay at the ready. . . ."

I didn't move. " 'Twas what Lark said. 'The Breeders come.' "

"And they do. The wisps were nothing." He'd packed his food items and was already rolling his cloak with quick, efficient moves. "You should not have worked *any* spell. 'Twas foolish. Leave off your gown and cloak; they're too wet. We'll fix them to the saddle." He picked up the bridle.

I was piqued by his reprimand. "Did you not understand? I make my own way."

"To where? For what purpose?" Laurent fed the bit between Arro's teeth, murmuring to him, "More stubborn than her cousin."

"I bid you *not* to follow!"

He only tossed over his shoulder far too matter-of-factly, "I do not follow. I accompany."

This was all wrong. I rued my spell making, but it was not for Laurent to say. If these Breeders wanted to punish me for overstepping my Healer rank, so be it. But I could hardly travel with this Rider, salting raw memories. And that he did not ask—as if there would be no issue of him coming with me! While he saddled his horse I picked up my sopping clothes and satchel.

"You erred, my lady. Now the dangers will be fast one upon the other," Laurent was saying. He heard me leaving, called a little louder: "If you stop one terror, the Breeders will use another, and another, until they have you." I ignored him and walked away.

Laurent called again in warning this time, and so I walked faster, disturbed more by the sound of his voice than the threats he described. It was like a balm, his voice.

And then he was coming after me, feet drumming the earth, so I said fiercely without turning: "Know that if you force your companionship, I will escape. Just as I know how to heal, I know as well how to hurt."

Maybe he already knew that. Laurent slowed but kept pace behind me, silent. Then he said simply, "I cannot force, it is a choice. Do you insist on being alone?"

"I do."

"Then"—his hand was on my arm, pulling me around to face him—"there is something I will have before you go."

The Rider was too close; those clear blue eyes depths to swim in. He would kiss me, I thought crazily; his lashes cast down as he looked at my mouth, then flicked back up to catch my gaze again. His hand slid up my arm, tugged the narrow strap of the undershift, and slipped it from my shoulder. The cloak and frock fell from my slackening grip. He leaned forward, touching his forehead to mine, his breath hitching ever so slightly, like a dusting of sandalwood against my skin. I had no breath of my own, no speech. I melted like wax in his hands.

Laurent's brows lifted at my willingness. I knew it too—

somewhere—that it was absurd, I was absurd. Except I wasn't thinking; I was reaching to meet his mouth. For a blistering moment his lips nearly touched mine, but then the Rider pulled back, gaze traveling down to my neck and along my arm to where his fingers held. He gripped my shoulder, not gently, and drew it toward him, putting his other hand to my back—

I screamed as a lightning flash of yearning exploded inside, dropped to my knees under its weight. Laurent had stepped back, shaken. We stared dumbly at one another. But he recovered himself first and straightened, very sober and formal, and maybe angry.

"Now, my lady, if you wish to travel alone, at least you are not exposed." And he turned away and strode back to where his horse patiently waited.

7

I PICKED MYSELF up, gathered my things, and stumbled after him, limbs all jelly and a strange keening in my ears. "What was that?" I gasped. "What was that? What did you do?"

"A bond seeking," Laurent said grimly. He reached his horse, made an adjustment to the saddle. "An informal one, but necessary."

"Necessary? Wait!" I lost my grip on my clothes and stumbled on, disoriented. The almost-kiss, the absurdity were lost in the hugeness of this feeling. Something sweet, something bitter, something beyond simple yearning—'twas a lifetime of emotion compressed into that single flash, and I was undone or fulfilled, hollowed out or completed by it, I couldn't tell. I wasn't sure I even knew my own name. I found the horse somehow, fumbled for the reins, and leaned into Arro's flank to hold them there while I caught my breath. "You cannot go, Rider, without explaining."

Laurent stayed rigid still for a moment, gathering his own breath, then with a seeming flick of wrist touched me just by my left shoulder blade. I trembled. "There," he said. "Your mark. I woke your calling. And that, my lady, was *my* choice. One I could not leave for you. Farewell." He mounted and nudged his horse. My jaw hung slack; the reins simply fell from my hands. I had no muscles.

"That . . . is not . . . enough," I panted. The keening was turning shrill, hammering into my head. I put my hands on my thighs and leaned over to shake the sound away, confused, maybe enraged that he'd made me feel something first so strangely beautiful and then so awful. "What calling?" I yelled after him. "What bond? Why your choice?"

"Those are questions that will only open more questions, my lady," he called back, as if he knew of my effort not to ask any. "You would do well to leave now, before the dawn breaks."

"And you would do well to tell me what I ought to know," I chattered. But he didn't respond. Laurent trotted a few yards off and then paused, waiting—waiting for me to leave. The Rider was doing my bidding, letting me leave on my own. Yet he also stayed, as if to make sure—of what? That I was safe? So far, the Rider was the only thing that made me vulnerable; I was unnerved by his presence, by the bond seeking that now made me sick.

I turned my back and staggered off in the opposite

direction. Which way I'd decided to go I couldn't remember. But I saw my garments tumbled on the ground and so wandered over to pick them up. I started to pull the frock over my head then stopped. My head was spinning from that incessant sound. Wet undershift, wet gown—I stood half in, half out— 'twas all a cold, sodden mess. I dropped the frock at my feet, wanting to crumple beside it. But since I could still stand, then so could I walk—and I did, gathering the clothes and satchel and dragging them behind me. The shrill was near unbearable, stabbing; I pushed into the noise the same way one pushed into the headwind of a tempest.

I made it halfway around the pond before the keening dropped me to my knees. Intention forgotten, Rider forgotten—just a desperation of helplessness that I didn't know how to guard myself, how to fix this complete undoing. My hands were shaking, grinding into my ears to shut out the maddening sound.

What had he done? Needles boring into my skull. I was on my knees, then on the ground, rolling onto my back, crushing my temples, railing at the sky while the shrieking only intensified.

Shadows swooped in against the dawn light. If the wisps were back, I didn't care. They could take me away, shred the skin from my bones—anything, anything to stop the sound. The ground was shuddering under my back, hooves pounding, shouting.

"Stop!" I screamed, begging anything that could hear

me. "Stop!" But then I was nearly bounced from the ground as the world exploded. A dark thing in the sky became a sudden ball of fire, a harsh burst of light and noise—the way that hideous bird exploded in the Insight spell. For a brief second the shrieking was drowned out and I could see Laurent, off his steed, guarding me, waving his shirt and sword like signals— but no, not signals. He was hitting the dark shapes before they reached us, and they were exploding one by one, with Laurent standing in the midst of confusion tall, focused, and unafraid. . . .

"Evie."

Blessed silence. A soft *brrr* from a redwing, a whisper of breeze.

"Evie, open your eyes."

I did, squinting. Laurent's face was hovering just above. My eyes wandered. The sky was a dull gray but clear. There were no shadows, no clouds.

My jaw was hard to work, stiff from being clenched so hard. "What happened?"

"Swifts. Breeders' birds," he said a little grimly. "I told you they'd move quickly."

The Breeders again. "You burned those things."

"Swifts explode if they are touched by anything earthbound—fast destroyed but nonetheless a great threat. To Healers especially they cause madness."

"That sound . . ." I'd thought Laurent had done that when

he touched me. It had all happened at once. But my head was clearer now that the horrid creatures were gone. . . . What remained was the warmth from that bond seeking.

"Wisps, swifts—Breeders have chosen things that will herd you, or pin you down."

"Pin me down?" I sat up quickly then, to prove I would not be pinned. Everything spun.

The Rider caught my arm, letting go easily enough when I tensed. "So that you may be found, and collected."

"If they are after me"—I did not like his certainty—"you haven't explained why."

He arched a brow. "I think it is you who've refused to ask."

A calm enough remark but it carved a strange heat along my throat. "I have eyes," I retorted. "I can see that there is a darkness come over us. The drought, Troths, dead villagers and frightened survivors, and now . . ." I gestured at the sky as if wisps or those swifts would simply reappear. "What did Lark not tell me?"

"My lady, you wanted to leave, remember? Do it now while your hair fades so well against the gray light of dawn. You will be less visible—to the eye at least."

He was baiting me. I worked my way to my feet, insisting, "What did she not tell me?"

Laurent did not answer, but offered a hand again, which I ignored. I straightened, testing my balance. The jellyness of earlier had faded, except for where he'd touched my mark. That still tingled. So did the little burn in my throat, and the memory that I'd expected, nay *wanted* a kiss . . . and the absurdity.

I put my hands on my hips to be fierce. "I should know what dangers are to be faced."

The Rider looked me up and down—my stance, my glare—and said softly: "What is it that you hold so tightly against? It isn't fear."

"Hardly." I snorted.

His mouth curved ever so faintly. Anyone would blush under that look; I forced my gaze steady. He said, "You do not have to prove your bravery with me, my lady. I know it well. Good luck to you." He turned and walked to his horse.

A standoff. We'd reversed postures. The Rider knew I had no destination and far too much curiosity. And I was fairly certain he had no intention of letting me go on alone. It remained who would give in first. I moved off a little, but then turned around and came back. I could not pretend to be coy.

"If I let you walk with me, you will answer *all* my questions."

This faintest victory shifted the Rider's posture, but he only called over his shoulder, "The dawn breaks, my lady. We should find better cover before we talk." He mounted his horse.

I looked away from the marsh. To the west the sky was paling from smoke to pearl. There were few trees nearby. I wondered what would count for cover. I looked back to the Rider.

He reached down his hand. I hesitated. "*Walk,* I said. I do not know how to ride."

"That," he returned, "matters not." Then Laurent gave me the first full smile. "Your cousin took to it rather quickly." He pulled me up with one sweeping move and set me before him on the saddle. I swallowed, teetering, before his arms came around and took the reins. His bare chest was warm against my back.

"I'll not let you fall," he said.

I'd misjudged. Hiding places dotted the route. Laurent chose our cover carefully, bypassing several copses.

"Why oak?" I asked, when we finally halted.

"Best protection from Breeders," he said, dismounting. "We can stop here for a time, dry our things." He put both hands around my waist and lifted me down, then set me back from him a little awkwardly since somehow I was still gripping his arms.

I dropped my hands to my sides and he turned back to his horse. "So, have with your questions, my lady."

"Then I start with *them*. Who are these Breeders?"

"Foes," he said, unstrapping our wet things from the saddle.

"Why?"

He grinned. "Necessity."

"Since when is it necessary to have an enemy?"

"When it is your calling." Laurent handed me my satchel and went about the business of hanging clothes from the boughs of the trees to dry. "There are those whose duty it is to protect the Balance of Nature, and those who wish nothing more than to destroy it—enmity is inherent to the task."

That made me laugh. "Who could be Nature's *foe*?"

The Rider glanced over, a look that quelled any humor.

"Keepers of Balance and Breeders of Chaos, the opposing powers," he said. "You do not know?"

I shook my head.

"What thrives on this earth is a result of Balance—the balance of the primal forces of Life, Death, Dark, and Light. The Keepers' duty is to protect this Balance while the Breeders will ever try to upset it." Laurent finished with the clothes and walked back toward me. "A struggle through the ages. Keepers hold tightly against the Breeders; Breeders search for opportunity to unleash Chaos—"

"The Riders," I interrupted. "Are the Riders on the side of Balance?"

It was his turn to snort. "You sound uncertain."

"Well," I said, "you kill."

"Since when is killing not part of Nature?"

"Since it is used to harm on purpose—in, as you say, a battle."

That stopped him. I saw that dark shadow flicker across his face. "I'm not a Healer," he answered flatly. "Nor am I from Merith. Do not compare me to your innocent . . . upbringing."

Upbringing was not what he was going to say. Regardless, his tone stung. I said right back, "And I am not from your violent world, so do not assume I understand it."

Laurent pulled the saddle from Arro. "True," he acknowledged, a little softer. "Sometimes there is no choice but to wield a weapon, especially if life as we know it is at risk." He walked away to heave the saddle over a limb. "You should know that the Breeders have gained advantage," he called back. "The battle is renewed with a vengeance. This drought is but a sample of the upheaval. 'Twill only get uglier."

I thought about that for a moment. "Does this battle have to do with finding a shell?"

Laurent dropped his chores, came from under the boughs of oak straight to me. "You said you did not speak with your cousin."

"I didn't. But you say the drought is part of this, and there is a bit of verse: *find the shell's song; bring rain upon—*"

He had my arms, tight. "Where did you hear that?"

I tugged reflexively, astonished at his grip. "You do housekeeping whilst speaking of the Earth's survival and now you are violent over some words?"

"You know of things. *How* do you know?"

The Rider was too close, his eyes so intensely blue. "I met an old man, a seer," I said breathlessly. "He said that the darkness comes, that I need to find a shell." *And that I was hiding from something I could not yet see.* I wished suddenly that the seer had been wrong about all of it.

"This seer." Laurent was terse. "Did he have a name?"

"Harker."

His stare hardened. "You should stay far from him."

I pictured the old man, sadly lonely and in pain. "He's harmless."

"Harmless?" It was almost barked. Laurent released me and walked away. "He is the *cause* of this."

"How? Why?"

"Harker offered the Breeders something he should not have, something they parlayed into this new attack." His tone was scathing. "I suppose he omitted that part of it."

I rubbed my arms, for his touch lingered. "Even so, why would he tell me to find a shell?"

"I hope out of guilt," Laurent muttered. "My lady, the shell you ask of—'tis an amulet, one of four which belong in the Keepers' protection, safe in castle Tarnec. But because of that seer's traitorous indiscretion they were lost to us, stolen by Breeders." His mouth hardened. "They are scattered now, hidden, used to taunt us—"

"What are these amulets?"

"An orb, a shell, a stone, and a blade. They represent Life, Death, Dark, and Light; the primal forces."

I'd lost my own breath somewhere. "What—what do they do?"

"They are linked together under the Keepers' watch. 'Tis how Balance is preserved, the essential cycles of these forces protected. If the amulets are separated, the forces become unstable and all life is at risk."

"Why?" I shouted it, surprising the Rider. But I was suddenly angry at this blithe talk of battle, not wanting to believe such power could be so recklessly placed in trinkets: "Why so simple—that our lives can be risked because amulets are separated?"

"Simple?" The Rider sneered. "You know nothing of the

Keepers' endless vigil!" He stalked off to wrestle some emotion privately, came back. His voice was even then, and more powerful for it: "Think how necessary this Balance, the ebb and flow of the primal forces, and yet we take it for granted; you, Healer, treat by it. A dawn, a dusk, a growing season, and a fallow one. . . . We assume that each day, each year the cycles will repeat. Why? Because it *must* if we are to thrive. If one force dominates or disappears, we are undone. You've seen what's happened in three months of drought, now imagine if it never rains again."

The words jerked out of me. "'Tis rain you speak of! Not light or dark . . . or death!"

"No rain," the Rider insisted, but softer. "The Breeders' choice. Do you understand? The primal forces are what bind Nature to the Earth. They must be in balance so that Nature is in balance, the four elements—Earth, Water, Air, and Fire—in equal share. But in the Breeders' hands the amulets become playthings." His stare narrowed. "So yes, they can deprive water . . . if they wish."

I heard my little gasp, the full impact of the threat hitting like a physical blow. This drought was by design, a whim of malice.

"You see it now, how they may toy with our lives." Laurent came close again to murmur it: "They cannot destroy the amulets, but the Breeders can manipulate, use Nature against itself. Ravage the Earth and madden its creatures. They rise against us with a strength we've not seen for many ages. The amulets must be reclaimed if they are to be stopped."

I nodded, I think. Humor gone, anger gone. There was still that tingling at my shoulder, running through me like a thread of warmth—

Laurent tilted his head, studying me. "I see it in your eyes— you hesitate. You've asked every question but the most essential. Shall I ask them for you?" And he was even softer: "Why do the Breeders look for you, Evie Carew? What calling was awakened by the bond seeking?"

"My mark. It means something—something I didn't know. . . ." I faltered, thinking: the seer had reached for my mark, frightened by it, asking what it was I shared with Lark. I looked at the Rider with new concern. "My cousin. What is she in this?"

He said, "Ask instead why your cousin was chosen to seek help for Merith."

"Because she received the signs!"

"But who sent them, my lady?" When I shook my head he answered, "Lark was summoned by the Keepers, by those of Castle Tarnec, because we need her help. We need your help as well." The Rider was so close; his nearness, what he was saying, made me catch my breath. "Each amulet has a Guardian, the one who can save or destroy it. Four amulets, four Guardians—our Guardians of Tarnec. They alone can find the amulets, return them, restore Balance. Lark is one such Guardian."

Lark—timid, sweet Lark. How could it be so? And yet there was sense in it.

I whispered, "I know my cousin well enough, her

connection to all things, to know that she is your Guardian of Life."

A single nod. Something was hurting my chest, making it hard to ask the next question. "And if Lark is the Guardian of Life, what, then, am I?"

"You, my lady, are the Guardian of Death."

8

I FELT THE heat rising from throat to cheek. I moved away.

"It is not what you think," Laurent said behind me.

"How do you know what I think?"

"Because your eyes burned just then, before you turned, as if you wished it away. As if it shamed you."

"Not the calling, Rider, but the title." That he noticed such detail unnerved me. "I am a Healer. How is it that I am *Death's Guardian*?"

"You speak it wrongly. As if you see death as an evil."

It burst out: "I've never seen death as evil! It is the necessary end to life!" And yet, since Raif, there was too much of it, so senseless and *unnecessary*. Death followed me—or I'd followed it, and now this young man had just draped it over me, crowned me with the word. I was galled by the idea. If a

Guardian, why could I not have been the one for Light? Or even the one for Dark? Anything but Death.

But Laurent said softly, "Not *Death's* Guardian, lady, but the *Guardian* of Death, of Death's amulet. Of course you are a Healer. You are *the* Healer. The one of ones."

"Harker called me that. You and he speak the same, and I thought him mad."

A snort. "Crafty, not mad. He spoke true. The Guardian of Death is the most powerful of Healers. You are the last stand between life and death. You allow only the passing of those who cannot be saved."

Only those who cannot be saved? The shock was physical. Frost bit through my spine, my knees quivered, something horrible burrowed in my gut. I felt brutal, suddenly, bursting into laughter and scorn: "Was I there to save the villagers of Bern, or any of the dying in other ruins I walked through? Was I there—?"

To save Raif. I couldn't say it out loud, though Laurent hesitated as if he heard it, understood. He said quietly, "But you can find the amulet, return it, and thereby save so many."

I sat down, hard, still laughing; I couldn't seem to stop. "You make it sound easy." Laurent shook his head at that, but I only laughed more. "Yes, of course. Why, *certainly*, Rider. Let us go to the waterfall, retrieve the shell, and so save—"

Laurent said sharply, "Waterfall?"

"Yes—a waterfall." I wiped my nose, giggling, "Why? Was

I not supposed to know that? Oh—yes, 'twas supposed to be hidden. The Breeders chose poorly if they meant so."

The Rider muttered, "How do you know?"

"The spell. That is what it showed—a lake, a cliff with streams of waterfalls pouring down." And then that too seemed ridiculously funny, and I was off, helpless in this drunken hysteria, completely disturbed by my behavior even as I laughed, shoulders heaving, even as I saw Laurent stride toward me, serious and urgent and purposeful, kneel in front of me to say, "Evie, you speak of Gren Fort. They are allies of Tarnec. To place the amulet openly, in safe environs—'tis too easy. Are you sure?"

I gasped something, thinking I was saying yes. Laurent repeated hard, "Are you sure?"

Then he was gripping my shoulders—the way I'd gripped the brown-bearded Rafinn to wake him from his panic. Now I was that frantic man and the Rider me, shaking me back to reason, making my skin burn under his touch, until the laughter fell out like pathetic hiccups.

"Enough!" I pushed his hands away. Exhaustion flooded in at his release, and I dropped my forehead on my knees with a shudder. *Guardian of Death.* I was needed—Harker and the Rider both said—and so be it. But retrieving a small shell seemed an overwhelming challenge, suddenly, like having to upend one of these oaks.

I wondered what Lark had thought when she was told.

Laurent did not apologize, only got up and moved off a few

paces. He watched me for a moment before saying once more, "Cliff, waterfalls. You are sure."

"'Twas an Insight spell. It does not lie." I sounded dull, remote.

"Fair enough," he decided, frowning. "I will bring you there."

I shook my head and sighed into my knees.

Laurent came back to urge, "A day's journey, perhaps less if we make haste."

"And then what?"

I heard the pause, as if my ignorance still surprised him, or as if he did not trust the ease of the task. "Retrieve the shell," he said at last. "Return it to its rightful place in Tarnec. One cycle of Balance will be restored."

"No."

"You are not still afraid of a horse!"

I looked up. "I said no, Rider."

Another, sharper pause, and then: "Look at you, refusing transport. Or . . . is it that you refuse to help?" He was angry. "You cannot mean to be so foolish."

I lifted my head, barely. "I mean that I am *tired*, Rider." The day of the spell, the night of wisps and Rider, and now this dawn of Guardianship were crashing down as one weight that I suddenly could not bear without sleep, rest, some moment to breathe. And I said it rudely: "Affix whatever reason you like; I cannot make any journey right now, be it with or without you."

Laurent's jaw tightened, but then he simply nodded, retrieved his cloak, and threw it on the ground next to me in a space of dappled light. "My lady." He gestured. It was less than gracious, but he did not mock.

I crawled to the cloak, lay down, and turned on my side away from him. I did not know if he would share, but I left him room enough. I closed my eyes, glad I was too weary to think—

But then, curious, I murmured, "Did Lark find her amulet?"

"She did."

Healers do not dream. We are too present-minded to be caught in the fabulous workings of sleep. I woke, though, disoriented. Something about the late afternoon play of light on the grass, the way the breeze ruffled through the green reminded me of Merith, of lying beneath the apple trees in late summer breathing in the smell of ripening fruit.

He was leaning against the trunk of a tree, silhouetted in the shadow, chiseling some bit of wood with a small blade and pushing the hair from his brow with a careless gesture. He must have felt my eyes on him, for the blade paused. There was a heavy silence within the copse, as if even the birds had stopped singing.

I said in a whisper, "Raif?"

It was soft enough, yet the Rider heard it. He looked to me, shifting a little where the sunlight caught him. I sat up quickly and rubbed my eyes. *Of course*—'twas oak not apple, and the cloak was all wrong. Even his silhouette was taller, if I'd truly thought.

Laurent went back to his wood. But I stayed watching him, wondering if I should apologize, and feeling strangely unmasked, like I'd accidentally shared a secret. Laurent was calm, intent on his work. His eyes were downcast. In the light, the differences between the Rider and Raif were more than obvious, but I went over each feature anyway. If he knew I studied, sorted out such details, he pretended ignorance.

I had no reason to ask it right then: "The scar along your temple, Rider. How did you come by it?"

"It was long ago." Which meant I was not to pry.

"'Twas healed by a White Healer, wasn't it?"

Laurent stopped whittling.

"Man or woman?" Another question I had no honest reason for asking.

But this one he answered: "Neither." He offered nothing more, only put his blade away and stood, saying politely, "Our clothes have dried."

I collected my frock, pulled it on. It was stiff but sunsweet. Laurent approached and held out the oak he'd been whittling—a spear, the point brutally sharp. My second spear in as many days. He said at my expression, "There is no Healer rule against defending yourself."

I took the spear. I could not help touching its tip, wondering what thing I'd have to stab to survive. I said a little hoarsely, "I need to eat something before we go. There should be acorns. . . ."

But Laurent was already holding out a piece of his own fare. "Hardbread is quicker."

I took that from him as well and wolfed it down in two bites, which seemed to amuse him. "Is there something funny, Rider?" I asked with my mouth full.

"Only that you are as ethereally lovely as the faerie queen, my lady, yet so very . . . human in your actions."

That stopped me in surprise. " 'Tis good for you, then, that I am no faerie, Rider Laurent," I answered after a moment, swallowing. "I've heard they break men's hearts."

"True enough." He nodded and walked away. He pulled on his shirt, strapped his pack onto the saddle, and mounted Arro. I picked up my own satchel and cloak and followed. Then I went back and retrieved the spear.

"I'll sit behind this time," I announced as he reached a hand. He swung me up behind him obligingly, and I was glad he asked no questions. It bothered me that he'd called me lovely, bothered me that he did not seem to know my retort was meant in jest and I did not want him to see me wrestle those thoughts. I hiked my frock above my knees and adjusted my seat. I tucked the spear into the saddle straps then tentatively put my arms around Laurent's waist.

"Where is this Gren Fort?" I asked against his shoulder.

"South," he called back. "The ancient quarries in the West-run Downs. 'Tis a hidden colony carved into the limestone, set up as defense in a long-ago battle with the Breeders."

"How many battles between Breeders and Keepers?"

His shoulder shrugged beneath my cheek. "Balance is always challenged."

We left the copse far behind. I hung on, clinging tightly, deciding I'd chosen the worse option, pressed so against his back. *A day's journey*, he'd said. Like this.

Landscape blurred the same as my thoughts. Sometimes I spotted specific plants—the makings of a digestive, something for aches. I wondered at the fortification of the hardbread, that we did not need to eat again after such a small piece. The sun dropped, the downs skidded by. A tea . . . a poultice . . . Laurent's hand was gripping my arm to keep me from slipping from Arro's back, for I was no longer clinging to stay upright but lulled by the steady gait.

But then Arro pulled up suddenly and veered hard left, pounding toward a flank of trees. We ducked under some branches and stopped. I turned, but Laurent squeezed my arm to signal silence and pointed up. Between the leaves the sky was peppered with crows, spiraling and cawing alarm.

"Something's coming," I breathed. He did not need to reply.

These woods were sparse. Laurent guided Arro into the thickest brush, then jumped down and lashed the reins tight to a branch. It was the first time the Rider had tethered his horse, I noted. "Stay—" Laurent began, looking up at me, then eyed my turquoise garb with a frown. He pulled me off the horse, marched me to a linden tree. "Can you climb?"

I nodded. A hoist and I was up, then Laurent went back to Arro, unsheathed his sword, and took the spear, which he brought to me. "High as you can. Tuck up your skirts."

I climbed, one-handed, found a high branch sturdy enough to perch on, then looked for the Rider. He'd chosen a wide hickory at the edge of the road. He leaned his back against it, both hands on his sword, and went utterly still. I watched him, waiting, feeling my own heart slow, each beat echo. A fevered hush . . . anticipation pulled a bead of perspiration down my neck.

There was a thrumming—not ponies, but the heavy tread of feet, a clanking of metal. A half run, it sounded, steps synchronized. I saw Laurent lift his blade. I gripped my spear and craned forward to see.

Soldiers—armored ones, ugly aberrations from a blacksmith's fires. Helmets, breastplates, shoulder guards, and thick-fingered gloves; the shape of metal disfigured them, as if they wore their bones on the outside, all pitch-black and heavy and hard-edged. They hoisted weapons—flails and poleaxes and falchions—vicious examples of what I'd once seen demonstrated at a fair. And painted on the armor was something familiarly ominous: a circle within which there was a Z slashed through—the same brand that had been scorched on poor Ruber Minwl's severed hand.

Ten in all, hardly an army, though by tread alone they sounded tenfold greater. The road curved along the gathering of trees; the soldiers marched closer while the crows shrieked above in protest. Massive and purposeful, they strode with gazes locked forward, dust clouding up from beneath their boots creating the illusion they rode the air. I found myself clenching my lip, not daring to breathe, though their dust and sweat still found a way into my nostrils. Life force was strong in that sweat. Too strong—the emphasis was on force, not life.

They pounded by, every branch shivering with their steps. I glanced down at Laurent; his head was turned, watching. Even after they disappeared he stayed fixed. Time passed. The crows stopped their noise and settled and still we held. I watched the light shift between the leaves, smelled the sweat dissipate. Finally I felt Laurent's sword touch my sandal and I scrambled down.

He took me by the waist to lower me from the last branch. I could feel his anger. "A forward guard from Tyre," he said, frowning. "They scout."

"The battle is near? *Now?*" I asked, surprised. "Are they fighting the Breeders?"

"Tyre is aligned with the Breeders."

"I thought . . ." But whatever thought I'd had trailed off as those words sank in: *aligned with.* Bile stung my throat. I knew the harsh rumors of that city, but it did not seem real that men would add their might to this darkness that was coming, would aid the thing that intended to destroy their world. 'Twas silly, plaintive, even, my question, "Why?"

"Greed. Aggression."

His words in turn were slapped, mouth tight—as if the Rider had painful history with such things. I started to ask, then remembered something Harker had said: *This begins as a violence of Nature and becomes the violence of Man.*

"It takes over?" I whispered.

"Like a virus. It finds your vulnerability and decimates."

I must have moved or flinched, for Laurent suddenly touched my arm. "Chaos is the easy option," he said more gently. "It is Balance that is the challenge. That makes us fragile. Remember that."

I nodded. *Fragile.* I'd heard that too from Harker—he'd tried to frighten me with a fierce voice asking me where I was weak.

"So." Laurent straightened. "Tyre is seeking."

"Gren Fort?"

"A fool's errand if they only send ten men," Laurent said. "Besides, this road only tracks our route for a league or so. From here on, though, we will take caution." He reshifted his sword to his left hip and started to push through the brush to where Arro waited.

I called after him, a sudden, ugly thought tightening my belly. "They—the guard—is it me they seek?"

Laurent paused, then shook his head. "There are things far better suited to tracking a Guardian." But he added something, which didn't sound quite like relief: "For now you are spared the Breeders' focus."

❧

The Rider was right. I was not the focus. At the bend where the road curved west we found them: twenty-three men and boys armed with farm tools as rude defense, all tumbled like rag dolls facedown in the dirt.

Blood stained the road.

9

I WAS OFF the horse and running for the first body, the second. Laurent galloped to the other side, dismounting before Arro even halted. "Anyone?" he shouted.

I felt for pulses, looked at wounds, shaking my head no and no again. I found one old man, wheezing pink spittle, and propped his head in my lap, using the hem of my cloak to wipe the blood and grit from his face, smear it from his white hair.

His eyes flung open and he cried and lashed out, as if he were still trapped in battle. I cried out too. "It's all right!" I tried to catch his focus. "You're safe."

"They're taking us. We couldn't stop them." The man's hands waved, reached out for me to pull him up.

I gripped his fingers and held them hard. I could feel life escaping him—sighing from his palms, his throat—beyond any ability to restore. "We can help," I urged. "Tell me how to help!"

"Take me back. My village . . . We won't be slaves. . . ."

"Slaves?" The word soured my mouth. Those were the rumors of Tyre I'd not been able to believe.

"Take me back," he begged. "I have to stop . . ."

The man was dying; it was cruel to force information. I spit out the disgust, then shifted and took his head gently between my hands, waiting while his skin warmed, Healer's energy dispelling the fear. "You are safe," I hushed. "Your village is safe." I hoped it was true. "You will go home. You'll see that all is well. All will be well." I repeated that until his face softened, pain lulled by voice and touch. The heartbeat shuddered, slowed. Then it was done. I closed his eyes and shifted his head to rest on the ground, ill for it. *Another and another and another . . .* I couldn't count how many dead I'd seen, soothed, could not help—

"Evie!"

I stumbled up and raced to Laurent. He cradled a boy, no more than nine year'd, with a vicious rip down his front from a falchion. "He breathes," the Rider said.

Carrot hair, a fair sprinkling of freckles, and ginger eyelashes that shut on so bright a face. "The soldiers were coming for slaves," I hissed, ripping open the blood-soaked shirt. "It cannot be—it can*not*!" I threw all my anger toward Tyre. "Where is there a place where you are forced to do another's bidding?"

"It's for the mines."

"What mines?" It was too quick, how the Rider answered. I wiped some of the blood away to see the wound, and for the first time my hands shook. The gash was long and deep, not unlike what had killed Raif. I swallowed, then set my jaw. This boy I would save.

"The gem mines of Tyre," Laurent was saying. "It's not territory they take, it's people."

"You cannot *take* people." I tore up the boy's shirt. "Stanch the blood," I directed, pushing the pieces at the Rider. Then I ran to Arro, pulled my satchel and the flask of water from the saddle, and raced back. "Press harder! Stop his bleeding."

I opened the flask, soaked a remaining bit of shirt, and used it to wipe around Laurent's hands. Then I dug in my satchel for my little vials of herbs, forgetting I'd finished them all in my spell making and for the seer. The only thing was the empty jar of minion, which I threw away with a curse. Laurent looked up at me.

"Minion." I was brusque. "*Quickly!* Does minion grow here?"

"I do not know, my lady."

The Rider's sudden formality warned me I was too late to help this boy. But I wanted none of it. I got to my feet again, ran to where the green met the road, then raced along the border. There was clover, and chamomile, and spurge—no minion. And why should there be? Minion was rare, not a roadside weed. Thwarted, I pulled some spurge as a poor substitute. I stuffed it in my mouth, chewing as I ran back, and spitting it into my palms.

I threw myself at Laurent's side. Blood was soaking the cloth, his hands, everything. "You're not pressing hard enough!" I cried.

"It cannot be stopped," Laurent said quietly.

"That's not true! He's just a *boy*!" Of course the Rider was right, but I would yell anyway—at him, at anything to ease this anger that was eating at my chest, my heart. "We *must* save him!" I gritted, then corrected: "*I* must save him."

Laurent did not respond, just drew his hands away and moved back. I smeared the wound with inadequate medicine. Blood ran into it so that the green became one mess of black, my hands black with it as well. I pushed hard on the wound, teeth clenched and silent, willing my hands to keep death at bay even as I felt the young life ebbing. And it was ebbing.

"No, *NO!*" On impulse I leaned over and placed a kiss on the freckled forehead—what was wrong with me that I was so despairing of a life? *"Stay!"* I shouted at him. I knew I was too upset for this; I brushed off my palms, pressed his wound again, asked softer, "Live." But it was already too late. This boy, who most likely had run through a field that morning, drawn well water, and gathered an egg for breakfast, now lay red and still.

All of them did.

I stood up and stalked away, wiped my hands on the grass, then came back and started to drag a body to the side of the road. Wordlessly Laurent went to another and pulled him to the road's edge. One by one we laid them there side by side, we as silent as the dead. It was not our place to bury or burn. We should leave these men, young and old, for their own families to collect. But when Laurent reached for the red-haired boy, I stopped him.

"He comes with us." I was fierce. "We are bringing him back to his village."

"If there is a village," Laurent murmured. But he did not argue. He wrapped the boy in his own cloak and rested him gently over the saddle. Then he offered me his hand to help me mount, but I shook my head.

"I'll walk."

"We both will walk," Laurent said. And it seemed a special respect that two led one home.

We stayed west on the road, following the sunset. I was miserable with questions, anger compounding. How could people kill other people or enslave them? Who would burn homes and livestock, ruin any bit of cultivated land? What inspired such senseless violence and disregard for life?

What Laurent's thoughts were I couldn't tell, but his jaw was set as hard as mine. We did not speak.

Smoke was in the distance—innocent at first, like the sweet smoke of kitchen fires. But there was too much of it and I'd seen too many burnings to be so fooled. "Their homes," I bit out, lunging forward. "We have to help."

Laurent gripped my shoulder, halting me midstride, and nodded at the field of corn that wound alongside the road. "Best we approach through there. We won't be seen."

I led, pushing into the stalks that rose high, then curled brown-dry, suffering like everything else. The smoke grew thicker, spiraling in the breeze, and I put my sleeve over my face at the stench, bitter at all of it. What matter that we were hidden when the dead leaves rasped, hardly disguising our approach? What matter that we approached at all? We were too late.

At the rim of the cornfield we stopped, faced a ruin where the village should have been. 'Twas empty of people, of animals—except for sheep carcasses strewn like puffs of fallen clouds. Eighteen cottages and three barns were in ashes, too fast, too complete for this to be from a normal burning, if there was such a thing. The nineteenth cottage, closest to the common well, stood untouched.

"They left it on purpose," Laurent murmured.

"Then let us see why," I said, and started off.

Again Laurent pulled me back. "Not so fast, my lady. That the soldiers left the cottage means they use it. They will be near."

I returned hard, "So? The smoke will hide me. I am nearly the color of it." And I was. My skin, hair, and frock were all rank gray.

We held gazes for a moment. My teeth were clenched, his mouth a hard line. Then Laurent's frown softened. He began, "You hurt, I know—"

"*Don't.*" I stopped him fiercely. "You were the one who said I only allow those who cannot be saved. So *do not* pity me."

The Rider hesitated, then said simply, "Be on your guard, my lady. I will see to Arro and join you quickly." He faded back and drew Arro deeper into the cornfield.

An acrid stink of charred wood and stone and straw. I picked my way over rubble—all steaming hot. The smoke was the same, but I'd never seen remains of a fire like this, what burned so totally, so quick. 'Twas nothing like the Troths' wild and clumsy destruction. I scanned withered, ash-gone gardens, trying to see what herbs or flowers or even weeds I could use for medicine if needed. There was little left.

And then I peeked in the window of the standing cottage, saw a kitchen fire burning, a stew pot over it, and an old woman tending to it, impossibly ordinary in the midst of devastation. She was alone. I ducked and skirted around the side to the door, then whispered, *"Mistress."*

The old woman straightened—as best a hunchback could. I must have looked like a ghost, for she clapped a hand over her face and nearly lost her balance on her crutch. "Law, lass! Who be ye?"

"Where are the soldiers?" I hissed.

"Near, must be—"

"Hurry, then." I beckoned. "Come with me!"

She looked stunned. "With ye? To where? I canna travel." She waggled her crutch.

"We have a horse."

"Horse!" She hobbled closer to study me in the dying light, suspicious. "Who are '*we*'? Magicians?"

I shook my head and reached my hand to her, but she shook her head as well. "They be coming fer their meal. Get on with ye. Go—or hide. Quick! Afore yer seen."

"Meal!" I stepped inside even as she waved me away. "You *feed* them?"

"Ye canna think I want to! I had no choice but prepare it! Where could I go?" The old woman's face was grim. She gave up trying to shoo me off and turned away. "Curse of deformity. Else I'd be with the rest."

"No curse, you're lucky for it! We'll take you to the next village."

"Lucky?" She barked. "Yer not understanding! There's no next village! Which ones they've not swallowed will fall tomorrow or the next. *Lucky* is to be bound, off to Tyre."

I was stunned, and blunt for it. "How can you speak blithely of wanting slavery? Those men on the east road died to save you from—!"

"Dinna say that!" She interrupted, bitter as I and colder than stone. "I *know* my neighbors be dead! The stink of it was on their axes! Them metal men roped the rest like cattle, herded 'em off. And, aye, I'd rather be with my people than stand here servin' tormentors our food!" She limped back to the pot.

I followed her. "We came to help."

"Help!" It was sneered. She'd gone past the point of believing there was anything worth helping, or that she was worth helping—and hadn't I thought the same? "Ye come from nowhere like some spook, whisperin' *Escape!* Well, it's too late fer that!"

I took a breath. I was sorry for being hard and we were foolish for arguing. "We brought one home to bury," I told her.

She spit, "An' who's left to do the buryin'?"

I plowed through anyway. "A boy with the brightest red hair."

Her crooked spine stiffened to retort, reject it all, but then she just sighed, sagging. "That be Ben. He shouldn't have gone. But what do ye say to him: Be a slave? Nay. He wanted to fight with his da. I shouldna blame him fer that, though I'd not a done the same." She shook a fist at the sky in breaking desperation. "They took my whole village! What use is an old body in a mine? Or a babe? But they took them *all!*"

The woman railed but she'd already given up, was waiting for the end. And it *was* an end; there was no one, nothing left. I looked at her shelves. Emptied but for some elderflower honey and rock salt. I looked at the pot; whatever she had left was in there. Food for the tormentors, she said. One final meal.

"*Wait*—they've not left." Why had I not thought of it before? "They're coming back for the stew!"

"Feed them, then be killed." She swallowed. "I serve my use. Nothing left, ye see. If any village still stands, if anyone comes lookin', it'll be a sign to them—they be next. Maybe they'll know, then, not to fight, an' the soldiers might na burn it all."

I hardly heard her. "'Tis almost dark. Where are the soldiers?"

"Can only be south, in the gully at the river. Not much of a river now, been so dry. But there's water deep enough, an' a cliff high enough ta keep a crowd from escaping."

"How many?" I asked. "How many soldiers?"

"Thirteen. Three came first, then ten more." She'd been

averting her head, but now she turned to me as if she wanted to study my expression as she said this. "I heard of the slave soldiers before but never did they come fer us like this. A kidnapping here or there—wantin' a strapping boy or girl fer their mines, but now they took all that weren't killed. So greedy! An' *still* they left me!" She smacked her cane against the bubbling pot.

The pot sloshed, making the fire spit. I glanced at the window. "How soon before they return for the stew?"

"It canna be long. See, I told ye ta hurry off!"

"Never mind that," I said. "We're going to help you; we're going to free your neighbors."

The old woman snorted. "Ye an' who else? Ye've a sweet face—earnest. I dinna know where yer chased from, but ye best run now or you'll be another prize fer Tyre. Ye canna fight the metal men." And then she started and gasped, "La!," her eyes on the doorway where Laurent had slipped in.

"Mistress." Laurent acknowledged her with a nod and said softly to me, "The boy is at the well. Feet to the water, head to where the moon will rise."

The old woman could not tear her eyes from him. "Ye know our customs, but 'tis wasted kindness. There be no one to bury poor Ben."

"We *will* free your neighbors," I repeated. I knew Laurent looked at me.

"Can ye?" The woman turned to the door, waiting, then back to me. "Is there no one else?" And when I said no, she shook her head. "Even wi' him!" she said. "Him 'n that sword. It's not enough."

"No," Laurent agreed. "It is not enough."

"'Tisn't the sword," I said quickly, looking over at Laurent. He raised a brow but I only smiled. "Hide him," I told the old woman quickly. "Add the honey and a handful of salt to the stew. Don't let the soldiers take it yet. I'll be right back." And I was out the door before the Rider had any opportunity to say not to go.

I'd seen some of it growing in one of the wrecked gardens: valerian. And jimson weed I was sure I could find in among the rows of corn. I stayed low, skimming from garden to garden, then into the cornfield, stuffing my skirts with what I could rip from the ground. Valerian, jimson weed, and certainly chamomile, which was an easy find among the trampled grass. Easier, of course, would have been the heliotrope that I'd brought from Merith, but that was a wasted wish. I wondered if Harker had used it. I wondered if he'd found an easy sleep.

The smoke was lifting, but so was night falling. Either way, I was nothing more than a shadow among the ruins, gray and quick. But as I pushed out of the corn, I froze. A steel-clad figure stood at the dim-lit doorway of the old woman's cottage. Did she know? Was the Rider safely stowed?

The old woman came limping out, followed by another soldier. She said something, which I could not hear, and they walked off, silhouettes against the red haze, two of them immense in their thick armor, one stooped over a crutch. Despite the heaved shoulder, the old woman kept her head high. And, crippled or not, it seemed she took extra long in walking—'twas to give me time, I was sure. I watched, touched by her small act of defiance, that maybe she hadn't given up, and yet I could not stop the doubt: to *what* end, this defiance? It was rubble, all of it, and she was alone.

I shook myself, then raced to the cottage, practically falling into Laurent, who met me at the door with drawn sword. He was frowning, ready to lecture, but I pushed him back from the entrance. "What are you doing? They'll be back in a moment."

He allowed my shove, it barely moved him anyway, but murmured with a none-too-sweet smile, "You expected me to hide while you flit among the ruins?"

I swatted away his concern. "Here, then. Help shred this into the pot." I shook my skirts so the greens fell to the floor. "Tiny bits. The taste is bitter."

Our humor was grim. Laurent's hand was close to his sword. This business of waiting went against him. He wanted action, bloody justice against the soldiers. And I was ordering a puny task where broad strokes of the blade would have been more to satisfaction. Still, he bent willingly enough for the weeds, ripping them into small bits, tossing them into the bubbling stew. We worked quickly. The dried blood and dirt on our hands worked off on the greens and so they were black even before I stirred them into the heat. They looked like savory bits of herb. *Choke on this,* I thought, brutal.

"They're coming," Laurent said, low and sudden. He grabbed my waist and half dragged me up a tiny ladder in the shadow of the cottage as the door banged open. Voices—three soldiers with the old woman now. I was panting, tucking my skirts, scrabbling to fit on the ledge of the loft, an empty shelf for the storage of grain and dried fruits barely wide enough for one person. Then Laurent wrapped his arms around me, forcing me still against him, my face in his chest. Behind the dirt of a day's turmoil, I could smell his skin like warm oak and that faint dusting of sandalwood. I swallowed and tried to turn my head away, for it made no sense in this moment to be enticed.

"Don't move," he mouthed in my ear. I felt his fingers in my hair.

We waited, still as stone, hearing the armored figures clunk across the floor. Two supported something between them, which was dropped heavily by the hearth—I could smell it: a wine cask. The old woman said loud, daring, "Is it enough? Ye got the last of everything. The stew, the wine. Is it *enough* yet? Or will yer shadows return to take the very sun from our fields?"

Her hostility was ignored, though she gnashed at them, taunted. Other noises—of metal, of thick crockery—a jug most likely—thunked on the floor, then the thunk, too, of an axe in wood, and slops of wine spilling everywhere. And then the old woman's voice was stopped. There were retches and whimpers as if she was being forced to drink the remnants of wine, and guttural laughs as if it amused the soldiers to watch. I tensed, thinking to shout, leap down—

The whimpers ended abruptly on a sigh. There was the scraping of a stool being pushed away, and then the clatter of the old woman's crutch. And, after all the harsh clanks and crashing, the following thud was quite soft.

The old woman was dead. Killed below us as we hid silent and still, and did nothing to prevent.

I jerked in reflex. *"Wait"* was the breath against my ear, a command like I'd never heard. I couldn't have moved anyway; Laurent's hold was like iron. I could feel the heat of his blood, the fury. I wanted to hate him for his caution, but he was forcing himself to stay still as much as he forced me, maybe more so. As if he'd had to swallow cruelty before. I pictured his scar.

The jug was collected, the pot from the fire lifted on its long brace. I was so strained against Laurent's grip that I thought my bones would break, but he held me hard, waiting until the soldiers clanked out of the cottage. The last one kicked the burning logs off the hearth with his metal-shod foot, for we heard them scatter over the floor, and smelled the smoke rising.

Still, Laurent held me for a count of fifty before deeming the soldiers far enough gone, and then we were both scrambling down the ladder. I ran to the old woman; Laurent pushed the logs back into the fireplace, then beat out flames with the hook rug and stuffed it into the wide fireplace as well.

"She's dead!" I hissed at him. "Stabbed straight through while we lay there!" I whirled in disbelief. "We just *lay* there!"

Laurent said grimly, "We'll carry her to the well." He stamped on an errant flame.

"The *well*? So we can lay her out the same as the boy, as if that is some honor? We let her *die*, Rider!"

"More would die if we'd intervened—"

"More *already* died! We waited in the woods while the

soldiers tripped past and slaughtered those men and boys! We did nothing to stop that either!"

Laurent rounded on me, gritting, "And you think my sword and your little spear would have stopped it, any of this? You don't even *have* your spear!"

"I wasn't—"

"*Thirteen* soldiers, my lady! Ten of them took twenty-three villagers with barely a struggle and rounded up the rest." The Rider leaned too close. "You might be a Healer, the Guardian of Death, but you are just as easily and softly killed as she was, never mind how grotesque the weapon." He reached a finger and touched the hollow below my collarbone, making me shiver. "There, my lady." His voice dropped to a bare whisper. "The tip of an arrow, a spear, a sword—just there. And then where would we be? We need *you*. That is my duty above all else." Laurent dropped his hand and moved so the old woman lay tumbled between us. "Take her feet," he said. I swallowed and bent to lift her.

We placed her next to the boy at the well in the market square. Laurent left immediately to get Arro. I stayed for a moment longer, wanting to be alone. I looked at young Ben, whom Laurent had carefully laid feet to the water. I reached out and smoothed his hair, a final tidying. The glowing embers of the burned cottages gave light to the ruined village square, to his shuttered face; I wished it had been completely dark. "I'm sorry," I whispered.

My hand rested on his forehead, warm against cold. For a

moment it was Raif lying there, lifeless. And I was helpless once more. I'd saved no one.

"I'm sorry," I whispered again miserably before running on.

Laurent stood with Arro, strong figures against the brittle corn. He was watching my approach, so I squared my shoulders and lifted my chin. "The river's south," I said, striding past him. "That's where they've taken all their captives."

Laurent let me walk ahead for a while, but then without difficulty he caught up with me, saying: "You know it's all right to be angry."

"I am not angry," I lied.

"You've seen little violence, tucked away in Merith. There is much you've endured just in two days. It cannot be easy to take it all at once."

"I am *fine*." I bit the word, adding, "You've endured just as much."

He ignored that. "What was it that you put in the stew?"

"Sleeping herbs. They should put down the soldiers fast enough."

"Sleep?" It burst from him. "*Only* sleep?"

I turned on him hard. "What—did you think 'twas poison? That I'd killed them? I can*not*."

"I didn't mean—"

"Do you not understand my wretched duty, Rider? *No harm*. 'Twas born into me; I cannot reject it! I would not have killed those soldiers in the cottage; I'd have tried to stop *them* from killing and, yes, probably died for it! And do you think it makes me glad? You can wield your sword, slay for good, for evil, for whatever you wish! But I cannot. No matter what I *feel*, I must respect life." I caught my breath, tried to lower my voice, but it hurt too much to sweep emotion back inside when I was already so stuffed with it. "Do you know what it's like to let someone die when you could have saved him, and not even be able to avenge his death?"

"I know it."

"Then do *not* say I should kill!"

"I do not say," Laurent murmured softly. "I trust you."

No one had ever said that to me before. No one had ever needed to. It unnerved me. I'd called being a Healer wretched, which unnerved me too. I slumped, put my hands on my thighs, and tried to breathe.

"But I would ask," Laurent added, "if you have thought what to do after they have gone to sleep?"

"We'll tie the soldiers, take their armor, weapons. . . ." My voice faded then, for the plan seemed childish against such vicious things. Laurent looked at me, waiting politely. "Anyway," I insisted, "I have an idea."

We approached the top of the gully as silently as we could. Laurent had his sword out; my heart was in my throat. Had all the soldiers eaten? Were they all passed out as they should be? The glow from a campfire was visible at the edge. Laurent motioned Arro to stay where he was, and then he and I crept to the overhang.

A river, reduced by half, glittered by firelight. Below us, bound and lassoed together, huddled the villagers. They were chattering, struggling, and trying to break from their bonds, unafraid of their captors now, for stretched out by the bank of the river lay thirteen soldiers. Their armor gleamed darkly.

I gripped Laurent's arm. He turned to look at them, at me, and I gave him a triumphant smile. We went over the edge, sliding down the sandy sides to a tremendous shout from the prisoners. Laurent took his sword and sliced the ropes and vines used to bind them—old men, women, young children, three babies. I ran to the soldiers and began unbuckling the armor, clamping my mouth against the foul stench beneath it. *They must live in this armor,* I thought. Their skin was pasty pale, overly soft and molded by the hard plates.

Others joined me. We removed the metal and the weapons, piling them at the edge of the river. No one asked yet why we didn't slice the throats of the soldiers, but I heard one woman quietly gasp at one, "He still breathes!" and fear was palpable after that. I called out, "They will not wake! Do not worry," worrying myself how I could find some way of ending this fear without murder.

And then I saw: fishing skiffs were neatly tethered some paces downriver by a small dock. The dock stood stick-legged in a dry portion of the riverbed, the boats beached. I left a soldier and thrust out into the river, wading toward its center, judging. Neck-deep, maybe more—was that deep enough to carry a heavy-weighted boat? The villagers paused to watch me. "Does it stay deep?" I yelled. "How far does it go?"

Someone called back, "These are the only shallows for many leagues. It goes on to the sea."

"Those!" I called then, pointing at the boats. "We need two of those!" And Laurent was running with two of the children to the dock, cutting the moors and dragging them into water. Then he too was wading chest-deep in the river and pulling two boats behind.

"What is all this?" one of the men growled from the shore. "What do we need the skiffs for? Take their weapons! Finish them!"

"No!" I shouted from the water. "No! Do not kill them!"

"Not kill?" I'd sparked a little fire—murmurs of unrest. "An' what? Have 'em come back again?" "They'll slaughter us—" "Nay, they'll torture first—"

"No! Do not strike first." I slogged toward the beach. "It makes you no better than they!"

"Who counts the order of strikes?" The shouts were piling up. "Who are ye ta say?"

"Others will come at you with greater force!" I cried. "They'll show no mercy!"

"And these metal men won't? I've nothin' left but my anger!"

"My home is burned!" Others shouted in agreement: "They killed my son!" "My da!"

I saw a figure—the youngest of the old men—make the first break from the pack and race for the soldiers' weapons we'd piled. He pulled the first thing he could, some wicked-looking axe.

Laurent was already on shore, unsheathing his sword as he ran. "You will not strike!" he commanded. "The lady says we spare them."

"Lady! What *lady* makes demands?" The man raised the axe over his head, stumbling under the weight, and swung it at the nearest slumbering soldier. I screamed. It was worse, this, than the terrified little group with the Troth. Those villagers had been frightened into inaction, but these would take their fear straight into the slaughter of sleeping men.

The Rider was faster than I could have imagined. Laurent sprang with a rounding kick, sweeping the man's feet out from underneath and bringing him down at the side of a soldier.

"*This* lady." Laurent panted, his sword tip at the man's throat. He whirled back, sweeping the blade at the restless group. They shuffled back nervously, and he pointed at me. "We do as she says."

Someone had the temerity to ask, "Who is *she*?"

Laurent said, before putting his sword down, "She is the one who will save us."

We bound the soldiers' hands and laid them in the boats, six in one, seven in the other, then pointed them downriver. We watched the boats slide away, firelight glinting on the sterns. The villagers were silent; I was the only one who wanted this mercy. One by one we scrambled back to the top of the gully, hoisting the children, hand to hand, pulling, pushing. . . .

There were more cries at the sight of Arro. Laurent told them to calm, but for naught. There was too much shock and now distrust to react any way but frightened. One old man, though, broke through the group and stepped nearer.

"A horse!" he exclaimed softly. He went to Arro, reached a tentative hand to his nose. Arro gave a soft bluster. A few of the children immediately reached to do the same but were yanked back. "Yer a Rider?" the old man asked, turning to peer at Laurent in the dark. "I heard o' ye. Never seen one o' yer kind, though. It bodes ill fer us."

"You have time, yet," Laurent said, then called out to all: "Bury your dead. Melt the armor into shields; take the weapons. Then move on. Tell others what has happened. Prepare."

"Do they come back?" a woman asked.

Laurent adjusted the saddle. "If you band with other villages, you have more of a chance. Learn Tyre's weapons; learn to defend." He turned to me, murmuring, "We have a journey, my lady," and lifted me onto the saddle before mounting. Laurent gathered Arro's reins and stepped him sideways. "Use this time wisely!" he called to the villagers. "Food, shelter, and protection."

And then Laurent urged Arro into a canter while I caught my arms around his waist, and we were away.

He was angry, his back stiffly slanted away from my cheek. "You wanted to kill them," I called out. "The soldiers. You wanted them dead too."

A nod. Terse and final.

But I did not let it go. "*Why?* Why kill?"

He let Arro run and turned his head; a gleam of moonlight caught the edge of his cheek. "There is no good that will come of keeping those soldiers alive. They will return; they have to. Soldiers cannot go back to Tyre without slaves or they themselves will be forced to the mines. So do not think you've spared anyone, my lady."

"But they have no weapons, no armor now!"

"Them or the next wave. Tyre is a bastion of Breeders. They will not be stopped."

I was stunned. "And so you kill and they *still* come? Then why not tell those poor villagers there is no point? Why bother giving them hope?"

"Hope is what keeps life worth something!" He was furious; he reined in Arro and turned fully in his seat, gritting out, "What would you tell them: Chaos is upon us? How do you beat Chaos? That struggle is *forever*." I felt his breath—short, hard. "Few should bear that burden. 'Tis better to give these folk something to fight: soldiers and famine. Things they *might* defeat. Things that have an end."

He nudged his steed forward. I had no retort; it upset me that this different view of violence opened a cavern between us. But there was something else, something that bridged the cavern that bothered me more. "You accepted my way of it, Laurent. You are angry and disagree, and yet you let me spare the soldiers, helped me tie them to the boats."

He did not turn again to answer, but his breath sighed. "You are the Guardian, I am the Complement. Ultimately, I must trust your choice."

And then we rode on. How many miles, how many hours, I do not know, except that we did not stop again. Anger drained.

Thought drained. I fell asleep against his back; he held my wrists tight around his waist to keep me upright. Somewhere it occurred to me that the Rider had used *Complement* not as a description but a title.

Healers do not dream. But I remember the soft thudding of hooves, the brush of wind, and finally the smell of water, as if they were vestiges of some other world unlocked when my eyes closed. And then I felt hands lift me down and the wrapping of something warm and soft.

I missed leaning against Laurent.

10

'TWAS THE COMFORT that woke me. I lay still for a time, feeling the give of goosedown beneath, blinking at the rafters above. *Rafters.* How long had it been? A roof *and* a pillow. Light streaked in, there was a steady rush of water. . . . It lulled me back to sleep until I woke again, this time with a start.

Room, bed, rushing water—incongruous after months of wander and drought. I got up, pulling the quilt with me since my clothes, I saw, were gone, and went to the window—not a true window, but a narrow, open rectangle cut into stone as thick as the length of my hand. I wedged my shoulders into the space, and peered out, down, then jerked back, heart hammering.

A moment to catch my breath and prepare, and then I peeked out again in awe: I was midway up a steep limestone cliff—some manmade territory within a manmade quarry, forced into the landscape by ages of stonecutting . . . and from where water sprang like leaks in a bucket.

Gren Fort.

From what I could see 'twas part of a wide, curving quarry filled with waterfalls. Above, below, from thin trickles to great torrents, waterfalls were everywhere. The spray was shot through with sun colors, rainbows shimmering in the mist. They spilled into some inaccessible lake far below while the fort itself was hewn right into the rock, halfway up, halfway down. It snaked along the idiosyncrasies of the rock cutting, so was built in levels—stone steps, wooden ladders, narrow footpaths, and rope bridges leading between stages and portions. The zig-zagging passageways scored the face of the limestone like teeth.

I turned around and looked again at the room I slept in, realizing 'twas all cut from stone, even what seemed like rafters were merely stained to appear as such, and the ceilings and walls only looked of yellowing plaster because the limestone was so pale. A dugout. A cave. Spare; function without detail—as if no one was meant to grow attached to this as a home. I wondered how many years Gren Fort had taken to carve, when the Keepers fought the Breeders from this hideout from which they could attack then disappear, and how they'd kept so hidden these years. I thought of the image of Tarnec that also appeared in my Insight spell, and how earth and rock seemed an important place for Keepers' dwellings. They built from things that could not be undone. Solid, and purposeful—

Like Laurent.

His name burst into my thoughts, more dizzying than

the height. I shook my head to clear it. For better measure, I stuck my head through the window and studied the fort again. A young girl was hurrying along a narrow edge, balancing a tray of food. I yelled, *"Take care!"* There was no railing—to fall from the steps would be a dead plunge to the rocks and lake so far below. But she paid no mind, whisking up a set of narrow steps with no eye to me or to the drop.

The girl disappeared into an interior tunnel. Moments later she was at my doorway—no place to knock, for there was no door. She smiled, doe-eyed and shy, bobbing a curtsy, making the stiff little braid at the back of her head bounce. She was not as young as I first thought, maybe only a year or so behind me. But she was all lightness and fine bones; she seemed a child.

"May I put this down, please?" she asked, holding out the tray. I nodded. Bread and goat butter and fresh-pressed juice—peach, I thought. My mouth watered at the sight. I'd not eaten for more than a day—strange that I didn't remember until this moment. When had a Healer forgotten to eat?

The girl entered almost on tiptoe and set the tray on the footstool, the only bit of furniture besides the bed. I hiked up the quilt, plunked down on the floor, and attacked the food.

"Thank you," I managed between bites. The bread was dark-crusted, studded with fruit and hickory, and dry as sawdust. But I worked through half the loaf before I slowed and considered the girl who kneeled by the door quiet as a mouse, politely waiting.

I wiped my mouth. "This is Gren Fort?"

She nodded.

"How many are here?"

"Seven families founded this dwelling."

"So small . . ." Even Merith had twenty households. Seven hardly seemed a worthy amount to defend a fort.

But she laughed at me and her mouselike posture evaporated. "Small? Seven families over seventy generations! But, I suppose 'tis what you think, for the fort can only support a hundred people at a time. The rest are spread out"—she waved a hand—"somewhere. Anyhap, you'll see everyone at evening meal. You are supposed to be left alone to rest for now."

I was done with resting. "How long was I asleep?"

"You arrived in the wee hours. It's past noon now." She jumped up. "I can show you where to wash if you're ready."

"Please, the—" I stopped, suddenly awkward. I'd not expected to ask news of the Rider, the question came of its own accord and foolishly so. We'd argued through our time together, I should be relieved he was not here. I swallowed and said carefully, "I came with someone else."

"Oh!" The girl jerked, her face going bright pink. "You did! But he sleeps still." She made some bashful gesture with her shoulder. He's very han—very tall."

"He is."

'Twas how I said it: spare of emotion, while she ducked and blushed. It surprised her. She cocked her head and studied me. "You're not wed or you'd share his room. Are you . . . Do you know him *well*?"

"Not at all." I swallowed. That was mostly true.

"I thought so." The girl shifted a little closer and whispered conspiratorially, reverently, "He is one of the *Riders*."

Her little move relieved me, made me grin, for she reminded me then of silly Cath from Merith and her flirting, rapturous infatuation with each of the young men of our village in turn. Even so, I wouldn't acknowledge Laurent's looks or share impressions in front of this girl any more than I might have gossiped with Cath about Raif. I changed the subject. "Tell me something of yourself."

"I'm Lill. I help out in the kitchens. Now *you*." She insisted rather than asked—I'd failed her thus far with my studious disinterest in Laurent, and she was waiting to be impressed.

"Evie. I'm a Healer."

That brought a smile. "I baked that," she whispered, nodding at the bread and flashing a sly little glance from the corner of her eye—waiting for a compliment. Lill was dark-haired and very pale, pixielike with her pointed features and slant to her wide eyes, and the way her braid scraped her hair so tightly back behind her ears. Cath had auburn curls, was peach-plump and syrup-pretty. Lill was a different sort of pretty, more haunting, richer.

Something twisted hollow in my stomach then, sending a strange little burn into my shoulder blade, into the circle of my birthmark. A longing, maybe, but I wasn't sure exactly what I was longing for. I was thinking of Cath and Laurent and mixing home with here. But Lill was not the Cath from home, and this was not home, and what was home anyway?

"Well?" Lill nodded at the bread again.

"Yes. Oh. Thank you." I said it blandly, and Lill only looked further disappointed. So I buttered another hunk of her bread and stuffed it in my mouth. "*Truly* delicious." I chewed hard, willing her to smile again. This was so unlike me—the neediness, the discomfort, the feigning to please another.

I drank up the juice and wiped my mouth against my arm, looking at the streaks of dirt and blood dried there. The strands of hair falling over my shoulders were filthy gray.

"You said I could wash?"

She jumped up. "I'll take you. It's a bit of a trek, but it's too impractical to hike buckets around here to fill any tubs."

"I don't mind." I unwound myself from the floor slowly, still stiff from the riding and tangled in the quilt. "Is there anything to wear? I've no clothes."

"They're drying," Lill answered. "Just bring that. Come."

So I followed her, quilt and all. We went through the little doorway into a dim tunnel, down three steps, and out onto the path. The sunlight dazzled; the drop was dizzying. Lill noticed none of it as we proceeded. She chose an upward route and ran lightly up the narrow steps on her rope-soled shoes, turning around often to stare at me. I tread far more carefully, aware of her curious gaze and the steep pitch . . . and the utter treachery of the bulky wrap. We wound our way up the face of the quarry, working sideways, climbing behind walls of waterfalls and up ladders and stairs until we came to a wider, flat path where we could walk side by side.

We stopped there to let two women pass. They had cropped

hair and were dressed alike in weighted shirts of linked metal and deerskin leggings similar to what I'd seen Lark wearing. One carried a bow and quiver, the other a short sword in her belt. They cast sharp glances at me, nodded at Lill, and strode by, withholding whatever conversation until we were out of earshot.

I turned to Lill. "Who are they?"

"Gren guards," she said with a shrug. "Couldn't you tell?" When I shook my head, she added impatiently, "The weapons and chain mail, silly."

"They're prepared for battle—? Oh, for goodness sake, Lill, what *is* it?" I could no longer take her staring.

"Why do you not know chain mail and ask of battle? Weren't you just in one?"

There was a pointed little thrill behind her question, expecting that I'd give a violent account for the blood and dirt that was dried all over me. I shook my head.

"Oh." Lill sighed. "Well, there's talk of great battles brewing, that we are at war with a very dark evil. I was hoping you'd been in a scrap or two. After all, you were traveling with a *Rider*. They don't come down from their hills unless something needs fighting." And then there was new eagerness in her tone: "You know the Breeders and their collaborators are massing, don't you? Breeders are our *greatest* threat. I heard that the Keepers are waking the Guardians and mustering all allies. The Guardians—have you heard the legends? They've not been awakened for ages and ages! We'll need all our might to push back the enemy this time."

If the Guardians were no secret, was I supposed to admit that I was one? Lill would be disappointed to learn it. I was all questions and boring answers for her, hardly as wondrous as she imagined. "I've heard this as well," I said as neutrally as possible, wishing suddenly that Laurent was with us. "But I've seen no battle."

Lill sighed again. "I suppose that's why the blood rinsed out of your clothes so easily; battle blood is harder to remove. They were washed this morning, I saw—Oh!" She was onto a wholly different subject. "Your *clothes*! How can there be such *blue*?"

"Indigo and alum," I said. "Common enough. Haven't you any?"

She shook her head. "We don't have such colors."

"But you are surrounded by blue!" I waved at the falls.

Lill shrugged. "Not like that. Colors are drab here." She skipped ahead, pointed to the wall of rock, and up. There were clever terraced plantings running up the sides of the quarry: narrow levels stacked up the length of one long waterfall (espaliered fruit trees at the bottom, then vegetables and berries above in decreasing size), close enough for the chiseled troughs to catch the constant spray of water. A rope ladder ran up the other side as access to the gardens. High above us a man was working; his legs hooked into the weave of rope as he leaned far out to cut some lettuces. He stuck them in a large pouch and hiked himself farther up.

Lill was used to the acrobatics and paid no mind, coming back to grab my arm and move me on. "We only dye from onion and spinach—all greens and yellows and browns." She groaned. "So dull! I remember being surrounded by color once. . . ."

"You didn't grow up here?"

She shook her head. "Refugee. Some of us are not descended from the founding families. I was rescued ten years back. There was a battle then. Not like this one coming, but . . ." Lill shifted suddenly before I could ask about it and changed her tone. "Healers are supposed to know all the workings of plants and minerals. Tell me which plants would make someone sweet on me."

She was so like Cath. I had to laugh. "There's someone you're fond of?"

"I want to catch his eye." She flitted ahead and then ran back, all hushed with rumor. "I hear Guardians don't need to be sweet on anyone, that they have someone already. . . ." Lill looked at me sideways, then lowered her voice, though there was no one else in sight, and said, "I hear it's a powerful bond created—that a Keeper or ally makes the bond with a single touch! Mark to mark and then they are connected: Guardian and Complement, the Complement protecting the Guardian to the death with heart and sword! Unless of course a Breeder catches the Guardian first. . . . What sort of bond would that make?" She leaned a little toward me, very serious. "Do you think so? That a simple touch could make so passionate a bond?"

Everything inside of me seemed to lurch. My grin faded. *Complement*—Laurent had not told me that part of the bond seeking. He'd only called it necessary. I looked over the edge of the path as if I'd find my thoughts somewhere below. "I think . . . I think a bond made is not always for love."

"No fights, no news, no imagination . . ." I was useless as far as Lill was concerned. She snipped, "So then why have you come to Gren Fort?"

"A journey," I answered vaguely.

Another disappointment. She shrugged. "Well, you will find no battles here. Nothing to heal . . ."

Lill ran a little way up the path and I hurried after, to where she stopped under hanging boughs of a birch that had somehow rooted in a crack of limestone and drooped like a screen for what lay behind: a wide ledge with two pools of water and a fall. The bigger pool was glass smooth—it collected the trickles from the waterfall. The closer was more a puddle where the water splashed into a shallow well in the rock and spilled over. It was not the one I'd seen in the Insight spell.

"You bathe here," Lill was instructing. "Leave the quilt outside the branches; I'll bring you something to wear." She turned to go.

"Wait, Lill!" I called her back. Her thin bright face appeared between the leaves. "There is something I'm looking for: a shell. Something"—I didn't lie—"that would be of great use to Healers. 'Tis said it's been hidden where there are waterfalls. Have you heard anything of it?"

"What sort of shell? Like from a tortoise?"

"A seashell."

Lill shook her head. "I have never heard of a sea-shell. But you can ask Eudin at supper. He is our captain. He knows much."

I nodded, and then she made a fierce little giggle. "I hope he does not tell you to travel to Hooded Falls. That would be very bad."

"Why?"

"Because if you go in, you cannot come out."

"Well then it seems unlikely that someone would be able to hide something in Hooded Falls, for they would still be there, wouldn't they?"

She shrugged and disappeared, then popped her head back through the curtain of leaves, thinking of something else. "About the plants. How can I make him sweet on me? Will you help?"

"Sneak a daisy into his pocket," I said. "They are past flowering, if they flowered at all this year, but you might find one or two if you look hard—are there fields nearby?"

At last I'd served a purpose; Lill was delighted. "I'll climb. I can find one!" She dashed away only to return a moment later. "I won't forget your things, though. I'll be back." And she was gone.

Within the quarry, in the little bower that the birch screen provided, it was hard to remember the dying landscape above and that it had not rained for months. There was water everywhere, pristine and sun-warm. I stepped right under the shower and let it pour over me while I watched the sun shift farther down and draw the shadows up from below. I searched around for a loose chunk of limestone and scrubbed the old blood from my skin and hair.

It mocked me, that stone. Limestone was the choice of blacksmiths to clean impurities from metal before forging, which seemed a fallacy. Armor and weapons—however shiny—had black hearts. 'Twas how I felt: scraped clean on the outside, but all this spilled blood was staining my soul. No limestone could erase that.

I lifted my hands and watched the water beat into my cupped palms, wondering if it might wash away violence like it did magic. Or perhaps water was stained as well—quicksilver when running, but when stilled the things it washed from us collected beneath. Maybe as a Healer I was like running water: I cleaned away a person's ills. But then as Guardian of Death I was also the still water—where the ills settled.

The water beat steadily, turning my palms red.

After, I sat in a shaft of sunlight to dry, to think more practically. Lill had come back with my cleaned undershift, which she politely left outside the leaf curtain. I stayed where I was, chin propped on my knees, trying to sort out all that happened and consider what had been requested of me. Would I find the shell amulet? Where was Tarnec? Would it be as the little verse said—that the shell could bring the rain? And if I were the only one able to do these things, what else did such a calling offer?

Shivers rippled along my back. I stayed hunched, imagining special abilities, none of them pretty. *Awakened,* Laurent had said. It might be for powers not yet realized, but for me it meant something more: that I was to be vigilant against the darkness consuming the world, one of those to bear the burden. It felt like the weight of the water.

Everything was changing, my little world expanding—I'd cut my ties to home; I'd expected to disappear, to release the pain. Instead, I had a new title and new purpose. New pain.

And, as Lill had unwittingly confirmed, I had a *Complement.*

The mark still burned warm. A full day or more, and still it burned—not firebrand painful, but enough to keep me aware. And whether I'd wanted it or not, I could not help the strangeness I felt now that Laurent had touched me. That he'd chosen to make that bond, even if only out of necessity, that he'd been at my side, that I'd rested my head against his strong back, that I'd nearly kissed him. . . .

That I wished I *had* kissed him, and been kissed back.

I bit my lip; half wanting to grin at the discovery, half wanting to reject what felt a betrayal to Raif. I decided upon rejection. Desire was hardly useful in such grim circumstances. Especially when I'd prided myself on being so impartial a Healer.

I should be neutral, should focus on the rescue of the amulet. I should concentrate on intent rather than need. . . . Hadn't the seer told me to beware my needs?

Besides, there were only so many challenges I could face at one time.

The walk back to my quarters took twice as long on my own, in part because I had to inch my way past a small herd of mountain goats blocking the route. Unlike me, they were indifferent to the steepness, jostling for the best lichen on the rock face. "'Tis lucky your milk is useful," I scolded when they nosed me to the outer edge of the path.

It was dusk when I finally returned. Torches were being fitted inside and out, so the carved doorways and windows glowed like honeycombs. My spare little room glowed prettily too. Lill had taken the old quilt when she left my undershift at the waterfall; a fresh one graced the narrow bed. All my things were piled on it, washed, mended, and smelling faintly of myrrh. A comb had been slipped in as well, and so I dressed, then sat in the little frame of window to work it through my hair, the way we did it back in Merith—Lark and I—before each bedtime.

I missed Lark. I missed her sweet and serious face, remembered that moment of seeing her running madly to the cliff's edge. I wondered about the leggings she wore, so similar to the Gren guards', wondered if she was preparing for battle—

"Good evening."

I nearly fell off the sill. The Rider stood in my doorway.

He smiled and I stared—a Cath's-infatuation stare—I couldn't help it. Perhaps I'd not seen him clean, or so refreshed. Perhaps the torchlight burnished his skin, made his hair gleam to some dark perfection. But those were not the reasons; he was handsome under any circumstance. Stunningly so. I'd just forgotten, or didn't want to remember, or . . .

Neutrality flew out the window.

"I've interrupted," Laurent murmured after a moment, deferring to my silence. He turned to leave.

"Yes—*no*. I'm—I'm just . . ." It was ridiculous, this being tongue-tied and embarrassed for it. I steadied my voice, forced my eyes away. "'Tis all right, Rider. Come in."

And he did, easily enough, ducking to enter. "You rested well, I trust?"

I nodded jerkily. "You?"

He nodded. We seemed at a loss after that, more used to arguing than pleasantries. I thought of Lill acknowledging his "height" and wondered if I was turning pink like she had. I never blushed, truly. . . . But then I couldn't stop from looking at him again from the corner of my eye. Laurent leaned against the doorway, gaze on me. My breath caught in a guilty lurch.

A corner of his mouth lifted. "What tumble of questions do you sort through this time, my lady?"

Anything—*anything* to distract. I thrust my hand out in some flurried gesture to indicate the space. "Tell me about Gren Fort."

"Ancient." The Rider shifted and looked around. "'Twas settled the last time the Breeders had the amulets."

"*Last* time? How often have the amulets been stolen?"

"Twice before." His eyes fell back on me and he grinned. "That's not a poor record, my lady, as you undoubtedly think. We cannot hold the Breeders off indefinitely."

I remembered the comb in my hand. "You got the amulets back, though," I said, and began tugging through the last strands.

"We have to," Laurent answered. "The first attempt was

quickly over. But the last battle endured four ages. Enough time to build this fort, certainly."

"Four ages!" The comb was snared in a tangle and I struggled with it, with the calculation of lives. "But the people— Was there a drought? Where were the amulets taken? Did the Breeders not want the Guardians to find them? And how *did* the Guardians survive all that time?"

He chuckled at the onslaught. "Guardians don't . . ." But then he stopped and said, "Forgive my staring. You are very beautiful."

My hand stopped. If I'd never intended that this Rider should affect me, I was so utterly wrong. I'd been called beautiful before, but this time the word sent flutters through my stomach to shiver straight up my spine. A vibration, a sensation—cracking open something like a door in my mind, something that had been locked tight, key tossed. It took too long to swallow, force the comb through, and ask, "Guardians don't what? Survive?"

"You are part of a line," he answered, calm as anything. "If a Guardian is lost, there will be another to wake."

That was enough to erase self-consciousness. "Good to know we are expendable." My tone was more than wry, but the Rider shrugged, unapologetic. So I added pointedly: "And what of Complements? Are they expendable?"

"Never," Laurent replied lightly. "You only get one."

He jested. But then again he seemed comfortable that I'd learned our connection, and unconcerned how. I had no witty response. I put down the comb and wove a braid, feeling heat rising again from chest to throat. "What has brought you to my room, Rider?" I asked. "Surely it is dull to watch me do up my hair."

"Your hair is caught by both the torchlight and the rising moon. 'Tis not dull."

"Still . . ." I was certain now my cheeks were pink. "It cannot be why you are here."

He raised a brow, then pushed from the wall, straightening. "Unfortunately, no. I am to escort you to supper."

All of this for an escort. I said a little tartly, "Only? I would have thought you'd be arming for the trek to find the amulet."

"Why? Do you know the way?" He was amused, not eager. I shook my head.

"Then perhaps *after* supper," he said with a grin. "You of all people should know the merits of a good meal." He gestured toward the doorway. "My lady?"

The center hall was above us. We zigzagged our way up the quarry; Laurent following me, most likely making sure I didn't fall. But I felt his gaze as something more—or maybe that was my own treacherous thinking. The walk was lovely, the moon sailing above in the deep blue and the punctuations of torches guiding us along the steps. The face of the quarry was riddled with lit doorways and balconies, like a sprinkling of fireflies. "How is this a fort?" I asked suddenly, laughing. "There are a *hundred* entrances."

"It cannot be reached from below and you were not awake to see how well hidden it is from above," Laurent said. "The quarry is quite open but can only be reached from the top by footbridges, and they are easily downed."

I craned my neck to look up but could not see the edge. "Where is Arro?"

"The bridges are slingbridges. He cannot pass over. There is a small outpost above where watch is kept. He stays with them."

And then we reached a flat ledge where a set of wooden doors—the only doors in the fort—was flung wide to the night air. The Great Room, Laurent announced, the largest of the tunneled spaces. Cave or no, 'twas the most formal space I'd ever seen. Torches made the rock glint gold. The walls were hung with weavings. An enormously long wooden table ran down the center of the room, laden with dripping beeswax candles and food in dishes carved from wood and stone. It made me smile. "It's beautiful!"

"It's copied from Castle Tarnec," Laurent said. "*That* is beautiful."

Despite the elegant setting, 'twas more brawl than banquet. If Lill said a hundred people remained at the fort, then the table was crafted for everyone to fit, and everyone did. They were already at supper—an event as wild as Dann's ale festivals. Some were deep in private conversation, but most shouted along the length of the table, boisterous and rude as they exchanged trays and bowls of food and dug into their meals. I spied Lill somewhere in the middle, sitting next to a boy her age with blond hair and a handsome face. He would be the one she was sweet on; she was yanking at his sleeve for attention. I wondered if she'd found a daisy.

Our arrival was ignored. Only a few nearest the doors turned briefly to see who entered. But at the far end of the table, the most enormous man I'd ever seen was rising from his seat and waving us forward. "Come down! Come down!" he boomed.

Laurent and I worked our way along opposite sides of the table; people shifted down the benches to make room. "Eudin," our host bellowed over the din when we reached him. "Captain of Gren Fort."

Up close the captain was even more impressive, wider than he was tall, with a thick beard that ringed a blinding, full-toothed smile. He radiated strength, exuberance . . . and risk. His body was studded with welts and scars. I was fascinated . . . a little horrified.

"You have felt your share of swords." I pointed as I reached him. "And axes."

"A curious greeting!" Eudin's laugh was deafening. "Could be a worse showing for one my age."

I looked at Laurent. "Three score and ten," Laurent murmured, and my jaw dropped.

"Welcome to you!" Eudin shouted. He turned first to Laurent and gripped forearms with him like old friends, then turned to me and took my face between his huge hands like an elder might pat the cheeks of a child. "Welcome, Evie Carew." He beamed, then said under his breath, which was hardly a whisper: "We'll keep your Guardianship to ourselves here, eh? What the clan does not know will keep them safe. Best not to know where the treasure is hidden, I say!" He gestured for us to take our places on the bench, announcing, "We neither wait nor stand on ceremony for guests. Just tuck in."

I looked down the table at the feast—fowl and fish, mostly, things that did not require space to herd. But the vertical gardens and the abundance of water provided a bounty: greens (the spinach that Lill had been so disdainful of among them), varied squash, and roots. There were fruit jellies, sweet and savory sauces, and bread with fresh honey. Hard cider and ale spilled from wet-beaded flagons. I touched my finger to one of the pitchers; 'twas icy cold. "Chilled in the lake, our beverages!" Eudin said proudly when he saw my interest. "We sink the casks and draw up what we need!" Both were favorites, I guessed, looking at his florid cheeks and double set of tankards.

Plates and knives were produced from somewhere and shoved over to us. Then there was a general rumble as people began passing things, heaping our plates, making me laugh at the ordered *dis*order. Someone sloshed cider into a cup and plunked it in front of me. Then everyone turned back to the revelry.

"*Eat,*" the captain directed, and I did. I gorged. Mouthfuls of bliss. I could not stop, not even in the spirit of regret for those who suffered beyond this fort. Food, drink, company— 'twas a privilege to have any and all, and I glowed from being so sated. There was near as much pleasure in this meal as the last solstice feast in Merith. And I remembered, then, Raif sitting next to me, our hands touching as we passed platters or reached for wine. It was sharp, that memory, but brief. For I was aware too of the Rider who sat across from me, aware of his hands as he tore a heel of bread or lifted his cup, aware of the smile that showed him amused again that I wolfed my meal.

I turned back to my plate, very daintily speared a piece of fish with my knife.

"Now, my friend, what news?" Eudin asked Laurent beneath the din. "Do not save detail," he added. "Better we talk honestly in a crowd. A quiet place begs for eavesdroppers."

"The good news first," Laurent said. "Tarnec has its queen once more."

Eudin nodded and raised his tankard in salute to that. "Guardian of Life returns her amulet and reign begins anew. May all the amulets be restored; may she reclaim the Balance and hold it long."

The fish fell off my knife. My cousin, the Guardian of Life—she was also *queen* of Tarnec? I pictured the castle hanging over the cliff, from where she nearly threw herself in her attempt to reach me. Lark was queen of that realm.

What a journey you've had, I'd told her. But, truly, I'd had no idea.

Laurent caught my expression. "The Life Guardian is always queen," he said gently. "She has found her home."

Home. I couldn't dispute it, but it stung to think home would nevermore be our cottage, our village. I wanted to keep the image intact—of Lark roaming the fields with her dog, Rileg—not to imagine her bound up by crowns and thrones.

Eudin was nodding, pleased. "So the queen is returned, and already you've found the next Guardian." He flicked an eye to me, then said to the Rider, "Let us hope this bodes well for a quick end to the trouble. Two Guardians proved so quickly."

"We had help." Laurent said it without emotion, but there was a tightening of his mouth—something I now recognized.

"Why does having help make you angry?" I asked.

"Because we shouldn't have had it." Laurent turned to Eudin. "I do not believe such ease bodes well. The Breeders know we were loaned the books of Fate; they'll simply wait for us to find the Guardians and then make their move. And if the return of the first amulet was a brilliant win for Tarnec, why offer the next amulet in such plain sight unless they want it easily found? So, no, I do not trust this freedom with which we travel."

"Freedom!" I laughed. "There were wisps, and swifts, and soldiers in all directions. How do you call it freedom? Certainly it wasn't ease!"

"Those were minor obstacles, comparatively." Laurent shrugged. I scowled at that.

But Eudin agreed with the Rider. "We've had message doves from Heran. They've seen disturbances on the Myr foothills, raids on the outposts. Breeders are slinking their way overland, summoning their worst." He lowered his voice more. "Not just Troths. They think—"

"I know what Heran thinks." Laurent stopped Eudin from telling, throwing the smallest warning nod in my direction. "It isn't enough that Troths have run through Merith and Crene and Bern and Littlefen and however many more. Now Tyre is on the prowl—they are stealing entire communities, not just the slave-aged." He cast an eye to make sure no one was listening. "They've sent scouts. They are not far."

"Aye, no secret, we've killed a few." Eudin nodded, grim. "And since Tyre is eager, so does Dorgrun seize opportunity. Those sod dwellers will scavenge the land in Tyre's wake. They both amass armies—already we've had reports of skirmishes to the north."

I was shifting in my seat, unsettled by how businesslike they discussed conflict—past or impending—Laurent and Eudin reeling off names of whole villages and cities like a scattering of individuals, and leaving some things unspoken—for my sake, annoyingly. "How many come to fight?" I asked.

"One, a thousand, tenfold that . . ." Eudin took half his ale in one swallow, then smacked the tankard on the wood. "For you it does not matter."

"How *not*?"

He leaned close. "It only takes one to change fate, to start a war. You shake your head, young lady, but the source of upheaval is what you must focus on, not the hordes that follow. Take out the source by finding the amulet."

"And if I don't find the amulet, what happens? The Breeders of Chaos win?"

Laurent made a noise and Eudin glanced at him, then shook his head. He said to me, "You will find your amulet, Guardian.

If the Breeders win 'twill be because of what happens to the amulet once you've found it."

"I return it to Castle Tarnec," I said flatly.

The large man laughed and sat up with a slap to his knee. "*Aye.* Be it that quick for all the Guardians!"

"What else would there be to do but return it?"

"You have a choice, Evie," Laurent said. "You may also destroy it."

I snorted, but Laurent was serious. "You might have the best intentions, but beware how the Breeders manipulate. Yes, they toy with the amulets, bring upheaval to Nature. There are earth rifts and drought. They can suck the air from a room or lash out with flame—"

"They've done all of this?"

"Here and there. This dearth of rain is the most wide-spread." Laurent leaned forward. "But all of that is just *toying*, Evie; I told you. They cannot truly hold or use the amulets; they just take pleasure in seeing how the upheavals distress us and turn us upon each other." He touched my cup as I reached for a swallow, holding it. His eyes were dark blue. "Ultimately, the Breeders need you to claim your amulet so that you may destroy it."

"But I wouldn't!"

"Masters of manipulation," he said, low and grim. "You wouldn't even know you had until it was too late. And if any of the amulets are destroyed, then the upheavals are permanent. Chaos unleashed."

A breath of cold flicked the back of my neck. Save or destroy. The Rider had said that before, but not that a Guardian could destroy without knowing. He wasn't just reminding, he was warning me. I found myself nodding, as if I had to promise.

"So." Laurent softened then and leaned back. "Beware the Breeders' intent. For if the shell is here as we think, isn't that a bit simple?"

Eudin broke in, "Do not scare our girl, Rider. *Let* it be that simple. We can manage the rest."

I turned to Eudin. "Manage means battle."

He grinned. "What else? The amulets are not for negotiation."

"You do not fear it?"

"Fear battle?" A guffaw. "'Tis what Breeders would hope! Have us cower before them!"

Then Eudin shouted to the table at large: "Heads up, ye of Gren Fort! Do we fear battle?"

A rousing shout of *"Nay!"* followed—young and old, women and men alike. The captain beat his tankard on the slab, beginning a chant quickly taken up by all:

"Chaos and Gren: their loss, our win! Chaos and Gren: their loss, our win . . . !"

Over and over they shouted and drummed until the table shook and the walls rang with victory. I put my hands to my ears; Laurent looked over at me, raised a brow to say, *See, Healer? Allies of the Keepers can be as aggressive as any Breeders' bane.*

I yelled to Eudin, "Is there no other way? Not everyone is as prepared as you! There are those villages that don't even have weapons!" I looked at Laurent. "You said that not everyone should carry the burden—"

"That's not—" Laurent started to object, but Eudin jumped in: "Nor should you!"

"But we *do*!" I cried. "We all must help. You speak of cities mobilizing to conquer and things from the Waste creeping in to destroy. How can you think a hundred people from Gren Fort can stop this? It is *all* our burden!"

Eudin laughed out loud. "We are *not* but a hundred swords, young Healer!"

"Evie," Laurent said. "No one is asking you to fight."

"It's not for me; I do not speak as a Healer. Merith, my village—we . . ." I swallowed. I could hardly bear to think of my friends in Merith trying to wield weapons again. "We don't know how to fight. We cannot fight. And there are more like us as well."

Laurent half smiled. "You are the lucky ones."

"Says the man with horse and sword!" Eudin snorted. "Lucky is the Rider!" He reached over and patted my shoulder. "There is no shame for your Merith friends. There must be some who travel life unweighted by the knowledge that Chaos lurks in a simple shift of power."

Like Lark and I were before, I thought. Unweighted. When we looked at the world with wonder, not fear. 'Twas the way I still wanted to—why I couldn't help arguing that it should be other than it was.

I wondered what Lark had thought when she learned of all

this darkness. I wondered if she'd missed Merith as much as I suddenly did; I wondered if she was afraid.

I wasn't afraid; I was sad.

Eudin was still watching me. He chuckled. "Do not be so severe in your thoughts. 'Tis not all doom. There is always choice, there is always hope, there is always sanctuary in the worst of places. Remember that as you travel."

I frowned at him. "Now you too are warning me for a purpose. You mean as I look for the amulet."

His laughter boomed. "I do not frighten you, my lady, do I?"

"I do not frighten."

"Exactly! And so here you are." He drew us in and spoke low, "And now to task: the Rider says that you believe your amulet hidden within a waterfall."

"Of which you have many," I said. "But I cannot claim it is here for certain."

"How did you perceive its hiding place? Was it in a vision?"

"I cast a spell."

That surprised him. "It is said that the amulets speak to their Guardians, that they reveal themselves when ready."

I shook my head. "What I saw I manufactured." I looked then to Laurent. "I forced the reveal. So perhaps all of this is wrong and I am not ready."

Laurent did not protest, and I worried suddenly that he agreed that it was done wrongly—that it was a rushed mistake, this touching of marks and claiming of Guardian and Complement. Hadn't Eudin just said that we needed to be thoughtful in the choices we made? It had been a messy business with the wisps, and Laurent had fallen, and what if he too impulsively forced the bond seeking? What if—

Eudin insisted, "Your birthmark was proved. The verse claimed you as well."

"But I do not *feel* anything. There should be a bond, no? Something more than a spell's hallucination." It was a disappointing thing to admit aloud.

Laurent murmured, "Perhaps you have not taken the time to listen." He said to Eudin, "The lady has had a rough time of it. We've worked our way here through a number of challenges"—he winked at me—"easy that they were. Perhaps we should give the Guardian a chance for silence."

I'd *been* silent, I thought. I'd spent the afternoon alone; I'd spent nearly two months alone. But Laurent was looking at me, a brow raised as if he knew that thought and challenged it. And maybe he was right. Maybe I'd been in silence but had not listened.

I slid out from the bench. "May I go?"

Eudin nodded. I put my hand on my heart, bowed to the captain, and started to leave.

Then I came back to swallow the last of my cider. Fortification.

11

THE MOON WAS high and bright as I crossed the length of quarry and followed the path back to the waterfall. Doves nested in crevices—their cooing suspended at my footsteps. I threaded my way under the leaves of the birch and walked past the first pool where I'd showered, to the wider basin of still water. I didn't choose this site for any reason other than I knew how to find it, but it felt a good place for privacy. I breathed in deeply. It smelled of cool, wet stone—of night. I unbuttoned my sandals, pulled my skirts out of the way, and sat on the rock facing out over the quarry. The faint spray of the waterfall brushed my bare legs.

Listen, I directed myself, settling in. And so I listened, hard, to the silence, to the undersong and odd calls of night things. And then I wondered at the different ways creatures made their sounds. I stared at the moon, a lopsided circle on the wane, and counted the days 'til the dark moon—

Listen. I closed my eyes and breathed more slowly. Breathed the metallic tang of the rocks, considered which minerals emitted that scent. I thought of the scents filling our herb shed and then of Grandmama and Lark. I pictured our hands plunged into the mixtures of Grandmama's recipes for soaps, spreading the mash into the trays for curing, and us laughing and reeking of lavender and lemon balm—

Listen! I was terrible at this. This would be what Lark loved. She could drink in the peace of night or sunny meadow, sit in contemplation of raindrops spattering on the casements with no thought to time. I wanted the bustle and chatter of market day, where others would tell their stories, not mine—

Evie! I pushed myself up from the ledge. I couldn't listen. I couldn't. I'd divined something about a shell, and that was done before I even knew what it was. Now the moment was lost, and how many waterfalls were here in the quarry let alone through the land? Would I have to search each one? What if it had nothing to do with a waterfall?

Always a question. I turned my back on the moon and the gaping quarry, and kneeled by the pool, angry that my mind wandered so. And then I was angry that I was angry. Where had the calm Healer gone?

Lark would have heard her amulet right away.

The moon poured light into the little pool. The water was looking-glass still. I leaned forward a little to see how my reflection was caught, to see my own frown. My hair shimmered silver in the pool like a trail of moonlight. *Moonlight on water brings Nature's daughter . . .* floated back from memory. If that was true, then what of the rest? *Swift-bred terror and sorrow of slaughter. / Silver and sickle, the healing hand, / Find the shell's song; bring rain upon land. . . .* Rain. There was no rain. The Breeders had taken it.

A leaf from the birch screen was falling. There wasn't any breeze, yet the leaf drifted sideways, lilting down in slow death until it came to rest on the pool. I leaned over to clear it away, and my braid slipped from my shoulder and dropped heavily into the water, breaking the mirror surface. My face disappeared. "Guardian," I called myself back. *Guardian . . .*

The pool stilled, the reflection resolved, but I was no longer the picture. The swirls of my braid were weaving into something else entirely. An apparition suspended in the water. A shell. The whelk shell.

I held my breath and watched. Whorls—pearlescent spirals of shell folding and unfolding. A house, a hiding place, a gift, a remnant—constructed and then discarded. I reached my hand to hover over the image, understanding. . . .

A shell as Death's amulet. Like a tiny window to the in-between of worlds, the remains of what once held life. It was itself a passing through, in exquisite miniature.

If I plunged my hand in, would it be there for me to take? But then it seemed my hand *was* stretching, dipping beneath the water to pull the amulet from its hold. And I thought with childish delight: *I am having a vision. . . .*

A cave. Almost dark. Oppressive walls of rock, a torrential pounding of water behind me. I stood hip-deep in water, staring at the little shell. It was tossed on a narrow ledge—so out of place, so abandoned. I felt the deepest yearning to pick it up, to take its care into my hands—as any mother to a lost child. The ache pulled me straight to it, a thread of heat in a cold space.

A vision, I reminded myself. Pay attention. Learn where you are.

My gaze went elsewhere, looking to identify. The walls were dank, slimed with algae and something more. My hand reached then, not for the shell, but for its stone coffin. I felt the cold wetness, the hard chipped edges, the mustard-yellow algae, and the slickness of whatever else was smeared there turning the algae brown in places. The water swirled at my hips as I moved to touch then draw away, to shift into the feeble light where I could look at the residue on my fingertips. Blood.

My breath caught and my head shot up, for I heard something else. . . .

I was not alone.

There was a sharper sound, a splash, and I was back on the quarry ledge, panting for breath. My hand had dropped into the pool, ruining the vision—but maybe I'd seen enough, maybe. But the blood, the other sound . . . ?

"Evie."

It was soft, the calling of my name, just beyond the curtain of leaves. I yanked my hand from the water, turned to hold it out under the moonlight. "I'm here." My voice shook.

Laurent pushed through the canopy. "I heard you gasp,

heard the splash." He stopped and looked at the pool, the falls, at me.

"You followed me?" *Clean.* There was no blood. I swallowed and wiped my palm on my sleeve.

"Only to be sure you were safe. I was waiting just beyond."

"I thought the fort was very safe." 'Twas rude, but I wasn't thinking very clearly.

There was a pause. "And so it is," he said softly. "I'll leave you to your silence."

He turned to leave. I blurted: "Rider . . ."

Another pause. His back was to me. "Lady?"

"I saw it." My hand was out. A gesture of need, of *something*. It dropped into my lap. "I saw the shell."

He turned around, saw I was wide-eyed with awe, with accomplishment, and then he smiled. I shifted, making it clear that he could join me, and he did, coming over to sit by my side. We both hung our feet over the edge and I described what I'd seen. I was breathless, I knew, excited and proud now that I'd achieved a vision; wound and set running like a jabber toy. "It needed me, Rider! It *needed* me." As if that could express the depth of what I'd understood: that in the midst of burden or despair there was beauty to be found in caring for another.

The Rider said softly, "Remember that, Evie."

There was a hint of warning in those words, stilling my jittery energy. I looked over and studied him for a moment. "Do you honestly think a Guardian could destroy her amulet?"

"We must be vigilant that they don't."

We. Keepers, Riders, those of Tarnec. I was hushed. "Would you kill a Guardian if she made that choice?"

"It has never yet come to that."

"And what if it did? And what sort of *choice* is it to return or destroy her amulet if one of the options is a death sentence? And why would a Guardian *ever*—even accidentally—destroy her amulet?"

"One needs a shield . . ." Laurent sighed at my barrage of questions, then chose to answer one—or all, I wasn't sure. "We do not always act with clear mind."

"Well . . ." I brushed my hands again and stood up, jitters back. I did not want to dwell on vulnerabilities; I was ready to save. "My mind is clear now. If Eudin knows the waterfall I describe, I can make my way there. The moon is bright enough."

"Now?" Laurent chuckled, a faint mocking of our first encounter. "What happened to your need for sleep first?"

"The sooner claimed, the quicker the end. And I am not sleepy."

His humor retreated and was replaced by a gentle grin. "Ever eager to mend, Healer. To spare pain," Laurent murmured. "But do not take any moment of peace lightly, Healer. It allows for strength later, when we will need it."

A different *we,* this time: he and I. The Rider meant to go with me, I knew, and yet that simple word seemed so powerful. *We.* I liked its sound.

Perhaps the Rider was tracking my thoughts. He asked, "In

your vision you were not alone. Do you know who or what was there?"

"No." I looked at him. "Maybe 'twas you." I swallowed quickly, made light of my presumption. "Well, since you are my Complement."

He gave a low laugh. "Is that a complaint?"

I shook my head. I wouldn't lie.

"Good, for it would be unseemly for a Complement *not* to protect his Guardian."

"Or likewise," I murmured, and he grinned.

"Really?"

" 'Tis only fair." I looked at him full on, how the silver light sank into his dark hair, how it made the white of his shirt gleam. Then I grinned too. "You need protection, perhaps more than I. You are already under siege, Rider."

He cocked his brow. "Am I?"

"Do you not see what is in the pocket of your tunic?" There was something small shadowed there I'd just noted.

He looked down, reached into the fold of fabric, and drew out a withered-looking stem. I laughed. "Do you know what that is?"

"A daisy, by the look."

"That, Rider, is a hopeful love charm." I'd not expected Laurent to be Lill's choice, and it seemed a foolish one, for she was so young. But then my laughter caught in an odd squeeze of my heart. What did I know of Laurent? What if Lill *was* special?

I said quickly, "The girl, Lill. 'Tis hers. She fancies you."

"She would."

I stared at him. Laurent said, "The Riders saved her some ten years back. Soldiers were taking her family as slaves for Tyre."

"Ah, so you saved them and she has adored you since."

"I was not there and we did not save her family." It was terse. "Her father and mother were killed. Her sister was lost to the slavers. And I was not there because—" He changed his mind. "Because I will not return to Tyre." Then he seemed to relent, letting the past recede. "But I suppose I fit her imagination."

Return. The word leaped out. "I do not know your history."

"You've seen what there is to know." I waited and he looked at me sideways. "I am a Rider. Those of Tarnec who are chosen—the strongest, the bravest—"

"Most modest . . . ," I couldn't help chiding.

Laurent shrugged. "I only speak truth, my lady." He drew a knee up, rested his arm there, and looked out over the quarry.

"Why do you not speak of your past?"

A snort. "'Tis a hard enough road for Riders—to be present, always at the ready, my lady. Past has no place in it."

"Then I will imagine that scar along your temple holds the past for you. Does it have to do with Tyre?"

No answer to that. Except that he said, "I do not hold the past as dear as you do."

"Then there is hope for Lill." I pointed to his daisy.

Laurent glanced at it, smiled—a smile that dazzled. Brilliance and light. A warning. "Hold it for me," he said, pushing it at me, then turned back to face the quarry, leaning forward on his hands. "This night is beautiful."

I tucked the sprig into my pocket. Looked out. The moon was very high over the quarry, the limestone pearl-white.

"I am thinking about the shell." I broke the now too-quiet space. 'Twasn't exactly true, but I was trying to sway my thoughts from Laurent and Lill . . . and Laurent.

"And?"

"A shell is a carcass. It makes a good amulet for Death. But there's more to the choice isn't there? If the primal forces bind Nature to Earth, then mightn't each force be tied with an element?"

The Rider nodded. "Life with Earth, Dark with Air, Light with Fire, and Death with Water. Nature is the way to commune with the intangible."

"And so the Guardians—we too are tied. Lark in the gardens, my love for swimming—"

"Swimming." He laughed. "Proclivity for certain talents is not what binds you."

"Nay, but it's here." My hand was on my chest as if I could pull out what I meant. "That *something*—Life or Dark, or Water or Fire—it's primal to us as well. You said that Guardians are awakened to seek their amulets. But the forces that we champion, they were always inside of us—what we would be drawn to, awakened or not."

There was quiet. My heart was beating against my palm, slow, steady. Then the Rider spoke. "It is your truth."

He said it not to me, but to the moon and to the wide sky, as if he meant that truth for all of us. It made me strangely happy that he understood.

And it seemed, too, a good opportunity. I asked, hopeful: "The shell's song. How do I find it?"

Laurent glanced over and smiled. "How many questions, my lady, before you are sated?"

A flush. He'd drawn it from me again. I said, as lightly as I could, "As many as you have answers."

He nodded. "Well, then. I will say the amulets are for Balance, no more. It is something to your Guardianship, to your story, that asks of a song."

"How so?"

"Guardians' stories do not repeat. Only the amulets are constant. Each awakening will pose unique challenges— different people in a different time. The verse is how we found you, proved you as Guardian, no one else. So it is for you to discover."

"But surely—"

"Look," Laurent interrupted smoothly, pointing down far to our left. "Night fishing."

Pressing the Rider would yield nothing more. I leaned over to see. There were men lowering lanterns into the lake—fat globes of glass, lit with candles, descending slowly on contraptions of poles and ropes as thin as reeds. Some globes already bobbed gently on the water, casting a blue-green halo in the deep.

"The nets are cast," the Rider said softly. "The light is bait; 'twill draw in the curious barrow fish."

It drew me in. 'Twas like a dance, lyrical and fluid, those lanterns. I watched. I forgot about the too-quiet space.

"How lovely," I whispered, "the way they glow on the water. It's as if the moon was captured in each."

"You've captured a bit of the moon," he murmured. I looked up at him. "Your hair. Like strands of moonbeam."

His voice was so rich it took my own from me. Below us the men began singing, music floating up, faint and melancholic. Laurent reached a hand and lifted a loose piece, tucked it behind my ear. The whisper of a touch.

Now I barely breathed, frozen by this act. Like an arrow, desire pierced deep, fast and foreign, and I did not know what to do with it. Laurent pulled his hand back as I tensed, and then shifted to give me more space. "My apologies."

"For—for what?" I swallowed. *What is it that you hold so tightly?* he'd asked once. If he asked again . . .

But Laurent only said, "I disturbed you."

"How?"

The smallest hitch of breath. "There is another who claims your feelings. Please know that I do not presume his place."

He spoke of Raif; he did not presume. 'Twas another sharp and sudden hurt—memory and desire all crushed together by this Rider. I said hoarsely, "What you presume is that your tucking my hair reminded me of him."

Laurent was quiet. Then he nodded, pushed himself from the rock to stand silhouetted against the moon. I looked away.

"We should take your news to Eudin now," he said.

I nodded, relieved . . . and yet not. I got up far slower, regretting our talk was done and the "we" separating. "I hope the captain recognizes what I describe."

"Eudin knows the quarry. He'll guide us well. We can leave on the morrow."

Laurent held out his hand, friendly enough, and so I reached for it, glad to feel it close warm and strong around mine.

With his other hand he held up the curtain of birch leaves for me to duck under. I passed near enough to inhale the faint sandalwood of his skin.

12

"HOODED FALLS!"

The shout flung me awake. It took a moment to remember where I was; the soft pillow, the quilt . . . I thought, *Merith!* but then the light resolved and I recognized the hewn walls of Gren Fort and the bright face of Lill.

I blinked at her, and she said it again eagerly: "That seashell you want is to be found in Hooded Falls!"

I pushed onto my elbows. "That's what Eudin said. The cave that glitters, the mustard algae—"

"And the blood!" Lill nodded brightly, setting down my tray of bread and tea. " 'Tis what's *most* whispered, the blood on the walls. That is the legend of Hooded Falls, you know, that it weeps blood."

"More algae," I told her. I brushed my hair from my face

and scooted to the end of the bed for the tray. "It only stains to look like blood."

She dismissed that. "Those who go in do not come out. It is *their* blood."

I grinned, morbid as it was. "You are glad 'tis the most treacherous choice. I think you wish you could join us."

"I *do* join you!" She bounced a little. "I volunteered to lead you to the falls. I know where it is and I am quick."

"Lill!" The tea sloshed, scalding my fingers. "'Tis too dangerous for one so young!" Not the paths, I was thinking, but what if Breeders were watching?

"Young!" Lill tossed me a towel, scoffing. "I am hardly younger than you, and I know my way around this quarry as good as any founding family. Besides," she said with a sigh, "I lead only. I do not travel into the falls; that is for you." Then she was brightly eager again. "So we say goodbye today, for you will not return!"

"Well," I took a piece of her dry bread and slathered on extra jam. "I can hardly imagine I won't come out—what would be the point of finding my shell?"

"*Your* shell! If it's your shell, how did it get so lost?" She watched me eat for a moment. "You don't scare easily, all my talk of blood and dead ends?"

I shook my head. "But I think it scares you."

"Hah! I am wily. I am fast. I am a survivor." She listed these as attributes, things she'd been told, obviously, and she was proud of them.

"I imagine you are. I heard you escaped the slavers from Tyre."

"Yes! We were being taken for the mines. But I got away."

Not quite as Laurent had described, but then, he'd not been there. "I was faster than my sister," she added. "She was not saved."

"Is she in the mines?" The bread stuck in my throat. I could not imagine being a slave.

"That's where they all go." Lill's voice was hushed now, and her eyes gleamed with her story. "But the Riders brought me here."

"Would you save her? Can you save her?"

"She's probably dead, since the mines are killing places. 'Tis like Hooded Falls, the mines of Tyre. If you go in, you won't come out. But mayhap I'll seek revenge someday." She twirled in the center of the room, suddenly, and wielded an imaginary weapon. "Mayhap the Rider will teach me how to use his sword." And she thrust forward as if to spit me on its tip, grinning. "Smite the enemy, leave no prisoners. Revenge for the wrongs done."

I felt the stab. "Be careful," I said. "I've been told your passions can be turned against you."

She shrugged. "Or make you fierce." She dropped her arm. "The mines yield the most *beautiful* of gems. People kill for them. Sometimes—only *sometimes*—one or two are smuggled from the city. I will take a few of those as well when I avenge my sister." She spun around, showing off an imaginary bejeweled gown. "Wouldn't you want to be drenched in such color?"

I laughed. "Flowers are just as pretty and they're freely harvested."

"Maybe." Lill stopped spinning, then sniffed. "But flowers die."

So do slaves. I worked at the bread, watching her. Lill was restless, picking my clothes from where I'd laid them last night and waiting for me to finish, so I dropped the piece of bread on the plate with a clatter and swallowed the last of the tea. I drew my hair quickly into a braid, thinking about what Eudin had told us the night before when Laurent and I returned to the Great Room.

"Hooded Falls," he'd announced gravely when I described where I'd seen the shell. "Not part of Gren Fort, exactly, but a day's hike from here at the northernmost tip of the quarry. One of us will guide you to it. I fear if we send more it shall spark interest. Grackles have been spying on the plains above."

"Do you know how we might navigate the falls?" I'd asked. "I've heard that those who go in do not return."

The large man had nodded and handed me another cup of cider. "That is the rumor. I hope you prove it untrue. I can't say I've met any survivors." He'd turned then. "How's *that* for a challenge, Rider?"

Laurent had snorted. "You leave much to hope, Captain."

But Eudin had grinned and said generously, "My friend, know this: Hooded Falls is beyond our regular patrol, but should you need help, we will come—"

"*Evie!*" Lill waved her hand before my face. "'Tis time we moved."

I nodded and stood. She held out my frock, gave it a final shake, and handed it to me. The daisy—Lill's daisy—that Laurent had passed to me fell out of the pocket.

There was silence. Lill looked at it, then at me. Her face darkened. "You told me it would work."

"I didn't," I protested. "Daisies can enhance feelings if they already exist, but you cannot make someone love you. You should not want to."

"But he noticed me! If—" Her voice had a sharp little edge before she shut her mouth.

Piqued, I returned as harshly: "Lill, he must be five and twenty! Ten years your senior at least!"

"And you? He's much older than you as well," she retorted.

"Me? This has nothing to do with me!"

"No? What magic trick did you save for yourself?" Lill muttered. She scooped the wilted stem from the ground, crushed it in her fist, and threw it out the window. "Never mind. We'd best be going, Healer." She hit the word with such venom she might as well have called me Breeder.

No one watched us go. Lill led the way up the narrow path; I followed, and then Laurent. The rasping of footsteps on rock, a sharp call of a bird . . . There was little noise to entertain. There was no conversation. Lill was angry with me about the daisy. I concentrated on my footing, ignoring Laurent for Lill's sake. Laurent was studying the skies.

'Twas a steep climb. Insects droned, the sun burned hot—more so than usual, for I felt a grimness seeping in, which had less to do with Lill and the supposedly impossible task than my own temper. I tugged my braid off my neck, reshouldered my satchel where it stuck to my damp skin. More than once we paused by a waterfall to cool off; I stepped right under the streams to soak, the sun quickly drying after each reprieve, but it did not make me feel better. Once, I stumbled, and Laurent's hand shot out to catch my waist. "Careful," he murmured.

"I am being very careful," I gritted.

"I'd rather not lose you over the edge."

I bit out, "Breeders have not got me yet, so you can hardly think the drop is a challenge."

Laurent released me without another word.

From her farther position Lill sniffed and said, "We'll not make it in time if you dally. We'll lose the light."

"Better than we don't make it at all," Laurent returned easily enough, which seemed to mollify her. But she did not turn around. My head ached.

We reached the height of the quarry just past the sun's midpoint. "It's straight from here on," Lill said, "except . . ."

I looked to where she pointed. There, just ahead, were some of the slingbridges that Laurent had mentioned. They spanned a series of splits in the ground. Gren Fort truly was impenetrable—unreachable from the bottom *and* from the top, if bridges were downed. And they were easily downed. These were rope bridges, for foot traffic only, suspended over the deep fissures and swaying in the breeze.

"One by one," Lill announced, and then practically skipped

across the first. I held on to both sides and stepped carefully from sling to sling, while the breeze buffeted the bridge and rocked me, even though Laurent and Lill tugged the ropes at both ends to hold it steady. I got over safely enough, and I think Lill was peeved that I didn't panic. Together we pulled on the ropes as Laurent traveled over. It was only then that I swallowed hard, for I could see how the bridge sank and stretched beneath his weight.

Laurent arrived on our side. He shielded his eyes with his hand and looked up—to judge the sun's position, I thought—then gave us a grin. "How many more?" he asked Lill.

There were four bridges, all told. We crossed them without incident. Twice more, Laurent took a position of the sun. "You waste time by judging it," I said crossly while he squinted at the sky. "We'll need to camp at the falls tonight before attempting."

"I say we try today," he said. Then, "How long, Lill?"

"Not far." She beamed at him. "Straight on this path." She started off again with a flounce of skirt. I wiped my face with my sleeve and followed, feeling a hundred years older.

Any trace of the fort disappeared behind us. The path was wider hereon; the insects more shrill. Laurent walked at my side. I looked over at him and pointed. "Your hand is on your sword."

He only nodded, and so I said, "You can hardly think there is something waiting to attack." I swung my arm at the flat, broiling trail. "Not even a tree to hide behind."

"You acknowledged something back there," Laurent said, refusing to quarrel. "Something that troubles me. The Breeders know who you are, and we are nearing their hiding place for the amulet. Why did they bother with wisps and such in the marsh if they do nothing else to stop you?"

"Because I give them no opportunity." I didn't know why I was so contrary. I wiped my forehead again as if that would clear away my anger, or at least the droning of insects. Laurent did not snort as I anticipated, but it was hardly out of respect for my prowess. So I added, "You were the one who said Gren Fort was well hidden."

"We are beyond Gren Fort."

He looked to the sky again, and I left him there and stalked on. I thought I could see some sort of rock formation ahead, past Lill's lithe silhouette. It would be good to arrive, to stand under water again and soothe my aching head. I should even take time to be worried, maybe, of what lay behind Hooded Falls—I'd hardly given thought to it all the way here, letting peevishness claim everything. I was worse than Lill.

I set my jaw and tried to storm through the irritation by quickening my pace.

But I got no farther. "Something's wrong," I gasped. 'Twas as if I'd smacked into a wall. A whine—a hundred scythes honing on whetstones—filled my head, sinking me to my knees. "Swifts . . ." My hands dug into my ears; I slammed my head on the stone to shut out the pain. I heard Laurent shouting my name, running up from behind, heard Lill screaming only a moment later, "What are those?" And then Laurent was yelling at her, "Run!" He'd scooped me up and was running too.

I went limp, bouncing like a doll in the Rider's arms. The

whine was louder, unbearable, and Laurent was pounding forward on the hard ground so my teeth chattered. Somewhere farther Lill was still shrieking, and Laurent shouting, "Get under the rock! *Under!*" A shadow passed over my face and I thought we'd reached protection, but then there was an enormous explosion, heat, dust spewing up—and I was flung to the earth.

The whine would eat through my head.

Hands grabbed and dragged. Laurent's voice was hard, commanding Lill to push under the rocks as far back as she could, and I was pushed too, painfully so. Another explosion, and another, and something garbled. Laurent was saying, "They touch earth on purpose—" and there was a roaring sound coming closer, and Lill was screaming Laurent's name, and somehow that sounded soothing against the fierce-pitched whine, and then I heard nothing at all.

Hands again. Gentle on my shoulders, shaking me. "Evie."

I pushed against the pressure, slapped it away, but the hands returned harder. "Evie, wake up!"

And I blinked against blinding sunlight and saw the silhouette of a boulder looming over my head at such an angle that I jerked away from the hands and rolled, coming hard against rock.

The hands righted me. "Evie, it's all right, they've gone."

"Let me . . ." I shrugged free, then pushed onto hands and knees, dizzy and aching, a dull roaring in my ears. But the whine was gone, so too the gripping irritability—and though my mind was raked bare by the sound, the relief was breathtaking. I stayed hunkered for a time, breathing, trying to remember details. Then I shook my head and crawled out from under the rock shadow to where the sun hit full on and where Lill sat crying.

"What happened?" she sobbed.

"Swifts." Laurent slid out behind me. "The sound destroys Healers."

"They were birds but not birds." Lill's teeth chattered. "They had eyes—*human* eyes!"

"We were safe enough; we found cover."

I looked at Laurent, at where his shirt was singed by the explosions. "Safe enough?"

"Laurent *saved* you!" Lill jumped to his defense. "He ran with you to these boulders, to hide you. He was nearly struck!"

"I'm sorry," I said. And to Laurent, "Thank you." Then I rubbed my ears, wincing at their tenderness. "I should have recognized the sound earlier."

"*I* should have," he corrected, then shook his head in disbelief. "No method to the attack, a suicide mission. The swifts made no effort to avoid the rocks. I wonder if my comment brought them"—then softly—"just for fun."

I stared at him and realized his face was pale beneath its tan, that he was worried—for the skirmish, for me—and that it made Lill angry. I said quickly, "I'm fine," and turned to Lill. "Hooded Falls?"

"Just beyond the outcrop." She nodded in that direction, envy and residual fear making her snip: "'Tis *obvious* we're here."

My ears were clearing; I could place the roar of water. It *was* obvious. "I'm ready," I said.

Laurent snorted. "Hardly."

"I am *fine*." I pushed my hair off my face. "The day is wasting."

"You need time to recover."

"This, to a Healer!" I scoffed. "I think I know my strength."

"I think you pretend it."

That last retort unnerved me, for he looked at me so keenly that I was sure he could read me straight through. And read what? That I liked him too much? That I wanted *not* to like him?

"The Healer is right, Laurent," Lill said sharply, making us both look to her. "The day *is* wasting."

Laurent's mouth tightened. "Then we go. But at the site, my lady, you will take a moment to eat, drink, and rest."

"Fair enough." Though I glared at him for his presumptuousness. And he was only making Lill angrier by attending to me. This was hardly any way to heal.

The Rider stood, leaned over, and pulled me to my feet. Lill lurched up and stomped off. "This way," she ordered.

The roar grew louder. We climbed over the cropping and found ourselves at the top of a smooth slope, one side of a V. Centered between spewed Hooded Falls.

The torrent of water gushed from above, where boulders

piled tall and jutted out. There was no trickle or stream of origin—water simply exploded out and over this hood of rock, and spread like a sheet that was as wide as three men were tall. Yet it wasn't a sheet, for that implied softness and pliability. This fall pounded as unyielding as a wall, its sound ferocious. It beat straight down upon a narrow half saucer of stone and cascaded over into a mist of oblivion.

Somewhere behind that crushing water was a cave, and somehow too the shell.

Laurent made a low whistle under his breath. With a triumphant flourish of hand, Lill said, *"See?"*

I understood why people did not return from these falls. They couldn't. Even if you were fortunate enough to make it through the force of water, there was no footing on that tiny lip of glass-slick rock upon return. The torrent would shove you straight over the edge for the long plunge.

"My mistake," Laurent murmured. " 'Tis not easy."

I murmured back, "How could the amulet even be placed in something so . . . so impossible?"

"Conjuring. Or summon a creature; work a spell . . ." He glanced at me. "Breeders have many tricks at their disposal without having to confront an obstacle head-on."

I would have to confront the falls head-on. We stood together considering the shape of the entrance, the surrounding rock. Slab, mostly, with few footholds. Laurent had brought ropes, but they seemed now of dubious use—fragile against such an assault.

"Well?" Lill called, impatient.

I looked at her; I looked at Laurent. I still felt queasy from the swifts' attack, but said simply, "We eat."

We sat at the top. The relentless sun baked the slab, but a faint mist from the falls cooled us before evaporating. Lill had carried the meal and now she spread it out to share: plums, apples, squab legs, and bread. I ate, studying the falls. Laurent watched me.

"What are you thinking?" he finally asked.

I grinned a little. "How to survive."

"Impossible," said Lill, fully convinced that this was our last meal and she would soon—and now happily—bid me good riddance.

Laurent frowned. But I only winked at him and said louder, "I am thinking that this fall is of the same way a wound gushes blood. As in a severed artery or an amputation—"

"Ugh," Lill said, and threw her plum over the side and got up.

We watched her leave. Laurent raised a brow and I smiled back serenely.

"That takes care of one thing," he said with his own hint of smile, "but not the other."

"'Tis true, though," I answered. "If one suffers a wound, the first thing to do is to stop the bleeding. So it is with this water; the answer is the same. Apply pressure. Or a tourniquet."

Laurent laughed, "And do you have a tourniquet for this, my lady?"

"As it happens . . ." I pointed up at the jutting boulders.

"The water bursts from above those rocks. If we moved one, would it not shift the direction or at least lessen the flow?"

Laurent looked at me, looked at the fall, then was on his feet, disappearing up the tumble of boulders. I watched two or three heavy-looking stones go flying over the cliff, shot away by the water. Moments later he was down again, drenched and panting and grim. "Nothing that can be moved will hold, but I might give you just enough time to exit the falls."

"What do you mean *you*?"

"I will help you from out here."

"How?" I waited for him to explain, but he didn't. I said, "You will not come with me, then, into the cave?"

He shook his head. Strange as it was, I was disappointed. I pushed away the twinge and asked, "What can I help with?"

"Nothing. Just work fast. Was there anything in your vision that showed an obstacle?"

I shook my head. The shell had simply sat on a little ledge of rock.

"Then I will count three hundred paces for you, in and out, that should be enough time. Here . . ." He was moving brusquely—dropping my satchel over my head and drawing one of the ropes, looping it at my waist, and knotting it tight. "You will slip, so keep a hand on it."

"Enough time?" I looked at him, ignoring his directions. "What are you going to do?"

"Just go, Evie. Be quick, will you? And—" He took my hands, pulling me closer, our gazes locking so that my breath caught. It was nearly as powerful as the first time, when through the smoke and haze and terror I looked into those eyes. . . .

"Evie." Laurent shook my hands to bring me back to the present. I blinked at him, started to pull my hands away. But he held them firmly and kept his gaze fixed, making me focus on what was here and now. "You will come back safe."

"Safe," I echoed. I was thinking suddenly, what if this were the last time I would see this young man, this Rider? I opened my mouth, not knowing what I would say, or if I even could say—

Lill was suddenly back. Laurent squeezed my hands and abruptly stepped away, nodding for me to go. So formal, then. My Complement. *Remember what you told Lill: a bond made is not always for love.* I looked at them, smiled as if I were fine. My fingers curled to hold the warmth from his touch.

"She can't come back," I heard Lill yell to Laurent. Then the roar of the waterfall took away the rest of her words. Laurent wrapped the other end of my rope around his waist, worked his way to a thin fissure where he could dig his foot in to brace, and nodded at me.

I scooted down to the half saucer, straightened, and tried to edge closer without stepping into the rush that tore away from the fall and over the cliff. But Laurent was right about slipping. One foot skidded into the wash. 'Twas so fast-moving and cold, I stumbled at the shock of it. The water rushed between my sandal and the rock, tipping and dragging me away, over. Then the rope went taut and I grabbed for it, gasping, felt it drag me sideways and up to a drier spot where I could find some purchase.

"Evie!"

I looked up at the two figures: Laurent pulling hard on the rope, Lill holding hard to him. I managed a wave, and turned back to Hooded Falls on my knees. With some mix of crawling and wriggling, I worked along the bottom edge of the slope, this time reaching the side of the fall. I stayed crouched, as if that somehow made me more solid, and reached out to test its strength. The water pounded straight down—the sheer force smacking my hand back the instant my fingertips touched it.

I took a deep breath, readying. Hesitation was death; so was slow motion. There was only one way to enter—meet force with force.

I ducked my head and, with a great spring off the slab, dove through the falls.

13

I LANDED BELLY down in the backwash, slid backward toward the torrent, then thrashed my way forward until there was no drag left to fight against. Choking, coughing, I worked my way to my knees and held there. My head hurt. Every muscle hurt. Slowly, gingerly, I felt along my limbs. Bruised, but not broken. I sucked in deep breaths, waiting to steady. Then I struggled up, hip-deep in tepid water, and looked around.

Low ceiling, dank air, murky light . . . and a strange sort of quiet. The waterfall's roar was muted, absorbed by the rock rather than echoing off it. There, against the left wall, bobbed the muck and bones of a body long stranded—one who'd preferred starvation to other unfortunate endings over the cliff. Only one body, for which I was grateful. I lurched to the opposite side, felt for the wall, for support, and waded into the darkness. *One. Two. Three . . .*

Three hundred paces. Laurent would be counting—slowly, I hoped. It suddenly didn't seem like much time. How deep the cave, where the shell might be ... things I'd wondered, unable to plan for. 'Twas a blind venture into a foreign realm. Already there was the urge to retreat: the Healer needing to orient toward survival.

I fought instinct and sloshed on. *Thirty. Thirty-one.* The water was much colder away from the entrance. My hand slipped a little on the wall. Algae—what I'd seen in my vision. I pulled away, squinted at my palm. The stone, the slime—something was not quite right. I wiped my hand over it again. 'Twas not blood-colored as in my vision, though imagination could have distorted truth. Honestly, what did I know for certain? I peered into the dark. Ahead to the right I thought the wall dimpled, forming a natural shelf just above the water. I struggled toward it, remembering the ledge—

A dagger stabbed deep into my chest. I sank to my neck, yelping, clutching, grabbing for the blade. But there was no weapon, only the cold—thin and sharp. It pierced straight through, began to throb. I gasped, lunging for the wall, the shelf, and dragged myself up to sit, to huddle, to chafe my legs and arms back to warmth. A moment later, though, I forced myself back into the water. No time to waste; I had to embrace the cold—however far I had to go. I touched the sodden rope at my waist. Laurent was counting.

I shuffled forward, hugging the side, the chill intensifying with every inch in bitter, agonizing stabs, until I could hardly bear it. I hunched over, willing myself to accept the pain. I gritted my teeth, closed my eyes, and let the cold burn through. . . .

And then the burning became heat, and the blade a line—a thread of energy, giving the gentlest tug. I straightened up, gasping, remembering.

'Twas a signal, not temperature. The thread gathered me, pulled me from the shelf, the wall, and drew me through the water. I waded toward the opposite side of the cave, following that lifeline of heat, feeling the water warm with each step. *Sixty, sixty-one, was it?* And then I could see that the cave was split into two tunnels. I'd been going in the wrong direction and was being corrected. The amulet was reaching for me.

I lurched forward. The heat grew, drawing me into what should have been utter darkness, except it was not dark, but more like moonlight—as if day had changed to night and I was open to the sky. I moved faster. 'Twas the shell that lit the space; I knew it. Heat, light, growing with every step. I squinted, trying to see. *Seventy-eight, seventy-nine?* Cursing that I'd forgotten the count—

And there it was, suddenly, the little whelk from spell and vision. Unassuming, unique, and . . . just *there.* I drew abreast, laughing with relief, with delight. "Oh, look!" I cried, sharing the moment with no one. "I found it!"

Death's amulet, abandoned on a narrow ledge. How simple it was! How bereft in isolation, in its displacement. It gleamed faintly—light emanating from the pearly insides. Strange that so little a thing was what held Death in balance, charged against the other primal forces. It looked so fragile.

A little tug, a little hitch of breath. The shell wanted to be held, not studied. I reached out my hand, then waited, but no rush of darkness, no hideous roar followed. Gently I took up the little thing and cradled it. It stayed cool in my palm, serene—if a shell could resonate such a feeling. Open, secret, succor, bone . . .

It shook me then: an emotion I could hardly identify, didn't understand. A knot in my throat was growing, tightening. That something so seemingly insignificant could be so extraordinary, could inspire tears that belonged in no Healer. Could inspire such tenderness.

"Little thing," I whispered to the shell, "I will bring you home."

I lifted my head, listening. The cave echoed my voice, soft as it was, repeating back as music. "Home," I whispered to the shell again, to see. The word hummed—the prettiest, sustained note. And so I leaned and whispered the word into the curved opening, wondering if the shell would sing something back. . . .

It did not. But I smiled anyway, proud to have accomplished this goal. I opened my satchel and put the shell inside, fastened the cord tightly.

And then I paused. Tensed.

Something was in the water.

Sweetness dissolved, spell and vision crumbling together—

I'd been forewarned; it should be no surprise. *Undulating water, stench, consuming darkness* . . . Even if I'd retrieved the amulet, it did not mean I'd succeeded. Laurent had said it: this was too easy.

The backwash rippled. I dropped my gaze. Circles expanded around me. Whatever it was, 'twas rising up from beneath, near enough to touch. My hand tightened on my satchel. Kelpie? Scum sleagh? Or some Breeder creature I'd never heard of? What would be my defense? And what did any of that matter? It was already too late.

A head broke through the water, then the rest. Human in form, but so scrawny—more a pile of stick-thin bones and joints. Sunken eyes were dark holes in the gaunt face. Dripping rags served for clothing, wrapped around like bandages. What hair remained was wet string.

And then I knew what it was: a Bog Hag. But this was no bog.

She drew up nearly as tall as I, silent and peering. Her teeth were bared, if they could be called teeth. She smelled of rot.

"You are not afraid." Her voice was a whiny hiss.

I stayed where I was, kept my gaze steady. I knew enough not to show fear to these sorts of creatures, to keep my eye on them and speak firmly. And I wasn't afraid anyway. A weedy Bog Hag could hardly be a Breeder's conjuring. She was out of her territory, same as I, and I already had the shell.

"Not afraid," the Bog Hag accused, and leaned forward—I thought she wanted to study me. But she suddenly flicked her fingers in my face, shrieking, *"PAH!"* to see if I might cower. Water splashed in my eyes, but I refused to even blink.

She frowned and pulled her hand back. "Not afraid."

This was testing—she knew something. I folded my arms. "What do you want here?"

"Want?" She cackled at the word. "I want nothing *here*. Though this . . . I like."

The Hag reached out to touch my hair with those fingers, but almost as soon as she did, she jerked back, shrieking, as if I'd burned her. She tried to run in circles, flinging her arms in every direction, hands fisted tight, but the water was unyielding. She wallowed and splashed, shrieking, "It is you! It is you! Ow, ow!"

"Stop it!" I had to shout over her dramatics. "Why are you here?"

"You—" Now she cringed, elbows and wrists all curled up against her chest. "I am here for you, Guardian. *She* forced me, cruel thing. The *other* one." The Hag straightened a little, squinted at me. "You are like her."

I gasped. "Lark!"

"Queen," she spit back. "But you are not her. She *glowed*. You . . . you are deep. Darker."

Darker. Heat prickled over my arms, soured my stomach. "Why have you come?"

"She called me to a task. She has that right." And the Bog Hag growled at that, but still she leaned forward and sniffed me, then sniffed again, liking what she smelled.

"Of Water, not of Earth." She cringed a little. "*Not* of the growing, but the transience. You . . ." The Hag hung there, holding me hostage with the want of knowing. "You are the passage to decay. I like this. We are of the same."

"What *same*?" I managed.

The Bog Hag grinned horribly. "You are the correct one. I give this to you, then. Hold out your hand."

I shook my head, holding my satchel tight against me. The Hag unfolded her arms slowly, reached out one hand toward me, one she'd kept fisted tight. She turned her palm up and slowly opened her stick fingers. There, crumpled in her hand, were sprigs of green with purple blossoms. Minion.

"You take this." She pushed it at me. "You will need it, the *queen* says."

"Lark sent you with this? Why?"

"She bound me to give it to you. *Take* it!"

I gathered the minion from her cold hand, and she whimpered at my touch. "Now this." The Bog Hag reached under her skimp of rags and drew out a small knife. "For you."

I took the blade, and the Hag screamed, *"There!"* She whipped her hand away and spun in a circle, sloshing waves, gleeful. "I did my task; I am unbound!" She turned back to me, stuck her face close, no longer wary, and said, "You have your help. You might be sorry." And her face split into another garish grin and she cackled as if misfortune brought pleasure.

"You still have not told me why," I said sharply. And then more desperate: "Take a message back for me. *Please!*" But she was already sinking back into the water, back the way she came, with no interest in my wants. Bog Hags had no hearts. And she owed me nothing.

I watched the ripples recede. I put the minion and blade into my satchel, unnerved. 'Twas Lark who'd done this summons, but why? The Sight had never before revealed me to her—we were too close—so what prompted this? It should be enough that I'd had a sign from my cousin in the middle of this dank and lonely space, a whispering that we shared a task in retrieving these amulets, that she understood. And yet this wasn't a sign or a connection, nor were minion and a knife any promise of good things.

I turned and slogged my way back toward the entrance, finding only moments later that I was trying to run, fighting my sopping skirts, needing suddenly to get back to the light. I'd used all my paces, I was certain. But more, I was sickened by this place.

Ahead was the entrance, water relentlessly pummeling rock. I approached—lopsided in my rush—hands out, thinking I'd dive out as I'd dived in and the rope would catch me. But the force spit me back so violently that I fell and went under. I rolled, struggled upright, hands and head raw from the beating, and found myself face to face with those bone remains. I thrust away, grabbing for the rope, trying to yank it taut as a signal. I only fell over again when its shredded end came up abruptly in my hands.

Of course. Fragile against such pounding. Yet I sat stunned, staring at the chewed piece, as if only now I'd learned this place was deadly.

How far, Laurent, had you counted?

I stood up slowly, facing the wall of water. A million thoughts raced through to fix, to help, until I wrenched my hair in frustration at these stupid Healer efforts. I cried out in shock. Despair. I shouted, "Laurent!" Useless reactions too, but I had nothing, no other offer. Why had Lark sent me little trinkets that had no power to open the falls?

"Hag!" I begged. There was no point.

And then, shivering there at the boundary of dark and light, I saw the waterfall begin to change. The pounding curtain was thinning, spewing sideways, leaving a drizzling gap to squeeze through. Laurent had managed to block the flow. I had a moment's opportunity; the surge would quickly expel whatever obstacle he'd placed. I shouted, exhilarated, then eased one step and another out from under the shadow of rock onto the smooth lip where the water now pooled harmlessly, and then jumped for the dry slab. I crashed flat and lay for a moment, panting, feeling the glorious late-day sun warm on my back.

"Don't! Don't!" came Lill's awful cry over the sputter. "You can't!" I pushed to my hands and knees, then looked up, but I could not see her, and she was not screaming at me. My eyes raked the promontory, then the warped flow of water, and I thought suddenly, sickeningly: *How did this work? What boulder?* And in a moment that seemed an eternity, I understood it was not with a rock that Laurent blocked the waterfall.

It was with his body.

I scrambled to my feet. Above, near the hood of rocks, Lill

was screaming, the hem of her skirt twitching as she hopped up and down.

"Lill!" I hauled myself up the slope, yelling for her. "Lill!"

She turned, her face in terror. "I couldn't stop him!"

I reached the top, horrified. My stupid comment about applying a tourniquet had given the Rider the idea—he'd tied himself with the leftover ropes, lashed them to either side of the hood of boulders, and thrown himself as the block, the obstacle against which the water pounded and changed course. Laurent was being battered against the force of it, bounced like a puppet at the mercy of this rage. His own sword sliced at his leggings, flashing and spraying the silver droplets of water and the red of blood—a throw of confetti in celebration of death. For it would be death. He'd taken his sword with him so that the rope could not be cut and he could not be stopped until his body burst and broke . . . all so I could escape Hooded Falls with the amulet.

Lill was shrieking. "There's nothing—we can't stop this! I don't know how to stop this!"

Laurent would break. The ropes would break. And then he would go over the edge. Death first or death last, either way. There was nothing to be done. Horror, dread, then absolute terror all searing through, until a plea exploded from my lips: *"Help! Help me! Please!"* I screamed louder than Lill, begging that someone be near to save him, my own uselessness ripping me apart.

And it came back in those sudden, terrible moments, the

Bog Hag opening her hideous fingers. *She bound me to give it. . . .*

"Quick!" I tore the satchel in my haste, pulling out the little blade and yelling to Lill: "Hold this side of the rope with all your might! Do not let it go! I will cut through on the other—"

"No!" she shrieked. "I am not strong enough."

It was true. She was too small to support Laurent's weight if he was thrown free. So was I, but I was the better chance. I tossed her the knife. *"Run!"*

She was up, scrambling over the hood of boulders, feet flying, to the other side of where the water exploded from the rocks. I wrested my end of rope, braced it against my back, hands gripped on either side, digging my feet into a crack, like Laurent had done before. "You must *race* back when you've cut the rope!" I screamed over the torrent. "It will take both of us to hold him!"

I hoped she heard me. I watched her bending to the rope, the knife drawn. I held my breath. And like a slingshot, her rope released, the falls burst into life, and Laurent came flying. He struck me full force, then went skidding down the slab. I was flat, breath knocked out, being dragged down harder than I was able to pull up. My feet fought for another hold. I pressed my back against the hard rock—anything to stop us from sliding. The rope behind me was yanked taut, straining to break, to release the load into the falls. I screamed for Lill.

"I'm here!" she gasped behind me.

"Grab under my arms; pull me up!" I cried. And her hands

grabbed and locked across my chest, tugging. It gave me the barest chance to get my feet under me, push against the rock, slide up a fraction.

"Sideways!" I was ordering, yelling at her. "Together! Shift sideways!" And we did, panting and grunting. "Is he clear of the fall?"

"Yes!"

Then it was only his body weight to work against. "Pull!" I shouted. "As hard as you can, Lill! PULL!"

Slowly we gained on the rock, pushing to stand, to tug and drag the rope, burning our hands raw. But we got Laurent up to the top. Unconscious and bloodied, but whole.

"What did you do?" I hissed wretchedly at Laurent, fumbling at the rope wrapped around his hands. "What did you do?"

"He?" cried Lill. "It was *you*! This is your fault!"

"Give me the knife," I said, hard. "Give it to me."

"I'll do it." Her eyes were like daggers. She sawed at the binding on Laurent's wrists, and then his ankles. He'd trussed himself like a boar on a spit with knots and loops. It was only by luck that the rope had not cut through his joints. I bit my tongue against my thought—that he'd sacrificed himself with terrible ingenuity for the stupidly simple act of my picking up a shell. I was angry. I was scared.

Lill had no reservation in sharing her feelings. She threw the bonds over the falls and turned back to me, white-faced. "Is he dead?"

I was feeling for a pulse in his neck—his wrists too bloodied—leaning my cheek at his mouth, feeling for the whisper of breath. I shook my head in grateful relief.

"But he *might* die!" she spit. "He might! *Look* at him! He's so . . . there's so much blood!" I heard her turn, then whip back, furious. "There was no reason for this, no purpose!"

I looked up, jaw hard because she echoed my own fury. "What would you have had me do, Lill? Toss the shell through the waterfall and hope you might catch it? That is, if it weren't smashed by the torrent or lost over the edge!"

"Who cares about your shell?" she hissed. "It's not worth this!" She pointed at my satchel. "You could have tied that to the rope; we could have hauled it up. You could have sacrificed yourself, not let him do that for you!"

She was right, but that had never occurred to me since Healer instinct declined sacrifice. I hated myself for it, my selfish preservation. I said fiercely, "Never mind. We need help. You need to go for help."

"I go for help? And let you betray us all, like you have him?"

"Lill—!"

She said viciously, "Maybe you will run off as soon as I am gone! You have what you want. What's to stop you from leaving?"

"*Run?*" I grabbed my satchel, dug in and pulled out the shell, held out my hand, enraged. "Go ahead, take it! Then you can be certain I won't abandon the Rider."

Lill hesitated briefly, then moved to snatch the amulet. She didn't even get close. There was a blinding light, and the air cracked like thunder; Lill was flung back hard, shrieking. It took her a moment to recover, then she burst into tears, accusing, "*You!* You knew that would happen!"

I was staring at the little shell, stunned. I'd had no idea that was what Laurent meant when he said only the Guardians could collect the amulets, could return them. It sat in my hand like a trinket bought on market day; it had nearly killed Lill. I looked up, horrified. "I'm sorry. I didn't—"

"Who *are* you?" Vicious, teary, she curled away from me.

Maybe this was how she was when she was torn from her sister—a terrified child at the mercy of powerful brutality. I felt terrible that I'd hurt her, frightened her so . . . and we were wasting time. "Lill, please—"

"Just *stop* before you kill us all!" She spit it—not terror this time, but rage. I watched her—a little ball, her back so coldly turned, remembered the villagers of Bern and what Harker had said: *the violence of Man.* That same darkness was brewing here, in her, where fear and pain and even envy birthed hatred and its fury. There was no chance, no opportunity to change the course, unless we could save the Rider.

I said, with more calm than I felt, "Lill, you need to run back to the fort. You need to get help." I turned to Laurent, ripped the shirt from his chest and shoulders. Welts and bruises, already in lurid colors, peppered his front. His wrists were raw. There was a long, deep gash across his ribs. I put my hands on it. The blood seeped cold.

"You want me to go so you can finish him off."

Lill was crouched now, facing me. She was not thinking,

just baiting me, wanting a fight. *How easy it is to turn violent, how easy to let madness in. A Breeder's strength* . . . "I am a Healer, Lill; I cannot kill like that." But maybe I'd killed another way. My hands were worthless. *Bandages. Tear strips for bandages. . . . Something. Anything.*

"Look at him! You are no Healer; you bring *Death*!" She threw the word at me like a spear. "And you are no friend! Lying about the daisy, pretending you haven't—"

"Lill, there is no time! You have to go. *Please!*"

She set her jaw. I pleaded, "You know the way. You are quick, remember? Bring men back and a stretcher to carry Laurent. You can help save him."

"From *you*." She sneered.

"I promise, Lill. I *will* heal him! I promise you I will *not* let him die!"

And then I wasn't saying that for her, I was saying that for myself. I stood up and strode to where I towered over her like the feared death-seeker she accused me of being, gritting and determined. "I. Will. Not. Now *GO!*"

Lill stumbled up, frightened by my fierceness, and was off, clambering down the boulders away from Hooded Falls and then onto the path. It would be twilight soon. I had to hope she knew her way in the dark.

14

I STARED AT the wet lump of shirt; I stared at Laurent. Any determination I'd felt deserted me in a single exhale. The roar of Hooded Falls was sapped away with my breath, a false peace suddenly isolating the bit of rock we shared. And in that silence the past came rushing forward: the market square of Merith, Raif's lifeless body, and the utter bleakness of an ending—that moment when I first learned death had agonizing impact, was no longer a simple ease from life. And where I was completely useless.

My hands lay in my lap, listless. I turned my palms over and stared.

"Not algae," I murmured. Like when I held Raif in his puddle of blood, my hands steeped in it, Laurent's blood was just as red.

"I'm sorry, Raif," I whispered, and looked back at Laurent. "I'm sorry, Rider." Lill was right. I was going to let him die.

Love cannot die. The words jumped at me from nowhere. Words that Raif murmured to Lark for her to share with me. Words to prove his faith, that we had a bond that would withstand death—a bond I'd betrayed with my feelings for the Rider.

I wiped my hands on my skirt. Slow strokes. Smearing the blue to black. Always black.

Love cannot die. Now it was Raif's voice in my head, speaking not kindly but insistent, as if I was not paying attention. "I'm sorry!" I looked up, pleading to the failing light, "I am *sorry*!"

Love cannot die! The words were loud this time, angry at my obtuseness, my lethargy. I heard them as some threatening epithet, some proof that Raif would haunt me. And yet Raif was never that sort of person. He would not have cursed me with such a promise, imprisoned my feelings so that I'd feel guilty if they strayed. *Then, what, Raif? What do you mean?*

Cannot die. Cannot die. A riddle perhaps, and if so, then a challenge. My dullness stirred, elementary answers trickling in. *Cannot die*—what died returned to earth and enriched new growth. Healers knew that more than anyone. . . .

Meaning exploded inside of me; laughter poured out—in joy, release, all of it. It wasn't a prison, that promise, 'twas an *offer* to share those feelings! Love couldn't die because it was meant to be reborn.

Dearest, noble Raif. I closed my eyes; bowed hand to heart, so grateful for him. Then my eyes opened on Laurent, and there was an ache in my chest that was too beautiful to bear, and suddenly what love I'd kept hidden as a naïve girl, or ignorant Healer, or wretched survivor was spilling into my trembling palm, no longer to be held secret. The words came again, whispering, *Cannot die.*

And then with a shock came the further meaning: *Do not let him die, Evie!*

I snapped to attention. I bent to the Rider, brushed back his hair, and pressed my fingers against his neck. The pulse was there, still, but faint; that strong life force embattled. I swept my hands down his arms, across his torso, feeling for breaks, feeling the bruises, the tears. I'd done this before, but was half stunned then—by his arrival, his beauty, by my own confused feelings. I'd spent much of the time staring at him, wondering if I wanted him to wake.

Now I'd do anything to make him wake.

It was the gash across his rib that was the worst. I wiped it clean with his wet shirt, and again . . . and again. It had to be closed; the blood seeped too quickly. But I had nothing to use for stitching. I pressed the shirt against the wound, watching it stain dark, willing it to stop. I'd done this too often these past days, trying to heal people. I'd lost them all.

And now the light was nearly gone, a last highlight in the western sky and then I'd be in near darkness, working blind.

I gripped his shoulders and vowed to his shuttered face, "I'll not lose you!"

Then I shot up, gasping. The crumpled handful of minion

that Lark had bade the Bog Hag give me; she'd done it to help me save Laurent. The knife, the minion—whatever divination Lark used to know this, 'twas a more powerful act than any healing I'd ever done. I was breathless with hope. . . . Lark had given me the chance to save him.

Beneath Laurent's head was the leather pack that Lill had brought with her; she'd propped him with it when we got him up the slab. I slid it gently out from under him, then yanked it open, pulling out the food that remained from our day's journey. Bread, apples, a squab leg. I slipped the pack back under Laurent, then ran to the mouth of the relentless water, soaked my skirts, clambered back, tore the crusts off the bread, and dumped the soft insides into the cloth bowl I shaped between my knees. I rolled the hem up and mashed the fabric against the rock, making a paste from the bread. Then I took out the minion, carefully shredded each sprig, and sprinkled it into the paste, then mashed the whole thing over again. I squinted against the dusk to see if I could make out a faint tinge of green, a sign that I'd mixed well enough.

I wiped Laurent's wound, then smeared handfuls of the paste over all of it, and over his wrists and ankles as well, leaving it to dry in the night air while I soaked his shirt then tore it into bandages. I laid these to dry on the rock, which still radiated heat from the day.

Then the apples. I smacked them against the stone 'til they squished, slit the skins with my thumbnail, and squeezed the juice from both into Laurent's parted lips. The sweet and the tannins would help from inside. I flattened the skins and spread them on the sides of the wound.

The squab I ate, cramming it in quickly.

I sat back, panting, surveying what I could in the dark. I went over in my head all my knowledge, all the available tools, and checked that I'd effected all that I could. All of this I might have done alone, but the minion made the difference. The most healing of herbs.

"How did you know?" I whispered. "How did you know that I would need the knife, the minion?" Lark could not read me. Any visions that I appeared in were made from things other than her gift of Sight, like the Insight spell I'd done. . . .

Curiosity burned inside me. Curiosity and then too a bit of envy—that had I been born with Lark's gift I might have prevented Laurent from his sacrifice in the first place.

I looked down at Laurent. I could hardly see him in the dark, but his heat radiated close if not vibrant. I shifted so that I could rest Laurent's head gently in my lap, trembling a little again. I'd watched the Rider, back when we fought the wisps, studied his features, trying to absorb him into memory and be done. Now, his nearness inspired something so huge that I hurt with longing. To be done would be impossible. I breathed deep three times, then laid my hands—first on his temples, and then on his heart—using my gift. *Head, heart, head, heart.* I repeated the pattern over and over, counting slowly to ten each time until it became rhythm and my own heart was beating to that pace. Over and over, giving warmth, life—

Over, and over. And over.

At some point I faltered. It wasn't working; all the mercy I'd been spared was used up, my healing gift had waned. The Rider lay barely breathing.

What if Lill was right that I would take Laurent into death? What if I'd been right that a Healer should not be the Guardian of Death? Was this part of the upset of Balance—that I now led people through Death's passage, undiscriminating? That I no longer healed?

This is how it begins, seeds of fear. . . .

I shook my head to refocus. I pulled my hands away, clapped them smartly to shake out the bad things, then placed them back on Laurent's temples. And yet all I could think of when I touched him was that beautiful ache he inspired inside of me, and how impossible it would be to live without it—to let him die. Of course I wasn't helping—I was not giving healing energy, I was giving need.

I released his temples, pressed against the paste-coated wounds, pressed against where I remembered each bruise and scrape. I begged; I railed. And still there was but faint breath, faint heartbeat. *If he did not come back . . .* I was desperate with want. *Love cannot die!* Whispered, murmured, shouted against the roar of the falls, to the sky as the stars burst into the deep blue and dusted the small flat of rock with light. *Love cannot die!*

I don't know exactly how it happened, how I found my hand searching through my little satchel, reaching not for the amulet of Death but what I'd carried for love: the braided leather ring. I took it from my satchel, slid it on my thumb for strength. For aid. *Cannot die*—rebirth, yes, but so too memory. A circle, I thought, renewing without ever dying. And what was the cycle of Life and Death without love woven into it, anyway? From Ruber Minwl to Raif to me, the ring offered that thread to weave. I laid my hands on Laurent's temples again, the bit of leather pressing deep.

"I love you." I'd never said those words aloud but now they came out, fervent. I leaned over and skimmed my lips over Laurent's brow, wanting—needing—to say it again: "I *love* you." My throat was thick. *"Please."* I took his hand, pressed it hard against my heart. "Please come back."

A faint squeeze of my fingers.

"Laurent! *Laurent?*" I released his hand and cupped his face, searching in the faint light. "Can you hear me?"

There was silence, an aching length of silence. But then his lips parted. "I feel you," he murmured, with the faintest grimace.

I pulled back abruptly. "I'm crowding you!" Then leaned forward, almost into him, worrying that he'd heard my confession. "Do I crowd you?"

A groan, a sigh. A hint of smile, half caught by starlight. "My lady, you do not know . . ."

The Rider mocked, but suddenly it mattered not if he'd heard or if he teased. I was grinning madly. "You've come back!"

"The shell?"

"It's here. I have it!"

Another ragged breath. "Then," he said with a grunt, "we succeeded."

"We did." *Succeed.* A word rich with opportunity. I was laughing now. Relief made me giddy.

"Lill?"

"She's gone for help."

He winced, then reached up. I grasped his hand. His fingers brushed the ring and he caught it between thumb and fore-finger for a moment before dropping away. I didn't think any-thing of it, just smoothed his hair from his temples.

But Laurent's languor was abruptly gone; he struggled against my hands, trying to sit up, to understand. "How am I loose?"

"Gifts from my cousin, strange as that may be. Lie back! You are too injured!"

"Nothing," he panted, "is strange. But . . ." He grimaced, sinking back at the pain. "We need shelter, *now*, should the swifts return."

"They are not returning." I *could* make him rest. I had to make him rest. "Close your eyes."

He did, briefly anyway. "My sword—"

"Hush. I'll wield your sword, Rider." He snorted and I grinned—jest or truth, perhaps we felt safe for both. "Relax, sir. Trust your Healer."

"*My* . . ." He drifted for just a moment, but then his eyes opened to catch my gaze. He murmured, "The ring you wear. Was that one of the queen's gifts?"

"Nay, it belonged to Raif." I could not stop smiling. "It's

been passed between loved ones—it holds a special power, I think."

Laurent was quiet for a moment. "I imagine it would."

I said lightly, "Here, you hold it." I took the ring off, placed it in his hand, and closed his fingers over it despite his resistance.

"Evie—"

"Shhh, now. The circle is in your hand; your energy is in mine." I pressed my hands on his. "That makes for very special healing."

"Evie, do—?"

"*Breathe*, Rider." I moved my hands to his temples. "Deep and slow. Deep and slow." I felt on the precipice of something extraordinary. "Breathe." 'Twas passion charging. My feelings were out—exposed to the elements but uncaught by Laurent. "*Breathe*." A secret unburdened, not betrayed. It filled the air, surrounded and screamed in silence, like the space between a note's vibration.

Maybe he could not help but sense it. Laurent gave up his struggle. "Your voice is like music."

"So they say." My hands were at his heart—they were the vibration itself, for I was shaking.

"'Tis part of your power, my lady."

"There is . . . there is a healing song I can sing if you'd like." And then despite the energy, the touch, the closeness, and all the yearning that made me tremble—this suggestion made me suddenly awkward. I offered it shyly, as if I were of Lark's timidity.

A faint smile played at the corner of his mouth. "I'd like."

I nodded, looking away, trying to reclaim some Healer neutrality. Then I sang it low, barely above the rush of the waterfall, my hands still pressed against his heart.

> *Take of wind, of rain, of ember, of wheat.*
> *Flow through, surround, include, complete.*
> *Heal breath, heal bone, renew, restart,*
> *Raise me up, clear my eyes; make it whole, my heart.*

A lullaby. The first healing tool I'd learned to use. Grandmama had taught it to me when I was very young, when she first understood I'd inherited her gift. I had a memory, then, of our cottage in Merith, of the hearth and Lark's dog, Rileg, sleeping before it, and Lark and me helping Grandmama stitch sachets for market. The warmth, the golden firelight, and remembered smell of apple wood and lemon balm and lavender shuddered a pang of homesickness through me—and yet it was not homesickness, for stronger was the smell of sandalwood and oak, Laurent's scent, which to me had become something far more like home than I'd ever known.

I understood then, how Lark had found a new home. I felt at home with Laurent, even on that slab of stone, even with the relentless gush of water drowning any serenity. Even in pain. Life could never reclaim those sweet days of childhood, but it could be as beautiful. Maybe more.

He murmured once, "There is the matter of the ring. . . ." But then Laurent fell asleep while I sat watch, humming, holding him. Above us the stars danced their way across the night sky.

And, far later, when those stars were fading into the grayness of first light, there was a new sound, of feet treading up the path and a shout from Lill, "Laurent!" And the clamor of help arriving, hands replacing mine to lift and transport Laurent back to Gren Fort. Someone wrapped Laurent's arms over his chest to keep them from dangling. The ring fell out of his hand; I caught it against the rock, then picked it up and slipped it on my finger. And then I saw Lill was watching, looking at my hand and at the little braided thing there. She turned away.

15

THE SOFT BED was a luxury. So were clean clothes. As thanks I helped in Gren Fort's kitchen, keeping busy while I waited for Laurent to heal.

I would have sat at the Rider's side, but the minion repaired without me. In truth, I'd hardly be steady tending the man I'd touched with needy hands; whom I'd kissed awake. Besides, Lill had taken that vigil from me, making it clear with silence that I should stay away, preferably disappear altogether. I didn't argue her claim; I'd hurt her enough, and I felt sorry for her—a refugee who'd suffered cruel loss. So I worked far from the Rider's room. 'Twas worth the impatience, feigning indifference while waiting for posts on Laurent's progress, if I could mend a fragile peace with Lill.

Still, to her disappointment, I wouldn't leave. Eudin could direct me out of the quarry, I could find the way to Castle

Tarnec without the Rider's aid, but I waited. I did not want to return the amulet without my Complement. I did not want to be without him at all.

I liked the kitchen—'twas the busiest place in Gren Fort. Something delicious was always simmering over the fire, and gossip was passed as freely as bread. The room was the first carved in the quarry. Wide and deep, with the largest open-aired entry exposing a huge vista of distant plains and the blue-deep lake far below. 'Twas smartly situated on the rock face—where smoke from the cooking fires did not interfere with rest of the fort, yet dissipated before it could be traced from above. Fresh water spouted from three places—ease for cooking and washing that made the memory of drawing well water a crude drudgery.

I assisted with preserving fruit and curing barrow fish, but I was better at conversation and showing how plants from the fort's hanging gardens could be used in medicinal arts just as well as food. "Wash hands with rosemary before attending to healing," I explained. "Groundsel is good for toothaches. Ellhorn will cure warts. . . ." A noisy little crowd would gather around the table, reminding me of any market day in Merith, of our booth where I once held court, loving the banter of sale. The information was popular, the crowd expanded, and it helped take my mind from Laurent. 'Twas comic the efforts made with all the plants at hand and what was scavenged cliff-top, shreds of leaves and stems brought to me with eager interest.

"Weeds," I had to tell them most of the time. Though

nothing was truly useless, just easier than explaining too much.

I learned from the crowd as well. They taught me a potion that I'd not known of, a concoction of spices and goat's milk dried to a hard curd so that it could be traveled with—melted into boiled water to create a richly fragrant drink. "Balm," they called it, simply. "It helps clear the mind and give strength. 'Twas passed down through stories from the oldest realm, Tarnec. It is our most prized recipe." Castle Tarnec, I learned, was as much lore as land. The way to it was so long steeped in mystery, it seemed forgotten by most outdwellers.

And I learned of Gren Fort's history. The seven original families came from Tarnec; over seventy generations they'd carved the fort into the deepest curve of the quarry and spread their descendants through the realms, leaving the fort both as a bastion for the Keepers and allies as well as a sanctuary for anyone discovered seeking refuge. Of the hundred folk caretaking Gren Fort, twenty had been rescued only recently. Burned out of villages, barely escaping capture . . . Eudin and his men frequently scouted for such survivors.

On the second morning after our return from Hooded Falls they deposited an exhausted man in the kitchen, found unconscious near the quarry lip. His discovery caused a greater stir than usual, it seemed, for Eudin ordered all of us confined to the fort—no more herb gathering—and took a posse topside once more to track the man's path. The kitchen crowded with even more people who'd come to watch this ravenous stranger spoon bowlful after bowlful of barley mash with trembling fingers. Little Merrye whispered to me that it was a worry, this too-close rescue. Gren Fort had gone undetected for generations, and now to be so nearly breached!

Though 'twas not the man who was the worry, but who chased him.

"Soldiers," said Merrye, hushed and wide-eyed, far too young to bear such information. "We've heard they are looting not far from here."

"Not far from here, but far from home," someone else hissed.

"Try nearby." A surprising grunt from the stranger. Everyone turned. "Dark-armored men," he muttered. "Thirty of them. Razed everything in the vale of Pembrake four nights back, claimed the territory, and took the inhabitants. *All* of them."

"So close . . . ," gasped one of the mothers, hand to throat. "Why must they keep filling their mines?"

Another woman answered what the rest were thinking: "Because they work the slaves to death, those *viles* of Tyre."

There was a collective shudder at the city's name, and I thought of Lill's poor sister. But then surprisingly Blind Kerl, who snored the days away in his seat by the fire, lifted his head from his chest and said, "These are different days. Tyre does not venture this wide just to stock the mines." He focused his milky stare on the stranger. "They build a slave army."

The stranger turned back to his stew, silent, but another mother scoffed. "You dream, old man. Why *wouldn't* they go far afield for their miners? Eudin says the villages nearest the city have already been culled and others are destroyed from within, villager to villager. The drought has spawned many jealousies."

"Jealousies? Do you have an herb for that?" Merrye asked me. They'd been asking for herbs for everything.

I shook my head and turned to Kerl. "Why would they need an army to invade hamlets? A few soldiers do more than enough damage. I've seen it."

The old man gave a toothless grin. "To *see* has different meanings, young Evie. Perhaps you *saw* destruction but not the reason why. *All* inhabitants, he said." Kerl gestured toward the stranger. "Babes are of no use in the mines, but they can be reared into allegiance, taught the skills of violence and no more. Given new language so that they cannot communicate with any but themselves." He snorted. "An army built from those who know nothing but to fight for Tyre. An army for the future, raised for the longer battle."

There was general chatter; half of the group believing age brought wisdom, half believing Kerl's mind was addled. But then the stranger spoke, and silence fell like a pall over his audience. "It is not only a future army. Tyre masses troops to join the greater march."

We all stared at him. I asked, "What march?"

"The blind man is right," he answered roughly. "Tyre will use up villages to reap bodies for the mines. But the army is for another target. There is rumor that a path to Castle Tarnec has been uncovered."

The general murmur fell away. "That kingdom is long disappeared," someone said.

"But not gone," the stranger corrected. "Just well protected. And it is said they hold things more precious than any gem that can be pulled from the earth. 'Twill be a full-on war to bring down this kingdom of Tarnec, a long war, even if a weakness is discovered. Tyre joins with others to conquer it."

"What could be more precious than Tyre gems?"

The stranger wiped the stew from his beard. "Horses."

Tarnec—murmurs ran through the room, waves of curiosity that such treasures of the old realm were not just a figment of legend. Little Merrye cried in excitement, "Horses!" and one of the older women shushed her. She glanced at me as she turned back to hear the stranger. And I realized most in Gren Fort knew very well about Castle Tarnec, about the horses, but pretended ignorance. No one was going to expose the Rider and his steed to a stranger.

I caught Lill's eye then. She was watching me carefully so I made the slightest nod—understanding that we'd not speak, that whatever differences we'd had, we still shared the desire to keep Laurent and Gren Fort safe.

Lill brought my breakfast tray after that, ruined scones and all, as a peace offering. She wouldn't stay, but on the third morning after the stranger's arrival Lill entered my little cove earlier than usual, flushed and frightened, flitting like a wren. I pressed her until she burst out that Eudin had returned. His posse had killed four soldiers. And four was nothing, of course, when the stranger had implied so many more were nearby.

"They will find us," she fretted, pacing. "This time they will find us. They are too close."

I said, "Even so, you are well protected here."

"We are not!"

"Then well hidden," I tried.

Lill waved her hand and stalked on. "How can you understand? You are only calm because you know how to care for the wounded. We don't have your materials, your skill. If we battle . . ." She paused to give me a grateful, if fleeting look. "Laurent heals because of what you did. But you'll be gone, and they'll find us and we'll . . . we'll all bleed *dead*."

"Skill is learned," I soothed. "I can teach you."

"We know how to put a bandage on!" Lill rejected harshly. "'Tis the *herbs*. You've shown us what our gardens can do. But it's not enough. We don't have enough. We need to *eat*, we can't use all our gardens for wounds!" Her lips were trembling. "'Twill be like my family's capture in Tyre. Nothing to save us."

"Lill, we can prepare."

"With what you carry in that satchel?" she scoffed, remembering. "That only offers pain."

"Not this. We'll collect what's needed topside and then I'll show—"

"What? *No!*" Lill said it with such a gasp that she flumped on the floor. "No, Healer! You cannot go above. 'Tis too dangerous! Eudin forbade it."

"Because of a few sightings?" It was my turn to scoff. "You said it yourself: Eudin found only four soldiers in three days! Herbs are far easier to find."

A shrug. "What if you cannot find any healing herbs? Last

time Merrye came back with nightshade and you made her throw up and it was only on her hands."

I grinned. "At least tell me if you have seen something like vervain up there. That's especially good for wounds. Long narrow leaves—"

"With purple stalk flowers." She nodded dully. "I remember your teaching. I've seen it. It grows above."

"Then quickly out, quickly back," I said, knotting the tie on my braid.

"No. You cannot go alone, you don't know the way."

"And you are too scared to show me."

I knew that would offend her. "I'm *not*," she said after a moment. "I'll show you but you have to *swear* 'twill be quick. Even if soldiers do not find us, Eudin will kill me himself that we've gone topside."

"Then we'll be quick." I buttoned my sandals and slung my satchel over one shoulder. Lill balked at that, not wanting to be anywhere near the shell. "Must you always bring that . . . that *thing* with you?"

I hadn't opened the satchel since we returned because of what had happened to Lill. Still, I'd hardly leave it. "Safer with me," I said brightly, then grabbed my cloak. "We'll use this to hold what we gather instead of a basket. Then no one will think to be suspicious." I took a last swallow of tea, avoiding the stone-hard scones on the tray. "Let's go."

"It's a walk," Lill insisted with unfortunate generosity. "Take them."

We climbed to the ridge, hiked west and crossed two of the handmade bridges. The sun had not yet risen above the far treetops but 'twas already hot. There was bone-dry scrub along the top edge followed by knee-high weeds—most of it brown. I'd almost forgotten the drought.

"Are we near?" I asked.

"We have to cross the last bridge." And she added a bit tersely, "Don't wonder about the way; watch for *soldiers*."

There were no soldiers. I bundled my cloak more tightly in the crook of my elbow and followed Lill. She walked quickly, eyes darting back and forth, not trusting I was vigilant enough. I watched her, curious at her fear, wondering about the memories she had of Tyre, of losing her sister, her parents. . . . How skittish she was. How scarred.

We crossed the last bridge to the quarry. I thought of Arro and asked Lill if the horse was housed somewhere near here, and she shrugged. "'Tis well hidden, the caretaker's post. You would not find it."

"Do you not want to visit the horse?" I stopped. "You've never seen one, have you?"

She shook her head vehemently. "This is not an outing!"

I started to snap, "Neither is it a death march," but bit my tongue. Sweat trickled down my neck and I paused to wipe it.

She whirled back. "Don't tarry, Healer, it's not safe!"

"Which way then?" I looked around. We stood hip-deep in a swath of dead grass. Ahead was a stand of birch and ash.

"Through there," she said, and started quickly for the trees. I followed, looking behind as I entered the grove—the last bridge was completely obscured by the grass. Gren Fort and its outposts were all well hidden. Unless it was known what to look for the approach would be completely missed.

Lill was standing in the shade of the last trees staring out over a huge plain of scrub and weed, keenly looking, listening. Her face was white.

"Now where?"

She pointed off to the right. "Over there."

I looked, then turned back to her. "That cannot be right. Vervain does not grow near ash and it does not grow near ansel thistle."

"That isn't ansel," she retorted.

"Lill—"

She snapped, anxious. "To be sure, I saw it. I'll *show* you."

She made two tentative steps onto the plain as if she were testing the first ice on a pond. I sighed. It was not hard to recognize ansel thistle, it grew almost like a shrub. Still, it wasn't worth picking another fight with Lill. "Stay here," I said, and strode out those hundred paces to where the ansel grew thick and the vervain did not. "There's none," I called back, cross now that she'd led us on a goose chase under so harsh a sun. There weren't even any purple stalks to mistake. I could not hear her answer, just the steady rasp of burr beetles cutting through the silence, the heat.

But then I did see something. A few steps beyond was a heavy trampling of the scrub. I frowned, went closer. Trampled, matted, as if several had stood—nay, camped there. Animal carcasses were torn apart, gnawed and scattered; the ground was scored where sharp-edged metal might have dug in. There was a pit as well—I dropped down into it to look. 'Twas for a campfire, so sparks would not spit, nor flames show. I kneeled to touch a piece of charred wood. It was faintly warm.

"Lill!" I shouted then, at half voice. "Lill! The soldiers!" I scrambled out of the pit, my palm crushing brittle bone and fur. Violent deaths. I wiped my hand on my frock, repulsed.

"Lill . . . ?" I said it more to myself, for my eyes played tricks in the blaze of sunlight. Lill was not there. My heart quickened, but it was impossible to think she'd been captured. There would have been noise—screams, or the heavy tread of those armored soldiers, at least. I squinted, marking each trunk along the grove's edge. There was no one. I shook my head to clear it, to prove my instincts were not wrong, that I had not been fooled. "Lill?"

Only the burr beetles hissed back.

I ran then. Back to the grove, back to the bridge. I fisted my cloak in my hands to keep it close, tore into the shadows of the trees, under branches and over roots 'til I burst out into the sunlight again, panting, "Lill!" Scared or not, she couldn't have left me like this. "Lill!"

The bridge—where was the bridge? Hidden blind of course in the tall grass. But there—there was the faintest parting between the dry stalks—Lill's tracks. She would know I'd study the plants, could figure this out for myself. Surely she'd wait for me at the bridge. I could probably find the way back, but surely she'd wait. . . .

And she was waiting. There on the other side of the bridge, facing me, hands behind her back like a guilty child.

"Lill!" I stopped short, gasping. "You didn't have to run!"

And then I realized I was wrong. Her hands were clenched but there was no guilt in it. "You saw it," she said. "The soldiers' camp."

"They aren't here." I walked toward her, annoyed. "You should have waited for me!"

"Why?"

Rudely flung, dismissive, even, as if she hadn't been frightened! I scowled. It was too hot for this. "You make no sense."

"Don't I? They can have you."

That stopped me. A harder, ugly edge to her voice now—neither guilt nor child. If she'd lured me out hoping the soldiers would frighten me . . . I bit my tongue, grabbed for the bridge—

"I wouldn't!" she said sharply.

I felt the ropes give and jerked back, tumbling into the grass. The slingbridge broke free at my feet and dropped away to dangle limply from its stakes on the opposite side.

She said, "I warned you."

I scrambled up. There was no way I could cross; no way she could throw any part of the bridge back to me to catch. But she wouldn't have. I stared at Lill in disbelief. Her eyes were bright, her smile fiercely frozen.

"What have you done?" I cried.

"I've made the fort safe. You can't hurt anyone here anymore."

Lill pulled her hands away from her back and dropped

to her knees. One hand gripped something I'd totally forgotten: the little knife the Bog Hag had given me. The gift from Lark, the knife I gave to her so she could cut Laurent from the waterfall. "Safe?" I echoed, stunned. I looked down—at the posts where the ropes for the bridge had been tied. The knots were still there, but the little bits beyond weren't frayed, they'd been sliced just enough to carry the weight of one small person across before they tore free. She was doing the same to the other side, now, sawing the ropes.

"Lill!" I shouted, heart racing. "Lill, stop! Listen to me! The shell. 'Tis a precious amulet. You witnessed its power but don't understand what it's for." I was babbling, dumbfounded she'd cut me off from the fort, from Laurent. "Remember what you said about the Guardians being wakened? Lill, *I* am one of those Guardians! I have to get the shell to Castle Tarnec, but I need help—I'm not supposed to do this alone!"

She didn't stop. I don't know what my expression was—blank with shock or frantic—I'd never been lied to before. But Lill was terrifying. Letting out snorts of breath as she worked, her jaw hard; I could see her hands trembling, even, as if scared by her own intensity. As the ropes gave and the intricately knotted slingbridge disappeared into the crevasse, she choked in some sort of horrified triumph. And then, that the deed was done with such finality seemed to calm her.

Not me. "Lill!" I screamed. "I am a Guardian, Laurent is my Complement! Remember the bond? He *has* to come with me!"

She stood up slowly, facing me. "I know who you are. Do you think Laurent does not speak as I sit by his side? You—he talks of you. *You,* who said bonds were not made out of love! Yet now you tell me he is necessary!"

I couldn't answer; the breath went out of me, but Lill seemed to grow stronger, filled with enough hatred that its bile spilled out to fill the silence I'd left. She shouted across, victorious, "Eudin will know I saved Gren Fort! The soldiers are too close! He will understand I had to cut the bridge even with you on the other side! But I cut *you* off, Guardian of Death! You've brought us ill luck—your dark ends, your conceits, your pretense at magic. Take it to Tyre. The soldiers will be glad to escort you!"

"It's not magic! 'Twas never magic!" Something rustled in the grass behind me and I flinched, thinking the Tyre soldiers had already found us. "Please, Lill, for the amulet! It has to go back to Tarnec—I don't know the way! Please! It's too special—"

"Why should I care for your shell?" She sneered. "It can't free my sister. It can't make *him* look at me."

Laurent. He was somewhere far below our feet, sleeping maybe. I shook my head, for Lill was right. She could not have what she wanted.

A pair of ravens flew raucously out of the trees, disturbed by something. My breath caught and Lill smothered a scream. I looked up at the sudden chaos of wings, then back at Lill.

Rightfully frightened this time, she turned and ran.

"Lill, please—!" I watched her disappear, the grass swallowing skirt, shoulders, and braids.

And then I turned and ran too. Back to the trees.

For once that morning my cloak was necessary. I slung it over the lowest branch of an ash, grabbed the ends to help me climb, tucked into a crook of limb and held still. There was the faint rustling of leaves. And then there was a heavier rustling, the tread of boot.

And voices. Soldiers filed into the grove. Three of them.

I wasn't scared—at least not like Lill—of the soldiers. But her betrayal shook me to the core. I was cold for it, my joints brittle. Nothing from home prepared me for this.

Merith! I missed it suddenly, searingly. But then just as suddenly the voices and boot tread were closer, and nostalgia was a waste of attention. I hugged my cloak tight, holding still as they passed, so they would not look up and see me there as bright as an enormous robin's egg. Lark and I once laughed about hiding in such colors—my turquoise as opposed to her soft moss green.

The soldiers paused nearly beneath my tree. I held my breath against their foul sweat stench; celebrated each minute they'd not spied me. Yet it became obvious 'twas not fortune that kept me hidden. I could see them standing, speaking gibberish in guttural voices, staring out at the field where Lill and I parted—intent on something far more important.

"Pass" was a word I did understand. So was "quarry."

They knew of Gren Fort, or had gotten word, somehow, or tracked the stranger or Eudin's posse. They were looking for signs. And even though nothing could be seen from here, nor a hundred paces closer; even if they could not cross to Gren

Fort for lack of that bridge, they would find the severed knots and stakes, camp there and wait. People traversed this area, they'd know. And where there were people, there were slaves to be reaped. Or, if they discovered the outpost where Arro was attended . . . I felt my heart sink, then a challenge. None of this, *none* of this could happen.

I was glad, then, that I was not camouflaged in Lark's moss green; I wanted them to find me.

I counted how long it would take to cross through the grove of trees, to the scrub and silly ansel thistle. I was fast—I could outrun those armored men; I knew it. With axe and long sword as weapons they could do little harm unless they caught me. Still, I'd have to give them a worthy target; they'd have to want to give chase.

They faced the sea of grass. I climbed down the ash limb by limb and was on the ground running before I realized they'd not heard my escape beneath their thick helms. I ran back to a spindly birch, tied my cloak around my shoulders, and then jumped for as high on the trunk as I could reach. I was briefly suspended, with the cloak swirling wide and bright, before the tree bent over with my weight. I touched down and let go with a furious yell; the birch swung back, smacking another tree. I dropped to my knees, yelling my lungs raw.

Let them think I've fallen from my hiding place. Let them think I am scared.

And they did. They turned with shouts, came stumping forward. I waited until they were but twenty paces away before leaping up with great screams of terror, and then I took off, limping. *Let them think I've hurt my leg.* I came out of the trees into the scrub and checked that they had a good view of me, then hobbled to the first ansel thistle. I counted to three, and hobbled to the next. I was blatantly visible; nothing else moved save for the glossy blackbirds shooting between bushes, or a blundering insect.

And so it went, my taunting of the soldiers, leading them far from the fort. 'Twas a game of sorts, a sick kind of pleasure. I limped between bushes, snapping stems and leaving little ripped bits from the hem of my cloak to be found for a trail, and crumbs of Lill's horrid scones. *Let them think I am foolish. Let them think I am weak.* Even so, I grew the distance between us. They could not keep up, and after a while it seemed silly that they tried. And I wondered why they bothered for one limping girl. I wondered how they caught anyone at all—or if fear simply paralyzed escape.

Perhaps the soldiers did grow tired. Sometime late in the afternoon I heard a clarion call, startling the blackbirds altogether so they shrieked and swooped. I peeked around the bush I sat by. The soldiers were stopped. One of them had pulled out a horn—not of metal, but something thin and curved to such a degree it had to be from one of those fiercely ugly pin bulls. He blew into it again, sharp and loud in the dry air, summoning, and I snorted. What was the point of more soldiers when even a hundred of them under such armor would not catch me? I broke off a few of the soft-spined thistle heads, split them open to slurp the milky sap, and left the remnants in an obvious scatter before moving on. Above, the birds cried.

Gren Fort was far distant. It was late and I was restless, bored of this tease. I hunkered down for a time by a dead elderberry and drew a vague map in the dirt, estimating the distance between the last village the Rider and I came upon and the fort, and how far east I'd have to backtrack to find Castle Tarnec. If I could put Dark Wood on my right and then head north I'd be near enough, I thought. It was a semblance of Lark's travels, on the opposite edge of Dark Wood. I sat on my heels, arms hugging my legs to my chin while I studied my sketch—

There was a strange shrill and *hissss,* like a snake, a whirligig. A sound so odd, I popped up to look. As I did, one of the scrub bushes I'd hidden behind earlier burst into a fiery ball, the noise knocking my eardrums and pitching me over. I spit out the dirt, crawled to my knees to look. Smoke funneled up from the flame, sharp and hot. But then with a sudden *whoosh* the flame was snuffed, and the spot lay black and bare.

The soldiers stood like little toys in the distance—*the metal men,* the old woman had called them. I squinted to see. One was flinging something; there was another *hissss* and I clamped my ears against a second blast.

Before me another bush was seared from the earth, seared from my gaze.

They are erasing the hiding places. Even as I thought it, a third and fourth bush detonated. Blackbirds shrieked up, flew on. Hisses screamed through the air; I watched, stunned. Little balls were being flung; each soldier had them. They flew far— farther than anything without wings had the right to—then landed, rolling fast along the ground, leaving singed trails until they hit something solid and exploded. The birds were wild with distress, looking for safety, closing in on where I hid. They reeled above the fray, too bewildered to leave the plain, yet with no place to rest.

I remembered the little seabird with its damaged feathers. It must have been caught by one of those things. I remembered how fast the hunchbacked woman's village burned. Those had to be the reason.

The air grew hazy. It smelled of rust, of lead. One of the balls went spinning toward nearby brush—too close. The blackbirds flew up and I jumped up too, running for another hiding place. A lucky throw, I thought. But then I saw the birds alight on the last bush I'd hid behind—realizing with a jolt what these blackbirds were: grackles. Eudin said they'd been spying above the quarry. They weren't displaced by the explosions; they were showing the soldiers where to throw their bombs.

I picked up and tore off, knowing they saw me, but it hardly mattered. I would run, far from any ball of fire, any clarion call. . . . But a moment later I was stumbling, dropping to my knees as a new sound rocked the air, something huge and feral and far more terrible than fire. The hair stood up on my arms.

I held motionless, then looked back against my will. There, at the edge of the plain, the setting sun glinted off the armor of approaching soldiers. Twelve were coming, making a total of fifteen soldiers. But it was what the twelve soldiers wrestled— two to a tether—that made my heart skip. Dogs. Not dogs as I knew them; not Lark's Rileg, or Kerrick Swan's Romer, grinning, tail-wagging, unassailable companions. These clay-white beasts reached to the breastplates of their handlers, dragged the metal men toward the sound of the horn.

These dogs were weapons.

I didn't wait to watch. I knew what the soldiers had in their favor: a trail I'd so considerately fashioned for them along my course, and a landscape even more barren than before. I'd be tracked in a moment.

I whipped around, scanned the horizon. There were ripples in the distance where some granite hills heaved up. I took off. Enough of limping; I aimed straight in flight. Enraged yelps filled the distance. The dogs were already loosed.

I raced head down for the rocks. Better cover, at least—at best, water would be collected in their basins. Water was the method of erasing scent, any trail. But then, if water gushed even a half league away it would be too late.

It was stunning how quick their speed—in minutes the dogs crossed the plain that I'd navigated over hours.

Stunning how quick that soft bed at Gren Fort was a thing of the past.

16

BOULDERS, CRAGS, HARD drops into wells of dead grass, but any water was long gone. Lark had sent no trinkets for this. I cursed at the dry earth, at the lack of hiding places: "No good comes if the shell is lost here! Give me something to use!"

Lark had connection with the Earth, with its creatures, why didn't I? Wouldn't Earth want to help her champions?

Right back came my own reply, an echo of Lill's sneer: *You are Guardian of Death, not Life.*

And what help was that?

I raced on, clambering up the scabs of granite, mind running as feverishly fast as my feet. How much time? Would the dogs surround me first the way wolves challenged a deer, or would they rip me apart without ceremony? And what of the shell: Would I lose it, be forced to destroy it, or die before either?

Somewhere it occurred to me that these scattered questions were at last the beginnings of true fear, that this was what fear felt like: worry becoming dread becoming terror. And yet they kept my mind from caving to Healer concerns—that I was parched, and starving, and exhausted—and maybe that was a good thing.

It was nearly dark. The soldiers in their black armor had disappeared into dusk and distance, but I saw six pale streaks coursing over the land. I faced forward again, hissing at myself to stop gauging my chances, and scrambled up a ridge—

It ended abruptly, the ridge. With two stumbling steps and an impromptu leap I hit the other side hard, falling from its edge, grabbing for anything to hold, then dangling with breath knocked out, arms scratched raw. I'd caught an edge of stone, barely. I grabbed at crevices, grunting, tearing skin and nails, worked my way up onto solid ground and huddled at the brim to find my breath, soften the pain. The dogs howled closer. *Think, Evie!* I had to do something; I had to protect the shell.

The dogs . . . The dogs . . . Brutally loud as they closed in. The only defense I had was that deadly gap. I lifted my head, grim but resolute. I'd lure them, I *would*. Self-preservation trumped killing, didn't it? This was defense.

I crawled to my feet, sick with intent, forced myself to wait on the edge of the ridge. A moment later the dogs arrived in a ferocious tangle. Shaking, sore, repulsed, I dragged in a breath and raised my hands above my head to lure their focus so they wouldn't see the drop. And then they were there, running fast, coming straight at me with double rows of teeth and fangs as long as my fingers, and—

A dissonance of howls and snarls. Some went over the edge, most not, and a failure, all of it. My stomach pitched. I turned and scrambled up a ledge of boulder, hearing the remaining dogs leap the gap. I lunged for the next little ridge, crying out against the pain, anger, and yes, fear—

Then my cry was cut short as a hand covered my mouth and hauled me up hard. A voice against my cheek breathed, "Hush." Then: "Don't look."

Laurent.

He spun me around so that I faced away from the attack—an attack that never happened. I remembered how deft he was with his sword, how he spitted the Troth on his blade back in Merith that day. The Rider was deft this night as well. The dogs went silent, all at once. No, no attack at all. They were dead before the chance.

I sat down, numb. At length I heard Laurent approach, heard him wipe his sword, felt him kneel at my side and brush loose strands of my hair back from my face.

His voice was hard. "You are all right?"

I leaned into him, nodding, forehead against his shoulder, feeling how solid . . . how safe. But Laurent pulled away abruptly as the pin bull's horn sounded in the distance, and said, "Listen. The soldiers are calling back the reaping hounds. They believe you were taken down."

He stood and I was left off balance, surprised for it. My

hands went flat to the ground. *"Reaping hounds . . . ,"* I echoed. The name tasted brutal. All of it was brutal.

"Breeders' creatures." Laurent sheathed his sword. "Just one of many beasts they provide to their cronies in Tyre."

"And the explosions, those fireballs—Breeders' weapons?"

"Incinerators."

He was cold to me and I didn't know why. I stared at the ground, defeated by rejection, violence, and betrayal, by the fact that I'd have failed to save the amulet had not my Complement swept in to do the killing. At length, I mumbled, "How did you find me?"

"You were gone," Laurent said simply, as if it should follow that he'd be here. "You and Lill were spotted leaving the quarry by the west route. I crossed to the caretaker's post to saddle Arro and then tracked you, or rather the soldiers. I skirted wide ahead to wait for dusk. I left Arro in the gully so the hounds would not catch his scent. And then you ran up here. . . ."

Laurent offered the water from his goatskin flask sparingly— a drink for each. He handed me some hardbread; I looked at it strangely—Healer instincts all twisted, awry. I'd forgotten about food and that I'd been famished. Now I didn't even feel the bread pass my lips. I had to think to ask, "How are your wounds, Rider?"

"Well enough." There was a pause before he added, "We are on our own now, Evie, from here on. The bridge to Gren Fort has been taken out."

"The bridge." I waited. Laurent offered no reason. I could not tell if he knew why the bridge was gone. Should I say what

Lill had done? Tattle on a girl who'd been so bruised? She was angry and impulsive, but she believed she was protecting her home and her love. I'd behaved as impulsively by risking the Insight spell. Then my stomach knotted wondering if Laurent was protecting Lill by *not* mentioning her. I said faintly, "You do not ask about Lill."

"Why? She is not with you."

No emotion, not for either of us. The horn was blowing again. I called above it: "Does it not matter? What if Lill is lost? You do not want to turn back, to find her too? She's a child."

He actually laughed. "Do not mistake the Riders as saviors. We kill trespassers in Tarnec—even a 'child' such as you describe. My duty is to you, to see you and the shell safe to Castle Tarnec." It was disturbing how firm and clear he said it, competing with the noise: "Lill is not so young that she can't find her way to the caretaker's post."

Sacrifice for Balance. It did not feel right anymore; it did not feel a simple trade. Laurent, Lill, the dogs . . . I could not tame the emotions that were running through. Fear and anger, yes. But also need—an intangible, powerful yearning to pull something from this Rider. Whether it was love or mercy, I didn't know. All of it was mixing together, hurting my gut, my heart. I wanted to slough off my skin and expose the pain, let the night air scrub it away.

Above the horn came a whinnying cry. "And what of your horse?" I frowned. "Is he not important? He calls—"

My voice fell away at the ugly look on Laurent's face. "Arro," he gritted, leaping to his feet. "*Stay here.*" And he was gone.

I ignored that, was immediately after him, but I could not keep up. Laurent tore back over the rock, leaping jagged heaves with no mind to his injuries; I ran left to where the gap was easier crossed. A minute later I crested a little ridge and saw the scrub plain once more, dark and rough, the moon not up.

But there were torches hoisted by the soldiers.

Arro's cry was terrified. The black steed lunged and bucked, corralled by the metal men who circled and prodded with their axe handles, who tried to catch hold of his reins, to force him away with them. They cared not about the dogs, nor even if I'd escaped, only that they had a new and better prize and intended to drag him back to Tyre. *Rarer than any gem,* the stranger had said. A horse would bring unimagined wealth and honor for a soldier, more so than any slave.

Arro shrieked again and reared, towering above the helmets, his hooves striking and flinging two soldiers dead some lengths away. But one of their axes ricocheted back, winging wide to catch Arro full across the flank. He went down in a chorus of panic, the soldiers and I all screaming. . . .

But it was the Rider's shout that shook the very earth.

Laurent threw himself at the dark-armored bodies, knocking them back, striking them down. He was possessed by rage-strength, huge and terrifying, slashing his sword in every direction. Armor against flesh, one against many . . . The Rider managed to still two of the metal men, but eleven were left, and—as in a game of pins—they kept standing up. It was an impossible win.

I didn't think. I charged into the fray, yelling at the top

of my voice, and launched myself at one of the soldiers. Surprised, thrown off his footing, he fell with me on top of him. I stabbed at the base of his neck for the immobilizing pressure point, but it was protected by that cursed armor. I banged on his chest plate, held down his arms, or tried to. But he worked for momentum, like an upturned, filthy sap turtle, rocking himself over until I had to jump before he crushed me. A blow from another soldier's steel-cased elbow knocked me back flat. I scrambled up, a rock in hand, and lunged for another. If I'd felt anguish for the reaping hounds, 'twas no more. Energy was loosed, set wild in me. I would have killed if I could. *Killed.*

Still, I was a gnat to these giants, a minor annoyance as they swung their weapons at Laurent. They flicked me away with barely a glance as I leaped at them, until one decided to rid himself of the pest. He raised his double-bladed axe over his head to slice me through, but Laurent's sword caught him across the throat and the soldier went down, the flat of his axe glancing my shoulder. I stumbled out of the circle, arm uselessly numb, and dropped to my knees, gasping. And then I watched in horror as ten hulking masses of steel closed on Laurent. I shrieked his name with the same terror as Arro.

It slowed, the battle, before my eyes. Sound ebbed to a distant howl, the clang of metal, the grunts and shouts and thudding of earth all blurred. It was an eternity for each axe to rise and crash down, for the swords to stab. A tumble of legs and arms and weapons played like a slow dance, silhouetted in the flickering light of the torches. Laurent was ever valiant, but he had no chance against ten. Furious attack became desperate defense.

He would die, my Complement. He would die in this moment—saving Arro, saving me, while I watched useless.

"STOP THEM!" I screamed it aloud; I cried it within. My fists were filled with the sand-dry dirt of the plain, which sieved between my fingers like in an hourglass shedding time. *Stop them.* Arro bled; Laurent suffered. *Please . . .* There was no Bog Hag, no gift to use, no Lark. And I was nothing, not Healer, not Guardian. Simply nothing.

And yet . . .

It began as a breeze. Some faint whisper that ruffled through the length of my hair and stirred my cloak. Then the breeze became sound—a whisper growing into a roar of shouts, cries, pleas—voices of a crowd, memories of pain. Something of it gave the soldiers and Laurent pause, a brief shudder, but they quickly fell back to their fight. The roar grew louder, and still they did not hear what I heard.

Nor see. The air surrounding us was shimmering, thickening. A whitish haze against the dark . . . and something more. The haze was forming, coloring, resolving to figures—transparent, nearly, but figures in the shape of human, of animal and tree. Nay, they *were* human and animal and tree, advancing in mass toward the battle. One figure—a boy, carrot-haired, ginger-lashed—broke for a moment to turn and look at me and nod. And then I knew.

Spirits of the recent dead. Those whom the soldiers had so

brutally killed—humans, animals . . . the trees, even, which had been so painfully hacked and trampled and burned. Those ripped from any peaceful end were returning to exact revenge.

Because I'd asked.

I sat back hard, panting, watching these incandescent figures surround the fight; circle slowly. *Step, step, step.* An ominous drumbeat. My heart matched each thud.

Growing in speed. Faster. Running now. *Faster.* A humming sound whined from the circle. *Faster.* Like a ring of mist, a whirling top, they blurred. *Faster.* A single, wild entity, racing. My hair was whipped from its braid; the torches spit fire, igniting the bone-dry brush. And still they spun ever faster, raising a wind of such force it trumped weapon and muscle. The mist pushed in, then soldiers—armor, axe, and all—were yanked from Laurent, sucked into the spiral and flung far off, disappearing into separate distances. The Rider was left in the middle striking at nothing.

The wind slowed and the spirit mist feathered out, smothering the burning scrub and quenching all the torches but one—one flame spared so that I could see, bear witness to what I'd begged for. Then the mist collected around me, resolved once more into individual figures. I was on my feet, mouth open. Transparent faces, hollowed eyes, sheer branch and bough. The empty gazes all trained on me, poised . . . for something.

"What . . . ?" It fell out of me before I could gather any thought. Then I collected myself and bowed hand to heart: "What can I give but my thanks?"

The carrot-haired boy spoke. "Take us home."

I raised my head and looked at him. "Home," he repeated, and the surrounding spirits echoed in ghostly voice, in shake of leaf. "Home."

Home. The word resonated long and needful, shuddering straight through me. They meant solace, not place, and it hurt to sense such yearning. On impulse I reached both hands toward the carrot-haired boy. "Ben," I murmured, remembering the old woman naming him.

It seemed to be what was wanted. Ben reached for my hands—a wisp of smoke brushing my fingertips. "From your lips, Guardian." He smiled and was gone. One by one they reached for my hands, supplying their names, which I whispered back before they disappeared, *Carn, Logan, Hurd, elm, badger, fern* . . . Person, plant, and animal brushing by as if a single touch—my touch—could send them on their way, could send them home. This Guardianship seemed huge, suddenly, my hands connecting to the whole world and the stars above— the barest glimmer of the awesomeness of a *primal* force. Huge and beautiful, and cruel. This was not healing, and yet it was—I was helping these tragic-killed beings to cross the threshold into peace. The seer had said it; Laurent had said it: *the one Healer. You allow only the passing of those who cannot be saved.*

And then it was done. The scrub plain was empty of spirits, quiet but for Arro's panting.

17

ARRO!

I whirled. Only a breath of time had passed; Laurent was staggering to his feet, eyes on me, not understanding what had happened—except that the soldiers were gone and I was unharmed. "How . . . ?" he began, but Arro made a sudden and terrible noise. Laurent dropped his sword and stumbled to his horse. I raced to join him.

Swearing, he tore off his shirt and pressed it to the ugly gash that ran full across Arro's flank. It was too long, too deep; Laurent could neither stanch nor hold the wound closed. Each heave of Arro's breath seeped new blood. I'd never heard such curses. A strong connection between wounded and nurse would aid a healing process, but rage would make it worse. 'Twas bad energy, all of it, with no time to waste.

I sank to my knees, put my hands over his blood-soaked ones. "Let me, Laurent. 'Twill be better if you hold—"

"Let you what?" he gritted. "We do not rest here. We need to get past those ridges, find cover."

My jaw dropped. "Arro cannot be moved like this!"

"And you cannot stay. You are too exposed on this plain. You will be tracked."

"How? The soldiers are dead!"

"Not soldiers," he growled. "Breeders. Whatever magic that was, whatever made those soldiers disappear, will bring the Breeders like a beacon."

"No magic," I said under my breath. Then aloud, "If you worry for me, let me go on alone. Tend Arro here. Eudin and his posse scout these plains, they'll find you, help you take Arro back to the fort—"

"I stay with you, Evie Carew. There is no arguing."

"Arro will bleed out if we make him stand!"

Laurent's voice was bitter hard. "We *will* make him stand, for I'll not leave him for vultures—winged or armored. There will be stones enough up on that ridge to . . . to cover."

"*Cover?* You *bury* your horse instead of mending him!"

"It's too late for mending!" he yelled.

I yanked his hands away from the blood, squeezed them between mine, forcing him to hold my gaze. "No, Laurent. Arro will live. His life force is strong, just as yours is."

"I had the *minion*." The words burned caustic. "What is there among this dead-dry scrub that can save him?"

"Me," I said fiercely. I scrambled up, shouted to the night sky, *Do you hear me? This horse will NOT pass!* I would *not* let Arro die.

I had no herbs, no special medicine, but I had water from the goatskin and fire from the torch. I had my hands. And I dug into the Rider's clever pack, finding a needle and twining. I held the goatskin over the flame, heating the water as best as I dared, then washed and cauterized the wound and stitched the thing closed. It was hardly neat, hardly delicate; the snorts of the horse were harsh. I worked as quickly as I could; Laurent paced.

"Tell me what happened back on the plain," he demanded abruptly. "How did we survive?"

"Spirits," I muttered, jamming my finger with the needle. "The spirits of those killed by Tyre's soldiers. They'd not yet passed to death. They came to our aid."

"Our aid?"

"Mine then," I said grimly.

"That's not . . ." He was frustrated. "How?"

I sucked my finger, spit out the blood. "I called them. Blame me."

He stopped his pacing. "What blame?"

I would not talk anymore of death. I knotted the thread and bit off the leftover. "Finished," I announced, wiping my hands with the hem of my frock. I laid them on Arro's neck at his pulse, willing recovery. Laurent moved close, inspecting. I gave him a hard look. "You cannot say there was no time for this. No Breeders have come." I didn't mention the spying grackles.

"Can he walk?"

"We are not moving him. That will not help—!" I gasped as Laurent straightened, lifted me up by the shoulders, and walked me back a few paces. *"Don't!* He needs rest!" If the Rider was furious then so was I, furious at the readiness to sacrifice his horse, his kindred spirit. I'd never felt such exasperation before, and his steadfast refusal to listen and barely contained fury were so completely against anything I'd ever witnessed in Laurent.

But then I saw the Rider's own hands so gently encouraging Arro to stand, how he braced Arro's flank until the horse's hooves were stable on the earth, the tenderness with which he brushed the forelock back. 'Twas breaking him, this decision, and yet he was going to let Arro die. For me. I'd not let it come to that.

I took a deep breath and put my hand on his arm. "Rider—"

"Let us go," Laurent interrupted, freezing under my touch. "Move on in front where I can see you. I'll assist Arro."

"Nay." I swallowed his rejection, tucked feelings away. I would not care what the Rider thought or insisted. "We'll both walk with Arro." I shook his sleeve. *"Together."*

The Rider's eyes bored through me then, harsh and cold. And bleak. He opened his mouth to speak, but then shut it and turned to collect his sword and pack and the single torch. We each threw an arm over Arro—I tried anyway, finally holding my shoulder against his great foreleg. And the three of us shuffled our way up rock and dirt in silence.

It was an ugly trek. Laurent was keenly, angrily vigilant. I kept my own eye out for the grackles, but there was nothing I could deem any sort of threat—except my thinning patience as he pushed the pace, and I resisted. Eventually the land flattened out, made it easier to travel, but the tension between us was already the heavier burden. "There is our cover," Laurent grunted about some trees up ahead. "We'll rest within."

The trees were dying—sad, bare boughs of larch and elm entwined overhead. After the exposed plain, though, even a skeletal canopy seemed protective. There was a trickle of water in a small hollow, a thick carpet of fallen leaves underfoot. We washed and watered the horse as best we could; Laurent soaked some hardbread for feed, and we helped Arro to lie down. I walked to the edge of wood where we'd left the torch, which forced Laurent to break our rigid silence.

"Do not leave the trees!" he barked.

"We need to make a fire," I snapped back. "I'd hardly build it where everything is tinder."

"No fires."

"The water from the goatskin was barely hot before! I want to clean Arro's wound again. Clean it *better.*"

Abruptly Laurent stalked over to me, yanked the torch from my hand, and stubbed it dead in the dirt, leaving us in the faint sheen of moonlight. "Fires open paths for Breeders," he gritted. "I know it too—"

"Enough!" I shouted. "Must you force your sacrifices, Rider?

Look about! There are no Breeders! No wisps, no reaping hounds, no swifts!"

"They come when least expected. And not always in violent forms."

"So? Let them come! Let us save Arro until they do!"

"I save you!"

He said it fiercely, with no regret. It stunned me a little. But his anguish beneath the anger expelled my own frustration in a rush of breath. Impulsively I reached out, knowing full well he'd jerk from me again, so I caught up his sleeve in a hard grip. "Laurent—!"

"Do you think I don't grieve my horse?" the Rider bit out. "He saved my life once and there is nothing I wouldn't do to save his." He inhaled harshly. "Except sacrifice you."

"Being a Complement means you'd let everything else die if necessary?" I was astonished. A little sickened. "Then I unbind you, Rider!"

"It is not my—"

I shouted, "I am no longer your duty! *Go* to Arro! You are free to do what is in your heart."

"Heart?" he yelled back. "Don't you *know* what is in my heart?"

We glared, jaws hard, my hand fisted in his sleeve. Not anger, but stubbornness. A standoff. What came next was my doing. He was there, this Rider, so haunted and beautiful and pained, and I couldn't think anything but that I wanted him to not hurt—

Nay. I simply wanted him. I released his sleeve, took his dirt-smeared face between my hands, and kissed him.

Laurent gripped the back of my head, as if he could draw me in any closer, devoured the kiss like a starved one, and then broke free, hands to my shoulders, setting me a little away from him. His breath was ragged. "Lady—"

"*Don't!* Don't call me so." I reached for him and he took my mouth once more, before pulling back.

" 'Tis this moment." He shook his head to clear it, his hands clenched tight. " 'Tis but passion expelled by fear. I understand."

Passion. A feeling I'd hidden away, and yet it was there, mine to own, and I wanted it—wanted to feel this wild thing that shivered through me. My laugh tasted cold and sweet. "This is not from fear. Do not brush this away."

"Evie, you are not yourself."

"You do not know me!"

Laurent hesitated. I saw his hand twitch to reach for me then drop, my heart dropping with it. "This is how the Breeders toy with us," he said abruptly, and turned to the woods to listen. He walked a little ways. "By all accounts they should have found us."

"And neither are Breeders the excuse." My tone was changed again—another emotion to cloud it, the sharp bitterness of rejection. "You once said I hold something so tight. But so do you. It makes you push me away."

There was a terrible pause. I stared at his hard back, watched a tremor flick across his shoulders and his hands clench. "Rider—"

"You were over his body," he gritted, head bowed.

It took a moment—Laurent was staring at his fist, and then I realized he was not speaking of his horse but a far different memory.

Raif.

"You were undone," he whispered. "I killed the Troth, rode past—I saw you."

"I know."

"No," he hissed, eyes fixed on his fist. "You do not understand. I *saw* you." Head up, he took a harsh breath. "You burned straight into my soul."

He would not turn. But his words hit, drop by drop: "You . . . do . . . not . . . know."

I stared at him. *You do not know.* Like raindrops fizzing on parched earth, those words, exploding life—it sprang into my head then the picture of what I'd so badly wanted to erase: that horrible day, that moment of death, of running for Raif . . . and Laurent's eyes on mine. 'Twas only a catch of stares, only the briefest of moments. And yet—

"You mourn your Raif," he was saying. "I would neither taint nor damage that memory."

And yet. Laurent's eyes—that look as he galloped past in the smoke and grit. I remembered it there in the dark, dry night as vividly as if it were yesterday: something that was never acknowledged yet never forgotten, something the old seer had warned of and the Insight spell exposed. It was Laurent I'd seen. Eye to eye, soul to soul. The image burst from memory as if it *had* to be exposed. And now here we stood, spinning in reverse—I uncovering feelings and Laurent burying them deep.

"Taint?" I whispered. "How can you taint when you fill me with *this*?" My hand was already pressing against my heart. "I *love* you. I have loved you since that moment, even if I did not claim it then."

We stood apart, silent. Then hoarsely Laurent said, "You have his ring."

I started, and then laughed at the simplicity of misunderstanding. "'Tis Raif's ring, but not as you think!" I reached into my satchel, pulled the ring from it, held out my hand. "Look at it, Rider: Raif's *grandfather's* ring. I choose to keep it for them both, as memory, as honor. 'Tis a symbol of love, yes, but 'twas never betrothal."

Laurent's shoulders heaved once, hard. "You say you knew in a moment. I know what comes from moments." He was warning me, himself, us. "But it has to be real. I could not bear this as regret."

Regret? I rolled the ring between my fingers, then slipped it on my thumb. I didn't need to hide the ring away; it didn't hurt the way it once did. "Rider, I am glad for you," I said, eyes on him, my hand back at my heart clutching a discovery no Healer stoicism could have suppressed: "I am *glad*."

Laurent let out a breath like a shudder, a release. A hope. I said louder: "*Know* it, Rider: what I feel is more real than any token of memory. Can you not tell?" Louder even: "Shall I own it here and now?"

He still had not turned. I stepped back from him, brimming

with light, determined. Grandmama had said loving freely would not weaken my gifts. She was right. Love empowered. Here in this dark night, in the midst of drought and death, I felt so incredibly alive—things fervent, and rich, and bubbling up from inside all making me grin madly. "Rider Laurent!" I called out. "Rider Laurent, I love thee!"

There—he was turning to warn me back to the canopy. But I stepped away from the bare trees, flung my arms wide open and shouted up, waking the universe: "All you stars, hear my claim: I love the Rider Laurent. I love him!" And I was laughing, spinning in a circle, yelling to the night sky, "I love him! I *love* him!" Let the grackles spy, let the Breeders hear, terrors could not hurt us.

"Evie—"

Gasping, exultant, I looked back. Laurent had started forward, half ready, I think, to drag me back under cover. But I shook my head, laughing, emotions no longer to be contained or kept secret. "There can be no danger here," I cried, running to him. "For this is too good. Too powerful. Too pure!" I grabbed his hands and pulled him out under the sky. "This is love."

He stared for a long moment into my eyes, reading everything that I laid bare in a gaze—a luxury of time we'd not had our first meeting. Every sense was burning, every detail unfolding a thousand more. I felt his hands slowly pull out from mine. My breath hitched, but he was only moving to cover my hands with his.

"Then I would like to know this love," the Rider said. And he pulled me into his arms, and took me down with a kiss.

We lay on my cloak under the canopy of boughs. I fit into Laurent's chest, my head resting just under his jaw. Arro's even breaths soothed the quiet. There was no other sound. We were drunk with discovery, brimful and sated. It should have been, then, that we slept, but this peace was too precious and fleeting to let go of. And yet trying to keep hold of it left us restless and a little sad, our thoughts trailing to dark things.

"Evie."

"Mm?"

"Why did you speak of blame?" Laurent shifted his head so his lips were against my temple. "Spirits—those who've not fully passed through. 'Tis your power as Guardian to bring them forth. What blame is there?"

My power. He said it so simply, as if it were a simple thing that I could call back those whose lives had ended cruelly, that I could beg favors in exchange for passage.

"What blame, Evie?" Laurent repeated.

I whispered, "Because if they had no blood on their hands before, they do now. So I wonder that it was right. That I asked them to kill in my stead."

"They made a choice," Laurent answered. "You did not tell them what to do."

"Didn't I?"

"The dead are your allies, Guardian, not your slaves. They killed what killed them."

"At my beckon."

"It seems a fair trade. They aided you in your need. How they did so was their own making." Laurent shifted, thoughtful. "It is your Guardian right to be able to summon spirits."

"A *right*?"

"A strength, then—yours to call. Death helps its amulet's Guardian."

"I wish I didn't need to ask for help. I wish there was nothing to beg help for. . . ."

He raised a brow, "Or . . . ?"

"Or I should learn to do my own killing."

I heard him grin. "You cannot, Evie. It is not your nature."

"I could make it mine."

"Nay." Laurent turned. "You and Lark are the part of Balance that is not aggressive by *nature*. You cannot force it."

I don't know if that soothed, but it answered for my struggle at least. It also opened more questions: If the forces of Life and Death existed as calm equilibrium, then Dark and Light would have to be the balancing spears of vibrant energy. I thought of the missing two Guardians, tried to picture them. Did they sense a change inside themselves, or were they still naïve to what was coming? How would they fight?

Laurent said, "You ask no questions." He chuckled. "For once."

I grinned. And then I couldn't help but ask one: "Is it better to be a warrior or not?"

"We need both." He drew his arm away to sit up. Alert,

listening, as if I'd prompted him. He turned to give me a brief grin. "Arro's breathing is steady."

"Yes, but that's not what you attend," I said. "You listen to the night. You still expect the Breeders to find us."

Laurent was quiet for a moment. "Do you not wonder that the amulet was so easy to retrieve?"

"Why do you hold on to that suspicion? I could not have left Hooded Falls without your sacrifice—you nearly died! There was nothing easy."

"Nay, Evie, trust me. It was a suspiciously easy find."

"Reaping hounds, swifts, Troths, soldiers, wisps, incinerators . . ." I laughed a little; the list was longer but we were still whole. "What more could they do?"

Laurent seemed not to hear. His strong profile was etched against a starry sky—both hushed and still. But then came an unpleasant answer: "You ask what more? Any depravity of Earth and creature—beast or human. Whatever is spawned from the Waste."

"Tell me about it." I sat up to be closer. "Tell me about this Waste." I'd refused to ask of the Waste before. How different that all was now.

There was a longer pause. I wondered if he was choosing words carefully, if he thought he should spare me more horror. "The Waste is the realm of the Breeders. They hold Chaos there the way the Keepers hold Balance here."

"Here and there—'tis another balance."

He smiled. "It has always been as such. The Myr Mountains

divide the two: Breeders to the north, Keepers to the south. So yes, a natural scale."

"I've heard the Myr Mountains are an impassable boundary. How is it then that Breeders spread on this side?"

"*Near* impassable," Laurent corrected. "Besides, the Breeders can manipulate through thought, reach through flame, keep watch by spy. . . . What mountain can stop that?"

I had no answer, so Laurent nudged my shoulder, saying, "'Tis not so grim. Pockets of opposing forces are known on both sides. They might have collaborators in Tyre, but we have the white oak inside the Seth—the desert that surrounds their throne."

"That is a single tree," I said with a sigh. "They build an army."

The Rider's retort was surprisingly sharp: "You, Healer, know that a plant can best a man. And sanctuary is never gratuitous." He caught himself, calmed. "But if you wish: there is Heran as well, a Keeper outpost at a northernmost tip of the mountains. They keep watch." Laurent was quiet again for a moment, navigating violent descriptions. "Heran is as close to that realm as anyone can safely survive. The Waste is a savage wilderness. Things warp; become distorted beyond understanding. If you were to spend any length of time there you could not help but change."

"Why does that not work the same for the Breeders here? Why can those in Tyre be warped as they are—maraud, reap, kill—why wouldn't being on this side turn them *nice*?"

He laughed. "Do not look at this as good and evil, love, even if it seems such. By virtue of its stability Balance seems morally righteous, but it's not. It is simply Balance—both good and bad exist within it. And neither is Chaos inherently evil. It is just desire unbound."

"Regardless," I whispered, "Balance is the source of life. It must be saved."

"Yes." There was a moment so long that I thought the Rider let the subject go. But then he lay back on the cloak, saying softly, "Desire is a devious and powerful intoxicant." And the barest murmur: "They cannot help themselves."

His voice made me shiver. "You forgive it," I whispered. "People close to you—what happened?"

"What more to tell?"

"No." I leaned over him, hands propped on either side, and insisted, "Do not spare me anymore, Rider. This is your story, what formed you. I want to know."

He looked up at me, blue eyes dark in the dead of night, hair smudged black against my turquoise cloak. But his face—so fair, so strong-shaped—was neither dark nor black, just faintly shadowed by sorrow from the past.

Perhaps Laurent had a similar thought. He smiled and touched a gentle finger to my brow. "I would not mar this beauty with sad stories."

"I am not easily marred. Tell me."

He would have refused again, but I leaned down and kissed him hard, and so he sighed. "Your choice. Close your eyes, then, Evie Carew."

I did, nestling once more in the curve of his arm. And Laurent wove his tale, murmuring against my ear as if it were meant to be a bedtime story. And I pictured his rich details as if I were there myself—so very rich, but none sweet.

The spires of Tyre once glistened with the bounty of its mines: rubies, emeralds, opals, garnets, sapphires, silver, copper, and gold. . . . A city of astonishing beauty, renowned and celebrated for its artists and their creations. Craftsmanship was the source of pleasure, not the material, and those who came to admire the buildings studied the skill of design rather than its worth. Tyre soared up from the Dun Plains like a beacon, an invitation to all travelers who wished to trade knowledge and goods. And so the city was filled with diverse traditions and people. Keepers lived there as openly as anyone.

Centuries of beauty, of scholarship. But in this last generation came a subtle infiltration, a whispered thought—Breeders were working their own sort of skill, putting a value on materials that ultimately dwarfed inspiration. And what was once something mined for art became a source of greed, power, and the jealousies and vengeance that follow. Gems were hoarded, killed for, or sold, the bounty of which empowered a select few who titled themselves Genarchs. Beauty was forgotten in the frenzy to claim more wealth. Mines riddled the earth, the city decayed around its inhabitants. Gems and metals were ripped from every building, every furnishing; spires turned black with ash from innumerable smelters. Tyranny succeeded the communal governance—arbitrary rules were levied by whichever Genarch had wrested power from the last. Keepers were executed; any of their allies not killed either escaped or were forced into the mines. Families were torn apart by gluttony. . . .

"Mine was one," Laurent added softly, jerking me from the reverie. "I lost my brother to the Breeders, who in turn condemned my parents to the axe. Dragged from our home, executed in Tor Tower while the bells . . ." He trailed off, and then, like it was some curiously horrible discovery, said, "My brother forced me to watch their heads come off."

There was a moment of nothing. I swallowed thickly. "But he didn't kill you."

"For no sentimental reason. My brother is ten years my senior; his interests were long separate from mine." There was a dark humor in his tone: "I was eight, a ripe age for the mines. 'Twould have been a waste to kill me."

I sat up abruptly. "You were in the mines? You were a slave?"

"Six years."

"But . . ." Six *years* in captivity! He'd acknowledged it so calmly. "How—how are you here? I thought no one could escape the mines!"

"True. But that does not stop some from trying. And if . . ." Laurent's voice faded for a moment, weighted with some memory. "Miners are sometimes transferred to the Waste. If a Genarch believes more can be squeezed from slaves who cause trouble in the mines, they are carted to the Waste as offerings. For entertainment. For food." He paused, the faint smirk returning. He tugged a strand of my hair. "They *waste* no muscle."

A crude jest. I ignored it, exclaiming, "You—you were one of those transferred to the Breeders' dominion. That's why . . ." *Why he scolded me for doubting the necessity of the white oak.* "How did you survive? You are not changed from being there."

"I was not there long enough." A hesitation—his fingers threaded through the ends of my hair. He was not telling me all. Perhaps the journey *had* changed him. But then he murmured, "You ask what is the Waste? It is nothing of life. I remember the ash of a charred landscape, the tar of the barren Seth and the green-gray of choke weed. I remember open pits of flame, the stink of sulfur. I remember death—"

I waited, breath held. But Laurent ended abruptly with: "Some tales are not worth remembering. I escaped the transport. I made it back over the mountains; some of those from Heran's watch helped me through the worst of the Goram Pass and pointed me south to the hills. 'Twas Arro who found me there, bore me to Castle Tarnec." He paused. "When I healed, I joined the Riders. I was fifteen."

We both listened to Arro's soft whickering for a moment. Laurent grinned, then brushed back my hair, dismissing the dark. "Lucky for me that this horse took a liking or I'd have been slain as a trespasser in Tarnec after all that struggle."

"That is a terrible ending, Rider."

"But an end nonetheless," he said, pulling me back down. "Come, Evie, this is hardly the way to share a pillow. We are safe and Arro is still with us."

"Safe! So now you no longer listen for a Breeder attack?" I teased.

I felt him smile against my hair, though I could not tell if it was a happy smile. "A respite, then," he said. "And I hardly use it to purpose. I should woo you, my lady, with raptures of your beauty—your silver hair and smooth brow and the deep blue of your eyes."

It made me laugh. "And your eyes, Rider Laurent, they are as deeply blue."

"Then you may woo me," he said.

I rolled over to face him. I could hardly see him in the dark, but it did not matter. "You, Rider, have eyes the depth of the sea—"

"Have you ever seen the sea, Guardian?"

I grinned. "No, but it must be so."

"Good, then continue."

"Continue to woo?"

"Aye."

"Hmm." He was drawing me from my dark thoughts; I knew it. *Our precious peace.* "Shall I speak of your hair, Rider?" I reached to brush it back from his temple. "How it falls shiny black like a crow's wing—"

"Crow?" He snorted. "What sort of wooing involves a crow?"

"Blackbird, then? Raven?"

"Raven I accept."

"And this jaw." I touched the edge of his jaw. "Square and

grim-set, but you are now excused for that. Besides, your smile softens everything."

"And my mouth?"

I pressed a finger against his lips. "Your mouth is a yearning," I murmured.

"And if I kiss you, is the yearning sated?"

"Try."

And he kissed me, once, twice. Then I pulled back and said, "Nay, not sated. It leaves me wanting more. Always."

"Always." Laurent nodded. Then he said soft: "From the first time I saw you I was lost to you anyway." He turned a little and drew a strand of my hair back from my cheek. "Silver-haired, silver-voiced beauty."

There was that strange little thickening in my throat. I whispered, "I was bound in my heart from the moment I saw you too, Rider." I no longer needed to qualify with Raif's memory. My lost love had given me that.

Laurent moved suddenly, getting up on his knees, pulling me up to face him. "We will seal this." He was smiling, a faint gleam of teeth, his blue eyes so dark. He took each of my hands, pressed his palms against mine. My heart skipped, so full it was nearly bursting. I knew this gesture: 'twas the ritual of betrothal vows.

"Lady Eveline, Guardian of Death," the Rider whispered, "I pledge you me."

I whispered back—I could do no more, for my throat was stopped: "I pledge you me, Rider Laurent."

Laurent hooked my forefingers with his, locking them with his thumbs. I followed, fumbling a little, and both of us laughed. Like links in a chain, like two rings. Warmth of touch, glow of happiness.

Then he hesitated, added a little roughly, "I can't give you back what you lost, what you miss. But I promise you I will give my life to keep you safe, and all of my heart is yours."

I said, "I cannot want for more."

"So it is spoken," he whispered, and I answered, "So be it."

Laurent leaned down and kissed me, or I reached to kiss him—wherever it started, it didn't matter, for it had no end. Love would circle round and round, bind us forever. And we could cling to one another in this dark space in this darkening world, knowing there was still safe haven.

18

A MORNING BIRD announced the dawn; it was a lusty-throated thing. I burrowed deeper into Laurent's side, wishing her away. But she trilled on, and so I squinted against the light seeping through the tree canopy. 'Twas not hard to spy her. The remaining leaves rattled as she hopped from twig to twig, too dry for stealth.

"Where is your mate?" I whispered. Sweet as the song was, it was a lonely sound and there was no answering call. 'Twas all dying, I thought. Nothing thrived here. Still, there would be a reason that she perched at the edge of this grizzled terrain.

I sat up and pushed my hair back, reoriented. Next to me Laurent sighed, and I smiled for that, and for how my heart swelled even to look at him. The release of worry, however brief, had softened his brow, made him look innocent even though his sword lay by his fingertips. Arro too nodded in sleep.

Almond eyes shuttered by drooping lashes, his mane dusting the ground. I rolled carefully so as not to wake Laurent and crawled my way over.

The horse whickered into my palm. I felt his muzzle and cheek for any fever. I smoothed my hand along his back; gently probed the axe wound. 'Twas not pretty; crusted black between the rude stitching I'd done in torchlight.

We needed water. I looked up at the quivering branch and whispered to the bird, "You would know, little thing."

Had I been Lark, the creature would have flitted to my shoulder, most likely piped directions in my ear. Instead, the bird only cocked her head and let me search on my own. I took Laurent's flask with me, and the cloth from his belt and his blood-soaked shirt; I emptied his leather pack to use for a bucket. I shouldered my satchel as well, for it seemed wrong to leave the shell alone anywhere. I thought with another smile: *I am like its mother. It needs me.*

The trees thinned at a steep bank of grass and rock. I climbed, scouting, smelling. I followed valerian and thyme; I followed moss. Up a bank, down its back and up another. There was a stand of prickles and ivy clotting a shelf of stone, and then there, below my feet, was a crystal clear spring. Much had evaporated—maybe at one time I might have dived in from where I stood, but now it looked only chest-deep.

I slid down the bank, sank on my knees, and plunged my arms deep. I drank my fill and then some. I filled the flask and the Rider's pack. I washed my skin and hair, rinsed my undershift and tugged it back on wet. I scrubbed the blood from Laurent's shirt, watched it disappear in the pool. Where a stream would whisk away a blot, still water swallowed it. Saved it. The staining feathered out 'til naught was left but a sheen . . . and then was gone.

Either way, water absorbed secrets the way death absorbed life.

I reached for my satchel, for the amulet. I was alone; it could not harm anyone. I drew the shell out for the first time since the day I found it, amazed again at how simple it was, how small. How very empty. It fit in my palm, warm, nearly weightless. I ran my fingers over each knob and twist; I dunked it in the spring, brought it up dripping, and watched how the water glistened on its whorls, catching the early sun.

Find the shell's song; bring rain upon land. . . . I thought again of the seer's verse and that I had breathed into the shell's mouth once, to see. This time I lifted the pointed, hollow end to my lips like a horn and blew. A little whisk of air. There was no song, no other sound, and the sky was very bright.

Arro's wound needed cleaning, I told myself. I returned the shell to my sack and stood up to go.

The sun came sideways this early, and so the figure was in silhouette, seated on top of a rock, a cap pointing oddly on an already misshapen body. I don't know why I felt no surprise. I simply set down my load and walked straight to him.

"You wait for me, Harker. Why?"

The seer smiled. "Ah. 'Tis the mud poppet, all clean. And yet she still plays the fool."

"If you speak in riddles again," I warned, "I will not stay." The seer's hands were on his knees; my eye fell to them. They were still blistered red, but maybe he was numb to the pain now. "Did you use the heliotrope?"

He nodded.

"Beeswax," I said. "'Twill cover the spots, keep them from burning in the sun."

"Yes."

"Then I have given you all knowledge that I have. I am no White Healer. I can no more help you."

"Help!" His grin could not get any wider. "'Twas *you* who asked for it, not I."

I frowned. "How? I am here, you are here—mayhap by accident, but I think not, and I need nothing from you. I did not ask for help."

He stood. "But you did, Guardian."

"No games, I told you! Speak what you need."

Harker studied me for a moment and I him. He was so very ugly; his deformed shape and narrow features made even worse by his eerie little thrill at our meeting—a shiver of pleasure exposing those awful teeth. He knew what I was thinking. He whispered, "You could leave, Guardian. There is nothing to stop you, and your young man is more appealing than I. And yet you wait—wait to see what I might say. Ever curious, Guardian of Death. 'Twas how I left you."

"Maybe so." I pursed my lips.

"Curiosity." Harker squinted at me. "What three things did I share with you?"

"You said that they will strike where I am weak, that I hid not from grief, that I was to find the shell amulet."

"Ah!" He twitched a little, like a puppet. "Backward reasoning and wrong!"

"What?" I nearly shouted it, for every word he uttered seemed a trap. "What have I got wrong?"

"You did not finish—I said that you were to find the shell amulet, and . . . ?"

"And that if I loved my cousin," I shot back, "I would not ask for help."

"Yes," he whispered. "*No* help."

I stamped my foot. "I asked for nothing! I retrieved the shell amulet on my own, there was no help."

"Not so! Not so!" He stamped his foot right back at me and pointed his finger as well, accusing. "You received help."

"*What* then? Tell me!"

"Out of the water came things for you to save your pretty man."

"The knife and the minion. I did not ask for them!"

"But you took them, Guardian."

"So?" I walked away a few steps, frustrated and torn—I should return to Laurent, return to Arro, but I was compelled to stay, to listen to his nonsense until I *could* make sense of it.

"When did you use these little treasures?" Harker asked.

"*After!* They were useful, yes, when we cut the Rider from Hooded Falls, treated his wounds, but that was after—"

"It was because you asked for HELP!" he cackled, bony fingers pointing at me. "You stood on the rock ledge, crying '*Help me, please!'*" Harker pushed himself from the rock to stand eye to eye. "'Twas your first time, such a request." And leaning close he taunted, "Not even for Raif did you ask for help."

That was true. I stood there, shaken. "But the knife, the minion, they were given to me before I begged. I did not know that I would need it, I did not ask specifically—"

"Not specific? The knife and herb were the perfect choices, were they not? Why would your cousin Lark know?"

"She has the Sight!"

"But she does not see *you*!" he cried. "Nay, Guardian. That was the easy answer, and it is not easy."

"Then you tell me, Seer. Why did she know to send me those things?"

He shook his head. He was thrilled, and yet not for me. "Curious still, Guardian? Shall I show you what she's done? She defied the rule. For *you*. Now she pays. Now we all lose."

I shook my head, but then nodded. My heart was beating faster, anxious. Something was so very wrong in all of this: the seer's pleasure, his wagging his finger at me as though I'd misbehaved.

"I show you," he said, taking off his funny sky-blue cap. "I show you this, Guardian." He pulled the cap wide open, then pushed it to me. "Look into it. You will see."

And so I leaned over to look in what he eagerly held out. I think I was expecting a trove of coins. Instead, the cap with the sky-blue outside was deepest midnight within, so dark that it seemed a window into the night sky. It made me dizzy—a dizziness that took my feet so that I was falling into the cap, into the night with the stars all around me. I fell fast, far faster than Arro's gallop.

I heard Harker's words echo from a distance: "You must share the gaze of another Healer. You may watch through her eyes. . . ."

In the darkness were pinpricks of light that were not stars. I hurtled toward them; watching the lights form to windows, hint at the outline of an enormous structure. Castle Tarnec. The one I'd seen when I'd done the Insight spell. The walls loomed large and then I was inside, plunging straight down and jerking abruptly to a stop.

But hardly—only the barest breath to reorient and then I was speeding erratically through a long passageway layered in tapestries and lit sconces. Ahead I spied two young women running. That the first was Lark I knew immediately—her bright brown hair swung at her hips, and the gown was her favorite color of moss green, though far more beautiful than any frock we sewed in Merith. There was a little circlet of gold on her brow.

Queen, I remembered before looking to the other lady. She was taller, wore a rich russet color, and had dark curls that fell past her shoulders. She couldn't have been much older than Lark, no more than one and twenty. She wore no crown.

The Lark I knew kept her distance from people—but not here, not with this lady. Closer and closer I sped, and then I was no longer watching, *I* was the other lady, seeing through her eyes as Harker had said. Lark turned back to look at her friend—at me—and I tried to cry my cousin's name and reach to hug, but I could not. 'Twas gaze only; I could not participate.

Lark's face was determined, eager. "You need not follow, Ilone!" she called over her shoulder. "There's little time before the swifts return. Find somewhere safe where their noise cannot hurt you!"

Ilone answered. So peculiar that what felt my lips worked her words, and her voice—not mine—rang along the stone hall: "I know what you are after. You mustn't, you *mustn't*." The words quavered. I felt her throat clenching. "'Tis not part of the loan," she hissed at Lark. "You were told this; I *know* it. The king said we must leave them to choice. The books are not to be used."

"The king also said I must aid them as I can, Ilone! This applies! A Guardian is in trouble!"

Them. Guardian. "What trouble?" Ilone panted. Her behavior was so unusual for a Healer. She dreaded something. "You said you saw your cousin!"

Lark stopped all at once at the edge of a descending stairwell and wrapped her arms around her stomach protectively. "I saw Evie because she cast a spell." She looked up at her friend—at me—who'd stopped in front of her. "Why do you think the swifts attack? She cast a *spell*, Ilone."

Them. Guardian. *Me.*

"A spell!" Ilone looked down at her hands. "But she is not a White Healer."

"No." Lark's voice was hushed. "And 'twas a dark spell. She used yew."

Ilone's hands fisted, then wiped against her gown, as if even the word poisoned.

"It brought the Breeders," Lark whispered. "They spied her. Now they can find her, destroy her."

"Dark magic."

"I *saw* it, Ilone! I went to Trethe. We looked—" Lark clutched her waist, grimacing. "'Tis why they send the swifts to us, battering at these walls all day! We are forced to ignore the Guardian, while they do what they need to take her. Evie will be harmed! She cannot. She *cannot*." She started for the stairs, then paused, stiffening. "Run back, Ilone, please! Hide! I cannot bear that you suffer these creatures for me."

But Ilone reached for Lark's arm, holding her back. "The books are only loaned to us because of the betrayal. We will lose them if we look beyond each first page. 'Twould be *our* betrayal."

"What matter if we lose them, Ilone? Do you think I care about books over Evie's life?"

"That *is* Evie's life!"

Lark was shaking her head. "Nay, not life, her *fate*—"

"Gharain's fate was altered because his book was opened by the Breeders. Look what it did, Lark! You're here because of it! We all suffer because of it!"

"We suffer because the Breeders gained advantage. Let *us* gain the advantage now. We'll lose the books, not the battle. I'll use the Sight to find the other Guardians."

"Use it then for your cousin; don't do this!"

"I'm too close to her, Ilone! I cannot read her energy, I never could." Lark rounded on Ilone, fierce with determination. " 'Tis but the tiniest verse that we're granted out of each book of Fate! I did not need to use it to know Evie's Guardian bloodline—I can learn the other Guardians just as well."

"But you did look, you *did* read her verse. You shared it with us! Laurent—"

"Laurent will not save her if the Breeders get her first!" Lark turned and disappeared down steps that wound into the castle depths.

Ilone would not be left out. She ran as quickly as Lark, spiraling down and down. Just before the end, though, Ilone gasped, dropping on the stairs abruptly. I felt it: an invisible force, pushing her back.

Lark was at her side in a heartbeat, gripping her arms. "Are you all right? Is it the swifts?"

"No! No. I just—I can go no farther. . . ." Ilone panted. " 'Tis blocked."

"Of course—I'm sorry! Guardians and Complements only. I'm sorry." Then Lark smiled. "Wait here. You followed me this far, I'll not leave you out." She turned and ran back down the steps, disappearing.

How strange it was to see Lark so unafraid, so free to touch . . . so at home. I was the distraction, the cause of all her worry, and I felt twinges of what were envy and guilt. I wanted to cry out, *Here I am! Please do not worry for me!* And yet I could only see what Ilone craned her head to see, to follow what Lark was doing. 'Twas a room where she disappeared just below, bare of furnishings as far as I could tell, but for the edge of some intricately carved basin that stood in the center. Something was lit in that basin; it gave off a soft glow, different from any candle's flame.

In a moment Lark returned with a book in her hands. She ran up the steps and sat down next to Ilone, propping the thing on her lap. The book was smallish, ancient-looking and yet unworn. There was some sort of filigree design, but Lark's hands covered it.

"Please, my queen," Ilone pleaded, touching Lark's arm. She said what I was thinking: "Can you not sense something from it? Perhaps you do not have to open the book."

Lark shook her head. "I imagine this is where the Sight fails—I see what *will* happen, not what might be." But she clutched the edges of the book for a moment, as if to be sure.

A moment, 'twas all. She relaxed and smoothed her hands over the cover, studying it. "Handsome, but so simple a binding. To hold one's fate within the pages of a book, you'd think it would be made of finer stuff."

Ilone whispered, "What is precious is inside."

"Or perhaps it is like this just to say: *You are not special, Guardian. You might have lived your life simply, unaware, happy in your little garden. . . .*" There was a wistfulness in Lark's voice that I understood too well. But then she shook it off and pulled the book close.

Ilone inhaled. "You are sure of this?" And when Lark nodded she begged, "Then let me share the burden. Do not say no,

Lark. You will not tell Gharain; you will not tell anyone, I know it, but someone should share this. Let me." She reached out and took Lark's wrist. "This might help lessen any repercussion. Healer hands . . ."

Lark shook her head, insisting, "I will not let you sacrifice—"

But Ilone countered, gripping harder. "Is that not what you are doing at this very moment, my queen? Are you not sacrificing?"

"Yes!" Lark looked up and shouted to the air, to the stones around her: "To open this book is *my* choice! Do you understand? Let what comes fall on me! I accept the consequences!"

It caught my breath to hear Lark speak so vehemently. When had I ever heard her protest? Insist? Defy? Even those months ago when she stood in our village square surrounded by too many faces, too many energies, and confronted with the terrifying task of traveling into the unknown, Lark had stood, quaking but accepting. And when others offered to go in her stead she refused because she'd been chosen. She felt obliged to obey the rule. Now Lark was willing, eager even, to do the forbidden.

Because of my mistake.

Lark took her friend's hand gently from her wrist. "Thank you, Ilone." She shifted the book on her knees, considered it once more. "This is beautiful," she said, touching a finger to the filigree. I saw it then: the amulet shaped there, the shell. My book, my fate, was in her lap. Lark looked up and flashed a grin at Ilone, the same grin she might have given me any night at home as we braided our hair before bedtime—the coconspirator, the listener, the sharer. . . . Dearest moments that were all gone from us.

Ilone was silent. Lark took a deep breath and slowly opened the cover. The leather crackled. However old, the book had rarely, if ever, been opened.

"Here is the first page again," Lark whispered, lifting the book so she and Ilone both could see. "The one we are allowed." And she lifted it a little to read. . . .

"*Moonlight on water brings Nature's daughter. . . .*" Her voice was sweet, so unlike Harker's or Laurent's reciting.

"First page only," Ilone pleaded low. "Why can that not be enough?"

Lark ignored her and turned the page slowly, carefully. She murmured, delighted, "Merith!"

Ilone leaned over to see. I'm not certain if what played there were words or pictures. Mayhap it was both. But Lark was turning pages, recounting bits of my history: "Evie is making soap with Grandmama! There she is at market. . . ." Laughing: "Oh, the thing with Hurn's cow!" And more hushed: "There's Raif. . . ." The events were revealed slowly; still it seemed not many before she halted: "She makes the spell. Yew and minion and goat's milk."

Ilone's hands were clenched. "'Tis an Insight spell."

"Now I will look further to see what *will* come." It was hushed, this. Even I—with gaze only—could sense the darkness of this moment, the ominous pall that was seeping into this space. Lark shut the book suddenly, then ran up the stairs, Ilone after her. "I will not read there," she called back. Somewhere farther on she stopped, panting for breath. "Halfway up, halfway down. Neither in the castle nor the amulets' keep." And there, leaning against a wall, Ilone a few steps beneath her, Lark pulled open the book. She was trembling now, the place she'd opened was random, as if she wanted to do something quickly and be done with it. She gasped, "Laurent! He's torn by a waterfall!" Lark scanned quickly, murmuring, anxious, telling Ilone, "They've put the amulet where Evie cannot return from unless Laurent sacrifices himself. He'll die; she'll lose him! She's begging for help, Ilone! She has never done that!" And Lark's voice caught in horror. "There's another girl there. She's raging that it's Evie's fault—she means to push her . . . !"

Ilone was asking something, but it was lost, for suddenly there was a cracking sound, like rocks flinging together, and then the book was gone from Lark's shaking hands.

The young women looked at each other, shocked, then went tearing back down the stairs—Lark flying ahead of Ilone all the way back to the keep.

"They're gone! Ilone, all the books are gone!" came her cry.

Ilone tried to follow but was thrown back once more by the invisible barrier. "Lark!" she called, pushing herself up. "The loan is broken!"

Lark was back, running past her up the stairs. "We have to save them, Ilone," she gritted.

Ilone ran after her. "Them? The books?"

"No! *Evie! Laurent!* You! All of Castle Tarnec!" Lark stopped abruptly, her back to Ilone, shuddering. "Laurent will die. Evie will be killed. The amulet will be lost. She needs help.

She won't survive without it." Lark started up the steps. "*We* won't survive."

"What can you do?"

"She's in water," Lark called back. "Water is Death's medium—I can use it, Ilone! I know one from those realms who will help us. I have to find Trethe. . . ."

· And she was gone around a curve in the stairs, and then I was no longer seeing through Ilone's eyes but being pulled back from the stairs, from the castle, from the great precipice on which the castle towered, and flung back into the night sky where the stars shimmered and crowded in so brightly.

19

I WAS ON the ridge, sprawled flat. Harker was grinning his nasty little grin. He popped the cap back on his head, singing under his breath, "Where are you weak, little Guardian? Where are you weak?" The tune shivered through my spine.

"Seer." I panted. "Why do you show me this?"

He snorted. "You say it, but still you ask. *Seer!*" And he sang louder: "Seer, seer. *The* seer, *the* holder of fates. *Mine* to know."

I rolled to my knees, tried to get my feet under me. "Was it you who gave the books to Castle Tarnec?"

"Gave?" Harker shouted, "I was forced! They are my books! *Mine!* Never given! But now the girl of Sight, the Guardian, the queen"—he spit it—"has broken the loan, and my books are lost." He roared, *"NO!"* and then broke down in sobs. "I want them. I want them back."

"What can be done?" I gave up the effort to stand, still

dizzy, wiped my hands on my undershift. "Lark said as well that they are gone."

"And they call me the fool. They are *lost*, not gone! You should be vanished too if your book of Fate was truly gone." He turned, anger focusing his words. "This is your doing, Healer, naïve Guardian; 'twas *your* curiosity. You made the Insight spell, because you needed to know what I had not told you. But I *did* tell you! I told you everything you had to know. And yet you were not satisfied; you needed more to quench your curiosity! Now look what you have done!"

I stared at him. I didn't understand; I was horrified to understand.

"The queen saw you in that Insight spell. She knew you'd laid yourself open to harm, and so she chose to look at your fate to see. And there you were, *begging* for help." He barked an angry laugh. "You've ruined it for all! She will die and the amulets will never return! Serves you right!"

"Harker, no!" I gasped at his grotesque joy. "You cannot mean that!"

"You do not believe? Look!"

He tore his cap off his head and thrust it at me so that I had to look into it once more, had to spin back into the dark and stars and castle. I was seeing through Ilone's eyes again—she was crowding into a room along with a tumble of people all vying for a look, all crying, "Make way! Give space!" Between shoulders and heads I recognized Gharain, limping, thrusting through the doorway led by another man whom I remembered as another Rider. Ilone worked her way forward, coming to stand by that Rider; he took her hand. There was a bed; an older maidservant waited there. And there was Rileg, Lark's beloved three-legged dog.

And then I could see why Gharain seemed uneven. He was carrying Lark, hurrying as he could to the bed, laying her gently down. Lark's eyes were open, but her face was ghastly white. Her fingers gripped at Gharain's shirt. He did not let her go but kneeled on the bed and pulled her close. Ilone was moving, coming to lean over Lark, placing her hands on Lark's sweat-beaded forehead. Rileg hopped onto the bed and nudged his nose into Lark's side.

Worry enraged Gharain. "Was it the Bog Hag? Did she do this?" He turned on the maidservant. "How did the Hag come, Nayla? Was it Trethe—did she conjure her?" But Nayla was silent, shaking her head, wringing her hands. Gharain barked, *"Speak!"*

Ilone shushed him, but Nayla burst out, "'Twas not the Bog Hag, Master Gharain. She had no reason to do the queen ill."

"Why was that thing here, then?" And Nayla could only shake her head.

"Shall I find the creature?" asked the Rider standing near Ilone, and Gharain shouted, "Yes!" He was beside himself in fear and fury, but I saw his hands soft in Lark's hair.

The other Rider leaned to Ilone and placed a kiss on her cheek. "I'll leave now," he said. But Ilone gripped his sleeve. "Dartegn, wait. There's no need." She looked up at Gharain. "'Tis not the Hag, brother. Look." Ilone pulled Lark a little onto her side, then undid the lacing of her gown and tugged it off her shoulders. Nayla cried out. The left shoulder was rashed red. I knew what it was. The wound she suffered made by the hukon—'twas inflamed; the poison at work once more. Ilone slid the sleeve a little lower, and there it was—the small pin-prick made by the hukon spear—a black spot just above the circle of her birthmark. Already it oozed green-gray pus.

"Breeders." I didn't see who whispered it. Maybe it was only in my own head. But 'twas what we all singly understood.

Ilone turned to Nayla. "Please get Trethe." And Nayla hurried from the room while Ilone looked at Gharain and Dartegn. "The books of Fate," she said. "I could not stop Lark from looking. 'Tis why she summoned the Bog Hag for help. She saw Laurent and Evie dying, the amulet lost. She made the Hag bring Evie some tokens so that they could survive. That we all could."

Gharain and Dartegn's faces were terrible. I felt as dark as they—and yet I could only brace as Ilone braced as she admitted, "She broke the loan. She altered fate."

There was an ominous murmur in the room, then Gharain gritted, "*Whose* fate?"

"'Twas Evie's book she opened." Ilone grabbed Gharain's shoulder as he made a sharp move. "You cannot be angry, brother. Lark was only saving us by doing so. Her cousin had crafted a spell."

"What of it? Spells are done every day!"

"Evie is not a White Healer, the spell was not hers to make. It exposed her to the Breeders." She tugged at Gharain, forcing him to turn from Lark, rushing a little to keep his focus. "Why do you think the swifts attack us now? They've kept us inside these walls for a day—and will continue if they can. The Breeders are keeping us occupied, keeping us from interfering as they track the Guardian!"

Nayla was back in the room, a rail-thin elderly woman following. Gharain yanked from Ilone, growling, "What is this, Trethe?"

His temper did not cow the old woman; she approached with head high, declaring, "Yes, I brought forth the Bog Hag, at the queen's insistence. We bound the miserable thing to a task. There was no harm done; the queen has that right—"

"*Look* at her!" Gharain shouted.

"That is not the Hag's doing," Trethe returned evenly.

"Who then? What can we do?"

"Gharain," Ilone broke in, "Lark insisted the consequences were to be hers. She made herself vulnerable." She looked at Trethe, who nodded. "The Breeders have opportunity now—they are reaching through her wound." She paused, then, knowing what would come. "Since Lark already returned her amulet, she *chose* to sacrifice in hopes she might save the Guardian and Laurent—"

"Don't!" Gharain was fierce. "Don't say it! It will not happen! You will do something, Ilone. You are my sister, her friend. You are a *Healer*. And you, old one," he cried to Trethe. "You have the skill. You will make her well." His gaze flicked between the two, then he begged. "You have to."

Ilone said, "Gharain, we cannot cure hukon. No one—"

"*Don't!*" 'Twas brutal, his voice. Even Dartegn shifted a

little to shield Ilone. "Go! All of you! Go away!" Most in the room whispered off while Gharain pulled Lark up and hugged her close to his heart.

Trethe remained very calm. "We can keep the queen from slipping, Master Gharain. Ilone and I together." She moved forward, took Lark out from Gharain's arms, rested her gently back on the bed, saying, "You must trust that we will do everything we can. We'll not let her die."

She wouldn't. Whoever this Trethe woman was, she and Ilone would work as deftly as Grandmama and I had when Lark returned to us first wounded. They'd taken our role as Lark's family. They would protect their queen better than I had my cousin.

"Let us look in the books," Dartegn was saying. "Let us get back the amulets, all of them together, *now* before—"

Ilone stopped him. "The books are vanished, all. They are"—she gestured at the window—"out beyond, somewhere. If they are in Harker's possession again, I do not know. But if not, then they are vulnerable to anyone who wants to manipulate the Guardians' fates." She turned. "And so all our fates."

Gharain slammed his fist against the wall. "*Damn* the books!" Then, in whispered anguish as he looked down at Lark, "Damn me."

I was pulled from the room, the castle, and night sky, sent reeling into harsh morning light, where Harker thrust his face close to mine. "This is what you've done!"

I put my hands against the ridge, trying to find something stable to hold, fighting to breathe. "I didn't know, Harker! 'Twas but a simple spell!" Devastation would drown me. "I didn't mean any harm!"

"Harm? My books are lost! Your cousin queen is poisoned!"

"No!" I was wild. "They will save her!"

"The Breeders have struck you where you are weak, little fool Guardian! If curiosity kills a cat, then so too will it kill everyone because of you!"

"Stop it! *Stop* it!"

But he didn't stop. The hideous little man was writhing in his strange mix of anger and glee. "This is you! Your fault!"

I screamed, "Then I will fix it!"

Harker turned and limped off. "Tell me!" I pushed myself up and stumbled after him, refusing to be ignored. "*Tell* me how to fix this!" I grabbed at his filthy sleeve, taking both of us off balance. "I will not let my cousin die!"

"Hukon has no cure," he hissed back at me.

"I don't believe you! You hold people's fates; you know their futures! Surely you've seen one!"

"I do not know what happens, Guardian! How *would* I know, my books are lost!" He gave a pitiful whimper and pulled away from me. "My books. *My* books."

Lark was dying, the books were vanished, the amulets unlinked. I turned and stormed away, heart pounding. Behind me desolate sobs from Harker. My hands clenched against the noise. Against the pain—

I blurted with sudden force, "I will find your books, Harker. I will return them if you help me heal Lark."

The sobs cut away abruptly. "I cannot help you heal her—"

"*Harker!*"

"You do not *listen*, Guardian of Death!" And then he made me listen by waiting to speak. My fingernails scored my palms, his silence was worse than the crying. Finally the seer tilted his head. "*I* cannot help you, but there is a White Healer—"

I ran to him. "*Where?*"

As if he could doubt my determination: "Too far from where you are headed."

"That doesn't matter!"

"Not matter? What of your amulet? What of your handsome man?" And then coyly, "What of the *wounded* steed?"

I hesitated, then said fiercely, "I go alone."

Harker jumped a little, then came close to look me straight in the eye, to read my intention. "You will," he announced softly. "I see. 'Twill be your secret."

"Tell me where."

He stayed soft. "South to the sea, Guardian, to the last spit of land that curves sickle-shaped. You will know the White Healer." His hands stabbed out, cupped as if he was begging, eager now for me to hurry. I studied him back, eye to eye. And suddenly curious.

"Why do you help me, seer, when what I've done has made you miserable?"

The seer blinked. "Because you helped me once. Because you were kind."

I turned and ran down the ridge to gather my belongings. And then I heard him bleating piteously, as though he was sorry for saying it: "You were kind. You were kind!"

Laurent was still sleeping, but Arro's head was up, his passive eye clear and alert to my step. I stopped to watch, to hold the moment. The stand of dying trees was the same, the bird still sang alone. The sun had not moved more than a hand's width from the horizon. Nothing had changed.

Except for me. I'd changed. Not a fortnight ago I'd stood at the edge of Rood Marsh wondering what to do with the Rider and his horse—I'd not wanted companions, I'd wanted to die. Now I was standing here just as wrecked, heart ripped and guilt shredding every breath, only now I wanted to share. I wanted to *live*. I shut my eyes. Hard. If I could just recapture the beauty and peace of last night, nestle myself safe within . . .

A moment, 'twas all. I opened my eyes and looked down at what I held in one fist: valerian—roots and all—and a cinder stone. There was no question what I was going to do; I just wished that it did not have to be so.

I went to the edge of the trees and built a tiny campfire. Dead leaves flamed bright and quick, and in short time I was boiling water inside of Laurent's small cup. I drank the first hot cup myself, breaking off a piece of Laurent's hardbread as a meal. Then I set to boiling the second cup, crushing the valerian roots to steep in it. I smothered the fire and carried the drink back under the trees.

"Arro looks better." Laurent was awake, sitting up stiffly.

I nodded. "And you look in pain."

He grinned. "Last night took its toll."

There was mischief in his tone; I tried to match his grin as I handed him the cup. "Well, then. This will help." It wasn't quite a lie.

"You should not have looked for water without me," he chided. Then, at its heat, a double exasperation: "No *fires, Evie.*"

"It's done. The fire is out."

He took a swig of the tea, made a face. "You cannot be serious."

"I am, Rider." I walked to Arro, unwilling now to meet Laurent's eye, wishing he'd just swallow the brew in one quick gulp. "You have your balm, we Healers have our roots. It will ease the pain."

"Balm at least tastes good."

"'Tis not sweets I make." *Sound light. Be easy.* "Drink it. You can rinse your mouth after."

Laurent snorted. Pain or not, he was relaxed, in a merry mood, and I ached to share it. Instead, I cleaned Arro's wound with unnecessary detail, waiting for the Rider to finish.

"The spring is close?" he asked, wanting to talk.

"Just over the ridge."

"I wish you'd wakened me."

"Your sleep was beautiful," I said, being very busy. "I couldn't disturb it." Finally, from the corner of my eye I saw him drain the cup, then set it on the ground. The cloth stilled in my hands. I exhaled slowly. These were the last moments the Rider would trust me.

"Evie," he was saying, "by now you should know better than to go off alone."

"I was not alone." I pulled myself together, wiped the last bit of dried blood from the stitches, and put the cloth down. I didn't have to avoid any longer. The valerian was finished two breaths ago; Laurent had perhaps twenty more before he sank. "The seer, Harker, was there."

"*Harker.*" The merry mood was gone. "Has he followed you?"

I shook my head. "He won't." Then I turned to the Rider. "You told me the seer showed the Breeders something he shouldn't have. What is the story of Harker and his books?"

A shrug. "Harker is one of seven sentinels who are responsible for the books of Fate. Every person's story is in their keeping. They are sworn never to share the books, so that no one can manipulate outcome by learning of something before it happens." Laurent paused to swallow against the sour aftertaste. "But Harker was seduced by a Breeder; he betrayed his post, allowed a book to be read, and so the amulets were stolen. As recompense, the books of the four Guardians were loaned to Castle Tarnec."

"Loaned, but not allowed to be opened?"

"Only the first page of each." He rubbed the back of his neck. "Call it the gift of a shortcut. We lost the amulets because of the seer, so in turn we may use the clues provided in the beginning of each book to find the Guardians. It gives us an advantage over the Breeders, small as it may be."

Five breaths, at least, he'd taken. "Lark disobeyed the agreement," I said. "The seer told me."

Laurent hesitated. "You should not trust him."

"Perhaps not, but you trust me." I could barely say it.

A sixth breath. A harsh one. "Then the books are relinquished." He shook his head.

I asked, "Are they destroyed?"

"No." Another shake of the head. He was trying to clear it. "If they were destroyed you would never have existed." He squinted at me. "But pages that are not yet set, not yet lived, could be burned or ripped out. And then the person whose fate they hold would die."

Lark and I were both alive, which meant the books were somewhere—but unprotected. What time did we have left? "The Breeders have used Lark's act to reopen her wound," I said. "The hukon is infecting her again."

"Breeders," Laurent echoed a little dully. " 'Twas the queen's choice that let them in. Our last queen did something of the same. . . ." He sat for a moment, pondering. "Why would she disobey?"

"For me," I said. "I asked for her help. She gave me things to save you." And much more, I realized.

The Rider stared. His reactions were slowing, comprehension fuzzing. What did it matter, then, what I told him?

"The knife," I murmured. "And the minion. She sent them. At Hooded Falls."

"The queen shouldn't have done it." Laurent struggled to focus. "She should have let me be."

"Would you say that if what she did saved me?" I asked softly. I saw him frown, try to work out his thoughts. I said, "Lark helped me—for all of us. Now it is my turn to help her."

His eyes flared briefly, understanding. "You are not going to Tarnec. . . ." Then he said sharply, "The amulet—"

"Will be returned after I find a cure for the hukon."

"Evie."

"Do not say there is no cure. There is something—there *must* be something. I will not let her die because of me. I *cannot*."

Laurent's eyes flicked to Arro. He stood shakily. "Then we go."

"Arro would not survive the journey; you know it. I will not let you sacrifice him anymore than I will let Lark sacrifice herself. Not for me."

"None—nonetheless, Evie . . ." Laurent was staggering, trying to reach for his sword. "I will go. Regardless of sacrifice."

I said it softly: "I disagree."

Laurent looked at his hands; they'd fallen limply to his sides. He looked at me. "What did you do?" His knees gave out; he dropped hard to the ground, all the while staring at me. "What did you do?"

"It is but for sleep. Just sleep." Our last moments. My voice burned my throat. "When you wake tomorrow wait a second day and then Arro will be strong enough to walk. Go home to Tarnec. Watch for me. I will come."

"Harker . . ."

I thought, then, that Laurent would show anger, vague as it might be. That he'd insist I not be foolish enough to trust the seer. But there was none of that.

"I will find you, Evie," he said. "Know that I will find you."

I shook my head. I'd been careful to give no clue. "No, but you will try. After all, you are my Complement," I whispered.

"Complement." And then it was done, Laurent fell on his side, Arro neighing in warning, and I ran to the Rider, held his head, kissed his face. Longing flared, hot and bright. "I'm sorry," I murmured against his lips. "I'm sorry. 'Twill be all right, 'twill just take a little longer. But Lark and Arro will be safe."

I smoothed the curls back from Laurent's brow, laid his cloak over him, washed out the cup, and arranged his pack to be at the ready—an apology of sorts. I stroked Arro's neck to calm him. I pulled on my frock and my sandals, then took my own satchel and looked at what remained inside—the lark feather and the shell. One meager, one huge. I picked up my cloak, which had acted as our bed. It was ripped and worn but it was still worth the cover . . . and more so the memory. Then I went back and took Laurent's cup. He had the flask and I had nothing.

But I left him the leather ring, pulling it from my thumb and sliding it on the little finger of his left hand. Proof I would return.

I stood. South to the sea, Harker had said. I looked at Arro, who eyed me reproachfully. "I'll not fail you," I told him, then walked away.

That Laurent would try to follow me I had no doubt. But he had a horse he could not ride and I had a full day's head start.

20

I COULD SMELL the sea. Even a league away, the scent came creeping up. Salt and tin and earth decay . . . and something more, something fresh and cold and dark and alive.

Tales were told at market of the incessant sweep and drowning of tides, of rowboats standing nearly on end against a crest of wave, of finned beasts the girth of a cottage—tales that were meant to awe and leave giddy with imagined horrors.

But I held no such fear. The closer I came, the more I hurried to see it. The hills flattened, trees gave way to grass, then marsh grass, and then wide salt flats, where I took off my sandals so my feet could slap along the silver-dried mud, where little holes and bubbles exposed secret hiding places.

'Twas good that some creatures lived under mud. They survived, at least. All along my four-day journey were remnants of things killed by a heartless sun. The landscape was dry, the ground hard underfoot. I hadn't seen fresh water since the last moonrise.

The flats shivered to a dust, then dust turned to sand—white and fine and scrubbing away the silver from between my toes. A sharp clean smell; when I looked close I saw little bits of shell, not unlike mine, crushed into the sand.

But then all those thoughts were erased in one sweep, for the sea appeared just over a dune. I sank to my knees in the wispy grass and stared. Stared at the froth and foam curling into shore, stared at the blue-gray swells heaving all the way to the horizon—the way a blanket is shaken before it is folded. I'd never seen anything so extraordinary as that blue color, never breathed anything so extraordinary as salt air. It made my body hum.

The sand ran west to a tall rock outcropping that jutted far into the sea, blocking that side of my view, but to the east it stretched on seemingly forever—a thin, curved trailing of sand. And all of it was empty. I should have been disappointed, impatient at least, that I saw no village, no person, that the White Healer was not there waiting for me. But I was near; I had to be. And the sea was captivating. For a moment—if just for a moment—I had to feel what that water was like.

I jumped up and ran down to explore—to dip my feet into the crisp cold, to splash. It was different, heavier than fresh water. The salt dried quick and white-rough on my legs by the breeze, and I laughed.

I ran back up the beach, pulled off the cloak and frock, dropped them with my sandals and pack, then ran straight back into the sea, shrieking with delight. Chest-deep I waited for a wave, gasping at its size, hugging my arms close. It cocooned, then crashed over me.

So alive, the sea! It was all the waters: running and still. Incessant motion, silent depths—'twould both clean away ills and keep them. It buoyed, tossed, and teased with its surf. I swam quick strokes, skin tingling from the minerals—I could sense them too in the sea's weight, in the smell. My hair slipped like silk over my arms, down my back, billowed out pale against the blue. Glorious sea, glorious release. *Water is Death's medium,* Lark had said. My medium.

Release was brief. I swam for shore, slogged up the beach as the stiffening breeze dried my undershift solid and my hair in ropes. Then I stopped and squinted. Far off on the sands a person stooped, rummaging through my things. It was a man I saw, wraith-thin. I'd expected a woman.

"White Healer!" I started to run. "White Healer!" Then I saw his hands at my pack. "No! Stop!" I cried. "You'll get hurt!"

The man stopped, looked up. His mouth worked and he pointed at me, but his voice did not carry. He turned and grabbed for the satchel.

"Do not touch it!" I yelled. "Stay back!"

An explosion of light and sound. Sand flew, stinging my eyes and lips. There was nothing to wipe it away with, for my fingers and shift were coated with salt. I stumbled up the beach, rooted blindly for my frock, cloak, anything to help, then sat, spitting and scouring the sand from my face. Then I grabbed for the satchel to check that the amulet was unharmed. I looked around. There was no one—no one tossed, or cowering . . . or dead. I scanned the rock outcropping. 'Twas the only thing the man could have disappeared to. He must have sprinted in terror.

I sighed. No White Healer, just a starved man scavenging for food, of which I'd none. But I looked at the outcropping again, thinking there was some flicker of movement. I tugged on my dress and sandals, shouldered my satchel, and tied my cloak, then trudged toward the rocks. I faced into the wind, which blew stronger now. The salt made my skin itch.

I was wrong: 'twas not the man huddled in the shadows there, but a child. A scrawny, dark-haired girl, dressed in rags. Her face was pressed hard into the rock. I kneeled down, already sensing it: poison of some sort. The girl burned with fever.

I turned her gently. She wasn't more than five years, pale, eyelids fluttering, her stomach gruesomely distended. I felt for the pulse in her limp wrist—rapid and light. Then I shifted around my satchel so that it hung over my back and picked up the girl. This needed curing beyond what my hands offered.

She was fragile, nearly weightless. I climbed up the outcropping carefully to avoid her limbs brushing the satchel. We gained the top, then started down the other side—

A village spread below us at the edge of the tide. The remains of one anyway. The cottages were all gone except for a scattering of walls and door frames jutting from mounds of sand. Whatever had destroyed the town was done and done quickly. But 'twas not from any incinerators. There were no signs of fire, no burned-out carcasses of homes. No soldiers.

There were signs of life, however: lean-tos made from rubble, makeshift doors from blankets. A thin line of smoke trickled skyward. None of it looked hopeful.

The girl in my arms twitched, propelling me down the face of rock.

"Hello!" I cried, nearing the first curtain of blankets. "Hello?"

Movement. Draped covers pulled back, folk stepping from underneath. Dark-haired, pale and freckled skin pulled taut over heavy features, clothing filthy and threadbare. Adults, all, except for one boy who was barely seven. They offered stares for welcome.

"This child. Is she one of yours?" I held out the limp girl for all to see, though they looked only at me. "Please, is she yours? Anyone?"

There was a general uneasy shuffling. Finally one woman jerked forward, almost tearing the little thing from my arms before pulling back. "Mine," she mumbled.

Mine—like Harker and his books. I followed her. "Your daughter's ill. She's eaten something bad."

"Nothing to be done."

"Let me try." I looked around for any kind of support from the crowd. Traumatized, maybe from the loss of their dwellings or their obvious hunger, they stared mutely back. I turned to the mother more firmly: "*Please*. I can help."

There was silence, but then the boy offered, "Duni was at the 'stools up by the riverbed."

"Toadstools," grunted an old woman. "That's the end of it.

Put her down at the water's edge. Let the sea take her out. That'll keep *them* satisfied." Duni's mother nodded and headed off.

"Wait!" I yelled. The mother froze briefly, but then walked on. I had to run to catch up with her, already splashing to where the waves foamed. "What are you doing?" I grabbed her arm, pulled her back with me. "Your daughter can be healed!" I called to the crowd, "We have to move quickly!" Then I lost patience beneath their dull stares and demanded from the boy: "What color toadstool? Brown or yellow or red?" I hoped he didn't choose red.

"Yellow," he answered.

"There's time, then." I chose a face from the group. "*You.* Tell me if there is milkweed somewhere near." He nodded and I ordered: "Go and collect the fattest pods, four of them. *Hurry.*" He lurched away. "And *you.*" I picked the boy. "Where there's milkweed there will be the orange butterfly. I need you to catch one. Don't kill it. Just cup it in your hands and run back here."

He nodded but an older woman grabbed his shoulder. "Let him go," I snapped at her. "Or go yourself." I turned to another, gesturing at the trail of smoke. "I see a fire lit over there. We need fresh water at the boil." Then, at their hesitation, *"Now!"*

Two others stumbled. "Come with me," I said to Duni's mother, and marched off toward the smoke, thinking how silly it was that they all stood stupefied. As if the death of a child was standard and I the greater curiosity, as if mending ills was not something they understood.

And maybe it wasn't. They had no stores of food, let alone

herbs, and no effort made, it looked, to replenish. The small fire burned bare in what had been a kitchen hearth—chimney gone, walls gone, nothing repaired. I bit my tongue and directed the action—a pot for water, a blanket for a bed, building up the fire—urging people who seemed so reluctant to aid. They were hampered with disfigurements. Crooked limbs, scar tissue, things that might have been easily treated. Ailments of all kinds were left ignored—healing not even attempted.

Duni's mother laid the child on a blanket. I stuck the pot of water on the embers, asking: "What town is this?"

Finally someone muttered, "Haver. It was Haver."

Was. "What happened?"

A pause and then someone blurted, "The sea witches took it from us."

"Sea witches?"

"Come up in a big wave three moons ago. They took our homes; they took the rain. They ruin us."

I turned to look at them. *Witch* rang false in my ears. A blame word when something was not understood. I wondered if they'd heard of Breeders.

"I am sorry for your suffering," I said instead. No one replied.

The man was back, suddenly, handing me four plump milkweed pods, and shortly after came the boy, with his hands cupping a large butterfly. I asked for a container; a chipped cup was produced. I had the boy open his hands on the ground and turned the cup upside down on the sand, trapping the insect. I begged another cup, then remembered I still had Laurent's.

I took it out, split the pods, squeezed the milk into it, and added some of the boiled water.

"Prop the girl up," I directed. "Open her mouth." There was hesitation, but I said fiercely, "*Do* it. Time grows short." And then I dribbled the hot drink between the girl's lips. She started and gagged, and the attendees watched in eerie silence. I said, "The milkweed will expel the poison. Keep her upright."

I was effortlessly capable—scrutinized for it, I knew. I dribbled more until the cup's worth was gone, then used the boiling water to wipe Duni's fingers clean of any residue of toadstool and had them turn her on her side. Moments later she began to heave and retch, bringing up the bits of yellowed cap and stem. Duni sobbed, the mother moaned—more from fear than worry, I thought. Then all of the villagers joined in with the mother as they watched; a faint, discordant hum that wafted up and surrounded us.

"'Tis just a stomach's worth," I explained over the noise. "There's no lasting harm." I lifted the other cup, releasing the butterfly, and held it up to show. "Do you see the stain left by the butterfly's wings? 'Twill make her fever break." I poured more of the boiled water into the cup and swirled it; the water turned faintly orange. "Here," I said to Duni. "Drink this up." She whimpered, wasted and wide-eyed; the mother had a grip on the girl's arm that must have hurt. I smiled, cajoling, "Drink. 'Twill taste sweet. The butterfly has left you a bit of its magic."

The hum broke at that. I pushed the cup into Duni's hands in spite of her mother's grip, tipped it for her, and watched that she drank the whole thing down. There wasn't a sound—the villagers waited, riveted. The child dropped the cup, rubbed her brow, which was already sweat-beaded, and sat up a little straighter on her own. She even managed a tiny belch and a faint smile. Her mother snatched her up and moved away.

I pretended not to mind and turned to the villagers. "I am looking for the White Healer who lives somewhere near. Do you know of her?" I waited, heart sinking. "None of you? Is there another village nearby?" No answer. The wind blew sturdy, hollow-dry. I glanced at the sky and judged how soon nightfall, then how weary I was, and then turned back. "I am a Healer. I'll teach you the uses of any plants that grow nearby, in return for a place to sleep tonight and a share of your food."

There was absolute silence, flat stares. Finally one spoke: "Wait here."

They walked as a group down to the water's edge, the adults and two children, huddled in conversation as twilight cast the sky the same color as the sea. I looked around at the ruined village. It might have been pretty once, nestled close to the shore. They must have had boats too, but most likely were dashed to bits by that wave. I felt sorry for them. To rebuild from scratch would be a tremendous challenge, with their tools, materials, and even will all gone.

I looked back at the darkening water beyond the clump of villagers. Why would this take so long? When had any in Merith needed to discuss offering hospitality or the worthiness of a traveler? I wiped my brow, reshouldered my satchel, wanting to sit, to sleep. My hair chafed like straw against my neck, my skin scratched from all the salt. I wondered if it would be too much to ask for more water to wash with. And then I thought of Laurent and Arro, and of the pool of water where I met Harker, and whether he led me wrong as Laurent always assumed.

My mind was wandering, dejection creeping in. No sign of the White Healer, nothing accomplished yet by leaving the Rider and the path to Tarnec. I brushed my hands on my frock. So grim, these days, these months. The need to curl away, to shut out the dark of it all, swelled inside. Laurent had said if I saved the shell, I'd save so many . . . I'd saved one. One small girl. How misguided that her mother—the entire village—would have left it to fate that she recover or not.

There it was: Fate. I shut my eyes tightly for a moment, and then opened them. Fate was why I was here. Harker, the books, the forbidden reading, and Lark's wound reopened . . . All for me. All a loss unless I did something.

I turned. I would not stay the night in this village. Of course these sad people did not know any White Healer, or they'd not be so frightened of a simple stomach remedy. Harker had said south to the sea—and here I stood on that last spit of sickle-curved sand he'd described. I was annoyed with myself then, worried that time was wasting and that I did not know which direction.

I tied my cloak around my neck and started toward the villagers to bid them goodbye. They were no longer huddled but strung in a line like uneven fence posts, holding hands and silently watching the water—the taller adults, the smallish boy. How dull their ragged clothing, all the shades of black, gray, and brown, how opposite the colors of sand and sea. Like a barrier. Like protection. Warding against those sea witches—

I gagged, horror-struck, began to run. "No! *NO!* What have you DONE?" Laurent's words to me, a thousand times more ghastly. The figures were turning at my screaming, opening that barrier so I could see. "*No. No. No . . .*" Waves rolling in to shore, beyond which a small dark head was sinking. "*NO!*"

I shoved right through them, tore into the water, leaping over the surf, splashing headlong—but I was yanked back, hands grabbing, hooking my arms, dragging me up the beach and throwing me facedown onto the wet sand. I lunged up, screaming, tried to crawl between their legs. "Stop! Let me save her!" The villagers crowded in front of me—a wall. I clawed at them, scrambled up, trying to force my way between unyielding bodies. "You put her in to drown! You've killed her! She was *safe*—!"

A hard slap across my cheek shut me up. I fell to my knees, stunned. I'd never been hit before. It burned like fire.

"She's one. She's one of 'em! A sea witch!"

I spit some blood onto the sand and mumbled, "I am no witch." But it was lost in the gasps of fear and excitement at such a title. I looked up and around at the small crowd, recognizing the one who hit me, who accused. It was the scrawny, long-jawed fellow from the beach. The one who'd tried to open my pack. His finger stabbed the air, accusing. I pushed myself up; the crowd shuffled back. "No witch," I gritted, louder. "You lie." But the man yelled over me, "I saw her come out of the sea! Look at her!"

"I was *swimming*—my clothes were on shore. You were picking through them!"

"Clothes?" he cried. "Those things were all magicked!"

"What magic?" I thrust at the crowd again, trying to break through. They caught my arms and held me back from the tide, then pulled me around to the needle-faced accuser. I twisted back, eyes raking the waves—nothing but a swirl of foam— then screamed at them, "Why did you kill her? She was healed! She was *healed*—!" I had no breath left.

The man sneered while I panted. "Look at the witch: straight from the sea. Can't breathe the air. She's drying out." He reached forward and lifted a salt-crusted chunk of my hair, singing, "Sea witch."

I yanked back from him. "I'm not!" I tossed my hair over my shoulder away from him, looking down as I did so and see- ing that the fine coating of salt shone white. Hair and skin . . . fairly shimmering, powdery dry, as if turning to dust. I spit out the last of the blood in my mouth, thinking fast. I had to get away from these people. I could prove nothing. Already it was picked up as a chant: *"Sea witch. Sea witch. Sea witch."*

It came to my head suddenly: Raif's silly childhood trick. I pulled around toward the sea with a horrified gasp and shouted in warning, "Look out! They're coming!" The villagers all turned—'twas quick, but their grip on my arms relaxed and I wrenched from them, running for the only place I could think of: the rock outcropping.

"Take her!" They were on me fast, like the reaping hounds. I reached the rocks, climbing quick; one of them had fingers on my cloak, trying to tug me down. I jerked it away and whipped around, my back pressed against the rock, the satchel caught between. I tugged it to the front; thrust it out. "*Stay back!* This will hurt you!"

The needle-faced man shrieked, "See? Magicked!" But he hesitated.

"Foolish man!" I yelled at him, at all of them. "You know nothing!" With the satchel still lifted, threatening, I reached for a handhold on the rock and heaved myself up backward. They watched as I grabbed for the rock again. Another step, and another, gaining height. Finally I was far enough that I could turn away, scramble faster. I could outrun these people. I *would* outrun them. There were grunts that I was escaping, and I thought, *I am! I am!*

But then the first stone smacked against my head.

"*Ahh—!*" Reeling, I cringed, then yelled, "Don't! *Please!* Just let me go." A second stone knocked my shoulder, stealing my grip. I grabbed wildly for the rocks and looked back, stunned.

All the villagers held stones, but I seemed to focus only on one hand—the one scratching the next little weapon from out of the sand and lifting to aim—the hand of the boy who'd brought me the butterfly.

And then I was pleading, "*Why?*"

And then the boy's hand was empty.

And then nothing.

21

THE LIGHT WAS gray. My mouth swollen, and sticky-dry. I still had my pack.

Those things occurred to me before the rest: that I was bound hand and foot and lying on hardened sand, that my forehead was tender, my hair caked with blood, that thirst and hunger gnawed sharp. That I'd been struck by a child.

Full-on madness. Chaos catching hold. Or maybe this village was already one of those Breeder bastions that Laurent implied were among us always—gnawing away at reason, gnawing away our souls. I thought of Lill, of her abandoning me on the other side of the bridge to Gren Fort, of her wanting to push me off Hooded Falls. And then I couldn't think on any of this.

I rolled gingerly to my other side. I kicked my feet up behind, trying to reach them to my hands, get my fingers to the knots. The binds were tightly woven, sharp-edged sea grass; my fingers bled without making headway. All the while the gray light paled. 'Twas dawn, the sun creeping up. If the villagers had left me for the night, then I hadn't much time before they came back.

Damn the sea grass! Like blades they sliced into my wrists and ankles and fingertips and yet nothing would give. I was still worrying at it, fighting the bonds—stretching, scraping, fumbling, even—when two of the village men came for me, lifted the flap of blanket I'd been tossed under, and pulled me out into the morning.

I fought them. Hard. I think, even, I hoped to hurt. I was dragged over the sand, kicking and punching, over what must once have been a path between cottages, and propped up against half a wall. The two men pinned my shoulders back to keep me upright while the rest of the group shuffled over to watch.

There was some surprise. "She survives out of water!" was the general murmur. "How?" "Her fishtail has not grown back!"

"I am no witch; I have no tail!" I gritted. "Do you see my hair? My head? 'Tis *red* blood. I am no different from you!"

"Hush your mouth, fiend!"

That was shouted from the needle-faced man who'd first accused me. He pushed himself front and center. "We've caught a sea witch!" he proclaimed to the others. "We have advantage at last! We'll throw her back trussed—an accepted trade, else her sea sisters let her drown for their fear of us, of what we can do to them! There will be no more waves; the rains will come and fill our cisterns. Haver shall be free of their plague!"

"You kill an innocent!" I hissed. "Like you killed Duni! No good comes of that!"

"Quiet! You have no voice here, witch!"

"*Healer!*"

It was a useless term; it fell on deaf ears. I searched the eyes, the faces of this gathering. *Gathering?* This was hardly a communal debate. "Where are your elders?" I demanded. "Let me speak to them. Let me be understood!"

"I am your elder," the needle-faced man said. "I judge."

"What sort of judgment is a single opinion?" I shouted. "What sort of trial when I am already damned?"

"Trial?" He echoed as if he did not understand the word. "You rose from the sea, dripping water and seaweed. Your claim of swimming is proof itself. We on land cannot swim without a rope to guide us home! Where is your rope?"

"And if I say I need no rope, you will say 'tis because I am a witch." I looked around at all the haggard, tight faces, my own flushed hot with anger. "I am not from here, true enough, but I only meant to help! What harm was there in healing a child? Asking to share a meal?"

"You are crafty in your speak. You do not fool us!" The man pointed at my pack. "What do you keep in there that causes explosion?"

"Beyond your concern, what I keep," I said recklessly.

One of the men holding my shoulders had no patience for belligerence. He grabbed for my satchel, stuffed his hand in, and was immediately flung back in a brilliant flash of white and thunderous *crack*. It did not harm me, but the man was prostate, the crowd cowering and crying out in fear.

The needle-faced man was the first to return. He shuffled forward, snarling, "We *will* know what is in your pack." He gestured to another one of the men. "Cut her wrists loose."

The man hesitated at coming close, but did what was ordered, taking out a blade fashioned from a long thin shell, and yanking my arms far from the satchel before sawing through the binds.

The needle-faced man kicked at my skirts. *"Show us."*

Stiffly, I tugged the shoulder strap over my head, then dug into the pack while the others shuffled back. I took out the shell and held it up for all to see.

Shell. A collective gasp. Even I recognized how wrong this looked. I jerked my arm back, pushed the shell into the satchel. But before I could even tie it closed, hands gripped me and dragged me out of reach.

"Sea witch." The needle-faced man turned on me. "We take you back!" A cry went up.

I twisted, trying to shrug them off. "Fools! All of you! Don't do this!"

"To the sea!" the man crowed, and the group roared in approval.

"Hear me!" I managed to yank one arm free and lurched toward the stupid man, spitting threats before they caught me again: " 'Twill be *very* bad for you if you do not let me go!"

"Oh, we let you go, *witch*," he spit back. "We return you to the sea, but no more will you be able to leave it." The man called out some names and a few villagers came forward, hauling something between them. It was another roping of sea grass, this one thick and sturdy. Bound into the rope were stones—all large, all heavy.

"Don't!" I cried. But I was one against many. I was forced to my feet, wrapped in that weighted cord—over shoulders, neck, around my waist, hips, and thighs. And then I was tipped over, lifted, and marched down to the sea. "Don't! *Don't!*" I kept yelling, thoughts swirling. 'Twas insane. It could not be that all would end here, Lark unsaved, the amulet—

The *amulet*! It was back in the ruined village in that piled sand, abandoned. I fought, bucked against their hold but could not break free. They were wading now, and I was screaming, pleading for them to stop. Knees, thighs, waist . . . all the way to the neck—most of the crowd had dropped away, all but for the tallest of them, their arms raised straight above their heads so they could, on a collective *"Heave!"* throw me far into the sea.

I had one deep breath before the gray-blue closed over my head. Instinct made me struggle; fear made me struggle. So did rage. I could not clear my head of the wrong of this; I could not accept my drowning the way the villagers of Merith accepted death, with dignity. I wrestled my binds—hands fast to my sides, my ankles trussed tightly—losing to the weight. They'd not taken me far; it wasn't even particularly deep, only impossible to return to the air. I battled on, frantic to swim up, to touch that glittering light of sky that wavered just out of reach.

There was nothing noble in this stupid, ignorant verdict; it simply could not happen.

And when breath was spent, I bit my lips together. My head shook violently, insides roiling from the fight, the refusal to let go . . . and the terror and fury that I would not be able to stop myself from letting go.

My lungs would burst. It was the death-clouding, I thought, that shimmer of something pale at the corner of my eye. But then another swish flicked by and another, and then I truly looked, my body finally ceasing its struggle. Figures were coming toward me. Nay, not coming, but swimming to me—sylphlike creatures, four, five, six of them. They neared, circled, then came close. My eyes were bulged, staring. Recognizing.

They were not beautiful, these things. Perhaps at distance their seaweed tresses and grace of swim could be imagined as beauty, but face to face these were hollowed, barnacled, deep-eyed things, horrible and needy, like the Hag that had surfaced inside the cave at Hooded Falls. They were *her* sisters: not witches, but Sea Hags. One of them stroked my hair that flowed out around me as if she liked its special color; another ducked down and with her long fingernails sliced through the sea grass around my ankles. Three others did the same with the rope—razor nails that made their fingers look like the claws of the hermit crabs that sometimes crept along the edge of Dark Wood. My mind was swirling to these odd thoughts, fuzzing away. The Sea Hag who'd petted at my hair now tugged it hard with those clawlike fingers, forcing me to focus.

"You must ask for help, Guardian," she said. "Go back."

The last of the rope was pulled away and I was pushed, propelled forward to the shore, until my toes then knees scraped the bottom. And they left me there to struggle up on all fours, choking and gagging. My lungs burned, my throat grated, but every breath was a privilege. And the Sea Hags flicked back into the depths as if they'd never existed.

I sat in the surf, shuddering, not wanting to return to this village, this strand, but even if I'd had the strength to swim around the rock outcropping, to land somewhere far from this wretched place, I still had to get the amulet. There was nothing to do but crawl, retching, back to the village.

Shouts came fast and furious. The villagers swarmed back, enraged that I was emerging, whole, alive—all proof that I was *other*, that I was a witch. And if the sea would not claim me, something else would. They were splashing into the shallows to grab me, drag me to some new torture.

"The shell," I rasped. "Let me take the shell."

They wanted no part of the amulet. I was carried up the beach, then thrown down by my satchel. "Pick it up!" they screamed, and poked me with pronged sticks until I fumbled the strap over my shoulder and felt the lump of shell inside the pouch. And then they yanked me up and dragged me on.

There was no debate, no protest. My arms were half wrenched from their sockets; my feet scraped raw across the sand. I barely noticed. Somewhere in my head there was a song repeating—a little nursery rhyme young Healers learned the first set of herbs by: *Alium for hands, mint for toes, but all defer as the minion grows.* . . .

Mint for toes—'twould heal my cuts. Minion would be best, though. And where did I leave the minion? *Oh* . . . Laurent.

The villagers of Haver had a second plan ready in case the sea spit me out. A long timber from one of their ruined cottages was sunk vertically into the sand; thatch and beams and chunks of driftwood all stacked around it. I didn't understand, it was simply an upended plank—the sort a bow pig might be roasted on for a feast. But they were dragging me up over the scavenged logs and brush, fixing me to this plank with another length of braided sea grass. And then recognition dawned and I panted, dull and disbelieving, "You cannot mean this."

"Stack the pyre!" someone yelled.

My eyes rolled, trying to catch a gaze, any gaze—there was Duni's mother, who killed her own daughter. There was the seven year'd boy, who'd thrown his stones. There was needle-faced man, who relished this sentence of death. 'Twas stupid to think I could mean anything to these people. All the townsfolk were contributing things to the pile while shouting victorious affirmations: "The sea refuses you, so shall you *burn*!"

"We destroy them together, the witch and her magic!"

"The sea will be tamed!"

"The rain will come!"

"We will reap the fruits of sacrifice!"

Sacrifice was personal. It was unselfish. "This is no sacrifice!" I tried to scream. "This is *butchery*!"

But they ignored me, a new vitality infusing their efforts, as if indeed slaughter were bringing them rewards already.

Sorrow of slaughter . . . another hint of rhyme floated through my mind. I watched, dazed, as they piled more remnants of their cottages around me. *Sorrow of slaughter* . . . where did that come from? Ah. The little verse, which proved me the Guardian of Death—the one who'd reclaim the amulet for Tarnec and help restore Balance. Was this what those words had also presaged? That Lark would fall, the shell be abandoned, and Chaos unleashed. Innocents slaughtered, including me. Except . . . was I innocent? Was this because of what I'd done?

Sorrow. I should weep for it all.

My head was spinning, but now from something beyond exhaustion, beyond pain. Some little noise was boring into my head and befuddling everything. Thoughts were splintering into incomprehensible fragments, memories and nightmares—

I am chasing Lark through Krem Poss's lavender fields. Her brown hair flies like the wings of the bird she was named for, her laughter filters back through the waves of rich purple, and the perfume wafts lush and soothing. I am tying blue ribbons on our booth at market day. The soaps and balms are so prettily displayed on the white-clothed table—the rose glycerin, the hyssop and wood aloe. Quin is waving to me, piping a little tune on his flute; Cath is dancing behind. There is Grandmama at the door of our warm cottage. She cries: "Evie! Evie! Where are you?" And I realize I am gone. And then all the sweet things are disappearing and there is no more lavender, no more ribbons or song, but a bleak waste of land—a place where no rain refreshes the colors. There is no color.

The noise swelled and I gnashed my teeth at it, groaning. *Swifts*—after two attacks I recognized their mind-bursting shrill; they were coming and I could do nothing to evade it. Instead, I ground the back of my head against the post and watched in some disconnected, agonizing dream as the villagers attacked the pile of debris with flints, igniting the thatch. Flames licked fast, surrounded. A circle tightening, collapsing in upon itself. How much I wished for the cool of night, of water. How much I needed to tear the noise from my skull! I heard a last shattering scream. Mine.

But maybe not—heads were turning to the sky, bodies sinking in terrified helplessness. Specks of black against the harsh sun were growing larger, incessant, insane noise filling the space. And in a rush came the swifts.

The first one dove straight for the needle-faced man, who'd shaken from his surprise and was running—they all were running now. 'Twas their screaming. There was an explosion—bright, hot, vicious. And then I was hysterically laughing, while the villagers scattered and the swifts shrieked. Black upon black: wing against rough cloth, against dark hair. Panic for all . . .

But breaking a Healer's mind.

Swift-bred terror and sorrow of slaughter . . . I was alone—dying Healer, dying Guardian, crowned with silver hair and clothed in fading turquoise—inside a ring of fire in the center of a collapsed town. Smoke stung my eyes and warped the shapes of all the villagers 'til I thought they were the Troths and we were back in Merith on that ugly day, when Raif was dead and Laurent caught my stare. When everything ended and everything began.

Laurent! I imagined him in the haze, seated on the glossy back of Arro, healed and whole and sword wielding once more. "No, don't!" I was crying, not wanting rescue—then oh so desperately wanting it. "Come back! Come back!"

It was Laurent, wasn't it? There—whatever that whorl of smoke was? Whatever was creating that violent wind that seemed to whisk everything away—sweeping all the brutality under the sand, burying it deep.

So that I could burn alone like a splash of color—a drop of water.

There . . . and gone.

22

DAPPLED SUNLIGHT. WISP of breeze. The faint scent of oat bread fresh from the hearth. My attic bedroom in Merith—the way the light played through the window, and how the heat and smells of the kitchen warmed through the floorboards.

Home. My heart leaped with relief. Then somewhere I remembered that I'd left home, that home was in another place. The thought drifted, ethereal and fleeting, before I sank deeper into slumber.

A change of time. Warm glow of candlelight, scent of a chicken stew. *Thyme,* I murmured. *Bay.* A favorite supper: oat bread and stew. *A celebration of my return. Grandmama and Lark are downstairs.* And yet they shouldn't be. . . .

Night and day and another night. Or perhaps 'twas only a moment, for time held no bearing. I felt the faint warmth of candlelight again, smelled the fresh oat bread. . . .

This time my eyes cracked open, then widened. This was not my attic room, nor the cottage in Merith, yet it was a similar pretty space under eaves, an alcove of whitewashed plaster. I nestled under a sun-bleached quilt smelling of lemon balm—the same herb that Grandmama folded into our linens. A curtain of similar cloth acted as a screen. There was a glass vial holding a snip of goldenrod on the crossbeam above my head. A lit candle sat next to it.

Sweet scents, soft bed. To sleep and drift forever in such gentle comfort . . . I snuggled deeper under the cover. As my eyes closed I caught a glimpse of turquoise—my cloak and frock hung in the corner on a black coatrack. They were filthy, completely out of place. I blinked, saw my hands curled over the sheets, saw that I too was filthy—my hair was straw, my undershift stank of smoke, my fingernails shredded.

The last things remembered: drought, smoke, noise, panic. This peace made no sense. I pushed off the sheets and stood on tender soles, wincing, a little dizzy. I reached for the curtain; firelight played on the other side of it and for a moment I hesitated. Then I yanked back the cloth.

A crackling fire, a wide hearth. An orange tabby cat curled up on the near side; a short, heavy-bellied elderly man perched on a stool at the far. The man was muttering to the burning logs, scratching the wisps of white hair that ringed a shiny bald scalp and plucking at the little beard on his chin.

He paused from his mumblings to say clearly: "You are quite safe here."

I stared at him, then around, gave a little shudder of release. The fire was warm, the floorboards worn smooth, the furniture of familiar comfort—

"I expect two things," the old man continued. His voice was a little blustery but cheerful. He reminded me of Perdy Ginnis back in Merith. "I expect you would like to wash, and that you are famished."

Those were true. I took a step into the room. "There are two things that I expect as well." My voice was so very raw. "I expect you will tell me who you are and how I got here."

A chuckle. "A curious one, aren't you? Most people would be content with a meal."

"If you saved me then I must thank you by name." It was still hard to breathe, hard to think. "I want to know what happened."

"Ah." He stood up. He was no taller than I; the hem of his dusky purple robe brushed the floor. "Curiosity, my dear, killed the cat." He sighed at the tabby, who hissed back at him. "Nonetheless, the cat is still here." The old man turned to me then, eyes crinkling at what I think he supposed a joke. His eyes were dark and very piercing, but the crinkled edges gave him humor. He found humor in me, I thought. I looked back as straight as I could, given my wobbling stance.

"Have your wash first," he said. "There will be a meal ready for you when you are finished. I think Salva can have your garments all clean by then?" And then he wasn't looking at me, but at a stooped old woman who was darning a bright yellow stocking in the corner behind me. She laid aside her sewing, stood, and murmured shyly, with eyes downcast, "A bath, mistress."

When had I last seen a washcloth? I left the old man and followed the woman as docilely as a newborn chick. She had tucked her white hair in a bun, not unlike the way Grandmama wore it, though the rest of her was scrawny where Grandmama was sturdy. We went outside into a night sky, then across a short bit of grass to another building.

"An herb shed," I said, recognizing. 'Twas like the one we'd lost in Merith: a single room with a fireplace on one side, though instead of drying racks a tin tub was centered in the room. The tub was already filled with hot water—I was so grateful that I did not ask until later, when more steaming buckets were brought by two redheaded children who disappeared as quickly as they came: "Where is the water being drawn? There is a drought."

"Not to mind that, mistress. You are safe here," Salva murmured. It seemed she always murmured and ducked when speaking.

"And already warmed," I added.

To which she murmured again, "Not to mind that. You are safe."

The pleasure of being clean! That my hair was no longer the color of the ash, and the salt rinsed from my cuts—every curiosity paled to it, dissolved in the scent of milk soap. 'Twas only after, when I steeped in the still-hot bath waiting for Salva to return, that I began to study the walls of shelves—or what crowded the shelves: jars upon jars of things preserved. The print was too tiny to read from where I sat, and mostly they blurred in quantity, but certainly some were recognizable—the lily, orris, and pimpernel . . .

I felt a lurch of memory, a sudden thrill. I climbed out of the tub, wrapped the rough sheet around me, and wandered, dripping, to inspect closer. 'Twas all as I would have imagined Dame Gringer's shelves: the repeating tidy little rows, the labels all neatly inked. . . . I found myself grinning, gripping the sheet in excitement—

Salva was back with my undershift, all sparkling white and lemon-scented. "So quick!" I laughed, snatching it from her in my eagerness.

"Not to mind," the woman replied, looking down of course. But I didn't listen. I was dragging the shift over my head, mumbling thanks.

"I'll go back now," I said, and fairly ran to the door. But I stopped there just to check: "This enormous collection: it *is* his, isn't it?"

Salva ducked, nodding her head and murmuring. I turned and ran across the grass.

The old man was still near the hearth, but a crock of stew and a hunk of crusty oat bread were waiting for me at the chair next to him.

"Ah," he said. "Now I can see your face."

"And I see you," I said, breathless. "You are the White Healer. I've been searching for you!"

He looked deeply into my eyes again, the corners of his

own crinkling once more. "You have found me, then. Have your supper."

Night blurred into day, and what I remember was the relief of being safe and long-forfeited pleasures: favorite supper, bright hearth, sweet-smelling pillow, clean clothes and hair.

And then it was sunlight and I stood with the old man, surveying a little cluster of cottages that nestled close to each other. That it was a true village, I could not be entirely sure, there was no activity, so few dwellings, but they faced each other around a small square, surrounding a communal well. I drank in the picture like one parched. A scene—a way of life—that I'd thought was lost.

So tidy, so sweet! So like beloved Merith cottages, with the roof thatching evenly trimmed, the plastered exteriors newly whitewashed. There were neatly drawn gardens at the edge of each front doorstep. The White Healer's tabby was haunting someone's pretty grouping of peonies and delphs, my favorites. And if such early flowers were out of place at summer's end, it did not matter, for this was a White Healer's territory; magic was in play.

I wandered over to the common well centered in the middle of the square, perched on the sun-warmed edge like I used to at home, and squinted up at the sky. Too piercingly blue, so I dropped my gaze, looked down into the well, wondering if I could see a reflection of sunlight as I could in Merith, but it was far too deep. I brought my head level once more and sighed long. A smiling, red-cheeked woman stepped out of a doorway to sweep her entry stones. She looked vaguely familiar—it had to be the buttercup color of her apron. She waved at me and I waved back, thinking of silly Cath, and market day, and then more fleetingly of villages charred and smoking. Like a dark shadow, the memory whisked through—a sharp rending of this peace, but then blessedly gone. And, because it was so quickly gone, I put my hand to my heart, suddenly overwhelmed.

The White Healer was coming toward me. I said, "Your village—you've been spared by drought, spared from tragedy. There is color here, kindness." The words were thick in my throat. "I feel as if I've been in some dark dream for so long, and I've ached for this—this—"

"Innocence."

I choked as he said it. He'd taken the very word I couldn't seem to speak. I nodded, grateful, indebted for my rescue.

The old man held up a hand. "Not to mind the past," he said gently. "You are here. You are safe. When you are ready you may speak your needs."

This is my need, I thought. *This haven in the midst of chaos.*

Chaos. I jumped to my feet with a gasp. "I came to you. You have knowledge. . . ."

Questions sputtered then blurred, I couldn't make sense of what I was supposed to ask. There were things—desperate things that I'd somehow forgotten. When had everything gotten so muddy? I could feel the cold of dread tingling at my hands and toes, but then the White Healer smiled. "Breathe deep, my dear," he said. "There is time."

Time—that didn't seem right. I closed my eyes, trying to

draw up a memory. "Hukon," I blurted out. "My cousin, Lark, was stabbed with a spear made from hukon. Grandmama and I did our best to heal her, but the wound has reopened."

"Then your cousin allowed it to reopen," the White Healer clarified gently, a little gravely. "Hukon leaves a thread of connection. That is why it can never be truly cured."

"A connection . . ." I tried to remember what I'd learned about Lark's stabbing.

"A connection to the maker of the weapon. Who fashioned the spear, my dear, do you know?"

"Troths." *Troths.* I had sickening images of them, suddenly. They'd cut a swath of destruction. They'd slaughtered Raif.

The White Healer's voice cut in. "Where would a Troth find hukon in the middle of the Myr Mountains? Nay, someone provided it to the Troths."

"*Breeders.*" The word fell out of me. "It would be their weapon."

"Hmm." He looked skeptical. "Breeders have been long dormant."

"But they are gathering now, in force." Thoughts were clarifying suddenly; the dread was surging, and dark things tumbled over one another in a race to be remembered. Raif, Laurent, Lark . . . I begged, "Your knowledge is what can save her. I was told this. I was told to come find you. That you would help."

"You wish for a cure? My dear, I've just said there is no antidote—"

"Please!" The White Healer looked taken aback. I swallowed. "Please. Your little village has been spared so far, but the Breeders are rising against Balance. There is little time for Lark, for the—" I stopped, stunned, then said curiously, "For the shell." How had I forgotten? I said, breathless, "My satchel!"

"Your satchel hangs on the rack by the door. It is quite safe. What is this shell?"

But I'd already turned and was running for the cottage.

The satchel hung just as he said. I yanked it from its knobby hook, pricked by splinters in my haste. I brought it to the hearth, sank down with it in my lap, and hugged it close, gulping. My emotions were wild—in moments I'd gone from sun-drenched contentment to desperation, and the relief I felt now was extreme. I'd lost Raif. I'd abandoned Laurent and I'd possibly killed Lark. But I had the shell. I had the shell.

Salva was in the corner darning her stocking, crooning little things, and over that I heard the old man entering. He settled on his stool by the fireplace, waited while I rocked the satchel. "My dear?" he asked after a time.

"I'm just . . ." I stopped, not knowing if I was laughing or trembling. "I've lost so much, made so many mistakes. I'm just so thankful to have this still."

"Would you like to show me?"

After a moment I nodded. I straightened, undid the satchel, and lifted out the shell, holding it up for him to see. Little bloody streaks from the splinters stained my fingertips, but the shell was unharmed. All pinkish gray and nobbed. All as it should be.

The White Healer fixed his gaze. His eyes didn't crinkle;

there was no humor. And when he spoke, his voice was husky: "The amulet of Death."

"You know its history?"

"The legend of Tarnec," the old man murmured. "Yes, I know it. Life, Death, Dark, and Light—the orb, the shell, the black stone, and the blade. Amulets of the primal forces protected by the Keepers of Balance. Immense power entrusted to simple items."

"It looks like nothing in my hand," I agreed.

"Not true. Not true." He studied it for a while longer before saying, "My dear, you must finish my story: How is it that you have this amulet?"

I looked at him, looking at the shell. My shell. I said a little hoarsely, "I am the Guardian of Death."

He smiled broadly and sat back a little on his stool, as if contented. "And so you are. And so you hold the ability to save your cousin within your hands."

I leaped from the hearth. "You know? Why did you not say it?"

"Because you must acknowledge who you are first, my dear. Had I promised you something before you claimed your Guardianship, then any healing efforts would be weakened. There is far more power to be harnessed when one commits to one's *own* direction."

It was beyond music, those words. "So you can craft a cure!"

The White Healer pulled back just a little. He tore his eyes from the shell to look at me. "No, my dear," he said. "Your shell, your hands. You must do the crafting. But"—he smiled—"I will guide you."

Grateful—how many times, now, had I thought it? An ugly memory of Haver flashed through and I wondered that I could be so far removed from those terrible last minutes of being burned alive and the swift attack. The dark of the past seemed to slide away, weakened against the hope I now held. That I had the shell, still, and now the ability to save Lark . . . I bent my head again, unable to speak.

Only Laurent was missing. It cut then, hard, how badly I wanted to see him. I'd left him dust-worn and wounded. I remembered my last night with him, understanding how precious those hours—that we might never again feel so free of threat . . . of burden. And I wished he could know there *was* a place still free, wished we could share in the White Healer's peaceful little world.

"You look unhappy, my dear."

I shook my head. In the corner I heard Salva murmur, "Not to mind. She misses someone."

The White Healer considered me for a moment, his eyebrows twitching. He said a little sternly, "You understand of course that your mind must be clear of all concerns as you craft a potion."

I looked away, nodded.

"Good. Then you might wish to answer the door," he said.

"I'm sorry?" I asked. But the old man only gestured toward the door. I looked at Salva, who hunched over her stocking murmuring, "She misses." I put the shell back in the satchel, shouldered it, and got up. The knock only came as I lifted the latch.

I know that I glanced back at the White Healer, as if to say, *How . . . ?*

But that is the beauty of magic. It didn't matter how. I had everything I wanted. I was in the Rider's arms.

23

"A SERIOUS TASK, you understand. You must give over to the process with whole heart. *And* presence of mind."

I stood with the White Healer in the herb shed, eyeing the shelves of ingredients. Energy burned through my body so intensely that I trembled. Happiness, excitement, things I could barely contain. I'd tried not to show it before my host— he'd been reminding me since we left the cottage: "Dedication begins with focus. How you fare with this work shall determine the success of the cure. Show that your intention is sincere."

Dame Gringer had said that. I remembered thinking that when I prepared the Insight spell. I shivered deeper.

"See? Your mind strays." The old man sighed. "I should not wonder. You are very young."

Hadn't I felt so very old recently? I took a breath, then squared my shoulders to look taller. "I am ready."

He gave his crinkled smile. "Well. You have potential."

There were a multitude of ingredients to collect. The old man bade me take the ladder, to climb to the top shelves to search. I ran my fingers over the labels, naming as swiftly as I could, bringing down whatever he called out. Mostly the shelves were lined with herbs, but I spied jars with dried carcasses of reptiles and claws of birds—things I remembered seeing in Dame Gringer's books. They all seemed to merge after a while; I was up and down the rungs of the ladder, breathless, placing glass bottles in the willow basket we'd brought from his cottage without really acknowledging what I'd gathered.

"So many ingredients," I said a little helplessly. I reached for an item from the basket. The tabby cat, who prowled around the basket like a surly guard, hissed at me, so I pulled my hand back.

"This takes serious effort to create," the White Healer admonished. "Be patient." But then he added brightly, "I think we've enough. Let us return and begin preparation."

"Not here?" I asked. Grandmama never worked her concoctions in our cottage.

The old man sniffed and turned. "*So* much to learn . . ."

We were back in the lovely sunshine. Laurent was walking Arro over the far grass. The two redheaded children were playing by the well in the square. The woman in the buttercup apron stood at her door, waving. I waved back again, happily, wondering if she lived alone, wondering if she crafted spells inside of her cottage. Then I spied the White Healer far ahead of me. He'd moved fast. Was it but a moment ago we'd been in the herb shed? And neither of us had brought the basket—

"Here, mistress!"

I turned and promptly jumped. Salva was directly behind me, holding up the basket of ingredients, and then spilling it in reflex to my reaction. She immediately scrabbled to pack it back together before I could help her. "Not to mind. I will carry this." And the servant hurried along to the cottage, the White Healer just ahead of her, the hem of his robe dragging in the dust. I dusted my own hands on my skirts, shaking my head a little and thinking what an odd pair. But then Laurent was there and I ran to hug him before racing on to the cottage, thinking then I should be happy to grow old here like Salva.

The White Healer was unpacking the basket, lining up the little bottles on the table. "Now then, shall we begin?"

I went over to study what I'd collected for him. "All dark," I murmured. It was an obvious description. These were black herbs, little bits of leaf and twig each the color of night.

"True. Do you understand why?"

I shook my head.

"Dark for light," he answered. "When all the dark colors are combined you will see how 'twill be brilliantly lit."

I picked out a few of the names I recognized. "Nightshade, oxalis, poison sedge." I looked at him. "Dark and toxic."

He nodded. "Poison of one thing can erase the poison of another."

"Even the deadly ones?" I picked up one of the vials. "This is yew."

"Hukon is more deadly. Return that to the table, my dear."

"I—" I was picturing the little island in Rood Marsh, the wisps. . . .

"Pay attention!"

I flinched, confessing, "I made a spell with yew before I should have. Before I was ready. I've brought so much trouble upon everyone because of it."

The White Healer looked thoughtful. Then he nodded once more and gently reached to take the yew from my hand. "But here you are, so perhaps it was a good thing to have done."

I considered that for a moment, watching him rearrange the bottles, lift their tops and sniff, testing for freshness. "If I had not done the spell," I murmured finally, "I might have accomplished my task without incident. I might have already reached my destination."

"What destination, my dear?"

"I would have made it to Tarnec. I would be with the Rider." That came out of me so sudden, so certain—and so contrary.

A stillness passed over the old man. I worried what he was thinking, that he would tell me to leave off the spell making because I could not focus. But after a moment he smiled his merry smile. "Was it not your original destination to become a White Healer? And here you are, learning the craft, even if your mind is not where it should be. Perhaps this way you accomplish both missions?

"But now to task, my dear, *this* task." The old man pulled my attention back to the table. "Take three pinches from this one"—he indicated the sedge—"and crush the bits between your palms." He watched me carefully draw the appropriate amount from the jar. "Very good. Rub hard, make a fine powder."

A harsh smell, the sedge. Darkly pungent.

"Now spread it clockwise on the table."

My hand tingled as I smoothed the powder, staining the wood a dark metal color. I paused for a moment to study the pattern. "How is it that a poison lays the base?"

"Poison oft protects the pure," he replied, and he bade me repeat the step with three other poisons, all staining the wood.

"Does it work in the opposite," I asked, "that you would take what was pure to make something foul?"

"'Tis curiosity that fouls work."

Curiosity cracked like a little switch. I pressed both hands to the table; the black stained them as well.

"There now, that was quickly done." The White Healer was pleased. "Clever girl! Now you shall craft the container." He pulled a little blade from his pocket. "Just beyond our hamlet is a grove of sweet wood. Find the willow tree there and cut twelve whips the length of half your height. From them you will braid four plaits and then bring them here."

I nodded. The blade disconcerted me; it reminded me of Lill. But then, I'd also—finally—been complimented, so I dared not mention another memory since he would consider it a distraction. I waited politely.

"Go on, then," he nudged. "Your Rider can assist you."

I turned and left, almost tripping in haste. Salva bent over her stocking and murmured, "Not to mind, mistress." The tabby hissed.

Laurent rode me out of the village. I wanted to say that Arro should still be recovering, that we should walk, but somehow we were already seated on the horse, Laurent behind me. Neither of us spoke—reminiscent of the first time I rode with the Rider.

And yet hardly. That was when suspicion was ripe between us. Now I was happy to sit so close. I leaned back against his warm chest, wondering how he'd tracked me here, how he knew the direction for the willow, and then wondering why I should care. Then the grove was just ahead and I forgot to ask anyway.

"The willow will be inside," Laurent said when I dismounted, "beyond that clump of trees."

"You do not go with me?" I asked. It was that same sting of disappointment as at Hooded Falls.

He took my hands. "You will come back safe, Evie. I will look to the horse."

He waved and turned Arro, then trotted off a ways leaving me standing in a field of hip-high grass. I watched him, feeling a little strange, a little empty. Then I shook myself. *Attention to task.* Laurent was right to leave me, or I'd be fixed upon him instead. I turned and walked into the grove.

It was dark and cool within, bare earth beneath my feet, a heavy canopy above. I reached up and touched the leaves— leaves of all shapes and meanings splintering the light.

There was the pointed oval of the slippery elm—it stopped the voice. 'Twould be why the grove was so quiet. There was the dragon's blood tree of stiff bristles—its red sap stopped digestion. 'Twas a tree for arid lands and had no business growing in this verdant spot. And there grew the black locust, clumped with fragrant blossom on thorny branches. It could stop the heart.

A collection of trees to wither a soul. Hardly sweet wood as the White Healer called them. But perhaps, like the spell, poisonous trees together created a positive force that protected the pure. . . .

For there, in the center of these dark trees, stood the willow.

Steep the bark in heated water; bring them back their ceded laughter. A bit of Healer verse floated into memory. The willow: a tree encompassing love, protection, healing, and even a guide to passage for those who were dying, a tree that was earthbound yet sought water. It was a tree for both the Guardian of Life and of Death. And I thought with relief: *I am here; I am nearly done.*

I approached the willow and sat down a little way from it, thinking that I should pay respect before I cut its branches. My fingers brushed over the bare ground, feeling little stubs of something. I looked down; my hand was resting on sprouts of minion. I stared at them, confused—I'd not noticed them before; it made no sense for minion to be growing next to a weeping willow—two healing plants did not need to share space. And minion grew in sun, not this dark shade. I touched a finger to one of them; my hand shimmered, white beneath the shadows. I brushed them again, and again my hand shimmered, white under what seemed so very black.

Attention to task.

The White Healer's words jumped out, bold and stern. I stood, wiped my hands on my frock, and went to the tree. I slipped the blade from my pocket and sliced off the twelve whips, measuring as required, then sat back down by the tree to braid the four plaits. They were sharp, making fine little slices along my fingertips; beads of blood smeared a pattern, reminding me of when I pulled the satchel from the rack—

Attention to task! came the order. I made it a little song. *To task, to task . . .*

It might have been why I didn't hear him, or perhaps he made no sound. But I felt a presence behind me, a sensation that I was being watched. I said, without turning around, "I am nearly done, Laurent." And then, because there was no answer, I did turn around—

And I said something else:

"Raif."

24

HE WAS STANDING a little behind me. Whole, unwounded, and wearing the same clothes as when I'd last seen him, a cambric shirt and dark trousers. They were the clothes I'd dressed him in for burial. I stared, eyes my only anchor. I was falling, spiraling somewhere, I was sure, even if I'd not moved.

"Are you a dream?" I asked, maybe in a whisper, or maybe not at all. I fought the dizziness, fumbled my way to standing— the willow plaits were spilling from my lap; I was stepping to him, throat-choked and breathless. But then I stopped. Raif's expression was so solemn, uninviting.

I reached out my hand, uncertain. "Do I truly see you?"

"You see me."

He remained where he was, the space yawning wider between us. My hand fell back at my side, useless. I should be wild with happiness, but his face, his distance was catching the feeling, squeezing my heart with it. And then I could only ask, "How are you here?"

"You, Evie," he said softly. "You brought me."

I shook my head.

Raif did not argue; he rarely would. He simply shifted his gaze, looked about. "A pretty place. The little cottages, this grove."

"It's beautiful." My voice was husky.

Raif caught my gaze again, his eyes sad. This seemed all wrong. We were awkward. Strangers. "Evie," he said softly, "don't do this."

"Do this?" I echoed, and my fingers, disconnected, were somehow gesturing at the braids of willow. "It's for Lark."

He watched me; those eyes making me ache, and then I was somehow defending: "I'm saving her, Raif. I found the White Healer—he's showing me how." I told him this as if he'd been with me all along, as if he knew the story. Or maybe I was challenging him to know it; I was no longer looking on his sudden appearance in wonder . . . for it wasn't quite wonder anymore, but doubt.

Raif said, "What is this Healer?"

What, not *who.* I frowned. "I don't remember his name." What if Raif's appearance was meant as another distraction, my own challenge? *Attention to task*—what I was supposed to be doing.

"Evie." Raif was softly insistent. "You never asked it."

"Why? Why does it matter? Look at them, I'm nearly done—I'm healing Lark. We'll go to Castle Tarnec, return the amulet. Then we'll come back here where it's safe and sound . . . and beautiful." I was protesting, trying to prove my intentions. I should return to the cottage. I bent to pick up the plaits.

The faintest smile lightened Raif's voice. "We."

I gave a tiny nod. There was silence in response. And then the plaits and the White Healer fell back in significance, for I could not let Raif be so slighted. I straightened, meeting his eyes once more. They were no longer sad but warm. Kind. It hurt to hurt him.

And he said it since I could not: "You love another."

The grove was so quiet. The withering trees so very dark and still. I nodded again. The barest motion.

"Evie," Raif said gently. "He does not belong here."

"I don't understand."

"Yes, you do," he whispered. "This is not the Rider's place. This is where I belong."

"Don't." I stopped him. "*Please.* Don't." Sorrow was filling my throat. I was catching breaths like hiccups. "You *gave* me leave."

"But you did not leave."

"Not true! I love Laurent!" Painful silence—I shut my eyes and tried to say it evenly: "You died, Raif. I had to leave you." Then I shook my head. "Nay. You left me."

And suddenly the memory of losing Raif welled up, tearing into my body with needles of want. "You left. You let me go!" My hands pressed against my cheeks, my temples, trying to push back the hurt and longing, but it came out anyway. "It was supposed to be so sweet, our life! It was supposed to be unharmed! The cottage by the orchard where the apple blossoms drift and sprinkle the thatch like snow, Grandmama, and Lark, and market day, and happy babies—and you coming home to me each night."

"Evie . . ." His voice bared his own regrets. "'Tis as you say: that is the life I belong to, not the Rider. That life, that time is gone—and that is not *this* place."

"But it can be," I whispered, desolate.

"Open your eyes, sweet girl. You can neither bring those days back nor force another into that picture."

"No!" It sounded so loud. "Laurent told me he was happy here! There is nothing forced."

"This is *your* dream, Evie. Wake up. *Think.* Some part of you knows something's wrong—you've brought me back because you want the truth."

I slumped down on my knees. "Truth for what?" I asked hoarsely.

Raif smiled—the old smile, the one I used to fall asleep picturing was meant for me. The ache of loss burned through my chest, stealing breath, purpose. He said, "Do you know what I love about you? How curious you were about everything. You would not just look at the apple blossoms; you would want to know why they shaded from pink to white. How the mordant fixed Semel Lewen's dyes." He looked at me keenly, then looked at my hands. "You must make your own choices. I can only warn you to see what is, not what you want." He put out a finger to almost touch the white little bit of my knuckle, then dropped it, whispering, "Where is your curiosity now, Evie Carew?"

I looked down at my hands too. They were pale and clean—as they should be. "My curiosity brought this upon us," I said, husky. "I'm here because I have to fix it."

"If curiosity brought you here, then yearning makes you stay."

Where are you weak, young girl? They will strike you where you are weak. . . . Words from a memory I couldn't place.

"Yearning, Evie," Raif said. "Do you not wonder why this is all just as you wish? The pretty square and pretty flowers and the innocent—"

"Why is that wrong?" I pleaded, "Can't there be a haven where there is no brutality, no threat?"

"Do you not wonder at the ease with which you are saving Lark?"

A bitter snort. How many times had Laurent suggested the same? I held up my bloody fingers. "What *ease*?" It seemed odd, then, that I'd only just seen my hands as pale and clean.

He was shaking his head. "Change your fate, Evie. Be curious again. Ask the White Healer's name. You have to see." Raif repeated, urging, needing: "You have to *see*."

He held out his hand and I immediately reached up, trying to grasp it, feeling that need for him, for what once was, so very deeply. The bottomless ache, the same yearning the amulet inspired, that need to go *home*. I looked at Raif, thinking I could say it through my eyes if my voice failed, but then knew I had to say it out loud. He deserved nothing less. "I loved you," I whispered. "I so loved you and I never told you."

He smiled. "I know."

And then, as if the woods came rushing forward, Raif was gone, receding into darkness.

I sat still, my hand floating in empty space until I pulled it back.

What do I not see, Raif? What do I not see?

It occurred to me that there were no birds singing—where I thought the vision of Raif had brought the silence, it seemed the silence had been there all along. I looked down, unnerved by the quiet, then gathered up the plaits, rolling them into my frock so the whips would not sting my hands. I stood and walked back out of the grove.

Laurent was waiting for me. A surge of emotion propelled me straight into his arms. "Have you finished?" he murmured against my hair, and I nodded. He lifted me up onto Arro, climbed up behind, and wrapped his arms about me. I crooked my head to look at him and smiled.

The sun shone; I sat with my love. I held in my skirts the things to save my dearest friend. I could not be uneasy.

We trotted off; the air and light so warm, I dozed in the peace of it. Arro seemed to know exactly where to go; Laurent's hands barely moved on the reins. Laurent's hands—so strong and capable, sun- and wind-tanned.

And without Raif's ring.

I was almost asleep; I saw at first with only drugged curiosity. But then my eyes opened a little wider; I watched his hands. Watched how naked they rested in front of me. How they didn't move at all.

"Laurent?" I turned. "Where is the ring?"

He was smiling down at me, his eyes so very blue. "Ring," he repeated back.

"The leather ring. That I left for you."

He kept smiling. "It is just as you wish."

As I wish? "Laurent . . ." There was something else.

"Hush, love." He kissed me. "We'll be back soon."

And we were. Laurent was halting Arro before the White Healer's cottage. I asked him as he helped me from Arro's back, "Are you truly happy here?"

Laurent brushed back a strand of hair from my shoulder. He leaned to kiss me again, warm and luscious and as real as anything I could need. "I'm here, Evie," he murmured, smiling at me. "You are happy."

I was happy, though it didn't erase Raif's visit. I entered the cottage with my gatherings, seeing that all was sweetly the same: the fire in the hearth, Salva darning the yellow stocking in her little chair. The tabby cat sat on the hearthstone washing his paws. I looked to my left, to where my satchel hung at the door. I smelled oat bread and chicken stew.

The White Healer stood at the table pondering his herb selection. He glanced up as I entered, eyed the lump in my frock.

"Ah." His eyes crinkled. "You have made the plaits, clever girl. Bring them here."

Clever. I smiled at the repeated compliment. I hurried to him, then unrolled the four willow braids from my skirts and let them drop onto the sedge-coated table. The White Healer looked at them, at me. "You found them easily?"

"Yes."

"Very good. Was there any confusion?"

I wondered if he suspected I'd been confronted, been conflicted, even. I shook my head. And then I worried he *had* magically sent Raif somehow, and I should admit that I'd been visited, been warned—

Warned. I paused, my hand hovering at the willow braids.

The White Healer said gently, "There is not much time. You need to do up the braids, weave them into a pouch. Now, my dear, while the willow is most potent."

I picked up the braids. My hands were trembling—shaking—just a little. *Nervous,* I thought. The way Lark would react in a crowd—

I clenched my jaw. *Lark.* I would not lose focus. "Show me." The old man smiled.

'Twas a simple weave—over, under, over, under. Four braids made for a small mat, and then the White Healer instructed how to loop a braid back on itself. In no time I had a smallish pouch.

"Just the size for your shell," the White Healer murmured, pleased. "Needles of hemlock and leaves of nightshade we weave in now. Poison to root out poison." He sprinkled some of both into my palm. I pressed the dried bits into the braiding, so that the yellowish hue of the willow was interrupted with black. We added dark sprinklings from all the jars.

"You said it would take on all the colors," I murmured. "When?"

"Patience. You will see." The old man pointed to my satchel. "Bring the shell."

See. I shook off the word and retrieved my bag. The tabby cat finished his washing as I passed and gave me a doleful look.

"Here." The White Healer beckoned me back. "Here. You've not much time. Put it in all safe and sound."

Safe and sound. How comforting and strange that he'd used words I'd recently used. I took out the shell, centered it inside the willow pouch.

And there it was, the little amulet nestled inside a weaving of healing willow and black poison.

"Well done." The old man nodded. He was sweating, a sheen of moisture over his temples and brow.

"Are you all right?" I asked.

"Powerful magic takes much focus, much concentration," he murmured. "Salva." He called to the white-haired woman without looking at her. "Bring her the jug."

I heard her behind me, creaking out of her chair, shuffling to a corner. Little noises so loud. The tabby yowled suddenly, and I jumped. Salva's darning needle clattered to the floor. She murmured, "Not to matter." And then the White Healer turned, saying, "We are nearly done, my dear. You must fetch water from the well." Salva handed me the jug and I went out of the cottage, past Laurent, who smiled at me and said, "I am here."

The two little redheaded children were playing by the well; they ran off as I approached. I wondered that I'd never acknowledged if they were boys or girls, and that they were gone before I could decide. I dunked the bucket, drew it up, and filled the container. A shadow fell over the stones; 'twas a puff of cloud skittering across the sky, the first cloud in what seemed forever. I stayed for a moment watching, wondering at its speed when there was no breeze, but then the woman in the buttercup apron came out of the far cottage door to sweep her step and wave her hand at me.

The same, I thought. A variation of the same task each time. . . . A chill flickered through me. *Raif.* I frowned and hurried back to the warmth of the cottage.

"Here," I said, entering, and then stopped dead.

Around me the pretty whitewashed walls were dulling, as if color was being pulled from the space. But the table, in shape, color, and size had intensified; the wood, brushed with the poison, was pulsing and vibrant. The powder was no longer a charcoal dust but swirls of color. The black things in their jars were pulsing too with glorious color.

And the shell was glowing—a radiant, beaming white. A burst of brilliance.

The old man was smiling. "Do you see? You have done exceptionally."

See. That word again—haunting, worrying. I could not feel exceptional, for it came back, what Raif had said to me: *You have to see.* I glanced around the room. All was still cozy and familiar: the size, the furnishings, the old woman, the old man, and the cat. Laurent outside. Things were in their place, things clean and whole and unharmed. Healer needs—nay, *my* needs. A sweet respite, a safe respite from the brutality that leached into our world. The only thing reminiscent of those horrors was my battered satchel. It rested empty and deflated on my hip. I felt a sudden ache at that. The shell shouldn't be glowing so brightly, but nestled close to me.

Where is your curiosity now, Evie Carew?

"And now the final part of this spell making, my dear." The White Healer pointed to what I'd forgotten I held. "Fresh water, my dear. 'Twill erase any impurities. You will pour it into the shell."

The cat was meowing—guttural sounds. I looked at the jug, then at the old man, confused. "You cannot purify with this. Water only cleans when running along its own free path."

The old man was taken aback. "What is gathered from that well is exceptional," he insisted. And when I shook my head, he said a little more forcefully, "Who is the greater Healer in this room? Do you defy my knowledge?"

"But well water is *still* water, and still water cannot purify. Every Healer knows—"

He didn't let me finish. "That you doubt weakens the spell. Pour the water into the shell, quickly before it is too late." He took a sharp breath. *"Attention to task!"* Now there was no question that he was sweating; it trickled over his temple, beaded his brow.

"You are worried," I whispered, curious. "My doubt makes you anxious."

" 'Tis not anxiety, 'tis *effort*!" he barked. "I bind this spell for you! You have not the strength enough in your resolve to ignite this cure. 'Tis I who hold it by my own power. 'Twill break apart if you do not hurry!"

"Nay." The word came out of me of its own accord. There

was a shift; the room gave a little jolt. *You have to see.* Raif's voice repeating, insistent in my ears.

The White Healer peered at me. "You will not refuse, Guardian."

'Twas the first time he'd called me Guardian. It sent a shiver down my spine, that tone, that name from his lips.

That name. I gripped the jug a little closer, Raif's words flowing back: *Ask the White Healer's name. . . .*

I lifted my head, looked the old man straight in the eye. "What is your name?"

My voice was hardly strong, yet seemed to crack like thunder, spawning a fury I'd never before witnessed. *"You dare . . ."* The White Healer's face turned red, his eyes bulged from their sockets, and his mouth contorted—as if trying to hold back what he was compelled to admit by that simple request.

I was fascinated. I said louder, bolder, "Tell me your name!"

At that the old man's mouth yawned wide, wider than humanly possible, and a sound erupted, huge and deep, tearing fascination into horror. A name! Unintelligible, unpronounceable. Like nothing I'd ever heard; it took my breath with fear, as winter sucks away breath with cold. It rocked the walls surrounding us, the floor we stood on, and crashed over us like a wave. . . .

A moment frozen in time forever—the moment before impact. The moment when I understood the old man was never whom I'd thought.

He was a Breeder.

I didn't think—Healer instinct to protect. My hands flew

348

up, bracing. The jug flung from my hands and smashed against the table, splashing its contents over the table, the nest, the shell.

And immediately I knew what a terrible mistake I'd made. About everything.

25

THE CAT SCREECHED and leaped upon the table; Salva lurched to grab it back. His claws scrabbled, scoring the wooden top as the old woman dragged him off, leaving bursts of light. Everything else on the table was turning a lurid black—not a pitch black, but a swirl of darkest color, massing, spreading, trying to bridge and smother those glowing striations. And there was laughter in the wake of that hideous release of name. Deep, bellowing laughter—laughter that was for me, at what I'd done. It wasn't pure water that I'd spilled. It wasn't water at all.

I lunged for the shell, trying to wipe or shake the liquid off, but it was already thickening, like some brackish tar—not on the shell but over it, wrapping the nest in a little dome. I cried out—

The laughter quit abruptly. "Stop!" the White Healer commanded. He grabbed my arm. It was the first time he'd touched me and we both gasped at how violently the effort was repelled. His arm flew back from mine and my own arm smacked against the table in powerful reflex. He tried to grab my skirts but the cat got in the way, hissing and swiping, so he shrieked, "Do not touch it! Do not stop the spell!"

"What have you done?" I cried, wrenching away from him. "What is this?" I dug my fingers into the stickiness, struggling to pry the whole mess from the table, and crying out at the pain of it. The tar was resin, sap from some vile thing, yew by the smell of it, and the nest . . . the nest . . .

You have to see, Raif had urged. And I was seeing, my eyes truly opening. Everything around me was dissolving, like rain washing mud from stone. Only here 'twas the stone dripping away, leaving behind muddy filth. The sweet room and everything beyond were melting before me.

Raif was right. I'd seen what I'd wanted to see, what I longed for: the world to be as sweet as a sunny day in Merith and a White Healer to put everything right again. A little world invented from my own history, as if my mind had been gleaned, picked over for images—the dear cottages, the waving woman, the red-haired children, Salva . . . all creations stitched together from memories. And all wavered and blurred as I stood clawing at the table. I saw my hands, saw them as they truly were, covered in blisters and blood, and knew why minion grew beneath that willow tree. A warning I'd refused to heed. 'Twas *black* willow I'd collected the branches from—*hukon.* The most evil, deadly thing, and I'd cut and plaited and made a nest from it. I'd placed my amulet within and spilled yew resin to trap, putrefy, and seal the shell to the hukon so that it would shatter if I tried to separate them. Laurent had warned me that I could destroy the shell without knowing, and now I could not have done worse had I been the White Healer—

No: *Breeder.*

Still I tried, working at the nest while the old man tried to get past the cat. There should have been at least some grim satisfaction that he could not stop my efforts—but I was frantic, screaming, "Laurent! Laurent!"

On some perverse cue there was knocking at the cottage door, even as the door was melting away. Between the smears of wood, exactly as I might wish him, stood Laurent with his beautiful smile and clear blue eyes, except he was slurring in horrid monotone, "I am here," before he too puddled into nothingness.

My breath caught, ripping out its first sob. Raif was right. Laurent didn't belong. That was not Laurent, but some pretty doll I'd stuck into this dream repeating all the things I wanted to hear him say: of happiness and sweet endings—*nothing* that the Rider had ever promised. I should have seen. I didn't want to see.

"What have you done to me?" I shrieked at the old man.

But he was shrieking as loud as I—half in fury that I was trying to abort the spell, and half in struggle with the scratching, hissing tabby. "What have *I* done?" He screamed back, "Look at yourself, Guardian! This was your will, your doing!"

"Will?" It stunned me, spurred me. Any victory I'd assumed

had led me exactly to where the Breeders wanted me. From the moment I made the Insight spell to quell my curiosity to this grotesque fabrication. *Curiosity and need—they'll strike you where you are weak.* And so they had.

But I could still fight for what little was left. I still had a Healer's need to save.

I said viciously, "That was not will. *This* is will!"

And I ripped the poisoned clump free, dragged the nest up to my chest, the resin sticking my fingers to the shardlike hukon. I turned as the last of the cottage dissolved, revealing those barren salt flats that I'd trudged across days—or hours—or maybe only minutes ago. Imploding, all of it—this sick fantasy created to erase all the dark things was now erasing itself. The walls of the cottage were gone; the square was gone, the other dwellings gone. Whatever gentle sunshine I'd imagined turned to some harsh, gray bulk of clouds, leaving me with the Breeder, the cat, and Salva. Salva stood up as her chair melted away. She came to me, head down, saying, "Not to mind, mistress. . . ." And then the yellow sock she darned was shriveling into something snakelike, a twisted, limbless muscle of putrid yellow, writhing in her grip. I stumbled back. Behind me the Breeder bellowed, "Nahlgruth!" Salva's head whipped up so that I caught her eye for the first time: liquid and black. And then the eye was the only thing that remained of the old woman, for she was expanding into something huge and inhuman. *Nahlgruth*—the Breeder had named it, summoned a beast. It was growing, already towering above me in a shape I could not fathom: a gargantuan trunk, reptilian skin, a frenzy of worms sprouting from an expanding skull. That writhing thing was merging as part of a third appendage, a tentacle.

And the Breeder laughed at me, hideous and cruel. "You cannot stop what you've begun! You will destroy the amulet!"

"No!" I screamed back, desperate. *"No!"* The tabby sprang, yowling, and landed by my feet. It wound between my skirts then leaped away with a look behind.

I ran after it. It had to be an ally, showing me the way. The Breeder shouted and the Nahlgruth thundered forward in response—so huge now, the heat of its breath carried straight to my back. I kept running. My hands stung, the resin bonding them to the hukon. I rolled and rolled the awful thing between my palms, trying not to let it fasten to my skin, for 'twould shatter if my hands were sucked in. "Wait!" I yelled at the cat. *"Wait!"* I was losing sight of him—a streak of rust between the dull of the flats and the sky. I stumbled once, falling hard on my knees, seeing that even my clothes I'd believed so clean were frayed and filthy, and stinking of the fire that the villagers of Haver had set. I picked myself up, unstuck my hands from the nest, and ran on.

And I thought again: Raif was right. My yearning had kept me in this dream; it was what brought this ruined end. *Be careful what you need,* the seer had said. I'd been warned from the start.

I laughed at myself, a horrible and ugly sound. If Harker had warned me, he had also contrived this—finding me at the drinking pool, offering me the possibility of a White Healer to beckon me forward, to open me to mistake, and to leave my one champion behind in drugged sleep. I was a fool. A fool!

Ahead was the sea. I could hear it, storm-tossed and angry. Above, the clouds were massing dark and thunderous, the wind howling, whipping my salt-dried hair across my face. It stung harsh as nettles, but at least it deflected the worse pain of my burning hands. I gritted my teeth, groaned against all of it, and ran on into what stretched as gray upon gray. Behind me the Nahlgruth roared, shivering the very sand.

There! Out of gray rose the rock outcropping that I'd climbed before. The tabby cat was waiting—a tiny splotch of color against first heave of stone. "You!" I called to it. "Where do I go?"

In response the thing leaped onto the rock and skimmed right up the tall face. I clambered after it, hampered by the nest, by the vile resin, stopping almost every step to switch hands. I was lagging, too slow. The Nahlgruth roared again, loud, breath hot—I couldn't tell if the beast was behind me or already above, waiting to swallow. *Don't think, Evie. Don't think of anything. Just climb.*

Barnacles gave way to a smoother face of boulders. I sank on one for a moment, dragging in breaths, juggling the nest and trying to peer through the thickening resin to see the shell. I remembered the satchel, yanked it into my lap, and placed the nest on top, thinking some cloth between skin and hukon would help, protect. But the resin burned right through the satchel with a hiss and stink of yew. I flung the charred bits off my frock before it caught fire, then paused. In the smeared ash on my lap was the lark feather. I plucked it up, gasping, laughing, rammed it through the middle of the nest—

Any hope the feather was going to stop the spell was brief. There was a flash of flame—the same way the cat's claws had drawn fire across the table—and the feather was gone. My laugh cut short in defeat. And out of that same defeat came the Breeder's cry exploding in my head, "You cannot escape!"

I jerked back, jamming myself in a gap, flailed there while the whole sky resounded the Breeder's glee: "The amulet is finished!"

And I, who'd hardly ever been afraid, was terrified—terrified by what I'd done, terrified that this bellowing declaration was true.

No. No. No. I pushed fear from my head, refusing this ending, and wriggled free. *No.* I turned and crawled up the huge boulders, tearing skin on stone, staying low, for the gale threatened to pluck me up, dash me down. The Nahlgruth roared again; the wind howled. And behind that, somewhere far, far behind, I could swear my name was being called, carried along by the rush of wind. *No.* Dry sobs squeezed my lungs, or maybe I was just gasping for breath, for the air seemed to be taken from me. The clouds boiled black and huge . . . yet despite the ferocity of the looming storm, there was no rain.

And then I was up, on the top of the outcropping, tugging my hands from the nest. For a moment—just for a moment—I thought the wind paused, maybe in surprise that I'd reached the summit. I could see the wild sea, the salt flats on one side, and the ruined village of Haver on the other. There in the rubble the villagers clung together, shouting, bracing for the oncoming storm. I shuddered to look at them: to look and remember their misguided prejudice, to look and remember that I'd constructed a perfect little town to replace this rubble, and that my own construct was far worse than what they'd done to me. I turned to the sky, with the lightning streaks making silver what was black, with the crash of thunder that nearly silenced the howl of the Nahlgruth. And I was suddenly so sad for the villagers. They had no concept of what was erupting all around them, that Chaos was claiming our world. All they understood was that they were being punished, that the clouds above could boil and threaten and push wave upon shore to decimate their lives and it still would not rain. Whatever slaughter they offered to beg safety only drew them further into chaos. It took my breath, the realization that I'd helped sink them ever deeper.

It would never rain.

The voice boomed again and I ducked; the wind whipped up stronger, buckling my knees. "You cannot have the amulet!" I shouted.

'Twas meager defiance in the face of something so huge. I shifted the ruined nest from hand to hand, as if I could not have the amulet either. And in answer a harrowing sound shivered the outcropping, shivered the earth. The villagers from Haver were wailing.

I staggered toward the end of the point, where it jutted high and far out into the sea. The waves were in a rage, smashing at the rocks in fury, sending the spray arcing over the top.

"Evie!"

The cry was faint against the roar of wind and wave. I'd imagined it. But it was there again: "Evie! Stop!"

I whirled around, the wind snatching the rest of my hair from its braid, whipping the strands. I pushed them from my eyes, staring stunned at the figure scrambling up the last boulders. And then I knew I'd imagined it. *Laurent.*

"No!" I screamed. "Get away!"

"Evie!" He was panting for breath, holding one hand against his ribs; the other gripped his sword. "Evie, come back!"

"Get away!" I screamed again. "You're not real!"

Laurent lurched toward me. "Evie, I'm here. It's me." I couldn't see his expression, the sky roiled too dark and he was too far away, but how he said it unnerved me. He fought the wind, his own body, and staggered forward.

The roaring grew louder—the beast was starting up the rocks.

I stood frozen. This was not the perfect Laurent that I'd constructed, who'd melted before my eyes. He was exhausted, in pain, filthy, and more beautiful for it, but—

"Stay back!" I screamed.

The Rider stopped. "Evie—"

"Tell me something I don't know!" I begged him. "Tell me something of you that I wouldn't know." I could prove his realness that way, couldn't I? If he told me something that had not been raked from my own memory.

"The white oak!" he shouted. "You wanted to know what healed the wound on my temple! 'Twas the white oak!"

The lump in my throat was cut through by a whimper.

Maybe he heard it. Laurent took a step toward me. Somewhere behind I heard the Nahlgruth climbing. I should move. I should run. . . .

"The ring." I gulped. "Where is the ring?"

Laurent held up his hand. "Evie, it's here." The braided leather was on his little finger where I'd put it. Another step closer and another, and then he was telling me something else I'd not known: "You are the only one I have ever loved, ever will love."

I sank down on the rocks feeling the wind whipping my clothes and hair sideways, salt stinging my cheeks. It didn't matter. Racking sobs of relief, release. "You found me." I gasped. "You found me." I reached for him. I heard him running.

'Twas the briefest of joys. I was looking in horror at what I held—what held me. I'd forgotten to juggle the nest. The resin had sealed my hands into its poisonous mass, swallowed them so that I squeezed the searing hukon braids between my palms, and within them the little shell. Shrinking, drying, slowly forcing me to crush the amulet. Like stone, the resin solidified— the only holes in the glassy, soot-colored ball were where I'd stuck the lark feather through.

"Evie! What's wrong?"

I lifted my burden to Laurent. He was slowing, realizing what I was holding—I, like a supplicant, begging, reaching hands engulfed in tar, desperately trying to separate them. If I kept the tension, pulled hard against the shriveling resin, I could slow the end. I could not hold out forever.

"You have to kill me," I choked out. "Kill me before I destroy it."

Laurent froze where he was. His voice was awful. "No."

"You have to! It's the only way!"

He shook his head. "I won't, Evie. You have to stop it."

"I can't!" I cried. "It's nearly done!" I yanked, tugged. My arms already ached.

"No!" he shouted back. "You *have* to!" Then, fiercely, "I won't let you go."

A shout, a terrible roar. I jerked my head up, then stumbled to my feet. The Nahlgruth had reached the top, stretching to its full and awesome height. Laurent was turning, lifting his sword, racing for the thing's massive legs, the only place he could avoid a deathblow. The cat was back, leaping on the beast, climbing for its throat. I was screaming. There was no way out of this. The Nahlgruth would kill Laurent and I would kill the shell.

I remembered Lark's terrible cry as she spied me high above Castle Tarnec: *What have you done?*

"What have you done?"

It was the Breeder. He stood before me, mimicking my thought with a hideous grin.

"Spare the Rider!" I screamed. "Spare him!"

The Breeder only laughed, knowing he'd won, and I hated him for it. I didn't even think; I lunged at him, knocking the old man flat to the rocks and then doubling over, retching at my violent act. *Do no harm.* I was sick from it, and still enraged.

Before my horrified eyes, the Breeder stood back up, still laughing. "You cannot stop this."

I will. Then, out loud, fierce: "I will!" And it came quick, something I could do, what I hoped could stop disaster. I turned and pushed through the wind, struggled toward the edge of the promontory.

"Stop!" cried the Breeder. His command resounded above the gale, making the Nahlgruth pause. Laurent sank to his knees, dragging breaths.

"Spare the Rider!" I screamed it at the Breeder. I backed up, stumbling, threatening. "Spare him!"

The Breeder shrieked, "Stop!"

"Show me! Bring the Nahlgruth to me!"

The Breeder hesitated, so I whirled and thrust my way to the very edge of the rock, teetering with each gust.

Something was yelled, for with a roar the Nahlgruth turned to face me. A step closer, another, shaking the boulders beneath.

"Run, Laurent! *Run!*" I screamed at the Rider. But Laurent only staggered to his feet, yelling, "Don't, Evie! Don't do it! Stay there!" He'd not leave me.

"Crush the shell," the Breeder seethed. "Give up!"

I shook my head. I could hardly speak—my throat thick and raw, my body shuddering. The tar was sucking in my hands with excruciating strength.

"Crush it! And I will save your Rider!" He screeched as I shook my head again. "There will always be another beast, another Breeder. You cannot stop this. It is forever!"

Forever racked through me. The struggle of Balance, the Keepers' endless vigil. I looked at the Breeder, suddenly clear. "I know," I said. "It is our burden."

"Evie, please!" Laurent shouted, desperate, forcing his way forward. "Don't do it. *Don't!*"

"Rider," I called out. "I love you." My voice broke. I tried louder: "I love you!" The words were taken by sobs and I realized it was not salt spray on my cheeks but tears. I'd never cried but I was crying now, weeping both for what I'd lost and for what I'd found—for all the beauty that had been, and for all the beauty that could still be glimpsed in the midst of darkness. "I'm sorry!"

The last words Laurent didn't hear, for he'd reached the Breeder and stabbed his sword straight through. It caught the Breeder mid laugh, turning it into some curdled shriek. The Nahlgruth swung its hideous tentacle, tossing the Rider like a rag doll. I screamed, thinking Laurent had gone over the rocks, but he was there, clawing his way back, dragging himself to stand, hunched and pained and refusing to give up. . . . The Nahlgruth turned to me.

I shouted with relief that the Rider lived, laughing through tears. Then my gaze met the beast's and narrowed. "I'll take you with me," I gritted as the thing thudded toward me, huge and horrible. I closed my eyes.

Ask for help, the Sea Hags had said.

I raised my hands high above my head to lure his focus, the tarred shell strained between, took a step back, and another.

Help, I whispered. *Help.*

The wind gusted, raced around me between my arms. The shell tugged, wind whipping through the little holes I'd pierced with the lark feather, resonating.

Sounding.

Hollow, deep, a pure tone that made the resin vibrate. Everything else seemed to pause to listen. A moment's hush before the Nahlgruth bellowed in agony and leaped for me, a moment's hush before I stepped back into space, into wind, and Laurent cried, "Evie, no!"

My cloak billowed like a bluebird's wing, lifted me. The beast was in midair, writhing, swiping, and then dropping like a stone to the waves. It burst into flames as the water claimed it, swallowed in a hiss of steam. Laurent was running, shouting my name. . . .

But none of that seemed to matter. I was buffeted out and away, falling far and free into the arms of the sea, and thinking: *The song, the shell's song.*

And there—the sky, the clouds were responding, yielding . . .

And there—the first drops of rain.

EPILOGUE

TEARS. RAIN. SEA. One bleeds into the next. They taste the same.

I am warm, weightless. I am safe.

Far above, through blue-gray mist, a figure struggles atop a rock outcropping. He stumbles to the edge, then drops to his knees. He reaches down. The waves are violent; they surge and crash just beneath his fingertips. They can take him if he simply leans a little.

The figure strains, conflicted. He wants to jump, to fall. To save . . . to die.

I will him not to. I watch him fight.

I do not fight.

Blue of turquoise sea and lapis stone, blue of the bright sky and coldest flame. It surrounded and shimmered. Beneath was the silver of purest white sand. I was neither drowned by wet nor crushed by weight, but inside a bubble within the infinite blue. A singular droplet in a vast ocean . . . suspended.

Water—the element to sweep clean, to hold secrets.

It washed me clean, leaving me clear-eyed and understanding: I'd not failed. Curiosity and need and twisted fate mattered not, for if every mistake led me here, then I was here—one small victory against a tide of threat. There would be no shell's song if not for the Breeder, the poison, or the lark feather I'd picked from a path. If not for curiosity and need. Every mistake still offered choice, an opportunity. They were mine to own and mine to heal.

And I did heal. 'Twas in my hands all along, such power—when I stopped resisting and embraced the poison, bestowed my energy against yew and hukon. Warming through; wearing away. Thumbs, then fingers slowly freeing, hardened sludge peeling apart. The little shell emerged, whorls and knobs and pearly opening all as they were when first found. Another victory.

But once released, the shell was gone, secreted away by the sea. To where, I did not know. And the sea would hold me her secret too. How long, I did not know.

It wasn't mine to know. I'd only asked for help.

Water holds no intent, but I think it did bear a tiny prejudice to my plight, for it offered me something—a hope to hold on to, perhaps a window in. Words murmured, washed over and through like the tide, like a lullaby:

The deepest place, no light to spare,
A small thief sleeps who brings two to air.
Stolen book, broken bond, the dark city burns.
By wing and surrender the Healer returns.

I wrapped my cloak, sank down to wait, to sleep, and, this time, to dream.

Somewhere above, the rain was pounding, feeding the Earth. Somewhere above, Trethe was keeping Lark from slipping into darkness, and all of Castle Tarnec was watching over their queen. Somewhere above, the seer was searching for his books and a Guardian was awakening. Hope in all of it. The reason to endure.

And . . . somewhere above, Laurent was calling for me. I felt it in my heart, my bones. My soul. He would not let go. Nor would I. That was not hope. It was truth.

"Love cannot die, Laurent." I whispered up last promises. "It cannot."

Nay. It will not.

ACKNOWLEDGMENTS

THERE IS A path I sometimes walk. It leads through a narrow trail in a marsh, where reeds once grew so high you could not see beyond its bend. The reeds were cut down recently, I suppose to open the view. I miss their mystery. I miss what inspired this story.

But if inspiration created, then others supported and nurtured, and I am very grateful to them: the most wonderful editor, Diane Landolf, who challenged me with gentle voice and astute eye to make everything better; the intrepid and brilliant agent, Jenny Bent, whose encouragement has never failed to amaze; the authors in my writing group—Tatiana Boncompagni, Melanie Murray Downing, and Lauren Lipton—who offered honest opinions and good friendship along the way; and my husband, who was always there to read, and to calm.

Thank you as well to the artist Marcela Bolivar for such

exquisite covers in this Guardians of Tarnec series, and to art director Nicole de las Heras for all her efforts in bringing such gorgeous design to fruition.

Last but never least, thank you, Jonathan, Christopher, and Jeremy, for maneuvering around my inconveniently placed writing chair with humor, patience, and enthusiasm, despite my gnashing teeth. You are the loves of my life.

ABOUT THE AUTHOR

SANDRA WAUGH grew up in an old house full of crowded bookshelves, in walking distance of an old library that allowed her to drag home a sack of six books at a time. It goes without saying, then, that she fell in love with an old house in Litchfield County, Connecticut, because of its many bookshelves. She lives there with her husband, two sons, and a dog who snores. Loudly. *Silver Eve* follows *Lark Rising* in the Guardians of Tarnec series.